THE BUCKET

Arnab Ray, better known as Greatbong, is one of India's most widely read bloggers (http://greatbong.net). He is also the author of six books, including the horror classic: *The Mine*. Two of his books have been made into web-series on major OTT platforms: *Sultan of Delhi* in Hindi on JioHotstar and *Mahabharata Murders* in Bengali on Hoichoi. A Ph.D. in Computer Science from State University of New York at Stony Brook, he graduated from Jadavpur University in Kolkata and is currently based out of Los Angeles. Arnab Ray writes for *Times of India* and can be found on X (formerly Twitter) at @greatbong.

THE BUCKET

Arnab Ray

hachette
INDIA

First published in 2026 by Hachette India
(Registered name: Hachette Book Publishing India Pvt. Ltd)
An Hachette UK Company
www.hachetteindia.com

1

Print ISBN 978-93-5731-643-9
Ebook ISBN 978-93-5731-771-9

Hachette Book Publishing India Pvt. Ltd
4th/5th Floors, Corporate Centre,
Plot No. 94, Sector 44, Gurugram 122003, India

Typeset in ITC Galliard Pro
by Mukul

Printed and bound in India by
Manipal Technologies Limited

MIX
Paper | Supporting responsible forestry
FSC™ C043100

To Anahita

Contents

Prologue

Water is a patient killer. It does not rush. It waits. First comes the cold shock against your face, a thousand needles of pain that make your muscles seize and your mind fragment into bright shards of panic. Then the burning begins, not from heat but from its absence: your lungs, desperate for air, start to consume themselves. The world above becomes a wavering circle of light, distorted by ripples that seem to laugh at your desperation.

Do not trust what they say about euphoria before death. Your pain is not numbed. The most beautiful moments of your life do not flash by in an unending kaleidoscope of joy.

Instead, time drags like slow jelly. You struggle. You flail. You scream into the void. Water rushes past your ears in bubbles.

Your hair spreads out like seaweed, shrouding out the last rays of the bathroom tube light.

You jerk. You spasm. Your eyes move back.

And then, finally, it stops. The water enters you in a flood, dragging you down into its black depths.

You feel it. And then, *the end.* It tastes like liquid rust.

Water has a memory. It remembers the shape of things submerged. It remembers the final breaths of those who surrender to its depths. It remembers the paths their lives would have taken.

Most of all, it remembers the face outside, holding you down by the neck, looking down onto the now-still surface.

1

Rose at Dusk

Twilight split Los Angeles between earth and sky. Darkness pooled steadily in the canyons, as light still crowned the hills, each minute draining colour from the world below.

From the terrace of the iconic Yamashiro, its pagoda silhouetted against the fading sky, like a temple misplaced in time, Ranadeep Saha watched the transformation. The restaurant's dark wood and stone rose above Hollywood, like a feudal fortress. Its terraced gardens descended the hillside in careful tiers, koi ponds catching the last orange light as they waited for the stone lanterns to glow along the winding paths.

His phone buzzed against the table. Another congratulations text on his Rajya Sabha nomination, the fourth since they had sat down. There would be more. He knew that. The tide of supplicants and favour-seekers would swell with the news. He would have to decide who merited a word, who a sentence, who an emoji, who a voice call, and who would be left with nothing but a read receipt and the silence that followed.

Below the restaurant's terrace, Runyon Canyon was already surrendering its colours. Petroleum-dark ribbons of asphalt threaded through the hills, vanishing into shadow. Behind him, the century-old replica of a Kyoto palace kept its vigil over the descending terrain, its curved eaves and red trim etched sharply against the dimming sky.

Ranadeep sat at a black iron table on the lowest terrace, where only a low fence marked the boundary between the manicured grounds and the untamed slope of the canyon. Other diners lingered at tables behind him, their conversations drifting outward like untethered whispers. A server moved among them, refilling water glasses with a practised grace; each step deliberate and soundless.

The breeze stirred, and Ranadeep leaned forward, gazing down over the fence.

Eight hours earlier, he had finished arranging his son's dormitory room at Harvey Mudd. That was why he was here in Los Angeles, as a family: to settle Shayan into his new life. Monobina Saha had straightened the already-straight towels and kept going over everything once again, while Shayan had fidgeted, eager for his parents to leave before his roommate arrived. The room Shayan was going to spend the next few years of his life in was one-third his bedroom in Delhi. Ranadeep had picked up on a lingering smell, maybe weed, but at least the windows faced the mountains. His father's mind had found itself cataloguing every detail: the thin mattress, the metal desk, the bare walls, the shared bathrooms with their faint scent of industrial cleaner. Shayan, the only son of the Home Secretary, had grown up in huge palatial bungalows and under continuous surveillance, with attendants hanging on to his every order, drivers who took him everywhere, a father who called him when he left, and a mother who called him when he arrived.

And now all of that was going to change.

That morning, as he watched his son arrange his books with quick, impatient movements, Ranadeep had wanted to say something. To explain that Shayan was his own man now, that no matter how much he and Monobina longed to shield him from harm, they no longer could. Not for lack of trying. They would try, always, for as long as they lived. That was what it meant to be parents.

But they could no longer stand between him and the arrows life would let loose. Some would graze. Some would draw blood. Some would stay buried deep, aching long after the moment of impact. And it would hurt Ranadeep to see his son wounded, just as it would hurt Monobina, but those wounds would be his to bear: the weight of rejection, frustration, heartbreak and betrayal.

There was no way to deflect those arrows. They would come.

As they had, to Ranadeep Saha. And to everyone.

But the words never left his throat. Instead, he had helped hang a poster of the periodic table and a framed photo of the three of them in Paris, beneath the Eiffel Tower. He had checked that the tops of the frames were perfectly level, given his son a quick, awkward hug, and sniffled back tears on the drive back.

Now, Monobina was in the restroom, and he sat alone, watching darkness fill the canyon like ink in water. The city lights were coming on in waves, each light a decision, a switch deliberately flipped, each with consequences.

That is when he saw the rose, deep red, blooming against the dusty brush just beyond the low fence that separated the terrace from the slope. In Delhi, he would have summoned a peon to fetch it without a second thought. But this was America, where people drove their own cars, assembled their own furniture and bought their own groceries.

The fence was low enough that even at forty-eight he could vault over it easily. The rose stood outside the restaurant's boundary, technically not private property.

He glanced around. The other diners were focused on their meals, their faces glowing golden from candles that had bloomed into the dusk.

Standing, he straightened his jacket. A quick step over, pluck the rose, and back before anyone noticed. Simple. The kind of impulsive act his son might have found oddly charming, coming from his boringly predictable father, if he knew.

His leather shoes slipped slightly on the dry slope. Ranadeep moved briskly, the downhill grade accelerating his steps. The darkness here had settled deeper than it appeared from above.

He bent. The rose stem was thick, stubborn.

As he gripped it, something shifted in the brush.

Fast.

A sting to his finger.

Then a blur lifted and wheeled into the night.

A bat.

Blood welled from a sharp puncture on his index finger.

'Fuck,' Ranadeep muttered under his breath, cursing himself for the impulsiveness. He glanced around, hoping there wasn't some damned camera hidden nearby and that he wouldn't end up with a citation from Los Angeles County, for what, picking a rose in a canyon! Just what he needed right now.

When he climbed back up to the terrace, Monobina was already at the table. With her dark hair swept up into a neat bun that accentuated her high cheekbones and slender neck, she looked as much a part of the restaurant's curated elegance as the lanterns or the koi pond. The only thing that didn't quite belong here, Ranadeep felt, was him.

'Where did you go?' Monobina asked.

He placed the rose in her water glass. A single drop of blood stained his napkin as he pressed it to his finger.

'I saw something I wanted down on the slope,' he said. The words didn't land quite as warmly or romantically as he had imagined. 'And I brought it for you.'

'What if you had fallen?' Monobina turned the rose slowly between her fingers. 'A man your age, climbing fences. What would I tell Shayan? Baba twisted his ankle while trying to play hero?'

Ranadeep touched his finger. The bleeding had stopped, but the spot still throbbed. 'It wasn't dangerous. I am still in decent shape for my age.'

'Your cholesterol numbers from last month – that is your definition of decent shape?' she said, leaning in so the nearby diners wouldn't overhear. 'Also, is it even legal to pick flowers here? This is probably L.A. city property. And you are a long way from home, so don't think your Indian Administrative Service card can get you out of this one.'

A waiter appeared at their table, notepad ready. The terrace was half-empty now, most diners having moved indoors as the temperature dipped. His pen caught the light as he waited.

'The miso black cod,' Monobina said. 'And the wagyu toban-yaki for him.' She waited until the waiter left before pulling out her phone.

'Speaking of illegal things, have you seen this? My favourite true crime show is back. You know, the one I told you we should watch together, but you keep changing the channel to cricket? That one. It's back.'

Ranadeep was watching the place where the bat had vanished into the darkness.

'Hmm?'

'*Hidden Secrets*, the one about unsolved cold cases from around the world. The new season is called "The Murder of the Rose", and this time it's set in…Are you even listening to a word I am saying?'

'I am listening,' Ranadeep said, though his eyes remained on the rose. Despite being plucked and placed in a glass of water, it seemed more alive now, its petals curling slightly.

Monobina had gone quiet. The animation in her face from just moments ago was draining away.

'What is it?' Ranadeep asked, rolling the edge of his cloth napkin between his fingers. He glanced at the half-eaten sushi rolls between them. 'I said I am listening; this time it's set where?'

She slowly lowered her phone, her expression shifting, as if she had seen a ghost.

'Pramila Chatterjee,' she said quietly.

Ranadeep's fingers kept turning the napkin, tighter now. 'So that's the cold case they've chosen for this season.'

There was concern in her voice. 'Will they interview you too, for the documentary?'

The steam from her green tea curled up between them.

'Maybe,' Ranadeep said, watching the vapour fade. 'But it's Ishaan they're going to focus on. Of all the cold cases in the world, they picked this one because of him. The buzz. The coverage. They know exactly what they are doing.'

Monobina's expression hardened. 'You talk like he is the one being wronged.'

Ranadeep frowned, sensing the edge in her voice.

'I am sorry,' she went on, 'but I don't see Ishaan Chatterjee as a victim. If there's anyone I can imagine killing a woman and getting away with it, it's that Neanderthal.'

'Mono…' Ranadeep began, making a face. 'They found the murderer, you know that.'

'The murderer was not found,' Monobina said crisply, setting down her chopsticks with care. 'The police arrested a man, threw him in jail, and he committed suicide before trial. That's not closure. That's convenience. That's exactly what the documentary is digging into, they think there was a cover-up.'

She leaned forward slightly. 'But forget all that. Are you going to speak to them if they ask?'

'I do not think I have a choice,' Ranadeep said, dabbing at his mouth with his napkin. 'I could have the office stonewall them, but I have nothing to hide. Nothing new to say. Just what I said back then.' He traced the rim of his sake cup. 'But I am worried about Ishaan. This could hit him hard. He has had a rough patch lately. A string of flops, well, more than a string…'

'Oh please,' Monobina cut in. 'He will survive. He has got lawyers, PR, an army of fans. But what's with you? You seem to be more worried about him than anything else.' She studied him. 'I didn't realize you were still in touch.'

'I am not,' Ranadeep said, weary. 'I see him sometimes at Delhi parties, every few years maybe. I don't think we have exchanged more than a "hi" or a "hello" in decades.' He gestured vaguely. 'He is always flanked by bodyguards, paparazzi and a ring of people trying to bask in the glow. I keep my distance. Maybe if our eyes meet, I give him a salute, he gives a nod. That's it. Honestly, I don't even recognize him anymore. It is like looking at a stranger wearing the face of someone I used to know.'

'Well I don't like him.' Monobina shook her head, disapprovingly.

'And I had no idea,' Ranadeep said dryly. 'Truly, this is the first time I am hearing your opinion of Ishaan.'

Monobina didn't rise to the bait. 'He is exactly the kind of man who cannot take no from a woman. Isn't that what likely happened? She broke it off, and that same night she ended up dead?'

Ranadeep leaned back, a faint smile tugging at his lips. 'Well, I suppose you will just have to wait for your favourite true crime show to tell you.'

A breeze stirred across the terrace, riffling the corners of the dessert menus the waiter had just placed on their table. One of the candles flickered low, the flame thinning before flaring back to life.

Ranadeep exhaled slowly.

'Do you ever hear from the others?' Monobina asked, her voice softer now. 'The Musketeers. That's what you used to call yourselves, didn't you?'

'Ishaan, Basab and Krishanu. We kind of all fell away after Pramila died. It was never the same again. I don't know where they are: Basab, I think I heard, is some big-shot professor in the US, at MIT or Princeton or Caltech or one of them. My memory is not as it used to be, and Krishanu, I have absolutely no idea. Maybe it was all for the better. Maybe it was inevitable.'

'Strange, isn't it,' she said softly, 'how some deaths leave doors open instead of closing them?'

The words hung in the air between them, mixing with the scent of grilled unagi and the canyon's breeze. Below them, a helicopter's searchlight swept across the hillside, its beam cutting through the darkness like a blade seeking secrets in the night.

Ranadeep didn't answer. His eyes remained fixed on the city lights below, but he was seeing something entirely different, not here, not in this time or this place, but thirty years ago, of four boys just eighteen or not even so, the best of friends, the Four Musketeers, sitting on the park bench as the sun set, looking up, the bat propped on the side, the stumps put away in the bag with the pads, as they talked about Sachin Tendulkar and Vinod Kambli and Madhuri Dixit and Raveena Tandon and laughed among themselves, none of them knowing that their world was about to shatter.

Most people do not remember the last day of their childhood.

Ranadeep did.

It was the evening Pramila Chatterjee died.

Drowned in a bucket.

2

The Interview with Genius

Professor Basab Banerjee was staring at the divorce papers, when someone knocked gently on his office door. The afternoon sun angled through the Venetian blinds, striping his cluttered desk with bars of gold and dust. His coffee sat untouched, cold since the process server had left twenty minutes ago.

It was over. Twelve years, two children and a business that could have changed the world.

The memory intruded unbidden: his father in Calcutta, sitting cross-legged on the bed inside the ancient mosquito net, wearing his threadbare lungi and his torn, white undershirt, crumbs of arrowroot biscuit speckling his greying chest hair. Sandra had wanted to visit Calcutta to see Basab's 'roots'. He knew exactly what awaited: two unmarried sisters, three cousins and his parents, all crammed into spaces barely big enough to breathe. He knew what the one shared bathroom, slippery with grime and moss and decay, the mould-eaten walls with the peeling paint and exposed brick, and the suffocating summer nights would do to his American wife, descended from Boston's old money. He had warned her. Told her very plainly what she would find. She had insisted. After a night at his home, he had read Sandra's eyes and booked the Park Hotel for the remainder of the stay.

The ultimate betrayal, the way his father saw it.

'Will she be a good wife, Khoka? Will she adjust?' The old man's lisp had made the words even more grating. 'White woman, will she let you send money home? Will she stay?'

His five sisters had echoed the same concerns, each in their own way, some masquerading it as humour, others as wisdom. As if their world, defined by Doordarshan serials and Bengali melodramas, where noble sons sold their kidneys for their sisters' dowries and wicked foreign daughters-in-law destroyed joint families with their Western notions, could even comprehend the universe of Basab Banerjee, PhD in Physics from Massachusetts Institute of Technology.

Only his mother had stayed silent. She never cared either way.

And now, here was their answer.

She had not stayed.

Baba must be laughing somewhere up there, if heaven tolerated Communist trade unionists who denied its very existence.

Someone knocked again.

'Not now,' he called out, his Bengali accent still strong, despite thirty years in America. Adjusting his wire-rimmed glasses, the same style he had worn since class six, he tried again to focus on the legalese before him: Petition for Dissolution of Marriage, Form FL-100, Superior Court of Los Angeles County.

No, his father had been wrong. Like always. Sandra had tried her best. She had put up with his needy family and his failings as a husband.

The only thing she could not accept was his genius.

He would have fixed things with the company. He was sure of it.

But Sandra had done that thing, from where there was no coming back. She had lost faith in Basab Banerjee.

Another knock. More insistent.

'I said not now...' His voice cracked slightly. 'My office hours are posted.'

'Professor Banerjee?' A woman's voice. Unfamiliar. 'I am Maya Sen, from *Hidden Secrets*. We had an appointment.'

Basab exhaled sharply, smoothing the knot of his tie, a Christmas gift from Sandra, from some other life. He glanced down: khaki pants, worn at the knees; a checked shirt past its prime; scuffed brown loafers. More or less his uniform for the last fifteen years at Caltech.

'Professor?'

He shoved the divorce papers into a desk drawer, tucking them beneath a stack of ungraded quantum mechanics assignments. 'Come in.'

The woman who entered was young, professional and carrying sound equipment. Behind her, an older man with a camera. Basab's eyes went straight to it. He had never liked being photographed, much less filmed.

'Thank you for seeing us,' Maya said, extending her hand.

'Yes, yes. You are here about Pramila Chatterjee.' He did not take her hand but just gestured to the chairs facing his desk, both buried under physics journals. 'Move those anywhere. The floor is fine. Entropy wins in the end.'

As they cleared the chairs, his gaze flicked to a framed Disneyland photo: him, Sandra and the kids last summer. He turned it face down.

'Would you prefer to do this somewhere else?' Maya asked, eyeing the cramped space. Books lined every wall, equations covered the whiteboard, and a small bust of Schrödinger peered down from atop a filing cabinet.

'Why? Would it make for better television?' Basab's lips curled. 'This is where I spend my life. Seems appropriate to discuss death here.'

Maya began setting up. 'We understand this might be difficult…'

'Do you?' he cut in, soft but sharp. His eyes had landed on the manila envelope he had forgotten to put away, the one stamped: **'Service of Process: Divorce, Do Not Discard.'**

She was looking at it. Not long. But long enough.

'Ah. You noticed that. Divorce papers. But let us keep that out of your show, shall we? No need to mix melodrama with murder.'

Maya hesitated. 'We can reschedule if…'

'No, no. Let's get all the unpleasantness over in one day. Better than letting it drip from one to another. Like slow water torture.'

She studied him carefully.

'Professor, you don't have to do this interview.'

'Oh, but I must.' He lifted his eyebrows theatrically. 'Inaction, whether in a documentary or a marriage, is just another kind of guilt.'

'I am not sure I understand,' Maya said.

'You know I was the chief witness in the murder trial of Brajendra Das.'

'Yes, of course.'

He steepled his fingers. 'Since I was a minor, my testimony was sealed. But something tells me you have read it.'

Maya looked down, briefly caught off guard. 'We did. As part of our research.'

'Nothing to feel bad about. You have done your homework. Excellent documentarians always get access to things they legally should not. Indian law, who cares, right?' He waved a hand. 'But forget that. The fact that you have read it means you know why I must be on record now.'

She frowned. 'Why do you say that?'

Basab leaned back, his chair creaking. 'If I refuse to speak, what will people assume? That I am just someone who wants to leave the past buried? Or that I have something to hide? That maybe I got away with something thirty years ago and cannot bear the scrutiny again?'

Maya held his gaze. 'That's not what we're suggesting.'

'Oh, but you will. It is how these things work. Otherwise, where is the drama? This is a reality show, is it not, but set in the past?' He smiled. 'But don't worry, I am not one of those professors who publish in *Nature* but get skittish when asked to share the data. I am quite prepared to stand by what I said thirty years ago. Fire away.'

'Just so you know, we tape everything,' Maya said, voice steady. 'If there's anything you want to say off the record, we will turn the camera off. We will edit what we record, but we will keep and share the raw footage in case you feel your words weren't faithfully reproduced.'

She pulled a folder of release forms and placed them on his desk.

'Ah, a day for signing away my rights,' Basab murmured, with a wistful smile.

As they set up their equipment, Basab watched her. There was something about Maya Sen that tugged at his memory, something in the way she moved, methodical and exact. She had that generic, twenty-something look of so many grad students: smart casual clothes and the quiet efficiency of someone used to interviewing professors. Perhaps that was it, maybe he had seen her around Caltech.

'So, let us begin.' She settled into the chair across from him, notebook balanced on her knee. 'You were Pramila's tutor for maths and science, is that right?'

'I suppose you got that from the police transcripts.'

'It was there, yes. But that's not where I remembered it from. Her mother showed me her exercise books.' Maya's voice softened. 'The last one still has that week's homework, integration by parts. And in the margin, she had written: Basab-da will be proud of me.'

Something shifted in Basab's expression. 'Chatterjee-mashi kept her books?'

'Everything. Her school uniform. Her poems. The trophies from her singing competitions.' Maya hesitated, then glanced back down at her notes.

Basab turned to the window, adjusting his glasses. The sun caught the grey in his hair. 'You want to know about my student.'

'Yes.'

'Not about that night?'

'We will come to that. Of course we will.' Maya looked up. 'But first, we need to know how you saw her.'

Basab's fingers found the edge of his desk. 'I used to go to Pramila's house every Thursday evening at six sharp. Mathematics, physics, chemistry. A hundred rupees, first week of every month, in a white envelope. Paid in advance.'

'Aah, that must have been a lot back then,' Maya said, smiling.

'This was not the seventies,' he snapped. 'I may be old, but I am not that ancient. A hundred rupees was not much, not for home tuition, for three subjects, one-on-one.'

His voice trailed off.

He remembered why he had started teaching. That evening, walking home from the locked-out jute mill, his father had seen him playing carrom with Ishaan under the banyan tree's lone bulb. After dinner, he had been summoned to his parents' room. Every detail remained intact: a lizard perched on the wall, a cockroach in its mouth, while the tube light flickered above the rusted Kelvinator fridge. The mosquito coil burned eternally on the cracked windowsill, its acrid smoke mixing with talcum powder and sweat.

And his father's voice, soft but cutting: 'Ishaan's father is a smuggler. Everyone knows it. Black money. That boy can do what he likes; his father will leave him crores unless he becomes a Mumbai hero first. But you, Khoka, you are not Ishaan. God gave you a brain. Use it.'

The memory of his father fingering the frayed sleeve of his ironed shirt still hanging behind the door. 'If you have finished your studies, fine. Then teach. Make money. A sister's wedding isn't cheap. And there are so many of them. But you? You play cricket on Sunday mornings and carrom in the evenings. What kind of son leaves it all on his old father? You are not a boy anymore.'

Basab blinked. The voice faded. He turned back to Maya. 'Someone with my credentials could have asked for three hundred. But my family needed the money.'

More memories came. His father at the wobbly dining table, head in hands, muttering about school fees, the dowries already paid, and the two daughters still unmarried. How he would look up when Basab entered, eyes lit with desperate hope. 'Khoka, another family is asking for tuition. Their son is weak in maths, twice a week.' And when Basab hesitated, 'Pujo is coming. I need shirts and trousers for the sons-in-law, Raymonds, nothing less. Or they say things to your sisters. And Ramesh, the grocer's son, insulted me last

Tuesday, in the ration line, in front of everyone. Refuses to sell on credit now.'

Basab looked at Maya, a bitter smile on his lips. 'You know what they say about beggars and choosers. Whatever they paid, I taught.'

'So, Professor Banerjee, tell me about Pramila. How was she? I presume, as her tutor, you knew her well.'

'I would not say that. I was a quiet boy then, and so was she…a quiet girl.'

Knew her well. A shiver traced down Basab's spine at the very thought. Ishaan would have rearranged any boy's face for even harbouring such notions about Pramila. His girl, as he called her, and everyone knew it. Not that it stopped the furtive glances. Pramila's beauty drew eyes without effort. Even Basab, for all his textbook-bound existence, was not so lost in equations that he could not see what made boys' heads turn when she walked by. But he was no fool. He had seen what happened to those who looked too long, those who forgot that Ishaan's fists were as quick as his temper.

In fact, the only reason he taught Pramila was that, of all the boys, Ishaan trusted him the most. Betraying that trust, even in thought, never came to him.

And no, that wasn't because of fear.

It was because of love.

Ishaan was his best friend. Yes, they all were, Ranadeep and Krishanu, but Ishaan was different. For him, Basab would have given his life.

And he almost did.

'But you taught her for more than a year, once every week. Surely you have some story, some anecdote, some recollection…?'

'Just so you understand how things were, thirty years ago, in Calcutta. I went to a boys' school, St. Matthew's. Pramila went to a girls' school, St. Agnes's. I stayed in my circle of boys, she in hers. But our schools were right across the street from each other, so yes, friendships did cross that road. Ishaan, as I am sure you know, was…'

'Yes, we will come to that, Ishaan Chatterjee,' Maya said. 'And I understand what you are saying, Professor Banerjee. Given Ishaan's reputation for possessiveness, and your closeness with him, you were wary of any perception of impropriety. Given the times, I absolutely understand the caution, but still…'

'Pramila wasn't meant for science. Her parents pushed her into it, but it wasn't what she wanted. We were just going through the motions. I was there for my hundred rupees; she was there because she had to be. Music was what she loved. She could sing like Lata, like Asha, like Alka and even Alisha Chinai. How is that for range? Even I could tell how good she was, and I knew nothing about music. She did Bharatanatyam, but sometimes when I came to teach, I would catch her practising salsa steps from a book. I used to say, imagine if she put that much effort into physics…'

His shoulders tensed, as if against a sudden chill.

'Then came that *Woman's World* cover, and…'

'Yes. We will come to that,' Maya said. 'The pictures for that magazine…that was such a vital part of the case. But still, if there's something…'

'I actually saw more of who she was during our cricket and football matches than in those classes. Every neighbourhood had its club back then. We had challenge matches at the park. That was everything to us, before phones and video games took over. Pramila came to watch Ishaan, but she loved cricket. She had read all her father's old *International Cricketer* and *Sportsworld* magazines. She knew about everything: Len Hutton, Denis Compton, Sachin, Azhar…everything. Getting into Eden Gardens was impossible unless you knew someone. Her uncle worked in the Cricket Association; she got tickets for me, Ranadeep and Krishanu for the India–England match. Ishaan had his father's VIP passes, of course, and she sat with him in the clubhouse. We were at square leg, the perfect spot to watch Azhar's century. Krishanu kept jumping up every over, yelling at the English players in Bengali.'

Basab smiled at the memory.

'Then there was this sports quiz, Sports Galaxy, the biggest one in Calcutta. Krishanu, Ranadeep and I were supposed to be a team, but Ranadeep got malaria. Ishaan came to support us and brought Pramila along. She ended up being our third. She was incredible. She answered every question about cricket, even the weird ones, like what plane Gower and Morris took for that joyride in '91 that got them in trouble, or that Don Bradman was called the Boy from Bowral...That was Pramila.'

Basab fell silent, his gaze dropping to the desk.

'It is time to talk about that night, isn't it?'

Maya nodded. 'But, first, let us talk about what led to all of it, the magazine cover. The *Woman's World*.'

'You have to understand,' Basab said, his voice carrying the weight of decades. His fingers moved restlessly across the desk surface, tracing what Maya had come to recognize as equations, a physicist's nervous habit. The afternoon light caught dust motes dancing above his invisible calculations. 'September 1994. No social media then.' He gave a hollow laugh. 'Content wasn't immediate, wasn't...' His fingers quickened their mathematical dance. 'Wasn't disposable.'

His eyes took on that far-away dreamy look, as if peering through a window that opened onto the past. 'Durga Pujo was approaching. All year, we struggled to survive; every moment awake was taken up with the stress of studies, employment and where the next rupee was going to come from. And whatever wasn't spent on that, was spent on going from one place to another, in public transportation, buses and local trains, stewing in someone else's sweat, or at home, in hour-long power cuts, stewing in your own, or waiting, just waiting, for the bank officer to do his job, or the government babu to do his, or the doctor to write the prescription. Every man stole your time in proportion to their worth.'

'That sounds terrible.'

'A huge swarm of flies buzzing around a broken pot of jaggery, one that everyone could get a lick of but would satiate the hunger of no one. That was Calcutta.' His fingers went still on the desk, the equations falling away into silence. 'But not during Durga Pujo. It was as if the curse was lifted for a few weeks. School was out, people took their leave from office, and there was time, a light, pleasant few days to oneself. People had time then. Time to read.' His eyes flickered to the divorce papers lurking in his drawer like a guilty secret. 'The magazines would release their special editions. Thicker paper, glossier covers. The *Woman's World* was…' He paused, tasting the memory. 'It was everything in Calcutta.'

Maya waited, letting the silence stretch between them.

'Ostensibly for women,' Basab continued, his academic tone fraying at the edges. 'But men read it too. For the articles, they claimed. The centrefolds.' A tremor passed through his hand as he straightened his tie. 'Pramila was on the cover that Pujo.'

His shoulders tensed, as if bracing against an unseen weight. 'And the centrespread.'

'I was with Ishaan the day he found out,' Basab began, then stopped.

Dover Market unfolded in his memory with merciless clarity: fish laid out on green plastic sheets, blood seeping into creases, eyes like vacant mirrors. Each tailfin twitched at the touch of water, waiting for the *bonthi* to separate flesh from bone. The market pressed close, bodies and sharp elbows, a heavy shoe finding your toe in the crowd, voices rising and falling in haggling rhythm. That smell of vegetables between ripe and rotten, and dead fish. And finally, the metallic fish scales, water and blood that seemed to slip through your slippers, marking each step.

Through it all, Ishaan walked beside him, their shoulders touching in the crowd as they had a thousand times before. They spoke of Ashtami night, which pandals to visit, how to slip past the crowds at Maddox Square, whether to brave Mohammad Ali Park after midnight. Simple plans, spoken with the easy confidence of boys who thought they understood their world.

Then Ishaan's voice changed. 'Something really strange happened today,' he said, his face wearing that same lost expression Basab had seen during mathematics tests. 'You know those morons from National Boys School, Partha and Atanu? I passed them coming back from the gym. Partha, that little, fat dwarf, was laughing at me. And Atanu, who looks like his circus master, did something even stranger, he made this gesture,' his hand moved uncertainly, 'like jerking off, and rolled his eyes. You know what's going on?'

Basab had shrugged. National Boys School boys were jackasses anyway. They had just lost the cricket final.

They passed the typists, little balding men in identical check shirts, hunched over wooden tables, keys clacking in unison as they transcribed deeds, contracts, thesis submissions. Beyond them stood the magazine stalls, where *Filmfare*, *Stardust*, *Sportsworld* hung from twine fastened with wooden clips, pages ruffling in the last humid breath of monsoon.

Maya leaned forward. 'You were with Ishaan, go on, Professor Banerjee.'

And there it was. The *Woman's World*, Pujo edition, swaying slightly. Pramila's face emerged from a backdrop of roses, head thrown back, with a smile. He had never seen it before, the smile of a Bollywood actress. Her shoulders were bare.

The wooden clips knocked together, *tok*, *tok*, *tok*. Ishaan went still, so still that even the air seemed to pause. The magazine vendor's eyes met Basab's. He heard Ishaan's teeth grind, watched his hand lunge forward, yanking the magazine down.

'Professor Banerjee?' Maya's voice seemed to come from very far away.

'In physics,' he said quietly, 'we study moments of phase transition, points where matter changes state. Ice to water, water to steam. But we rarely discuss what happens exactly at that point of change. In that infinite moment of becoming something else entirely.'

Basab's voice came out as if a fishbone was stuck in his throat. 'That is what I saw in Ishaan's face. A phase transition. My friend becoming...something else. He started running, screaming into the wind, leafing through the magazine in a rage. And when he came to the centrefold, he tore the magazine apart, a bound Pujo magazine, this thick, into two, and threw the remnants of it into the air. I ran after him, but he was too fast. Not much makes a Calcutta crowd stop what they are doing and turn around. They did. They all did.'

'What happened then?' Maya asked.

'He went to her house.' Basab's fingers found the edge of his desk. 'Barged in. Slapped her in front of her family. Kicked down some furniture.'

'You saw this?'

'No.' Basab looked down at his hands. 'I was not there. I had to go give tuition, hundred rupees, remember? But the whole neighbourhood knew by evening. Where I grew up, news like that spreads faster than floods.'

'And after that?'

'Can we pause for a moment?' Basab asked. 'I need some water.'

When he was back with a glass of water from the water fountain in the hall, Maya asked, 'So, didn't Pramila's father call the police on Ishaan? Here you have another boy, a teen, coming and striking his daughter in his house.'

'No.' Basab lifted the water glass with careful precision as if the simple act required all his concentration. 'Some said he was afraid of Ishaan's father.' A pause, the water trembling slightly. 'Ishaan's dad, Siddhartha Chatterjee, wasn't just any businessman. He owned factories, produced Bengali films. Police officers at his command, influential people and…' his voice lowered to nearly a whisper, 'some of the types you do not want to mess with.'

The glass made a soft click against the desk. 'Others said Pramila's father was angrier at her than at Ishaan. That he beat her too, for bringing shame to their family name.'

'For modelling?'

'For modelling without permission. For showing her shoulders. For those "expressions".' The last word caught in his throat like a splinter. He swallowed hard, eyes flickering away for a moment. 'This was not something good girls from middle-class Bengali families did. Bollywood actresses, yes, but not our Pramila.' His eyes met Maya's, searching for understanding across the decades.

'Maybe centuries from now, they will look back at us, growing sentient beings with the ability to love, feel, and understand pain and death, yet still raising animals in industrial farms…' He shook his head slowly, a faint, bitter smile touching his lips. 'They will call us monsters too.'

Basab's reflection in the window seemed older suddenly, stretched thinly by the weight of memory. He blinked, breaking the silence. 'We all thought things would sort themselves out. We felt they should. Life would go on.' His voice lowered, almost resigned.

Maya leaned forward slightly. 'We were wrong, weren't we?'

He sighed, running a hand through his thinning hair. 'Breakups were different then…They needed more than a text message, cold and digital. Love, after all, is analogue. You had to put ink to paper, leave something of yourself behind.'

'The letter came on a Tuesday.' He paused, eyes distant, as if recalling the exact moment. 'I remember because that was the day our classes started even earlier at school. Ishaan found me during the lunch break, the envelope worn soft at the corners from his grip.'

'She wanted to meet Ishaan at Ramkrishna Park. To end it.' His voice grew heavier, thick with remembered pain. 'Ishaan couldn't comprehend rejection; it was not something that existed in his world.' He shook his head slowly. 'He kept saying it over and over: yes, he shouldn't have hit her, but then she had gone behind his back with those pictures. Her father hit her too, he said, even more than he did. Was she going to abandon her family as well?'

Basab remembered the words still, not that he would say them to Maya Sen.

'Actions have consequences,' Ishaan had said. 'Even I understand Newton's Third Law.'

Maya's brow furrowed. 'That letter,' she said. 'I couldn't find it in the police archives. Did Ishaan show it to you?'

Basab's jaw tightened. 'No.' His voice was firm. 'No one reads another person's letters.'

'Then why tell you about it?'

He looked down at his hands, folding them together. 'He needed someone to be there with him for that conversation. Not next to him, not listening to them fight. Just...present. A wingman.' His fingers stilled on the desk. 'I expected him to ask Ranadeep, our Jack of All Trades, good at everything, the perfect sidekick. The Deepak Tijori to his Rahul Roy.' A ghost of a smile flickered on his lips. 'Or even Krishanu, though no one took him seriously, called him too much of a clown. Our Johnny Lever.' His voice softened. 'But he chose me. The quiet one. The keeper of secrets. He knew I would have his back.'

And he had, for thirty years after that.

Basab's eyes darkened with memory. 'Ramkrishna Park. It was barely a park at all. Just dust and yellowed grass choking between buildings. The monsoon had left everything with that peculiar dampness, not quite wet, not quite dry, a state of perpetual decay. We lived in terror of rain before Pujo. It threatened to wash away the only days that made the rest of the year bearable.' He let out a bitter laugh, surprising even himself. 'As if the gods themselves might drown our little attempts at joy.'

'The benches.' His voice caught, fragile as a broken string. 'If you could call them that. Filthy metal planks streaked with rust and crow droppings, each with a light above that cast more shadows than illumination. A half-paved road bisected the park, and to the side...'

He paused, weighing the memory. 'There was what we called the ditch. Some corporation official's abandoned dream; they had excavated it for a children's playground, meant to install swings and slides. But then, it remained unfinished. Just a quagmire of mud and soil that seemed to grow deeper with each passing rain, as if it were slowly consuming whatever fell into it.'

The quality of light in his office shifted, taking on that same murky cast he remembered from the park, neither day nor dusk, but some liminal space between where truth could slip its moorings.

'That's where we met that evening,' Basab said softly. 'The last evening. When everything was still possible, and nothing was yet inevitable.'

Maya leaned forward slightly. 'Tell me about that evening, Professor.'

Basab's hand absently smoothed the edge of his desk calendar. 'That evening stays with me.' He closed his eyes briefly, swallowing hard. 'I stood by that half-dug ditch, and they sat a few hundred metres away on one of those broken, dusty benches, one of the few that had a working street light above it.'

Though he wouldn't share it with Maya, the memory unfurled in his mind with terrible clarity: Ishaan stooped forward, his palms on the seat of the bench, broken like a tin doll, tears tracking down his face. He had never seen his friend cry before, not when he broke his arm playing cricket, not when his father's belt left welts. But there he was, the invincible Ishaan Chatterjee, begging like a child.

But the most terrifying change was not in Ishaan. It was in Pramila.

In his tutoring sessions, she had been a ghost of herself, shoulders curved inward, eyes downcast, fingers trembling over equations as if each mistake might summon punishment. With Ishaan, she had worn a different mask: the adoring girlfriend, face upturned like a flower seeking the sun, her smile a careful performance of submission that seemed to both dread and crave his attention.

But that evening in Ramkrishna Park, as darkness pooled around the corroded benches, someone else entirely occupied Pramila's skin. Her face had shed its familiar contours, revealing angles that belonged to a stranger. The way she looked at Ishaan now carried neither hatred nor triumph but something far more devastating: the way an owner looks at a beloved pet they have decided must be put down, acknowledging the years of love and loyalty while remaining unmoved in their terrible resolve.

Gone was the girl who apologized for existing. In her place stood a woman who had crossed an invisible threshold, leaving behind not just Ishaan, but the very shape of herself that had made their love possible.

What frightened Basab most, though this too would remain unspoken, was the completeness of her transformation. As if the Pramila he had known had been merely provisional, a chrysalis waiting to split open and reveal its true form.

He watched her standing there, backlit by the sputtering street lamp, and felt a cold certainty: this was Pramila as she was meant to be.

He could not have known then that this would be her final form. That in a few hours, this newfound self would be submerged in water, her emergence cut brutally short.

But somehow, watching her that evening, he had sensed it.

This could not last.

'She seemed…different that evening,' was all he told Maya, his words falling into the afternoon silence like pebbles dropped into still water.

'Did you hear what they were saying?'

'They were too far for me to catch the words,' he said, his thumb idly working the calendar's metal binding. 'Just shapes in the gathering dark.'

'What happened then?'

Basab hesitated. 'He was…' The words, very distraught, felt hollow against the reality he still carried. 'It is not my place to say more. I didn't stay until the end. Their conversation went on way longer than I expected, and I had studying to do.' His hand moved to straighten papers that were already perfectly aligned. 'And it felt…wrong, somehow. Like I was intruding on something too private.'

The real reason for his departure stayed locked behind his teeth, how he had fled because he couldn't bear to watch his friend break apart. It reminded him too much of that day Krishanu fell during a match, his leg twisted at an impossible angle, screaming in pain. Some wounds were too raw to witness.

As he had walked home in the gathering dark, his mind had spun with one terrible question: How does someone like Ishaan heal from this? How does pride reassemble itself once it's been ground to dust?

'So I left them there. It was starting to rain.'

The silence that followed felt heavy with all he couldn't say.

'I didn't know then,' he said quietly, 'that it would be the last time I would see her alive.'

Maya waited, but Basab had retreated into himself. His fingers now methodically arranged and rearranged his pens as if perfect order might somehow absolve him of what came after.

'Your police testimony,' Maya said, shuffling through her notes. 'You mentioned seeing Ishaan after you left the park.'

The memory of that police station surfaced with startling clarity: a colonial relic with ceiling fans stirring thick air into visible currents of dust. The wooden bench where he had sat had an open handcuff still attached to one leg, a place where criminals were kept when the holding cells were full, where the sound of stick beatings still seemed to echo.

His school uniform had stuck to his back. The fear of being chained there if they didn't like his answers made the cotton transparent with sweat.

Two inspectors sat across from him at a metal desk. The older one, Bhattacharya, obscenely obese with a walrus moustache, chain-smoked Charminar cigarettes. Their sharp smoke mixed with phenyl and stale tea, while a rusted file cabinet loomed behind them, stuffed with yellowing papers, ready to burst.

The younger inspector, Roy, looked like he had stepped out of *Miami Vice*, lean and chiselled, a registration book open before him, its pages warped by humidity.

'So many times we have asked you, boy,' Inspector Bhattacharya said, tapping ash onto a grey-stained saucer. 'Think carefully. Which direction did Ishaan go?'

The ceiling fan clicked with each rotation. A Government of India calendar hung on the wall, the prime minister's face watching over the wrong month.

A peon shuffled past, rubber slippers making wet sounds against the floor, bringing tea nobody had asked for.

Inspector Bhattacharya leaned forward, dark sweat patches spreading under his arms. 'Your friend's life could depend on this. You understand? Be very sure.'

Somewhere in the building, a typewriter clattered like distant gunfire. Inspector Roy's leaking fountain pen left blue stains on his fingers as he waited to record the answer.

The question hung in the air like cigarette smoke, refusing to dissipate.

Basab looked at Maya. Thirty years later, another interrogation. But his story hadn't changed.

Basab nodded slowly, tapping his pen against the edge of his desk. 'The police asked about that too during questioning; if I had left, how did I know in which direction Ishaan had gone? After I left, I went home but couldn't settle. I opened a set of mock tests but couldn't focus. I was worried. After about an hour, I went back to the park.'

He paused, as if mentally mapping the old neighbourhood.

'They were gone by then, but I saw Ishaan walking in the direction opposite to Pramila's house. The layout of our area was...' His hands moved across the desk, sketching invisible streets. 'We had two distinct parts. Our middle-class section, where I lived, where Pramila's family lived, where Krishanu lived.'

He remembered his street. Houses growing upwards like rotting teeth, plaster crumbled at the edges, revealing brick beneath like exposed bone. Open drains running between the buildings, carrying things you had to grow nose-blind to survive, a stench cocktail of ammonia and phenyl.

His voice shifted as he continued, 'Then there was the other side, where Ishaan and Ranadeep's families lived. Newer buildings, multi-storeyed apartments with ground floor parking, security guards in pressed uniforms, and small patches of cement where children could actually play. You could tell where one neighbourhood ended and the other began just by the smell of the air and the fact that the drains vanished underground.'

'Was there any way he could have reached Pramila's house from that direction?' Maya asked.

'Well,' Basab said, rolling a pen back and forth across the polished wood. 'There was one route. A very long way around. You would have to cross the main road, circle past Dover Market and come all the way back through the lanes behind the temple. But that would have taken...' He frowned slightly. 'At least forty-five minutes on foot. It was not a path anyone would normally take.'

'Understood. But that still doesn't mean he didn't go to Pramila's house.' Maya let the words settle before continuing. 'According to police records, her parents were at R.G. Kar Hospital every day, morning till night. Her uncle had had a heart attack. Was it normal then, leaving daughters alone at home?'

Basab's fingers stilled on the pen. 'She wasn't alone. You have to understand what a Calcutta *para* was: more than neighbours, more than community. The shopkeeper at the corner selling bread and eggs and peppermint lozenges, the lady walking the street shouting, "Do you have utensils to sell?" in a loud, screechy voice cutting through concentration, street dogs barking at any strange smell, families in every window, kids playing cricket in the lane. A thousand eyes, a thousand ears.'

Then his voice softened. 'We looked out for each other, yes. Interfered in each other's lives, certainly. But no one was ever truly alone.'

He looked directly at Maya for the first time since beginning this memory.

'That was the tragedy. When Pramila was harmed, it came from within the *para* itself. And that's why no one saw anything, because there was nothing to see. Nothing out of place. Nothing that didn't belong.'

'So, we come to Brajendra Das.' Maya's voice dropped slightly. 'Her next-door neighbour. Part of her *para*. The man who was accused of her murder. Primarily on the basis of one person's testimony.'

Basab knew what was coming.

'Yours.'

'Yes,' he said, keeping his gaze on Maya's. 'Mine.'

'Tell me about him. And about what you told the police.'

'Before I tell you that,' Basab said, 'you need to understand the geography of the place.' His hands mapped invisible boundaries in the air. 'Three houses, pressed against each other like badly shelved books. On the right was Brajendra Das's three-storey house; he owned it, lived on the top floor, rented out the rest. The middle house was Brajendra Das's, but he rented it out fully. It had two floors, and Pramila's family lived on the second. To the left lived Krishanu.'

He paused. 'My place was the fourth house. It was behind Brajendra's. No street access. To reach the main road, I had to use this narrow lane through Brajendra's property. Barely wide enough for one person, walls on both sides, always filled with garbage. The stench…' He shook his head. 'But that is not important. What is important is that this lane ran along the wall between Brajendra's house and Pramila's. And there was a gate in that wall.'

'And that is where you saw him?'

'Yes. I was standing at my door, looking down that filthy lane. I saw him cross through that gate, from Pramila's side to his.'

'When?'

'That night. At two minutes after nine in the evening.'

'Yes, you gave the police that time. How were you so sure about the precise time?'

'Superhit Festival,' Basab said. 'A Hindi song countdown show. Everyone watched it. You could hear the theme song from every television in the neighbourhood. It plays for exactly two minutes; I checked the next week. He came through that door just as it ended.'

'What was suspicious about it? You said that property was also his.'

'If you recall, I had said there were two floors, with tenants in both. The first-floor tenant was an office, a travel agency at the time if I recall correctly, and it was closed that late. The second-floor tenant was Pramila's family, and she was alone at home. So why would a man, more than fifty years old, have any legitimate reason for going to that house? Suspicious, yes, but I might have forgotten it, if not for the other, more significant detail.'

'The detail was his state when he emerged,' Basab said. 'He was visibly distraught. His hair was dishevelled, his breathing laboured. He kept shaking, made this strange slurping sound. Bent over twice as if to vomit. Had to steady himself against the wall.'

He looked at Maya. 'You have my full testimony from that night in the police records. I was more...detailed then. Thirty years do that to memory, reduces everything to broad strokes and raw emotion. What I do remember, and will never forget, was the insanity in his eyes, flickering by the dim light of the distant street lamp, not a man, not quite, but someone, and I do not use the word lightly, possessed.'

He would not tell Maya how precisely he remembered every word of his testimony. Why risk an inconsistency that could be used against him? But the memory played in his mind with perfect clarity: that small room at the police station, the rickety table between him and the two inspectors, Bhattacharya and Roy. His teenage voice, cracking with nerves: 'Sir, I saw Brajendra-kaku come out through the gate. His hair was all over his face, sir, like when we run in the wind. He was not walking straight at all; it was like when my father comes home with a fever. His lungi was crooked, the edge dragging in the drain water. He was breathing so hard I could hear it over the sound from a TV, *hunh hunh*, like a dog in summer. Twice he bent down, his hands on his knees, like he would throw up. He made this sound, *slurp slurp*, like when you are trying not to cry. He had to hold the wall with both hands, sir, his fingers spread out on the wet moss. And his face…it was the face of a monster, a *rakhosh*, gleaming with madness.'

The officers had leaned forward then, the ceiling fan stirring cigarette smoke above their heads. Even now, Basab could smell the tea growing cold on the table and feel the wet patch of sweat spreading across the back of his shirt.

'They made me repeat this story many times, trying to check it for inconsistencies, so you will find multiple recountings of it,' Basab told Maya, pulling himself back to the present. 'What matters is that he went inside his house after that. And there was absolutely nothing normal about what I saw. Nothing.'

'And how many days after the murder did you tell this story to the police, Professor?' Maya asked.

'Story?' The word came out sharp as broken glass.

'By story, I meant your version of events. Mr Das, in his testimony, repeatedly denied being there.'

'Yes, he had to. Because he could not come up with a good enough reason for why he could have been there.'

'It says you told the police after they brought you in for questioning three days later.' Maya's voice remained neutral, but her words carried weight. 'Was this not important enough to tell them right after you heard the news, presumably the next day at the latest?'

'Oh, please.' Anger threaded through Basab's voice. 'No one wants to be involved with the police, not now, not thirty years ago. You go to the police, and you are trapped in a cycle of questioning and courts. And my father, if he knew this would require hiring a lawyer…' He shook his head. 'First, he wouldn't hire one, and second, he would kill me for not keeping my mouth shut.'

His voice dropped. 'But there was someone worse than the police. Brajendra Das. I was terrified of him after what I had seen. And then when I found out the next day what he had done...' He drew in a sharp breath. 'If he knew I had seen him, he would have killed me. If I went to the police and he managed to get out, he would kill me. I was a month short of eighteen, with no one to talk to about this, and you are questioning me about why I took three days?'

'Well then, if you were so afraid, why say it at all?' Maya asked.

'Because of Ishaan.' Basab's voice softened. 'The papers were all over him. The police too. Every morning there was the headline, "Movie Producer's Son Prime Suspect". They had his motive, his violence, his history with Pramila.' He looked at Maya, and for a moment his eyes held that old, fierce loyalty that had once bound them all together. 'I told you before, he was my friend. My best friend. And I was willing to go through hell for him.'

'You know how it is in Calcutta,' he continued, a bitter edge creeping into his voice. 'If a Mercedes hits a Maruti, no one asks what happened. The Mercedes is guilty. The rich man's son must be the villain. It is how people compensate for their own insignificance, by tearing down anyone who rises above their station. Since they can never have what Ishaan had, he must not deserve it.'

He straightened in his chair. 'The newspapers knew exactly what they were doing. Every day, another story about the "spoiled rich boy", another anonymous source speaking about his temper. They didn't need evidence. They had something better; they had what their readers wanted to believe.'

'The law is supposed to be blind to such things,' Maya said.

'Is it?' Basab's laugh held no humour. 'We like to pretend justice is pure, controlled only by statutes and precedents. But judges read newspapers. Police officers have opinions. The whole machinery of justice moves to the rhythm of social sentiment. And in Calcutta, in 1994, society had already decided who the villain was.'

Maya watched him carefully. The careful professor's façade had cracked, revealing something raw underneath.

'Besides,' Basab continued, his voice steadying, 'it wasn't just my testimony. The police raided Brajendra's house. In his terrace room, that *chilekotha* where he lived alone…' He paused. 'They found things. Pictures of Pramila from school trips to Digha and Darjeeling. Her old diaries, filled with poems and stories. Things that belonged to her, that should never have been in his possession.'

'The shrine,' Maya said.

'That's what the police called it. Their theory was that he had been entering her house when he thought no one was home, stealing her things, piece by piece. That night, he didn't know she would be there. When she discovered him.' Basab stopped, letting the silence complete the thought. 'The police said he killed her to keep his secret. A perfectly logical conclusion.'

'There's something else, Professor Banerjee.' Maya's voice shifted like a shadow across still water. 'I spoke with Inspector Roy.'

'Ah, the man who took an excessive interest in his appearance.' Basab's lips curved in a thin smile. 'Does he still work for the force, or has he found his true calling, playing cops in Bengali web series?'

'He is retired now,' Maya continued. 'Inspector Bhattacharya passed away ten years ago, but Inspector Roy…he remembers everything. Particularly you.'

'Does he now?' Basab's voice held the careful neutrality of a man measuring each word.

'He said that he believes that it was Ishaan who killed Pramila. That his father's money buried the truth.'

'Of course.' Basab leaned back slightly. 'That's the central premise of your documentary, isn't it? I knew the moment you walked in. Where's the drama in the simple truth that a madman killed Pramila, when you can suggest an Indian superstar has skeletons in his closet, literally? So, what did Inspector Roy say?'

'He spoke about those days of questioning,' Maya said, watching Basab carefully. 'Said you were remarkable, how you avoided their traps, how quickly you understood where they were leading. He said the other boys called you Genius, and he agreed. What he said was, and I quote, "It was like being the Belgian defence to a Maradona in his prime; the boy is feinting, going left while looking to the right, and every time I try to trip him, he seems to gather even more momentum, dribbling the ball away."'

'Wow, that must be the sweetest thing anyone has ever said about me.' A sarcastic smile touched Basab's lips, then faded. 'But such is my luck, I cannot even accept that compliment without damning myself.'

'He said he tried for days to break your testimony. But Inspector Bhattacharya always intervened, right when he thought you had painted yourself into a corner.'

'Oh, then I cannot be Maradona. Now he is saying I had assists, which makes me Gary Lineker at best.' Basab Banerjee was visibly enjoying himself now.

'Inspector Roy thinks his senior was bought. As a matter of fact, he said he was positive.'

'Ah! Inspector Roy, the only cop who couldn't be bought. That old Ranjit Mallick trope from Bengali movies from the 80s.'

'Then there is the question of money, Professor.' Maya's words cut through the afternoon air. 'Inspector Roy remembers your family's circumstances very well. Your father, unemployed after the jute mill lockout. Two sisters' marriages to fund. Financial demands from the three he had already married off. And yet…' She let the pause stretch. 'You made it to IIT Kanpur. Then America.'

'Interesting. And here I was thinking that being second in the All India Joint Entrance Examination, considered the toughest examination of that level in the world, getting into IIT Kanpur in computer science, and then transferring to physics because I did not find the computer science curriculum challenging enough, studying on a government scholarship given to one person in India every year and then getting a fellowship to do my PhD at MIT, given to one person in the world every year, was all because of my brains. I guess it was all because of Ishaan Chatterjee's movie-producer father. If Inspector Roy had his way, he would possibly insist that my current endowed professorship at Caltech, the "David Kirk Endowed Professor of Physics", be renamed "Siddhartha Chatterjee Endowed Professor of Physics" on account of Ishaan's father having paid for my position.'

His laugh held no warmth.

'I was just saying, in the interest of full disclosure, what Inspector Roy had to say about you,' Maya said. 'I do not mean to cast aspersions on your achievements or in any way offend you, Professor.'

'None taken.' His voice held the precise chill of liquid nitrogen. 'But as a documentarian, may I request that you find out how my education was sponsored? It should be a matter of public record since I have always been a scholarship student. If my permission is needed to get these records, I will be only too glad to give it to you.'

'That will not be necessary, Professor Banerjee. These are, of course, mere accusations.'

'So, what did Inspector Roy have to say about the shrine?' Something flickered in Basab's eyes, like light catching the edge of a blade. 'How did I manage to pull that off?'

'He has a theory,' Maya continued. 'Would you like to hear it?'

When Basab nodded, she went on: 'Inspector Roy believes you knew about Brajendra Das's…proclivities. Everyone in the *para* did. The strange old man, the whispers of perversion. Inspector Roy thinks you knew that he had stolen Pramila's personal effects. You had seen him go through the door when he thought no one was looking. Just not that day. You had figured out why he did that. That you and perhaps others, maybe Ishaan's father's lawyers… then made up that story.' She studied his face, searching for cracks in its careful composition. 'He hired Calcutta's finest, didn't he? Inspector Roy thinks you constructed the perfect trap, not just for Brajendra Das but also for the Calcutta police. Triggered a raid, knowing what they would find: Pramila's personal effects siphoned off for months or, who knows, years.'

'A theory,' Basab said, his words precise as equations written in chalk, 'but one with no empirical validation.'

'One last thing Inspector Roy said.' Maya leaned forward slightly. 'The media was there when the raid started. It was almost as if someone very powerful wanted to ensure that the police would not be able to hide what they had found from the public, someone powerful who knew beforehand what was in that room.'

'So, we are back to where we started.' Basab's voice carried the weariness of thirty years of remembering. 'When we began, I told you that refusing to speak would be taken as admission of guilt. So even though I didn't want to revisit what was the most traumatic day of my life, and I have had a few, I was forced to. Now, if I terminate this interview, it will seem as if I am doing so because I cannot, to use the famous line from *A Few Good Men*, "handle the truth".'

He looked back at Maya. 'This is the reality TV conundrum, and like the Grand Unified Theory conundrum, there seems to be no solution to it. All I will say is that I have said what I had to say, now, as I did thirty years ago.' His lips curved in a bitter smile. 'And to use Walter Cronkite's closing lines: "And that's the way it is".'

Maya stood. The video had stopped recording.

Basab remained seated, his office growing darker though the sun still hung high outside. As she reached the door, he spoke again, so softly she almost missed it.

'You know what the hardest part of understanding quantum physics is, Ms Sen? It's accepting that some things can be both true and false at the same time. Schrödinger's cat, alive and dead in its box. Until you open it. Until you look.'

She closed the door quietly behind her. Basab Banerjee knew it was time to go home.

3

Krishanu's Album

The crack in the *choubaccha* worried him. Krishanu traced it with his finger, feeling the rough edge where the cement had started to crumble. For a hundred years, this tank had held water, a hedge against the vagaries of the municipal supply. When the house was full of people, it guaranteed that no matter what other deprivations they faced, there would at least be water to shower, wash clothes and clean utensils. Now, only he and Sunanda remained, everyone else taken away by death, the promise of a better future elsewhere and a verdict of the Calcutta High Court which had let him evict his warring cousins and uncles. The corporation provided steady water now, making the tank in their tiny backyard nothing but a source of worry, the constant threat of leaks, the looming cost of repairs. Like my life itself, Krishanu thought, staring into its dark waters, no purpose left, just the burden of maintenance and the certainty of decay.

'Baba!' Sunanda's voice cut through the morning air. 'What are you doing out there?'

He did turn. The morning sun felt good on his back, and if he kept very still, the pain was almost bearable. 'Examining your inheritance, Rini. Come see.'

She appeared beside him. 'You shouldn't be out of bed.'

'The crack,' he said, ignoring her concern. 'See how it's spread? Like a river on a map.'

Sunanda knelt beside him, her fingers following where his had been. 'I will get some cement from Nitai-kaku's shop. Mix it this evening, and get it done.'

'No point wasting money.' His smile carried the weight of too many goodbyes. 'Just needs to last as long as I do. Then you sell this place and get as far away from this city as you can.'

'Baba, please.'

'What? Can't a dying man joke about dying?' But he let her help him up, both pretending his weight hadn't become so light.

'Baba, you have a new chemo cocktail now. You know what Dr Lakhotia said. This is the absolute best in the world for the stage that you are in.'

'Nonsense.' His voice hardened. 'I am just a lab rat. Dr Lakhotia is conducting tests for American pharma companies on poor people like us because they can't do it in the USA. New unapproved drug, remember. Why else would they make you sign a form? The only good thing is it's free, and that's the only reason I agreed to it.'

'Where do you get this information from? Your WhatsApp groups of bored uncles and retired grandfathers?' Exasperation laced her voice. 'I don't know what's worse, the false information, the ceaseless politics, or those "good morning, dear" images. And then there are your gambling apps...'

'They are not gambling apps.' The defence came quick, practised. 'They are skill-based games, cricket and football, patience and rummy. Real cash payouts.' His voice softened. 'And what else am I going to do? The chemo keeps going on. I am on the bed. Everything hurts. The television channels are unwatchable, and I can't remember anything, can't focus. These are the only things that keep me sane: reels, WhatsApp, and yes, mobile games.'

As they walked up the two steps from the backyard into the main house, Krishanu spoke suddenly.

'I am hungry.'

Sunanda's face lit up. 'Really? Not just saying it?'

He patted her cheek with a hand that trembled slightly. 'Really. The doctor said if the medicines work, appetite would return. Make me some toast? With butter.'

The smile she had inherited from her mother bloomed across her face. 'And tea?'

'With ginger.' He looked back at the *choubaccha*. Morning light caught its still surface, hiding the crack beneath. 'Everything breaks eventually, Rini. The trick is to know which cracks to fix, and which ones to let be.'

She helped him inside, trying not to think about how thin he had become, how his bones felt like bird wings under her hands, his old blue kurta swimming on his slender frame. Her father had always been big, with pudgy cheeks, a loud laugh and heavy footsteps that announced his presence. Now he was a fraction of that man, stooped and light, so light she feared one day he might simply float away, his feet forgetting how to touch the ground.

Krishanu settled gently into his chair at the dining table.

'Shouldn't you be at work?' he asked, examining the toast she had placed before him.

'You have forgotten again?' She kept her voice flat. The doctor had warned them, chemo fog, he had called it, one of the new drug's most prominent side effects. A state of confusion, of continuously forgetting.

'They changed the system last month. They call when they need me, pay hourly with some base income. Post-Covid, this is what the world is. Everyone orders phones online now. The shop is empty most days.'

He picked up a piece of toast, then set it down again. 'Jobs. In my time, they meant something. Like marriage, you stuck together through thick and thin. Employees didn't change companies for a thousand rupees more; employers didn't fire people after one bad year. You only lost your job if you had violated its most sacred rules, stolen money, broken trust.' His voice trailed off. 'Now it's all transactional, no loyalty. Are marriages becoming like jobs, or jobs like marriages? There's a term for it…I can't remember…'

'Gig economy,' she said quietly.

Krishanu picked up the toast again and bit into it.

'Actually, speaking of the gig economy…' She sat across from him, rehearsed words suddenly tangling on her tongue. 'Sneha's brother has this bike, just lying around. And there is this app, for food delivery…'

The toast dropped from his hand. 'No.'

'Baba, listen…'

'My daughter will not go door-to-door delivering food.' His voice carried an echo of its old strength.

'What's the shame in it? You are fine if I sell mobile phones in a shop, wearing a red T-shirt and a cap, but you are not fine if I deliver food, wearing another shade of red?'

Sunanda immediately regretted raising her voice. He sat quietly, munching at his toast.

'It's not a matter of shame.' His voice softened. 'A father who had to ask his daughter to quit her studies after her bachelor's so that she could support the family has no shame left to lose.'

'I didn't mean that, Baba. I meant…'

'No, let me finish.' He set down the toast. 'A father who sits at home at forty-eight is a man with no shame. But this isn't about shame. First, it's unsafe. You follow the news; you know how terrible the city has become for women. Late night, delivering food in strange places. No, I will not let you take that risk. Second, it's dangerous. They give you outrageous delivery windows, or you don't get paid. I read it on WhatsApp, and don't tell me it's not true. Delivery boys drive fast, and they die. Third, this is not a career. At the mobile shop, you are working for a big MNC. There is progression: junior associate, associate, senior associate, manager, executive. You have made it to associate, haven't you? Here, what's the career path? Samosa, then chilli chicken and then biryani?'

'We need the money. Career can wait.'

His eyes lit up with sudden animation. 'I told you the documentary will pay. When I first asked them for payment to speak, they said no, on principle.' He leaned forward, lowering his voice as if sharing a conspiracy. 'I told them I understood what the documentary was really about, digging up dirt on Ishaan Chatterjee, the superstar. That no one alive knows more about him and his childhood than I do.'

He paused to catch his breath. 'It was a gamble. Sure, Ranadeep knows as much. But he will not talk. He is a big government man now, about to become a minister. Maybe Basab knows too, but he's in the US, and "maybe" is the word; he was always lost in his books, barely understood anything that wasn't in the syllabus. Only I know things, and I am ready to do what they need to make their documentary a hit.'

Sunanda watched the familiar transformation – how his shoulders straightened, how his hands stopped trembling. The promise of money did this to him every time, as if possibility itself was a medicine more potent than his chemotherapy.

'Like we waited for Ma's life insurance? All those forms, all those trips to Chowringhee. And they denied it?'

The light dimmed in his eyes. Outside, a pressure cooker whistled from some neighbour's kitchen, marking time like it always had.

'There, we did not have leverage. We were small people, and they were a big insurance company, and they had figured out we did not have the money to take them to court. Here, I hold the cards.'

He said this with such conviction that, for a moment, Sunanda almost believed him. Almost forgot how many times she had seen this same certainty crumble.

'The collection agents, you know, they will show up at my work any day.'

'They cannot do that. The loan is in my name and not in yours. I called them and reminded them that we know the law.'

Krishanu's mind drifted to that morning, when the collection agents had appeared. They had waited for Sunanda to leave for work, a small mercy they had made sure he understood. He had stood at his door while they filled the narrow passage, two men whose corporate white shirts and black trousers were like costumes, poorly concealing what lay underneath.

'Uncle,' they had said, stepping in close, their smiles tight, 'you think your cancer is your protection, that you will die before you pay the bills. We know that's your game, but we will keep coming, again and again, as we are allowed to do under the law. The law says we can come between 7 a.m. and 7 p.m., and we will, but the law doesn't say how long we can talk, how high our voices can go. We cannot use abusive language, but I think we can both agree that

"I hope you die slowly and painfully from cancer" doesn't meet the definition of abusive language. We cannot disclose your indebtedness to other people, but there is nothing we can do if an anonymous phone number discloses that on your community WhatsApp group. You know people get disposable SIMs all the time; I am sure your daughter can tell you that since she works in a mobile shop. Just pay up, Uncle, do the right thing. Do you really want to die like a half-man?'

For a moment, the chemo fog in his brain had parted like monsoon clouds. And there it was, a memory bright as lightning: Ishaan's fists, Basab's planning, Ranadeep's silver tongue. One phone call and the Musketeers would come running, they always had. These collection thugs wouldn't last five minutes in their *para*, not against boys who had grown up defending their territory against rival cricket teams and National Boys School bullies. He had almost reached for his phone and said the words that would bring his friends charging in like avenging angels.

Then the fog returned, slow and silent, like dusk through an open window. Those boys existed only in photographs now, preserved in time on old Kodak paper.

He was alone now, in this time, in the place that had once been theirs together.

'Baba!' Sunanda's voice tugged him back to the present. She was studying his face with that worried look she tried so hard to hide. 'What are you thinking about?'

'Nothing.' He forced himself to smile. 'Just remembering how things used to be. You know, Ishaan wasn't always like what you see in the movies. None of them were what they became. Ranadeep, now he is going to be a minister, but back then he was just a quiet boy who loved music. Used to sing Rabindra Sangeet with that girl…with Pramila, what beautiful voices they had.'

'The girl who was murdered?'

'Yes.' He reached for his tea, his hand trembling slightly. 'That's what the documentary people want to know about. Not just the murder, everything before it. How we were. What changed.'

'And you are going to tell them?'

'For the right price.' His voice hardened. 'They think they are so clever, making a show about poor dead Pramila. But I know what they really want: the great Ishaan Chatterjee's dark past. Well, I will give it to them. Every bit of it.'

Krishanu finished his toast, stood up and then sat back down again, his face writ with confusion.

'Are you all right, Baba?' Sunanda asked.

'Bring me the album, the big red one.' Krishanu smiled. 'Behind your mother's dressing table, in the old trunk.' His voice softened at the mention of his wife. 'She kept all our photographs.'

Sunanda retrieved the album quickly. She settled into the chair beside him, something warm blooming in her chest. Baba hardly spoke of the past anymore, not since Ma died. The cancer had stolen his voice along with his smile, leaving him silent in his own house. But today was different. He had walked in the morning sun, eaten real food, and now his voice carried an echo of its old strength. Perhaps the new medicine was working, after all.

Krishanu opened the album, its plastic sheets crackling. The photographs had that sepia tint that old prints get with age.

He stopped at a cricket ground photo, four boys in whites, arms around each other's shoulders, squinting into the sun.

'Look,' he said, tapping the image with a trembling finger. 'The Musketeers.'

Sunanda leaned closer. 'I don't remember having seen this picture before.' The boy on the far left was tall, handsome in that unfinished teenage way, a younger version of the man she had seen countless number of times on the screen and in advertisement hoardings. She pointed to him. 'Ishaan-uncle.'

'Yes. And that's Basab next to him, the one with the glasses. Ranadeep with the cricket ball. And…' His finger hesitated over the last figure, a chubby boy with an awkward smile.

'Of course, I know that's you. You look so cute.'

'The word you want to use is fat.' Krishanu smiled ruefully. 'Funny how the world turns. There was a time when what would I not give to lose a few kilos, and now here I am; what would I not give to gain a few. Here is another bit of what you would call WhatsApp advice. Be happy with what you have, Rini, we never know what we truly want.'

She nodded, then turned the page. Another photo, the same four boys, but this time with a girl in a blue salwar kameez standing slightly apart.

'That's Pramila,' Sunanda said. 'I remember seeing this. She is breathtakingly beautiful.'

'Was,' Krishanu said softly. 'This was at Saraswati Pujo. Just months before…'

He coughed lightly, eyes fixed on the album, before straightening in his chair. Sunanda recognized the old rhythm: the straightening spine, the subtle clearing of the throat. Her father was never more alive than when he told his stories, half-truth, half-magic, and always just convincing enough to make you doubt what you thought you knew. They had stopped too when Ma died.

'Siddhartha Chatterjee, Ishaan's father, was more interesting than his son ever was. Could have been a film star himself, but he had other ambitions.'

'Wait.' Sunanda leaned forward. 'You have never mentioned Ishaan's father before. Not once.'

'You were too young then,' Krishanu said. 'Now you are old enough to know.'

'Ooh,' Sunanda said, opening her eyes wide. 'I cannot wait.'

'There is this stereotype of Bengalis,' Krishanu continued, 'Of effete men spouting Neruda, falling unconscious at the sight of blood and of being bad at business.'

'That stereotype exists for a reason. Bengali men are insufferably *nyaka*,' Sunanda said, with a smile, knowing that the way to bait more stories from her father was to challenge him. She had figured that out when she was three.

'Nonsense!' Krishanu scoffed. 'Your generation knows nothing of real Bengal. That is because you have never read Manik Bandopadhyay. He wrote about village life, how rough and violent it truly was. You city kids think all of Bengal is like Calcutta, and all Bengali literature begins and ends with Rabindranath Tagore.' His eyes lit up. 'Siddhartha Chatterjee was from the real backwaters, Purulia. A roughneck, through and through.'

'I can see an origin story beginning,' Sunanda said, excitedly.

'Siddhartha Chatterjee, or Sidhu-da as he was known, started his life smuggling arms across the border with what used to be East Pakistan, now Bangladesh. The Pakistani army officers there had weapons to sell, American issue, not the local-made ones that would explode in your hands. He would bring them west, through the Sundarbans. The Naxals needed guns, the criminals in Bihar needed guns, everyone needed guns.'

'Hold on, Baba, hold on.' Sunanda raised her hand. 'How do you know all this? You were not even born during Naxalbari; that was 1967, and the agitation went into the early 1970s. You are forgetting I had history in class eleven.'

Krishanu smiled, pleased at her challenge. 'You forget my father lived here, in this house, and my two uncles, who were elder to him. Everyone here knew Sidhu-da, and what he did for a living. The documentary producers think Ishaan is interesting, but for all his bad-boy image, he is nothing compared to his father. That is the thing I was telling you; to understand Ishaan, you need to know his father, and who is left but me to tell them his story.'

'If he is as famous as you say, they can knock on any door and find the stories out for free.' Sunanda crossed her arms.

'Aha, but there is no one left from those days to tell them the secret history of the Chatterjees.' Krishanu's eyes sparkled with the old mischief. 'Everyone from that time is either dead or has left the city. I am the one who remains, the last keeper of those memories.'

'Last keeper of memories, oh, the melodrama,' Sunanda said, and Krishanu nodded, with a smile.

'What do they teach you in history? Did they tell you about this place where you grew up? In the 50s, the jungle started from where the school is now, yes, and my father remembered when you could hear jackals howl right outside. Ishaan's dad cleared the jungles with his henchmen, and whoever protested was never heard of again, buried, they say, in the swamp on which they made Ramkrishna Park.'

'Baba, this sounds like one of those WhatsApp forwards. Like that UFO they spotted over Rishikesh. Bodies under Ramkrishna Park.'

'One more time, you act smart, and I am done.'

Sunanda nodded.

'Ishaan's dad seized the land. He took out titles in his name after bribing officials. Then he sold the land to refugees flooding the city from East Pakistan. Whatever money he made from that and whatever money he had left over from his gun-running, he put into factories and then into movie production, as a way to go "legit". As you can see, neither a man of poetry nor peaceful nor a bad businessman.'

Sunanda wanted to say something but thought better of it.

'You know who his rival was in his young days? The man who used to own a lot of property here, a man by the name of Harendra Das. This house was his, but my father bought it from him, and maybe that is the only good thing he ever did, bless his soul. This house may be falling apart now, but you will get a very good price once you hand this over to a promoter after my death.

'But remember that name. Harendra Das. We will come back to him later.'

Sunanda rolled her eyes. 'Always with the dramatic foreshadowing, Baba. You should have written thrillers instead of working at the bank.'

'Ishaan's father made a bungalow for himself. Two storeys high, with a big yard and a high fence. People said that the arrangements were not so much to keep those on the outside from coming inside, but those on the inside from going outside.'

'I am doubling down. You should have written novels,' Sunanda said. 'The new mall is there, right, where the bungalow used to be?'

'What a monstrosity, what an absolute monstrosity, to knock down that house and all the other buildings there, nice old constructions, and build that eyesore. Well, only

God will know how many bodies Ishaan's dad has put beneath the Starbucks and the Guchi…'

'Gucci, Baba, it is pronounced Gucci.'

Sunanda studied her father's face. Colour had returned to his hollow cheeks. His eyes, so recently dulled by pain and medication, now sparkled with their old mischief. She had not seen him this animated in months.

'Baba, would you like some *muri*? With chopped onions and mustard oil?'

His face lit up like a child's on Durga Pujo morning. 'Like your Ma used to make? With the green chillies?'

'And a squeeze of lemon. Yes.'

'Oh, that would be wonderful!' He rubbed his hands together. 'A story needs *muri*. Your Ma always knew that. She used to bring it out whenever I started telling tales. Said it kept my mouth busy between sentences, so I wouldn't exaggerate too much.'

Sunanda smiled. This was another good sign, his appetite returning. The doctor had said that would happen if the new medicine was working. She rose, feeling lighter than she had in weeks. 'I will make it just how Ma did. Then you can tell me more of your absolutely hundred per cent true stories.'

When she returned with a steel bowl of *muri*, white puffed rice glistening with golden mustard oil, flecked with green chillies and pink onions, Krishanu dipped his fingers in immediately. The familiar crunch filled the space between them.

'So,' Krishanu continued, licking oil from his fingertips, 'Siddhartha Chatterjee, now respectable and flush with money from his various enterprises, decided the next step to social acceptance was to start a community Durga Pujo. That's how Kumudini Boy's Club Durga Pujo started, named after Sidhu-da's mother, Kumudini, the only time I ever heard of her.

'Winner of Nordic Paints pandal of the year six years running, as their banner says.

'Such is how excellence is made.' A *muri* had come stuck to the corner of his lips. 'He went from shop to shop, asking for donations. Who could say no?' Krishanu smiled grimly, using his finger to slide the errant *muri* back into his mouth. 'Everyone knew what happened to people who crossed Sidhu-da. The shopkeepers gave generously. Even my father contributed with a "smile", though we could barely make ends meet.'

He took another handful of *muri*, letting the memories settle.

'The pandal was magnificent, they said. I was just born, so this is all that I heard later. Film stars came from Mumbai to cut the ribbon. The *Times of India* covered it. But that wasn't the most surprising part.'

Sunanda leaned forward. 'What was?'

'On Saptami, Sidhu-da showed up with a woman nobody had ever seen before. Young, beautiful, with the kind of complexion people whispered about. Not from around here, that much was clear. Some said Punjabi, others thought Kashmiri, my mother was convinced she was Sindhi. He introduced her as his wife.'

'Who was she?'

'Nanibala Chatterjee. Ishaan's mother.' Krishanu's eyes widened.

'Nanibala, that's her name. And she was Sindhi?' Sunanda asked, incredulous, on the verge of laughing out loud.

'Obviously, that was not her real name, and do not ask me why Sidhu-da chose a fake name that would be considered old school even in the 1930s. Nothing about her was real, from her beauty to her name. Until then,

Sidhu-da had been a bachelor, at least officially. A notorious one, with a bad reputation. Then suddenly, he appears with this mystery woman and a young boy, Ishaan, maybe a few months old then. Declared them as his family. In public! At Durga Pujo!'

'What was so strange about that?'

'Nobody had ever heard of her before. Not a whisper, not a rumour. For a man like Sidhu-da, whose business depended on connections, whose every move was observed and discussed, to produce a wife and child from nowhere?' Krishanu shook his head. 'Even for Sidhu-da, this was shocking. But who would question him? Not to his face.'

'Where had she been all that time?'

'That's what everyone wanted to know.' Krishanu lowered his voice. 'There were rumours, of course. Some said she was an actress from Mumbai who had failed to make it big. Others whispered that she had been kept hidden in his new house all along. The most interesting rumour, though…'

He paused, reaching for more *muri*. A cough shook his thin frame.

'Baba!' Sunanda touched his arm.

'I am fine.' He waved her concern away. 'The most interesting rumour was that Ishaan was not really his son.'

'But you have always said that Ishaan was exactly like his father.'

'As a person, yes. A dead ringer. But as a boy and then as a young man, he looked like his mother, with those sharp features and that complexion. But, in terms of how closely he resembled his father physically, I am not sure. Now that he has done so much work on his face, who knows who he looks like?'

'Wow,' Sunanda said. 'Are you seriously planning to drop this bombshell for the documentary?'

'Depends on how much they value me.'

'How was Ishaan's mother, this "Nanibala"-mashima?'

'Unlike our mothers, who slaved all their lives in the kitchen and in the house, she had the luxury of looking pretty and standing up in the verandah, looking down at the world below. Ishaan's mother was always bedecked in gold, always, as if going to a wedding, which on anyone else would be a magnet for criminals and thieves. But who would hit the house of the biggest criminal in the area?'

Krishanu paused, his eyes fixed on something far away.

'What happened, Baba? Story finished?' Sunanda nudged, impatient.

'Just wondering if I should tell you the next part.' His fingers traced circles in the remaining mustard oil at the bottom of the *muri* bowl.

'Why did I make the *muri* for you?' She crossed her arms, feigning outrage. 'Besides, didn't you say I was old enough to hear everything now?'

Krishanu's gaze returned to her, a shadow crossing his face. 'We must have been in class four. Maybe five. We played *pittu*, seven stones, in front of Ishaan's house, on that empty plot perfect for running games.'

He leaned forward, voice dropping. 'There we were, Ishaan, Basab, Ranadeep, me, a couple of other boys, chasing each other with the ball. Across the footpath sat this little cigarette–paan shop. Every afternoon when we played, this man would stand there smoking, chatting with the shopkeeper. A college student, a paying guest somewhere nearby. I think he tutored Ranadeep's sister.'

Krishanu's hand sliced through the air. 'So there we are, kids, running around when suddenly, CRACK! Something hit the lamppost beside this man. We all froze. A broken brick lay there. When we looked up…'

His eyes widened, bringing the memory to life. 'Siddhartha Chatterjee stood on the balcony, eyes bloodshot with rage, barebodied, muscles rippling in the afternoon sun like Bheema confronting Keechaka. He hurled another brick, bigger, that missed the man's head by this much.' He held his thumb and forefinger a hair's width apart. 'The man bolted...'

'Oh my God,' Sunanda whispered. 'Why would he...'

'We all looked up, terrified. Ishaan's face...' Krishanu shook his head. 'And she, white as a sheet, cried out, "You would have killed him!"'

Krishanu's voice deepened, mimicking Siddhartha's threatening growl: 'So what? Would you have become a widow if I had killed him? Do you think I am stupid? That I don't know why you come to the balcony, all dolled up, and why he stands there, every afternoon, always at the same time?'

Sunanda shifted uncomfortably. 'What happened to Ishaan? How did he react?'

'Ishaan worshipped his father. Always did. Followed him everywhere like a shadow, even to meetings where children didn't belong. All of us went through rebellious phases with our fathers, and you know yours has still not ended,' he gave her a knowing look, 'but Ishaan never rebelled against his father, at least not while I knew him. His father was his god, absolute and unquestioned.'

Krishanu's expression darkened. 'Sidhu-da had two personas. In public: charming, generous, larger than life. But inside that house...' He shook his head. 'People heard things. Even through those thick walls, across that vast garden. Shouting. Crying. The sound of his belt.'

'His belt?'

'First on his wife. Later, on Ishaan.' Krishanu stared into the distance. 'When Ishaan's mother tried to intervene, he would beat her even more severely. He had a mouth on him too, with words that would make teenage boys blush. And a temper that struck like lightning. One moment laughing, the next…' He made a slashing motion with his hand.

'He sounds monstrous.' Sunanda's voice fell quiet.

'He was.' Krishanu nodded. 'Everyone feared him. Even the party leaders, even the police.'

'And Ishaan still worshipped him? How?'

'That's the strange part.' Krishanu leaned forward. 'Because Sidhu-da was also the most involved father any of us knew. More friend than parent. He built Ishaan a gym when no one knew what gyms were. Hired trainers from Mumbai. Bought the best cricket equipment. Our fathers barely noticed us; we grew up like wildflowers. But Sidhu-da was protective, invested. He spent hours preparing Ishaan for a film career. And best of all, he would play cricket with us.'

'With you boys? Siddhartha Chatterjee?'

'Oh, yes.' A smile crept across Krishanu's face. 'I remember that enormous garden in his bungalow. He would sit behind the wickets, cigarette between his lips, keeper for one-drop-one-hand cricket. No other father played with their son's friends. Mine certainly didn't. Sidhu-da would swear throughout the game and tell off-colour jokes. We thought he was the coolest adult alive.'

'So Ishaan loved his father despite how he treated his mother.'

'Exactly.' Krishanu took another handful of *muri*. 'He wanted to be just like him: tough, feared, successful.'

'What was she like when you would visit?'

Krishanu's eyes grew distant. 'She would stand on the balcony, watching us play. Always overdressed, heavy silk saris, too much makeup, and as I told you, gold, so much gold. But her eyes…' He shuddered slightly. 'They had this hunted look. Like she was always waiting for disaster.'

'Did she speak to you?'

'Only to ask, "How is your mother?" Every time. The same question. I think she envied our mothers, ordinary women with ordinary worries. She would drift back inside right after asking that question, trailing perfume and sadness.'

'What a terrible marriage to an absolute brute. Is she still alive?'

'I wouldn't know. After Pramila's death, they sold the house and left the city. We all fell apart.' Krishanu seemed lost in thought. 'She always reminded me of an exotic bird in a silver cage. I don't think she was ever really alive.'

'You told me something about Harendra Das,' Sunanda prompted. 'You were going to come back to him.'

'Harendra Das?' Krishanu's eyes lit up with that familiar gleam he got when connecting pieces of an old story. 'Ah yes. Ishaan's father's old enemy. The vanquished king of our neighbourhood, the one who could have been.'

'Like in those old Bengali novels? The fallen zamindar?'

'Something like that.' Krishanu's fingers played with the remaining *muri*. 'Though his story ended without drama, without a final ride on the old, trusty steed into the sunset. Just keeled over one day from a rotten liver, too much cheap liquor, leaving behind property disputes and a younger brother.'

'The younger brother being…?'

'Brajendra. The Loon.'

'That's a terrible name to call someone.'

Krishanu shifted uncomfortably. 'You are right. But back then, we didn't think about how cruel our words could be. But I guess every neighbourhood still has its character, doesn't it? Ours was Brajendra Das. A big man, but stooped forward slightly, you would see him shuffling down the street in the middle of summer, wearing a thick, brown sweater and a monkey cap, muttering words to himself that we could barely make out. Sometimes, he would disappear into his house for months, just board himself up inside.'

'Was he always like that?'

'No, no. The story around him, and I have no way of knowing whether it was true or not, was that he was a mathematics honours student at Calcutta University. Supposedly, on a dare from his friends, he tried to memorize the entire table of logarithms. They say that's what short-circuited his brain.'

'Very believable, Baba.' Sunanda rolled her eyes. 'Sounds like you were in WhatsApp University even before the internet.'

Krishanu chuckled. 'Every generation thinks they invented rumours. In our time, we just spread them more slowly, over sweet tea and spicy paan and Charminar cigarettes instead of forwarded messages.'

He paused, running his finger along the rim of his teacup. 'Once he had that breakdown, he was never going to become a mathematician. His elder brother got him a job at Elite Cinema, selling tickets and working the projector. Not a bad thing back then, got to see all the latest films, meet the occasional star.' Krishanu smiled, remembering. 'We boys were terrible to him. Every time he would walk past, we would chant, "Dadu, what Hema Malini movie is running today?" He would ignore for a while, and then curse, before throwing pebbles at us. We thought it was hilarious.'

'That's cruel, Baba.'

'It was. But you know how boys are; anything different becomes a target. He owned some buildings in the area, the remnants of his elder brother's legacy. He lived off the rent. Mostly kept to himself. Some people considered him harmless…' He waved his hand vaguely. 'Some people said he definitely was not. He had a reputation, a bad one.'

Sunanda sat up straighter, recognition dawning on her face. 'Brajendra Das, wait. That name. Wasn't he the one who…' She paused, watching her father carefully. 'The one they said killed Pramila?'

Krishanu's face grew still. 'Yes.'

'Oh my God, Baba.' Sunanda's face lit up with realization. 'Everything you have just told me about Ishaan's father, the violence, the possessiveness, the beatings, and how Ishaan idolized him…' She shook her head slowly. 'It's like a pattern, isn't it? A son following in his father's footsteps.'

'That's what most people thought when Pramila was murdered.'

Sunanda continued. 'It is only in detective fiction that the least likely person is the killer. In real life, it is the most obvious one. And Ishaan has the motive and the opportunity and the pathology for the crime. If Ishaan's father could try to kill a man just for looking at his wife, couldn't Ishaan kill a girl for rejecting him? And who better to pin it all on than the neighbourhood madman who also happens to be his old enemy's brother?' Her voice rose with certainty. 'It's perfect, isn't it?'

Krishanu said nothing but looked up once at the ceiling fan.

'But there's something I don't understand.' Sunanda leaned forward, her voice dropping. 'It was Basab who testified against Brajendra, wasn't it? Your friend, Basab. The quiet one, always with his books. Why would he do that? Why would he help frame an innocent man?'

Krishanu's cup clattered against the saucer. 'You don't know Basab. Of all of us, he was the most honest. Painfully honest. Once, in a cricket match, he gave himself out when no one had appealed, saying the ball had grazed his glove. During our class ten examination, he was struggling with a question; it was in English, his weakest subject, and one of the teachers who was proctoring told him the answer. He left the question blank.'

'But if he was so honest…'

'The thing about Basab,' Krishanu interrupted, 'was that honesty wasn't just a choice for him. It was who he was. Like breathing.'

'Then maybe…' Sunanda hesitated. 'You said his family was poor. Could someone have offered him money?'

Krishanu's laugh came out harsh. 'Basab? Take a bribe? Like a cop at a traffic light?' He shook his head. 'Not like that. As I told you, Basab was a very straight kid.' His voice grew quieter. 'But then, some debts…' He paused. 'Some debts are more complicated.'

'So, you do think Ishaan's father got to him, don't you?' Sunanda pressed. 'That's what you are implying. But to lie like this, to set up an innocent man for murder, what enormous risk was he taking? I know Ishaan's father had the police in his pocket, but what if Basab broke under questioning from the prosecutor? Why would he put his entire future at risk with one lie?'

'I don't know,' Krishanu said, his gaze dropping to his hands. 'Or maybe I do.'

Krishanu's voice took on that peculiar rhythm it got when he was pulling a memory from deep within. 'We were playing National Boys School. Important match. They had beaten us the year before when their fast bowler broke Ranadeep's finger. Ranadeep was our best batsman, by the way.'

'Jack of All Trades – was that not what you guys called him?'

'Yes, and I was Master of None.' Krishanu said, with a sad shrug. 'But do not let the Jack part fool you; Ranadeep was actually pretty good at everything he did. Coming back to the game, though...'

'Where was this being played?'

'The park where that super-fancy luxury apartment complex stands now. What is it called?'

'The Retreat. Each apartment there costs two crore rupees, I have heard,' Sunanda said, in a whisper.

'Back then, it was just open ground, which was perfect for cricket. Basab was keeping wicket, as he always did. I was, of course, fat, and bad at fielding, so I got saddled with standing at slip.'

Krishanu smiled faintly. 'Their opener was Pritam Roy. He went on to play the Ranji Trophy for Bengal and went as high as to be a reserve player for the South Africa tour of the national team. That good. We needed him out, fast. Basab noticed him standing outside his crease, trying to get under our bowler's skin. So Basab did something clever, or what he thought was clever. Stood up to the stumps.'

'To bring the stumping into play.'

'Exactly. But for Pritam, standing outside was a strategic ruse. As the bowler delivered the ball, Pritam stepped back, deep into his crease. Basab realized too late what was coming. The ball was short, perfect for the hook, and Pritam's bat...' Krishanu's hands demonstrated the arc. 'The follow-through caught Basab right here.' He touched his temple. 'I was the closest to Basab. Heard it crack like someone had dropped a coconut on concrete. Blood everywhere.'

'It was like slow motion. Basab just...crumpled, like a bird that hits a closed window in full flight. No sound, no cry.' Krishanu's voice had grown hoarse. 'Everyone froze. Except Ishaan. He was already running from cover, like a train at full tilt, and before any of us could move, he had scooped Basab up like he was carrying a child. Then he ran with him, straight to Bengal Medical.'

'But that is far,' Sunanda asked, caught up in the story. 'Why did you not call a taxi?'

'Two kilometres at least. There was no flyover then. It was also difficult to get taxis; remember, no apps then. The taxis all waited near the market, and once there, there would be traffic in both directions. It was faster to run. So, he did it. Through those narrow lanes, past the market. Ishaan didn't stop once. Didn't even seem to breathe hard. I ran to get Basab's father...' His face darkened. 'Found him at home, reading the newspaper. When I told him what happened, you know what he said?'

Sunanda shook her head.

'*I told Basab not to play cricket.* Just that, over and over. Wouldn't even get up.' Krishanu's hands had begun to shake again. 'We all knew about his situation, two daughters to marry off, a joint family, a foreman in a locked-out factory. I realized he didn't want to go because he didn't want to pay the bill, and hospitals won't accept serious cases without money. He almost shoved me out, saying you boys got him into this, you handle it...'

'What?' Sunanda asked incredulously. 'What kind of father refuses to help his son, hurt that bad?'

'A very strange one. When I think of my childhood, and God knows it wasn't exactly happy, it was nothing compared to Basab's. Of all of us, he had it the worst. The very worst.' Krishanu's voice had dropped to almost a whisper. 'His father wouldn't even buy him textbooks. Basab used to borrow them from the library, copy entire chapters by hand into notebooks. His father would force him to give tuition; every hour of his evening was packed, well...' He caught himself, shaking his head. 'Let me not lose the thread of this story…for Basab's family can fill up many hours of storytelling, and I need another snack for that.'

'What happened at the hospital?' Sunanda prompted gently.

'Someone had called Ishaan's father. He came roaring up to the hospital in his Ambassador. Ranadeep was there; he told me later that Ishaan's father, rolled his kurta up, and told the doctor in charge "Nothing bad should happen to him. If it does, something bad will happen to you." Specialists came in from outside. That night was crucial; he could have died. Ishaan stayed at the hospital, never leaving Basab. In the morning, Basab was taken to Belle Vue for CT scans, money flowed like water, and Ishaan's father paid every paisa. Basab's sisters came to see him, not his father, and not his mother. As I said, Basab's family was weird.'

'Oh my God.' Sunanda's hand flew to her mouth. 'That's why Basab went along with everything Ishaan's lawyers and father wanted. What a monster.' Her voice hardened. 'Even Siddhartha Chatterjee's kindness was an investment, a way to ensnare someone, a boy, with gratitude. He is like the Godfather from the book. He does things for others so that he can call in a favour when he needs it. The hospital bills must have been nothing compared to what he got in return: his son's freedom bought with an innocent man's life.'

'But they found evidence,' Krishanu said weakly. 'Pramila's photos, her poems in Brajendra's house…'

'Photos and poems any boyfriend could have had!' Sunanda stood up, agitated. 'And who controlled the police in this neighbourhood? Who could have planted that evidence?'

Krishanu wanted to say something, but his voice trailed off; the story seemed to drain what little strength remained in his thin frame.

'Baba? Are you all right?'

The colour had fled from Krishanu's face, like water seeping through cracks.

'I need to lie down.'

His words came out barely above a whisper.

'The medicine…'

'Let me help you.' Sunanda rushed to his side, supporting his weight as he rose. She could feel the tremors running through him, worse than usual. Each step to his bedroom seemed to age him further, as if the very act of remembering had accelerated his decay.

She pulled the thin cotton sheet over him, adjusting the pillow beneath his head. His phone lay on the bedside table, and as she turned to leave, its screen lit up with a notification.

Sarah Blair (documentary): *Please let me know when I can call. We are ready to pay appearance fees.*

Sunanda stared at the message, then at her father's sleeping form. The light from the screen flickered against the wall like a second pulse.

She wondered about the stories her father had just told her. And the stories he did not.

4

The Empty House

The key stuck in the lock of 2147 Oakland Avenue. Seven years of resistance had worn grooves in the brass, but tonight the mechanism fought him with fresh spite. Basab Banerjee worked it back and forth, each scrape of metal against metal echoing down the empty street. The silence of the Pasadena street pressed against his ears. No Sandra's Audi Q7 in the driveway; the car movers had taken it away. No bikes scattered across the lawn. Just the garbage bins still waiting at the curb; he had forgotten today was collection day. The twins' bedroom window gaped dark and empty. He still looked up, out of force of habit, hoping to see at least one of them with their face to the glass, welcoming him home, but all that met him was nothing.

He had known they would be gone. That was what they had agreed on. But seeing the house like this, stripped of motion, of life, of family, made his chest constrict. 2147 Oakland Avenue stood against the darkening sky like a photograph of something that used to be his. The building remained his property, but the home had left with them.

The lock finally surrendered. The door swung inward on expensive hinges that should have been silent but weren't. They creaked a single sustained note, like the beginning of a dirge.

Empty houses have their own language: the hollow echo of footsteps on hardwood, the subtle protest of settling beams, the whispered conversations between pipes in the walls. But this silence had texture. It pressed against his ears like water, thick with unspoken words and accusations that had gathered like dust in the corners.

'What the fuck were you thinking?' Sandra's voice echoed through his memories. 'I would have never thought of you being capable of this.'

What would you know about what I am capable of, Sandra? What did you ever know about me?

His briefcase landed heavily on the marble foyer table, its thud swallowed by the darkness. The house stretched before him, a maze of shadows and bare corners, where the movers had removed Sandra's furniture. They had taken the family pictures too. Empty rectangles of unfaded paint marked the walls, like tombstones; each blank space seemed to watch him with invisible eyes.

The thermostat read 72 degrees but cold radiated from the walls. Not California's winter chill, but something deeper, as if the house itself had turned cold. The kind of chill that came with emptiness. Back in Calcutta, he had dreamed of a space like this, away from the cramped five rooms he had shared with his parents, five sisters, two widowed aunts and a cousin. They had lived in carefully negotiated inches, snapping and biting at each other, for each square foot, like animals in a mill.

Now, standing in all this space, he was not sure anymore what he had been running for.

He should have sent that documentary woman, Maya Sen, away. It was too much to have had to go back to the worst days of his life, on the worst day of his life.

Where had he seen her before? Oh right, he had settled on the answer. Somewhere in Pasadena itself, the generic American-Born-Confused-Desi face.

His feet carried him to the bar cart without conscious thought. The crystal decanter caught what little light filtered through the windows, transforming it into amber pathways across the Brazilian cherry floors. His father's voice echoed inside his skull: 'Drinking whisky, Khoka? Like some street drunk? Is this what I sent you to America for? And what whisky is this, single malt? How much did you spend on this, you irresponsible brat? All this money blown on yourself, so you could just drink it away, while your sisters struggle with the fees of their children, I would have never thought of you being capable of this.'

How would you know what I am capable of, Baba? What did you ever know about me?

The Scotch poured slowly, syrupy. His hand trembled, making the stream stutter against crystal. Something shifted in his peripheral vision, a shadow where no shadow belonged, quick as a startled cat. He turned, but the corner held only darkness. Yet the sensation of movement lingered, like ripples spreading across still water.

Ice cubes clinked like tiny bones as he swirled the glass. Each swallow burned, but it couldn't wash away the taste of failure lodged in his throat since morning. Back in Calcutta, walking between tutoring sessions in the heat, he would pray for money, America, physics, fame. Now his eyes found the last photo that was still hanging, of him accepting the National Medal of Science, the President's hand extended, both men smiling for history. He had gotten everything he had asked for. Like Macbeth's prophecies, every word had come true, and like Macbeth's prophecies, each truth had carried its own poison.

Basab reached into his right pocket and brought out an amber prescription bottle. Now that he was alone, he no longer needed to slip into the bathroom to pop in a few. He had started taking the pills since last December, once he had found a place on the dark web from where he could get them without leaving a paper trail. They had helped him sleep or kept him alert when he did not want to, that was their magic. Initially it was something he would take to calm himself down, after a confrontation with Sandra, in front of the twins, but over the months, he had become habituated to turning to it whenever he was stressed. As the final stages of the dissolution of his marriage had accelerated, so had his visits to that place on the dark web. He had not ever had the pills with whisky, but as he popped the lid casually with his fingers and poured out two onto his right palm, he could once again hear his father's voice coming to him from the past.

'What, Khoka! Drugs? First booze, now drugs. You are no different from those criminals who sit in the shadows below stairs and shoot up. Is this how I brought you up? Is this why I sent you to school? *Chi chi chi...*'

He took the pills dry. It left behind on his tongue an aftertaste, of Boroline, his father's solution to all problems, be it heat, heartbreak or heresy, and he took a sip of whisky to wash away that memory in an instant.

The grand staircase curved up into darkness. His footsteps echoed strangely as he climbed, each step slightly out of sync with his movements, as if someone was following just behind.

He had expected a note from the twins. Or a text on his phone. Something.

That is what children did, wasn't it? Left tearful goodbyes when their parents separated, promised to visit on weekends, said they still loved you even if you couldn't live together anymore. He had checked the kitchen counter, even the refrigerator door where the kids used to leave their messages, the phone, the inbox, the spam, the trash.

Nothing.

He remembered walking across the tarmac at Dum Dum Airport, the British Airways 747 towering above him like Goliath. His sisters had wept in the departure lounge. Ma had not come; of course, she hadn't. Even Baba had gone quiet, his usual criticisms finally exhausted. He knew he should have felt something: fear, sadness, the weight of leaving home for the first time. Instead, relief had flooded through him with each step toward the aircraft.

As the plane climbed through Calcutta's smog, he pressed his face to the window. Bengali soil shrank beneath the wings, taking with it his father's disappointed sighs, his mother's studied indifference, his sisters' theatrical affections he had never learned to trust. The lies would be simpler from a distance. He would send money home. Return every few years bearing the tributes of the West: electronics, perfumes, cigarettes, chocolates for an army of relatives whose names he had started to forget.

But his real life would begin at cruising altitude, somewhere over the Atlantic. He would never have to decode their faces again. And when he first saw MIT's Great Dome rising above Massachusetts Avenue, he knew he had found his home.

Now he wondered if his children felt that same lift in their hearts as the Uber pulled away. No, that was too harsh. Perhaps they felt nothing at all. More logical. His endless lectures about grades and artificial intelligence, his stories about cricket matches they had never seen, his reverence for

Hindi movies they couldn't understand, his insistence on Bengali food they wouldn't eat, must have seemed as alien to them as his mother's silence had seemed to him.

The irony. He had always wanted to escape Calcutta, but once he had done that, he had never left.

'You never checked into Hotel California,' Sandra would say, a gentle critique of him never integrating into the American immigrant experience of Monday night football, beer and barbecuing.

He looked at the wallpaper on his phone, the twins a few days old.

At least they were escaping young. If they had grown older around him, they might have learned to hate him properly. Or worse, this cool indifference might calcify, turning their court-mandated visits into the same dutiful rituals he used to perform in Calcutta all those years, for the sake of appearances.

Bitter laughter rose in his throat. Three generations bound not by blood but by the need to leave. His father's voice whispered from decades past: 'You will understand when you have children of your own.'

And now he did understand, with a clarity that burned worse than the Scotch in his hand.

The upstairs hallway stretched longer than he remembered. The master bedroom door stood slightly ajar, though he distinctly remembered closing it that morning. A draft whispered through the gap, carrying a scent he hadn't encountered in decades: the metallic tang of old pipes, the musty sweetness of the rains striking dry soil, and the cough syrup that stood on the side table of his mother's bed, each note distinct.

His office beckoned, a sanctuary of equations and order. But as he reached for the handle of the French door, a sound froze him mid-motion.

Somewhere in the house, chalk was scratching against slate with mechanical precision.

Someone was writing on a blackboard. But there was no blackboard in this house.

The sound stopped. In its wake came something worse: a giggle, high and young, musical with cruel delight.

Basab's throat closed. The sound was swallowed by the waiting darkness, leaving him alone with the echo of that laugh, a laugh he had not heard in thirty years, not since the day they had found her face down in the bucket.

The house breathed around him, patient as a spider watching its prey stumble into its web.

His office door opened without resistance. That was wrong. He had locked it that morning. He always locked it, a habit from not wanting Sandra to snoop through his things, not that she did, but then how would he know? The French doors had never failed before, their brass fittings imported from England, the kind of unnecessary luxury Sandra had insisted on during the remodel.

They had fought through it, the entire remodelling. Sandra was determined to maintain the level of high living, straight from lifestyle magazines, that she had seen growing up in Martha's Vineyard, while he had always leaned towards the minimum, the functional, what they could get away with. Sandra had won, or so he thought, till the court-mandated sessions where she had brought this up, as a sign of his 'my way or the highway' style of doing things.

The room beyond lay thick with shadow despite the wall of windows facing the backyard pool, where underwater lights cast shifting patterns on the ceiling.

The magazine lay centred on his mahogany desk, its placement too deliberate to be accidental. The *Woman's World*, September 1994 issue, price ₹15, the masthead proclaimed in that familiar 80s font. His fingers brushed the glossy cover. No dust. The paper felt cool, almost damp, like something recently fished from water.

Pramila's face stared up at him, caught in profile against a blue studio backdrop. Eighteen years old, hair swept back like Madhuri Dixit's in *Hum Aapke Hain Koun..!*, and eyes bright with possibilities about to be extinguished. 'The Rose of Calcutta, a Star Blooms', the headline announced in that particular shade of pink that magazines of that vintage used.

How was this magazine here, on his desk?

He had kept the magazine all these years, buried in a cardboard box in the garage beneath cricket scorecards marked with his precise statistics-keeping, the issue of *Sportsworld* when India won the World Cup, his school tie with its green and gold stripes, his copy of Resnick–Halliday never returned to the school library, and the fountain pen Ishaan had given him before the finals, one whose nib was broken, but he would never throw away. The box should have been sealed, hidden under Christmas decorations, his boys' old Halloween costumes and camping equipment they had never used. He had not opened it since moving to Oakland Avenue. Sandra had not known about it. He had carried it himself during the move, along with other remnants of Calcutta he couldn't explain: the Hawkins pressure cooker he had brought with him when he had first come here as a graduate student, together with spare gaskets, his father's dog-eared collection of Communist pamphlets from the 60s, the ruled notebook where he had kept an account of the money he sent home, a little sheaf of papers clipped together where his sisters had written down recipes, and his old wicketkeeper gloves, also a gift from Ishaan, disintegrating from use and age.

A drop of water rolled down the glossy surface of the magazine, leaving a trail, like mascara in the rain. Then another. The smell hit him next. What was it? A faint hint of chlorine, the sharp tang of rust, and something else, something more organic, impossible to place.

He touched the paper. Nope. Bone dry.

He sniffed his fingers. Nothing.

The empty chair across his desk, an Aeron that had cost more than his father's yearly salary, creaked.

And then, the sound again. Chalk on blackboard.

He ran his finger over the cover of the magazine. Immediately, a new scent hit him: Sunsilk shampoo, strawberry scented, the kind teenage girls used in nineties Calcutta, sold in tiny sachets for five rupees each. Beneath it, something darker: the reek of stagnant summer water from the open drain that ran to the right of their house.

His hand jerked back. The office chair remained empty, but the strawberry scent grew stronger. The water smell faded, replaced by the warmth of hot tea and Bourbon chocolate biscuits, the exact aroma of Thursday evening tutoring sessions, when he sat in Pramila's room with the door ajar, her mother periodically entering with tea and biscuits, a gesture as much about hospitality as about keeping an eye on him.

The magazine's pages began to turn on their own. Slowly. Deliberately. Each page exhaled a soft sigh, fragile as wings brushing the air. The sound of paper sliding against paper transformed into the gentle lapping of water against enamel, against skin, against hair.

Water dripped onto the pages now, each drop spreading like a bruise. The paper warped and swelled. Pramila's face distorted in every photograph, her bright smile stretched too wide, her neck elongated at impossible angles. In the centrefold, her bare arms reached toward the camera like dead branches submerged in water, the come-hither expression that had sent Ishaan into a rage frozen on her face. But her eyes, her eyes had changed. They were nothing but white orbs, no iris, no pupil, rolling slowly inward as if trying to turn away from what they had seen in those final moments. As if they were still watching something terrible unfold behind her skull.

A sound ripped from Basab's throat, raw and animalistic. The same guttural noise his father had made at the funeral home, when the man insisted on his father checking his mother's pulse one last time, just to be sure, before consigning her to flames. The kind of noise that lives in the marrow, waiting for moments when language fails.

The scream echoed through the empty house, bouncing off the bare walls where Sandra's paintings once hung. The force made Basab stagger backward, his knee catching the edge of the cupboard. Awards clattered against one another. Fellow of the American Physical Society, Distinguished Teaching, National Medal of Science, their metal surfaces ringing like temple bells.

He forced himself to look down at the magazine again. It lay innocent now, just glossy paper and celebrity interviews, Pramila's face composed and beautiful as it had been that day. But it shouldn't be here. It couldn't be here.

Maybe the movers had broken his box while taking out Sandra's furniture. The cardboard was old, probably rotted. They'd have found the magazine, placed it here, meaning to ask about it. Yes. He would figure it out tomorrow morning.

He was drunk; he told himself. Too much Scotch on an empty stomach. And then the pills had gone to town, too.

He stumbled out of his office, needing distance from the magazine. That's when he saw it in the passageway. A backpack. One of the twins' North Face bags, sleek and black, abandoned where it shouldn't be.

His throat closed as he reached for words that no one would hear anymore: 'Who left their...'

But as he stared, the sleek black fabric seemed to age and weather. The North Face logo blurred and faded. The modern zippers dulled to old brass. Padded straps flattened to simple canvas. Now a different bag slumped against the wall, worn cotton, fraying at the corners, that distinctive ink stain spreading across one edge where Pramila's cheap pen had leaked during third-period chemistry. The careful Bengali lettering emerged like a developing photograph: 'Property of P. Chatterjee, Class XI-A, St. Agnes Convent.'

He knew if he opened the flap, he would find that homework, the integration by parts written in her precise hand, and then that note the documentary lady said she saw, the words she quoted: 'Basab-da would be proud.' He knew what else he would find. Her blue Camlin pencil box with its scratched lid. That collection of lipsticks she thought no one knew about, the ones that had clattered across his desk that day as she dug for her Sarin and Sarin textbook. He had averted his eyes then, maintaining the fiction.

So much fiction he had maintained. These thirty years.

When he went to her house, he would see that bag lying near the door, cast away near her shoes, and he would know that Pramila was waiting at the dining table, and his heart, despite him not wanting it to, would beat faster.

As it did today, but for a different reason. He ran downstairs, not daring to look back at where the bag had appeared back into his reality, crossing over from one he had run away from.

His footsteps echoed through empty halls until he stepped into the kitchen. The refrigerator hummed, a steady anchor in reality. But even here, he caught the ghost of her perfume.

The refrigerator's clinical light spilled across the floor. As Basab reached for the handle, his father's voice slithered in from behind, close enough that he should have felt his breath against his neck: 'So much food, Khoka. Chicken, you have chicken on weekdays. Are you out of your mind? Oh, so you are a rich man now? Well then, leave some for your sisters; leave some for me. All day I was at the mill in front of the locked gates; the sun was overhead, and I had nothing to eat. What! There are grapes in your fridge, so many, and they are growing ripe, and you did not even have them, going to waste. Well, at least then give your old man some of that fruit; I am fine with those too…'

The words carried that familiar cadence of guilt, the same lisp that had haunted their cramped Calcutta apartment. Tears streamed down Basab's face, salt burning his lips. His hand trembled against the steel door.

This is not real. This cannot be real. The rational part of his mind, the physicist who understood quantum mechanics, who could explain wave functions and probability clouds, grasped for explanations like a drowning man holding on to driftwood.

The TV burst to life behind him, crackling through static before settling into melody. '*Madhumaloti daake aaye*', the song Pramila had hummed during their tutoring sessions, her pencil tapping softly against her notebook. The familiar tune wafted through the ground floor, but now the lyrics about flowers sharing secrets took on a darker timbre, as if the song had been waiting thirty years to reveal its true meaning.

So many secrets he had kept. These thirty years.

'Just my phone,' he muttered. 'Connected to the TV through the home wireless. I forgot to disconnect.' The words fell flat in the empty kitchen.

The song played on, its gentle romance twisting into accusation. The volume increased without him touching any controls, the sweet melody turning cloying, suffocating, like blossoms left too long in the vase, rotting in the stagnant water.

He yanked the cord of the television. The song stopped playing.

That Maya Sen. Now he saw it, the way she had adjusted her hair, that exact flick. Of course. That was it.

He had to warn Ishaan Chatterjee.

His fingers trembled as he pulled up WhatsApp. Ishaan's contact. He had saved it years ago. Was this his number anymore? Movie stars probably changed their numbers as often as they changed their looks.

The phone rang into emptiness. He had never called Ishaan, nor had he exchanged perfunctory festival greetings. He could not remember how he had even got his number, and maybe it was never his.

His mind drifted to the old rotary phone, mounted high on the wall where his sisters could not reach. Those precious minutes of calls, his father hovering nearby in his sweat-stained vest, counting seconds, muttering about the bill. 'Cut it short, cut it short,' he would say. 'The phone charges are robbery. Two rupees for a minute. I am not a black marketeer like Ishaan's father that he gets it from his business, nor do I work as an executive like Ranadeep's father that he gets it from his office.'

They had developed a system: Basab would call, let it ring once, then hang up. That was their signal. And without fail, Ishaan would call back from his father's deluxe push-button phone with the golden trim.

'I am here,' Ishaan would always say, those three words carrying the weight of their friendship. No matter what time, no matter where, if Basab called, Ishaan answered. Always.

His fingers moved across the smartphone screen, typing: 'This is Genius. Call me.'

The message showed a single grey tick. Undelivered. The number was probably dead, like everything else from their past. He stared at the screen, waiting, but nothing changed. Just that solitary grey tick, hanging in digital limbo.

As the California evening painted the sky in deepening shades of purple, Basab flicked on the backyard lights. Their sterile brightness carved sharp shadows across his pool deck, a luxury that still felt foreign after seven years in this house. He stripped down to his swimming trunks, his middle-aged, pudgy body a far cry from the skinny boy who had once played cricket under Calcutta's merciless sun.

The water embraced him, cool against his skin. He pushed off, cutting through the blue with mechanical strokes. Each lap carried him further from the present, from divorce papers and documentary crews and ghosts that shouldn't exist. The rhythmic splash of his arms, the steady kick of his legs, the regulated breathing, the peace of the water.

After twenty laps, he pulled himself out.

The swim had cleared his head. Maya Sen was just another journalist, her familiar gestures mere coincidence. His mind playing tricks, conjuring ghosts from guilt. He took another sip of the Scotch, ice clinking against crystal as pool lights fractured through the glass.

Only he knew what had really happened to Pramila Chatterjee.

Well, he and Ishaan.

That was how it would stay.

Inspector Roy's words to Maya Sen floated back: Basab had run rings round the police, the way Maradona danced through the Belgian defence. A smile tugged at his lips; most people remembered Maradona's second goal against England, but his absolute best was the one against Belgium. There were two gods: Maradona and Sachin Tendulkar, and being compared to one of them…

'I will drink to that,' he said to the empty night, pouring another measure. The crystal caught the light, dancing patterns across his hand.

He had always been the smartest in any room. Everything had gone exactly as he had planned. Except that one time. Just once.

And for that miscalculation, Sandra had left him. Money, it always came down to money, didn't it? The pattern had started long before, in that cramped Calcutta flat where his mother performed her monthly ritual of desperation.

He remembered her voice in those phone calls, the practised quiver as she described phantom symptoms to her brothers. 'Dada, the doctor says it might be my heart…no, no, don't tell Boudi, she will only worry.' The lies dropping like pearls from her lips, each one rehearsed in front of her mirror the night before. The way she would sit afterwards, staring at her reflection, touching the remaining pieces of gold, wedding bangles his father's family had given her when she had eloped, back when they still had hopes for the match. One by one, she had sold them off: first the golden bangles, then the heavy gold sets, then the delicate *nupur*, until only a thin golden chain remained. She fingered it absently during the evening serials, its weight a constant reminder of choices made and prices paid.

She had been beautiful once, his mother. The portraits in her brothers' jewellery shops showed a different woman, head held high, eyes bright with possibility. Not this silent ghost who moved through their flat, calculating which piece of gold she could pawn next. She blamed Baba for being poor, for never giving her the life she had been promised. But she never said it aloud, not even once.

Basab was not like his father, though, a man who had sat at home, moaning about misfortune; he had tried. He would have succeeded too, making enough money for generations to live off, if not for that 'black swan' event that had wiped out everything he had built.

Sandra left, just like his mother had, though his mother's departure had been a quieter thing. No divorce papers, no legal proceedings; just a slow retreat into TV serials, her body present but her mind gone, turning her back even on her children, giving their father effective custody of their shells.

History repeated itself, in a house thousands of miles from that Calcutta flat.

Different women.

Same story.

They lost faith.

The jacuzzi hummed to life, bubbles churning the water white.

As he lowered himself into the warm froth, he closed his eyes.

The Scotch loosened memories he had buried, the ones too raw for Maya Sen's camera. His mind circled back to that day at the magazine stand near the place where the typists sat. Ishaan's hands had trembled as he picked up the *Woman's World*, Pramila's face smiling from its cover. He remembered the exact moment Ishaan's expression changed. First, confusion. Then, disbelief. And then… something else entirely.

Pure rage had transformed his features, twisting them into something Basab recognized but never dared name.

'I will kill her,' Ishaan had whispered, the words barely audible above the street noise. Not a threat, not hyperbole, a promise.

And if there was something about Ishaan he knew, he never went back on a promise.

He had seen that expression before, on Ishaan's father's face the day Prabal-da's gaze had lingered too long on Ishaan's mother. Those subtle exchanges that most missed, but Basab caught. He always noticed everything. The way Prabal-da would time his evening walks with her shopping trips. The way she would adjust her hair when he passed. Small things, meaningless perhaps, until the day the brick sailed past Prabal-da's head. Everyone pretended not to see her bruises the next day. Ranadeep had caught on to their little afternoon dalliance for weeks too. Basab and he had discussed it in whispers for days before the brick incident, understanding even then what it meant, and wondering what Ishaan's mother was planning to do.

Basab remembered other moments too. The way Ishaan would grip Pramila's wrist when she talked too long to other boys. How Ishaan had once slapped her for wearing a sleeveless salwar kameez to the movie theatre and then bought her Swiss chocolates after. So many stories Basab could have told Maya Sen, but he would never.

Ishaan was a violent boy, and he took his cues from his father. Siddhartha Chatterjee's reputation was built on blood; everyone knew he had killed people, though such things were only whispered.

Like father, like son: jealousy, possession, ownership, control. This was the true Chatterjee inheritance.

When word spread the next morning about Pramila's murder, Basab did not need to ask who had done it. He had known with the same certainty that he knew gravity would pull an object earthward, or that entropy always increased.

But he also knew something else: he had to save Ishaan.

His friend was not eighteen yet, but only a few weeks away. What if the judge tried him as an adult? The noose or a life in jail, these were the only possible outcomes. Siddhartha Chatterjee's money and muscle wouldn't be enough this time. The justice system could be bent, yes, even broken, but not for this. A criminal knifed by a rival gang and left bleeding on the street corner. They would look away. But you couldn't murder a girl in her home, a good girl from a good family, leave her face down in a bucket of water, and expect to walk free just by greasing the right palms and calling in favours.

No, this needed something else. Something more than money. Something more than brute force.

This needed genius.

A crow landed on the string lights above the jacuzzi, its head cocked as if listening to Basab's thoughts. He remembered how methodically he had constructed his masterpiece of deception; each piece laid with the precision of a mathematical proof.

First, he had his reputation. Teachers' pet, best student, character certificates that spoke of unfailing honesty. When Basab Banerjee spoke, people listened. They believed. That would be the foundation.

Second, they needed a suspect. Not just any suspect, the right kind. Not a teenager who looked like a Greek god, not the genial uncle who read *Ganashakti* in his veranda. No, they needed someone who everyone already feared might do such a thing. A lonely man. Someone with a history of mental problems. Someone who, if found guilty, would comfort rather than disturb the neighbourhood's sense of order.

The one they called the 'Loon'.

The crow hopped closer; its blue-black feathers shimmered in the pool lights.

Third came the evidence. The textbooks had been key. As Pramila's tutor, he had access to her house, to her study materials. Her elder brother had left for college, leaving behind his old textbooks: Irodov, Loney's Coordinate Geometry, all the expensive ones. Basab had simply taken them for himself. No one would miss old textbooks gathering dust.

But he had not known then what Pramila had hidden in those pages. Between the pages, she had tucked away pieces of her secret life: photographs from her early modelling days, test shots from local photographers, magazine clippings she didn't want her parents to see. The kind of pictures that showed her transformation from schoolgirl to something more. And the poems, pages torn from her diary, filled with dreams and desires she couldn't share with anyone. She had chosen her brother's abandoned textbooks as her hiding place, certain no one would ever look there.

These weren't just pieces of paper; they were the perfect evidence. The sort of collection a stalker might keep. Intimate enough to suggest obsession, personal enough to imply surveillance. And Basab had them all, an accidental arsenal fallen into his hands through nothing more than his role as her tutor and his need for second-hand books.

Getting them into Brajendra's house had been calculated precision. He knew the old man's schedule, the evening walk that lasted exactly forty-seven minutes, the way he always locked his front door but left his terrace access open. From Basab's roof, it was a simple matter of using the plank that all Kolkata houses kept for hanging clothes. The photographs went into the bedside drawer, some poems scattered in the study, a few pictures pressed between the pages of Brajendra's own books. Not too obvious, not too hidden, placed exactly where searching police would find them.

When the police brought Basab in about Ishaan's whereabouts, he was ready. He had rehearsed his fake stories like his mother used to rehearse hers, practising his story in front of the mirror, calculating every possible trajectory the questioning might take. Like a chess grandmaster, he had planned twenty moves ahead, ready with counters for every possible challenge.

The crow cawed once, the sound echoing across the water.

There had been no risk.

None.

No one was smarter than Basab Banerjee. Certainly not those half-wit police officers.

Every variable had been accounted for, every loose end tied up. A perfect equation that added up to Ishaan's freedom.

The crow watched as Basab poured another drink, his thoughts circling back to Maya Sen's implications.

'Bribed by Ishaan's father.' He almost laughed at the crudeness of her theory. As if he, Basab Banerjee, would have done something so amateurish as accepting money. These documentary makers, with their simplistic understanding of human nature, always looking for the obvious answer, follow the money, find the payoff.

They couldn't understand that the perfect crime demanded perfect isolation. A suitcase of cash would have been the sloppiest possible move. Money left trails. Bank deposits raised questions. Even cash had serial numbers, transaction records, witnesses. Someone would have seen the handoff. Someone would have talked: a servant, a driver, maybe even Ishaan's father himself, in one of his drunken boasts. Or Ishaan, in a moment of weakness or spite. Even silence, when bought, had a price tag that could be traced.

No, his genius lay in understanding that true perfection required complete severance. No meetings with Ishaan's father. No conspiratorial whispers with Ishaan. No evidence of collusion, because there had been none. He had acted alone, moving pieces on the board while appearing to be nothing more than another pawn. His reward had been the elegant perfection of the plan itself.

The crow hopped closer, its head tilting as if questioning his logic.

That was what most people could not grasp. The most dangerous connection wasn't a trail of money; it was any connection at all. Every link in a chain was a potential break point. Every shared secret was a liability. Every conspirator was a risk.

In the end, the perfect crime isn't about what you do.

It is about what you don't.

Never take money. Never make contact. Never share plans. Never leave traces.

And never, ever, let anyone know that you were the architect of it all.

The crow's presence felt accusatory now, as Basab's thoughts sank into deeper waters. Why had he really done it?

The easy answer was gratitude. When the blow from the bat nearly killed him, it was Ishaan who had paid for the private hospital, the surgery, the scans. His father couldn't have afforded it; he would have taken him to a government hospital, where they would have left him to die, or live as a vegetable.

But Ishaan's generosity always came with a price tag. *Here, take this money for your treatment. Here, I am paying for the movie tickets. Keep this branded shirt; it doesn't* fit me anymore. Each act of kindness, a reminder of who held the power to give, and who needed to receive. Ishaan loved playing saviour, to Basab, to the other Musketeers, to Pramila. Until Pramila refused to be saved anymore.

The crow shifted on its perch, moonlight catching its eye, watching, waiting.

Hadn't Basab done the same? Used his power, his brain, his reputation, his carefully cultivated image of honesty, to save Ishaan? He had orchestrated the perfect salvation, crafted an airtight alternate reality where Ishaan was innocent and Brajendra guilty. Was that love? Or another kind of power play, the Genius proving he too could bend lives and reality to his will?

Perhaps that was what love was: a constant negotiation of power. Ishaan's money against Basab's brains. Pramila's beauty against Ishaan's control. Everyone was playing their hand, using whatever cards they held.

Love, power, money, different faces of the same die. Maybe he saved Ishaan out of love, or maybe to prove his intelligence was worth as much as Ishaan's wealth. Or maybe, deep down, he understood they were the same, both willing to destroy others to maintain control.

The crow's caw split the night air as it took flight, vanishing into the darkness beyond the trellis.

Then, the backyard lights died. No flicker, no warning, just gone.

Basab sat still in the jacuzzi, steam rising around his shoulders, eyes fixed on the dead bulbs. Motion sensors, he told himself. They had timed out because he had not moved. That was all. Nothing more.

But the dark thickened. Not just absence, it had weight, a living texture, like ink spreading through water.

Underwater lights still pulsed softly, distorting the surface with tremors of green and gold. Shadows danced at the edges of his vision. The hedges slouched like beasts, their shapes pooling under them. The garden trellis stretched across the grass in long black bars, prison shadows, whispering of Brajendra's final cell.

Then came the scent.

Strawberry shampoo.

Sunsilk. Familiar. Impossible.

It's the Scotch, Basab told himself. He should have stopped drinking an hour ago. Or maybe some flower blooming at night, its fragrance playing tricks with memory.

Then, another sound.

A chime. Delicate, unmistakable. The silvery rhythm of an anklet.

Pramila's anklet.

The sound transported him. Back to those Thursday evenings in her home. Textbooks opened between them, ink smudging fingers. She would emerge from her bath, hair dripping into a tightly wrapped pink towel. And before she appeared, always, always, that musical rhythm would arrive first.

Now, in the dark, he kept his head low, eyes on the shimmering water. His reflection fractured. The surface trembled.

Then came the laugh.

Not the sweet, polite laughter of a schoolgirl. Something else. Older. Knowing.

His fingers gripped the edge of the jacuzzi.

The water churned softly around him.

The laugh returned, closer this time. It had that same lilt Pramila used when she got an answer right in her homework, rare and triumphant.

'Not so smart now, are you, Basab-da?'

He flinched.

That voice. That teasing cruelty. The edge behind the innocence.

Thud. Drag. Thud. Drag.

Footsteps. Slow. Lopsided. Measured in pain.

And now the stench. Unwashed clothes. Desperate loneliness. The same smell he had described in his testimony.

He was breathing so hard I could hear it over the TV, he had told Inspector Roy. And now he heard it again: that ragged, wet breath. *Hunh. Hunh.* Like a stray dog in summer heat.

A pause.

Then the sound he had invented, the detail that made his story believable.

A man bending over. Hands on knees. Fighting nausea.

Slurp. Slurp. A noise like someone holding back tears. Exactly as Basab had described.

He had made it all up. Fabricated it with care, precision, mathematical elegance. Brajendra's guilt, assembled piece by piece like a machine built to hum with perfect deceit.

And now the lies had grown limbs. Breath. Sound.

They circled the water like sharks.

I made you up, he wanted to scream. *You weren't there. You never made those sounds. I invented you.*

But the footsteps continued their slow orbit. The breathing drew closer.

And his guilt, conjured from fiction, refused to stay dead.

Then came the third smell, cutting through the sweetness of Pramila's shampoo and the sour reek of Brajendra.

That unmistakable hospital smell. Antiseptic, yes, but only on the surface. Beneath it, something deeper, more human. The scent of endings.

It brought him back to that white, humming room where his father had lain for days, skin stretched taut over his cheekbones, eyes fixed on some point beyond the wall.

'Khoka, you are here?' his father had whispered. 'I thought you wouldn't come.'

Even now, the words held the weight of quiet devastation. Not relief from his father, surprise. Surprise that his son had rushed back to hold his hand at the edge of departure, surprise that his son had not begged off coming back, citing some conference or the other.

He remembered that smell: the sweet-sour tang of a body shutting down, one system after another failing in quiet succession. A scent that marked the moment when hope stopped pretending.

Now, impossibly, it drifted across the water. Across his jacuzzi. Thousands of miles from that hospital, but unmistakably the same.

Not just a memory.

A promise.

From the shadows, his father's voice returned, soft, threadbare, insistent:

'Khoka, you are here?'

But this time, the words carried a different meaning.

This is not happening, Basab told himself. *I am imagining things. All I need to do is stand up. Just stand, step out of the water, and the motion sensors will turn the lights back on.*

But his body didn't move.

The warm water clung to him. A velvet trap. The jets still pulsed steadily against his ribs. Soothing. Holding him in place. Inside this cocoon, logic still functioned. Physics still made sense. Quantum mechanics obeyed its riddles. The universe could still be explained.

But to rise, to stand, would mean triggering the lights.

And in their glare, he would see what he already knew was waiting.

The schoolgirl with waterlogged eyes, stepping forward to ask why he had let her killer go.

The old man with rope burns at his throat, demanding why Basab had sentenced him to death.

And his father, with hospital-sweet breath, wondering why his son had stopped coming home.

Then something cold and wet forced him down, hands, but wrong. Bloated. With too many joints bending in impossible directions. And they were not outside him, but inside.

His head went under.

The churning water turned the jacuzzi lights into a hellish theatre. Above him, the surface rippled like a membrane between worlds.

Pramila's face hovered before him, preserved in the moment of her final realization. Her hair moved in unnatural currents, each strand devouring light. Her eyes held thirty years of watching. Waiting. Knowing.

Beside her, Brajendra emerged from the dark. The rope marks on his neck pulsed with a sick, luminous glow. His jaw dangled at an impossible angle, dislocated by the prison noose, a grotesque smile stretched too wide, too far.

But what floated behind them made these horrors seem merciful.

Where light touched shadow, the world came apart. Faces appeared, then dissolved:

His mother, whispering lies rehearsed in front of a mirror.

His father, counting rupee notes with fingers made of bone.

Sandra, signing the divorce papers as her hands turned to ash.

His sons, walking away without looking back.

Each image twisted into the next, judgement given form.

The underwater lights flickered. With each flash, the figures came closer. Clearer. More wrong.

Pramila's school uniform swirled in currents that obeyed no natural laws.

Brajendra's eyes became bottomless wells where light, and sanity, vanished without a ripple.

The lights pulsed once more.

And then Basab saw what floated above them all: his own face, watching from the surface, twisted into a grotesque, knowing smile.

His heart gave out before the next breath could come. Before the next flicker. Before the next secret rose from the depths.

They found him at 8 a.m., floating face-up in the still-churning jacuzzi. His body had started to bloat. Fingers, pruned and white, clutched at nothing.

The coroner ruled it a heart attack, natural causes, accelerated by alcohol, heat, drugs in his system, and the stress of divorce.

They noted the expression frozen on his face, but medical reports have no column for the flavour of terror that stops a heart.

A single red rose drifted beside him; its petals open in the morning light.

When the police tried to retrieve it, they swore it had been there all night.

Yet the petals were perfectly fresh, as if just plucked.

No one could explain where it had come from.

The nearest rose bush stood on the far side of the property.

There had been no wind.

5

The Roast of Ishaan Chatterjee

Ishaan Chatterjee watched his fist connect. The comedian's nose exploded in a spray of blood. On the hundred-inch screen dominating his penthouse wall, the moment looped again, this time cut to the Rocky theme by some enterprising meme page admin. The savage crack, the gasps from the awards show audience, his own snarling face, rendered in slow motion, every brutal detail vivid.

'Two million views in three hours,' Anand Dwivedi murmured, sweat beading on his balding pate despite the arctic air conditioning. His pudgy fingers scrolled over his phone screen, leaving smudges on the glass. 'Totally viral, sir, superhit it is.' He had spent fifteen years forecasting Ishaan's moods, reading the air like a seasoned weatherman tracking tropical storms, but tonight, the barometer had failed him.

Ishaan stood impassive, his black compression shirt moulded to his shoulders like a second skin. Every curve of hard-earned muscle showed through the fabric, a testament to the brutal hours in his private gym with his team of trainers and sports medicine doctors. A jagged scar ran along his forearm, a souvenir from his first action film when he had insisted on doing his own stunts. At forty-eight, it took twice the work to keep that action-hero physique, but the results were undeniable. His cargo pants, deceptively casual, were tailored to military precision. A limited-edition Rolex winked on his wrist, a gift for attending the baby shower of a Mumbai industrialist. Presence, not performance, had always been his highest-paid role.

His face betrayed the perfection of the body beneath. Despite the artistry of a dozen Beverly Hills surgeons, something always felt…off. The skin stretched too tight, the nose too sharp, his hair a uniform black that seemed implanted with surgical precision. It was a mask of youth, applied desperately but never quite convincing. Only his eyes remained unchanged, dark and intense with a crackling ferocity, the same eyes that had stared out from countless posters and magazine covers, making women swoon and men copy his look.

He stood like what he was: Bollywood's last true Titan, as *Celebrity* magazine had recently called him, perched on Mount Olympus, refusing to acknowledge the younger gods circling his kingdom. His penthouse suite bore testament to two decades of stardom, awards gleaming in glass cases, movie posters from his blockbuster years, photographs with three generations of prime ministers.

The impact still rang in his knuckles, that savage, bone-deep satisfaction of cartilage giving way. The rush was pure, unfiltered, more real than anything he had felt in years. In that moment, he hadn't been a fading star, a middle-aged man in an industry obsessed with youth, the butt of jokes and barbs. He had been powerful. Feared. Larger than life. The kind that men had to crane their necks up to look at.

On screen, the comedian lay sprawled, clutched into a foetal ball. Ishaan towered over him, chest heaving, fists clenched, looking like a hunter in front of a downed deer.

Ishaan smiled to himself. Power. It still felt good.

'Play it again,' he said.

Anand shot a glance at the third person in the room. A silent warning threaded through the look.

'Play. It. Again,' Ishaan barked, each word landing like a strike.

The comedian's voice filled the room: 'Let's give a round of applause for Ishaan Chatterjee, the man who shows us that while money can buy a new face, it can't guarantee a successful movie! I recently watched your latest film, the one where you go undercover in a prison. Congratulations, sir, you succeeded in your craft. You made me feel what solitary confinement really feels like. I was watching it in an empty theatre, and I have never wanted to run out so fast.'

Scattered applause and laughter rippled through the awards show audience. The camera cut to several other superstars, one trying to suppress a laugh, another nodding sadly.

The comedian adjusted his tuxedo collar, leaning toward where Ishaan had been sitting. 'And what's with this new look, Uncle ji? Did the surgeon run off because the budget got cut midway, like what happens to all your movies now?'

Laughter turned to shrieks as Ishaan sauntered onto the screen and launched himself at the comic like a missile.

'Sir, I just got a text,' Anand said, his face tight with worry. 'He is filing a complaint.'

'It's all over the debates on *News Night* and *Hot Potato*, freedom of speech, the right of comedians to offend…' A female voice filled the room.

Both Ishaan and Anand turned to the woman sitting on the massive leather couch. She had spoken for the first time since she had introduced herself a while ago.

'Hold on, honey,' Ishaan growled, voice dripping with contempt. 'First of all, this stick with a tuft of hair isn't a comedian. Johnny Lever is a comedian. This punk is a little girly-boy from YouTube, a *chikna* Charlie whose balls have barely dropped. It's a sign of the times we live in that this punk gets to host *The Cinema Awards*, all because he has got a few million subscribers. I was filling theatres before he was a gleam in his mother's eye, all right?'

Ishaan stalked toward the window, his reflection looming large in the glass. 'Second, freedom of speech is what a citizen expects from a government in a democracy. It's not a free pass between people. Third, this is an industry event. We celebrate the people in it and our audience. Making a mockery of people like me, who are the industry, isn't cool.' He spun around, eyes flashing. 'Fourth, and maybe this is the most important, action leads to reaction. That's Newton's Third Law.'

His lips curled into a sneer. 'Anyway, let him file the complaint. I do not dance at the police's annual charity ball for nothing.'

He stopped, turned, and fixed Anand with a piercing stare. 'Fine. Send this twerp a cheque for twenty lakh. And with that, send a note: "This should cover the cost of setting your nose back. Maybe you can get some work done while you are at it too."'

Anand's fingers tightened around his phone. He had seen this before, Ishaan's relentless appetite for escalating public feuds. As his manager, he knew he should put his foot down.

'I am not sure that's the best idea, sir. Maybe we should just let this blow over…'

'I don't pay you to think,' Ishaan snapped. 'I pay you to do what I tell you. Send the cheque. Send the note. And make sure the press knows about it.'

'But you do pay us as your PR agency,' the woman's voice cut in, steady despite the tension thick in the room. 'And I would strongly recommend you don't do this, sir.'

Ishaan turned, his movement precise. His head tilted, that familiar angle from a thousand magazine covers, as he looked at her.

She was a striking young woman, light makeup, black tube skirt, crisp white shirt, pearl necklace. Ishaan remembered his best friend Rocky Chopra's term for this look, one he had never quite understood before: the girlboss.

'I am sorry, who are you?' The question hung in the air, deceptively mild.

'Sir, I gave you my card when you came in. I am Ria Raghunathan, VP of Crisis Management for Black Envelope Public…' she began.

Ishaan's hand sliced through her words like a blade.

'I didn't ask for your biodata, madam,' he sneered. 'I wanted to know who you are, and why you think you can tell me what to do or not.'

Ria didn't flinch. Her shoulders squared, eyes locking with his. 'Well, I am here to rescue your public image, sir,' she said evenly. 'Someone needs to tell you this: you do have a perception problem with the demographic you target.'

'Ennnhhh,' Ishaan drawled, tilting his head again. 'You, whom I have never seen before and will probably never see again, are going to tell me why I, Ishaan Chatterjee, have a…what was it, Anand, "Perception problem"?'

Anand, standing quietly to the side, made a face at Ria, a silent plea to retreat. The room seemed to shrink, the air thickening with an unspoken threat. Ishaan took a slow, menacing step toward her, then another. His bulk towered over her slender frame, but she remained unmoved, a stillness that spoke of something harder than mere presence.

'Yes, sir,' she said, voice clear and steady. 'That's exactly what I am telling you. And if you want to salvage what's left of your career, you will listen to me.'

Ishaan stared, jaw clenched, fists tightening at his sides. Seconds stretched, the moment balanced on a knife's edge. Then, abruptly, he threw his head back and laughed, shattering the tension.

'Black Envelope didn't hold back, did they? Sent their finest.'

Anand watched, eyes wide, caught between disbelief and relief. He had seen Ishaan dismiss countless professionals, tear through entire PR teams. But this…this was different.

'Looks like we've got ourselves a firecracker, Anand,' Ishaan said. 'Get the lady a drink. Scratch the plan to send the note. Send the cheque to the kid, though.'

For a moment Anand hesitated. This was unprecedented: Ishaan abandoning a plan to humiliate someone publicly. His tension eased slowly, shoulders dropping, as if a weight had lifted.

Ishaan noticed the shift. 'Yes, Anand-bhai,' he said, the honorific softening his tone. 'I guess I am getting old. The fight is going out of me.'

He moved to his single-seater sofa, a throne perched on a raised marble pedestal, his performance space, where directors trembled, young actresses grovelled, and producers kept their heads down, laying out their offerings. From this vantage, he looked down at Ria with new curiosity.

'Just water for me, please,' Ria said, gaze careful to avoid his eyes. 'I don't drink on the job.'

Ishaan made a faint, almost imperceptible face. When he offered a woman a drink, he couldn't remember the last time one had refused.

Ria sat upright in her single-seat couch, filling her space with quiet confidence despite his penetrating stare from above.

'First, sir,' she began, 'let's establish whether you acknowledge there's an issue with your public image. Accepting the problem is the crucial first step toward finding a solution.'

Ishaan glanced at Anand, a smirk twitching at his lips. 'I thought you said she was PR. But she talks like that anger management shrink you set me up with last year. "Accept the problem." What next? "Growth mindset"? I hope this isn't your roundabout way of putting me back in therapy.'

Anand said nothing. Ishaan snorted softly.

He leaned forward with a predator's focus, teeth visible behind his smile. 'When you say "issue with my public image", are you referring to the less-than-stellar numbers at the box office for my last few movies?'

She said nothing, letting the silence hang heavy as confirmation.

'Bollywood's Titan is now Bollywood's Titanic,' he scoffed, 'except the Titanic only sank once, right? Isn't that what that broken-nose comedian said? I will give the kid that; that was funny.'

Anand returned with glasses of water and flinched. He knew Ishaan's pattern by heart: first, the self-deprecation, bait cast out, expecting reassurance. When met with silence, the beast emerged, his rage exploding in the destruction of the nearest costly object. The price tag always matched the depth of his fury.

Anand started to intervene, hoping to prevent an outburst before the stranger, but Ishaan silenced him with a raised hand, eyes fixed on Ria, waiting for a contradiction that wouldn't come.

She sat motionless, a professional mask carved on her face, neither impressed nor intimidated.

Anand closed his eyes, bracing for the inevitable: the storm of motion, the crash of glass, the fallout.

But instead, Ishaan leaned back and exhaled, shoulders sagging beneath his tailored jacket.

'I will tell you what the real problem is,' he said, voice measured. 'India is a cost-conscious market. Going to the movies is just too expensive.'

His fingers tapped a quiet rhythm on the leather armrest, his only sign of contained energy. 'This isn't new. Ever since VHS, the industry has battled "video piracy." Why pay for a theatre when you can watch it at home for almost nothing? Back in high school, we would sneak off to Sneha Library after lunch when the adults napped. The guy would pull out worn tapes from under the counter, the magnetic strip scarred from endless pauses. You would get camera recordings, dark shadows moving across the screen, someone's head blocking the view, muffled sound, usually missing the climax because the recorder fought with the projectionist over money. Then VCRs died and cable arrived. Sunday afternoons for Hindi, late nights for English, Poltu-da would broadcast pirated films on local channels. VCDs arrived, then file sharing, but the problem stayed the same: pirated movies at home are a poor substitute for the real thing.'

'Now?' Ishaan continued, his own narrative feeding his fire. 'Streaming services are cheap. Perfect picture, crystal-clear sound, no legal worries, pause whenever you want. Why would anyone drag their family to a multiplex? Ticket prices, parking, concessions – that's a month's groceries for some families. Covid just confirmed what people already suspected: they don't need theatres anymore.'

Anand noticed Ria watching Ishaan with clinical detachment. Her eyes tracked his gestures, noted his posture, catalogued his expressions, an anthropologist studying a rare specimen.

Ishaan didn't notice. 'This isn't about me or my appeal. It's simple economics. Psychology.'

'Not all films are performing poorly,' she said, voice dropping like a hunter's snare.

Anand recognized the trap immediately. He had seen a hundred interviewers try this tactic: a casual contradiction meant to provoke Ishaan's legendary temper.

But Ishaan stayed calm, voice steady. 'True, some films succeed like spectacles, mass entertainers that need huge screens. But intimate stories? Slice of life? Family dramas? Mysteries? Romances?' He shook his head. 'For those, people watch them on their phones with streaming apps.'

'But the numbers aren't bad for everyone; they are consistently bad for you.'

Anand tensed. This woman was deliberately provoking him. Ishaan, though, seemed too absorbed in his narrative to notice.

'The numbers.' His laugh scraped across the room like broken glass. 'No disrespect, Ms Ria, but you twenty-something South Mumbai types who get your cultural cues from "phoren", you are the real problem.'

There it was, the first crack. Anand watched the familiar transformation begin: eyes narrowing, chin tilting forward, lips tightening.

Ishaan leaned in, afternoon light tracing the too-perfect planes of his face, a masterpiece of surgical precision masquerading as nature. 'All the creative VPs sitting in those chairs at studios and OTT platforms; they are like you. Your age, your type, that same shade of lipstick. Your kind has turned art into an Excel sheet. Big Data, focus groups, metrics, as if you could measure magic with maths.'

His fist pressed to his chest, knuckles white. 'Cinema happens here. Heart to heart. I paint with light and shadow. Make strangers cry, laugh, fear. You think that skill rusts with age?'

The spark ignited in his eyes, the flint before the explosion.

'Oh, I read what they write about me on Twitter and Facebook. Too old for roles, they say. But that's not the problem. The problem is these scripts. Hollow stories crafted by people like you to suit your sensibilities, which I end up doing.

'Here's some data for you: walk into a movie hall in Gorakhpur, Raipur, Patna. What percentage of the audience is male? Since you love numbers so much.'

'I don't know, sir.' Her voice stayed even, posture unchanged.

Ishaan raised a hand, cutting her off. 'Almost a hundred per cent male. Pure testosterone in those seats. No idea of feminist theory. And what are we selling them?' His laugh cracked like glass. '"Toxic masculinity must die." "Down with the male gaze." We ask hard-working men who provide for their families to pay good money to be told they are the root of all evil.'

He slumped back like a king on his throne. 'You know why the South films work? Because they know their audience. Give the people what they want, not what some Bandra coffee-shop ethically sourced latte-sipper thinks they should want while dreaming of a "crossover series like Squid Game".'

A razor smile. 'I know what you are doing, where you are going. Poor toxic Ishaan Chatterjee, a dinosaur from the 90s, needs sensitivity training. Should find his feminine chakras. Shouldn't punch comedians mocking his masculinity, no, no, he should laugh along, leave his privilege at the door.'

His voice dripped with sarcasm. 'Let me guess the prescription: a forty-eight-year-old star, who still can't take a morning run without getting mobbed, by the way, needs an image makeover. Trade the Ferrari for a Prius. Play doting father or evil patriarch in women-centric films. Advertise Pure Basmati rice and Star Super Specialty Heart Hospital. Date the mother, not the daughter. Marry a single mom, raise her kids, change diapers.'

He leaned forward, elbows on knees, veins pulsing at his temples. 'You think you are the first? There has been a parade of Priyas, Rias, Sonias, Alias, sitting exactly where you are, looking exactly as you do, selling exactly the same shit.' His smile was pure venom. 'So, unless you have got something new to say, we are done here.'

'So, to sum up,' Ria's voice was antiseptic, calm, surgical. 'You see no issue with yourself. The problems are poor scripts, industry changes and "woke culture" misaligning you with your target demographic. Have I got the essence?'

The clinical precision of her response seemed to deflate Ishaan. Like a boxer whose haymaker had swung into empty air, he slumped slightly, eyes flicking to Anand for some kind of support. Finding none, he ran a hand through his perfectly styled hair.

'Yeah,' he muttered, uncertainty crackling through his bravado. 'I guess.'

'I am not here to advise you about your movies.' Ria's fingers tapped sharply against her phone, silencing an incoming message. The sound echoed in the sudden quiet. 'My concerns are about your image, and the Netmovies partnership.'

Ishaan's expression flickered, a micro-movement, barely perceptible, but on a face trained to perform, it spoke volumes.

Anand shifted uneasily on the sofa. He knew how vital the Netmovies deal was. Ishaan's last chance at relevance, a five-picture production agreement worth $175 million that had taken eighteen months of gruelling negotiation. The streaming giant was aggressively expanding into India, pouring billions into original content. For Ishaan, whose last three theatrical releases barely recouped marketing costs, the partnership offered financial security and creative control. His production company would helm five films aimed at the global Indian diaspora, each with a $35 million budget. Unlike his recent box office flops, these wouldn't be judged by opening weekend grosses, but by engagement and viewer retention metrics.

The money was needed to cover Ishaan's mounting debts. Just yesterday, Anand sat with the accountant and stared at the balance sheets. The situation was dire. Ishaan insisted he didn't care for OTT platforms, 'turd water for people I don't care to understand', preferring to make movies for his 'army of fans in the badlands of Bihar and UP.' But Anand worried, not just about the money or Ishaan's volatile temper, but about his grip on reality. Ishaan still believed the old style worked, that billions loved him, and that producers lined up to sign him as a hero.

The Netmovies deal was a lifeline. The contract sat unsigned on some executive's desk in California, waiting for the board's final approval. Anand had been bracing for good news when, last Tuesday, Ishaan's international agent called. A new executive had raised concerns about Ishaan's public image, and whether they wanted him to be the face of their brand in India and beyond. That's when Anand had quietly reached out to Black Envelope, India's premier PR firm, without telling Ishaan, to see if they could help.

And then, last night, Ishaan had punched some idiot comedian at Bollywood's biggest awards show, live, in front of millions of viewers.

'What's your point?' The bravado had ebbed from Ishaan's voice, replaced by something harder, warier.

Ria looked down at her phone and this time she didn't look up. Anand knew how much Ishaan hated phones being pulled out in front of him, let alone someone looking down at one, but for now, Ishaan remained still in his throne-like chair, distracted.

'My point is: American studios don't just write cheques when they put that kind of money on one person. They conduct audits. Deep ones. It's part of their risk management. They'll review your finances, sure, but also your conduct. Your social media presence. Your press coverage. Especially,' she paused, letting the silence stretch, 'how you treat women.'

Ishaan's jaw tightened. The muscles in his neck corded beneath his shirt.

'Prerna Malhotra.' Ria's voice was neutral, almost gentle. 'Claims you threw a phone at her head during *Dil Ka Sitara* because she kept you waiting on set.'

Ishaan grunted, dismissive. 'She is two films old. I am fucking Ishaan Chatterjee. She shows up an hour late for her shot. Mind you, I show up on time, always have. If anything, she is supposed to wait for me, not the other way around.'

'Naina Kapoor's three-part Instagram story. Emotional abuse on *Pyaar Ka Junoon*. Regular humiliation in front of the entire crew, raised voice, bad language, mocking her English accent.'

Ishaan's hands clenched the armrests of his sofa. 'Couldn't remember her lines. Didn't come to workshops. No clue where the camera was. Kept talking on her phone during shoots. When I was a junior artist, we learned through public shame when we messed up. On my second movie, the director slapped me in front of everyone because I looked away from the heroine's face for a second during a shot. Wasn't even my fault – she had onion paratha before the shot and breathed it full on my face. You did not see me complaining. I deserved it.' His body remained rigid; only his face betrayed emotion, shadows cutting across his features. 'Now everything is "emotional abuse." And why the hell does her gender matter? It is all identity politics now. Can't perform? Raise the woman card. Boom. All women flock to social media. Men jump in too, hoping to look "sensitive."' His lips curled. 'Trust me, I have said worse to guys for far less. Spoilt brat, that Naina Kapoor.'

'The Cinema Roll after-party last year. There's a detailed Twitter thread.'

'I was drunk.' He shrugged with practised charm, a motion honed over decades. 'We all were. The difference?' A bitter smile twisted his lips. 'Ronit Kapoor and Armaan Khan's PR teams knew how to spin it. Mine didn't.' He spread his hands, never rising. 'The Women's Commission called me for hearings in Delhi over that; this is where we are as a country. It was an after-party. What do people think happens there? Poetry readings?'

'Now, let's talk about your public statements.' Ria's voice cut through his sarcasm like a scalpel. '"Women should conform to traditional roles, or the social contract will break down." Your exact words at the Mumbai International Film Festival.'

Ishaan stared at his reflection in the darkened windowpane.

'What? I don't get credit for knowing what a "social contract" is, me, the gym lunk?'

'Or perhaps,' she continued, each word measured and precise, 'you prefer the similarly intellectual "boys will be boys" from your *Bharat Online* interview? Then there's that gem on *Coffee with Arjun* during rapid fire. He asks, "Eggs?" You say, "Sunny side up." He asks, "Women?" You say, "Ass up".'

'A joke. They told me to say that. You think any of that rapid-fire shit is spontaneous?' His words hung heavy in the chilled silence.

'Freedom of expression,' Ishaan then mumbled. 'Don't I have that too?'

'As you said earlier, freedom of expression is between a government and its citizens.' Ria's fingers traced the edge of her phone. 'Not between a star and his paycheck.'

She scrolled down. The blue light from her phone screen cast sharp, angular shadows across her face.

'And then there's the matter of intimate partner violence, or rather, the accusations made by your long-term romantic partner, Pooja Asrani...'

Ishaan's hand shot up, a conductor silencing an orchestra. 'She never took my name.'

'You are very lucky she didn't.' Ria's voice carried the weight of unspoken consequences. She set her phone down on the glass coffee table, its screen now dark.

'Suo moto cognizance by the police would have meant jail. Punching a comedian for a joke is one thing. But punching your girlfriend for signing a movie with a rival hero?' Her gaze never left his face as she leaned in, voice low but lethal. 'Locking her in her own bedroom with your two pit bulls loose in the living room? You consider that "old-world" behaviour?'

Ishaan slumped deeper into his throne-like sofa.

'This alpha male persona?' She gestured at him. 'Maybe it works for your target demographic. Maybe it's exactly what the single-screen audiences in Gorakhpur and Patna want. I would dispute that, but that's not my brief.'

She sat straighter, spine unbending. 'But Hollywood?'

A beat passed.

'That's why I am different from your parade of Rias and Sonias and Alias. I am not here to fix your image for Bollywood. You and I both know that your career is flickering out. I am here to align you with where you might have a chance. Where there are meatier, main character roles for older actors, outside India.'

Her eyes locked onto his. Calm. Clinical.

'And right now? You are radioactive.'

The night had swept across Mumbai; its golden glow reflected in the infinity pool visible through the glass behind him. The city shimmered like something half-real. Italian marble caught the sharp outlines of imported modern art, their shadows long and judgmental.

'So now comes the lecture?' His voice carried the brittle mockery of a man who already knew he was losing. 'You are here to make me a better man?'

'No, sir.' Ria remained poised. Precise.

'I don't care who you are, what you believe in or who you slap around. My judgements stay outside that door.' She nodded toward the elevator lobby, its gold-leaf ceiling glinting faintly. 'I am a problem-solver. My job is to manage perception, at least until Netmovies completes their audit.'

A corner of her mouth lifted, cold, not kind.

'Think of me as your lawyer in the court of public opinion. I just need to know where you buried the bodies, so I can defend you better.'

Something shifted in Ishaan's face. A flicker. A crack in the mask. He leaned forward slightly, adjusting the strap of his designer watch.

'I am not sure where this is going. But I am intrigued.'

'And as your lawyer, I need you to tell me the truth. Without it, I cannot spin things away from where you don't want people to go.'

'What truth?'

'Mr Anand hasn't told you, has he?' Ria glanced over to where Ishaan's manager had retreated into the shadows of the vast room, nearly indistinguishable against the walnut panelling.

'Told me what?'

'About the documentary.'

Ishaan's eyebrows crept upward. 'What documentary?'

'*Hidden Secrets*. Their new season.' She paused.

'Am I supposed to know what that is?' Ishaan's voice was genuinely confused, wary. 'I have no idea what you are saying.'

'*Hidden Secrets* is a global true-crime web series. Twenty million viewers, give or take. Each season, they travel to a different country, digging up a cold case, usually one involving the homicide of a young woman. They study crime, yes, but also culture, society and public memory.'

Understanding dawned in Ishaan's eyes.

Followed, a second later, by something else.

A flicker. A cloud. A shadow.

Then, nothing. The mask reset. Smooth. Blank.

But Ria didn't look away. She had caught it.

'Yes, sir,' she said softly. 'This time it's going to be about Pramila Chatterjee.'

His left hand closed ever so slightly around his right wrist. A minor tic. A small betrayal.

'That's ancient history,' he said, tone even.

'So, you do understand why, sir, you are sitting right now on top of a PR volcano at a time when you can least afford it?'

The room went still.

'When were you planning to tell me, Anand?' Ishaan's voice was almost too quiet.

'Sir, I was waiting for the right moment. The information just came to me yesterday, and you were in such a good mood after the Omega shoot...'

'Why am I always the last to know?' Ishaan's voice rose, barely, but the tremor in it made Anand flinch. 'Why the fuck do I pay you? Once upon a time, you at least brought me the bad news before everyone else did: flop openings, shit reviews, cancelled endorsements. Now you don't even do that. What exactly am I paying you for? Your pretty face?' He gestured at Anand's jowls, which were beginning to quiver. 'Or that masterpiece of a moustache?'

'Sir, they contacted me only yesterday, sir.' Anand's fingers twisted the hem of his silk shirt. 'They said they had been trying for weeks. I thought it was just another random YouTube channel pestering for footage...Yesterday only I thought, okay, let me give them two minutes. I just saw they had twenty million subscribers, and I thought, okay, they have reach. Your latest, the buzz is not so good, na, so maybe...a positive interview...'

His voice trailed off as Ishaan's expression darkened.

'Then they told me something from your past in Calcutta...sir...murder...'

The last word emerged as barely a whisper. Anand's moustache twitched like a frightened caterpillar.

'And you didn't think to call me immediately?' Ishaan's voice was velvet stretched over steel.

'Sir, I was going to, but then...I thought...'

'You *thought*.' Ishaan smiled. The kind of smile that made junior artists flee sets and veteran directors hesitate before calling 'action'.

'That's the problem, Anand-bhai. Second time I am telling you within the hour, I don't pay you to think.'

He turned to Ria, who sat with the calm focus of a chess player mid-endgame.

'I don't know how much you know about the case. Pre-internet days, probably before your time.' His tone softened. 'Pramila was my girlfriend. Puppy love. Teenage romance. She was murdered by a man in our neighbourhood, Brajendra Das.' He paused, as if dredging up an old scar. 'Yes, that was his name. Creepy old pervert. The police questioned me, of course, standard procedure. Questioned all my friends too, the Musketeers. We were always together.'

He spread his hands, staying seated. 'That was pretty much it.'

'Black Envelope's research goes deeper than Google.' Ria's voice cut cleanly through the air. She leaned forward, the leather of her couch whispering against her elbow.

'Multiple newspapers, *Anandabazar*, the *Statesman*, the *Telegraph*, *Bartaman*, *Ganashakti*, all identified you as the prime suspect.'

A muscle in Ishaan's jaw ticked. Barely.

'She broke up with you that afternoon. Hours later, she was found dead. Drowned in a bucket of water in her own home.' Ria's gaze didn't waver. 'The papers described your behaviour: volatile, jealous, violent. The kind of red flags people ignored back then.'

'I did not kill Pramila,' Ishaan's voice rang with conviction. His eyes locked onto hers, controlled, precise, dangerous.

'As I told you, sir, I don't care whether you killed her or not.' Ria's tone was scalpel-sharp, cold and steady. 'Someone else was charged. Died in custody. The system closed the book. I doubt the police will find usable evidence thirty years later.'

She let the silence breathe.

'But the court of public opinion...that's a different beast.'

Something hardened behind Ishaan's eyes. The charm slipped, just enough to reveal the steel beneath.

'So, what do you want from me?'

'I want to know exactly what their research team will uncover. The truth would be a good place to start, not about the murder, but about the abuse.'

She watched him closely, waiting for the performance to crack.

His gaze drifted past her to the Mumbai skyline, but he wasn't seeing skyscrapers and sea-link lights. He was somewhere else.

Calcutta. Summer evenings.

The sun melting behind Victoria Memorial. Pramila in her school uniform, white ribbons fluttering in her braid. A shared chocolate ice cream at Flurys. Her laughter. When she would walk away, pretending not to notice him, but then glance back when she thought he was not looking. The way she would adjust her dupatta when nervous. Scrunch her nose while angry.

That monsoon afternoon under the umbrella, their shoulders brushing, her hands trembling in his.

The pride in her eyes when he hit the winning six at the inter-school cricket final. The rose she gave him, still heavy with dew.

The scent of her shampoo. The gloss on her lips. The song she sang at that singing competition with Ranadeep, '*Kon alo laaglo chokhe*', still haunting.

The onyx pendant he gave her for her birthday. The black of her eyes, darker still.

He blinked.

The past scattered like torn scraps in a storm.

'I don't remember much,' he said. Voice level. Eyes unreadable. 'It was so many years ago.'

'I can't help you unless you help me.' Ria's tone sharpened. 'You went to her home. You hit her. In front of her family. You kicked over a shelf holding her trophies. It was in the papers. And if it made the papers in the 90s, it means it wasn't the only time. I need to know what happened. All of it.'

'Well, since you have read the papers, you already know what happened.'

His voice thinned. And then, just for a second, the mask slipped.

He turned sharply to Anand.

'Call Black Envelope. Right now.'

'Sir?'

'Call them. Ask if they have a Ria Raghunathan on their payroll. If they sent her.'

He narrowed his eyes at her. 'Because maybe our friend here isn't who she claims to be. Maybe she is wired. Maybe she is working with the documentary team. Because right now, she is fishing for information. And I don't like being baited.'

The room went still.

Anand scrambled with his phone, fingers trembling.

Outside, the city shimmered in glass. Inside, shadows gathered.

This was not the first time. Years ago, a tabloid had sent a fake casting director with a hidden camera. Ishaan had caught on, nearly dislocated the man's shoulder before smashing the device.

'Sir,' Anand said, phone pressed to his ear. 'Yes…yes… Ria ma'am…credentials, yes…'

A pause. Then: 'She is legitimate, sir.'

He lowered the phone. 'Security followed full protocol. The lady guard frisked her for wires. Black Envelope confirmed; she's their VP of Crisis PR.'

Ria had not moved. She sat composed, her body language a masterclass in executive calm.

'Are we done with the theatrics, sir?' she asked quietly. 'Or would you prefer to search me yourself?'

Ishaan exhaled and leaned back, drumming his fingers once against the leather.

'Well. One can never blame a man for being careful.'

'No,' she said, locking eyes with him. 'But you can blame him for wasting time. And you don't have much of that left.'

'What the hell does that mean? Am I dying?' Ishaan shifted his weight, the sofa creaking beneath him.

'Your public image is. And with it, your deal.'

Ria stopped, waiting for Ishaan to reply. He did not. So she continued.

'If someone says you threw a paperweight at Pramila, your phone-throwing incident with Prerna Malhotra makes it plausible. If they claim you humiliated Pramila for singing off-key, your well-documented abuse of co-stars for fumbling their lines lends it credibility.'

She leaned forward slightly. 'This team will dig deep. They will talk to people from your neighbourhood. Your classmates. Your friends. You are a celebrity. People will fabricate, exaggerate, bask in their borrowed spotlight. A camera crew, global viewership, some will say anything to be on screen.'

'And they will build their fiction on the scaffold of your documented truths. Every slap, every tantrum, every blind item everyone knows is about you, that becomes their palette.'

A pause. Then, she went on.

'And yes, let's say the quiet part out loud. This season's success depends on how convincingly they can paint you as the murderer who got away.'

Her eyes didn't flinch.

'To protect you, I need to know what's true, what isn't and what lies in between. What we acknowledge, what we deny, what we regret, and what we weaponize.'

Ishaan's fingers paused on the armrest.

'And if I don't tell you?'

'Then I will be writing your obituary instead of your defence.'

He gestured to Anand. 'Fix me a drink. I cannot deal with this sober.' Then, turning to Ria, his tone softened. 'And, Ms Ria, can I tempt you? Something grown-up, a single malt? Maybe some food too. It's late.'

'No drinking, sir.' She didn't budge. 'I need you clear-headed. And focused.'

He almost made a joke. Something flippant. Something about not hitting her even if he got drunk.

But he stopped himself.

'Okay. Water, then, for both of us. And Anand, dinner. Are you vegetarian?'

Ria nodded. 'I am not hungry. Water is fine.'

'Right. Anand-bhai, get us water. Then my dinner. Today is my vegetarian day.'

Anand shuffled off. The sound of ice cubes hitting crystal cut through the silence like a ticking clock.

'Tell me about the violence,' Ria said, as Anand returned and handed Ishaan a glass. 'How many times did you hit her? How bad was it?'

Ishaan took the glass but didn't drink. He stared at the water.

'I don't remember.'

'There were so many times you cannot remember? Or are we still performing?'

He exhaled. 'I raised my voice often. Surely. But quarrels from thirty years ago, how is one supposed to remember every one?'

'I asked,' Ria said, her voice sharpening, 'how many times did you hit her?'

He looked past her, past the room, past the city.

'Okay...there was this time...she wore a sleeveless top. I grabbed her arm. Clamped down. Left finger marks. Maybe twisted it a bit.'

He stopped and thought, concentrating on his memories.

'And once...she didn't wear this top I bought her. I asked why. She snapped back. I might've...'

A vague flick of his hand. 'Slapped her. Open-handed. Once.'

He looked up. Ria was still. Watching.

Ishaan's smile carried generations of disapproval.

'For us, love meant forever. This birth and the next. May sound trite and filmy, but that's the way it was. When Pramila was mine, she was mine completely.'

His voice hardened with conviction.

'And yes, I know Neanderthal is meant as an insult. But those ancient men figured out something your generation has forgotten: that men and women have different roles. Man as the hunter and the woman as the child-rearer. Roles that helped us survive. Build civilizations. I will not apologize for what I believe in. I am the man, she is the woman, and no, we are not the same. I am expected to earn, to go to work. I will fail in my duty to be who I am if I quit my job and say, "I have decided to discover myself," or "I am taking a mental health break." Similarly, there are things that women should do, and are expected to do. And all cultures across the world have been aligned on such values. There's a reason for that. This social organization works. I have been cancelled for saying this, but I will say it again: strict equality isn't natural. It's not how we're meant to be. I take care of her, I provide for her, and yes, that means she listens to what I say. I am a man. And I will not apologize for being one.'

'"You may say yes, you may say no,"' Ria quoted softly, '"but you are mine." Sung by a man about obsession, oppressive obsession disguised as romance.'

'You said you wouldn't judge.'

'I am not,' she said. 'Not yet.'

She gave him space to continue his rant on gender roles. When he remained silent, she moved on.

'Tell me about the day you went to her house. The one with the violence. That one you must remember. It was in the papers. Her parents were home. You went in anyway. What happened?'

The magazine shook in Ishaan's fist as he burst through their unlocked door. Her face stared out from the cover, head tilted, lips open slightly, eyes direct into the camera, shoulders bare beneath flimsy designer fabric.

Pramila sat at the cheap Sunmica table, afternoon light catching her profile. She wore that blue salwar he hated, the one that made her look older, like an aunty. A brass plate before her held a small mound of watery rice, a half-bitten onion, too much salt, and bowls of yellow *daal* and a single fish floating in reddish curry.

Their eyes met. Recognition flickered in hers, not fear, but something worse. Acceptance.

'Is this what my future wife does?' Ishaan hurled the rolled magazine. It struck the table, unspooling like a dying snake. 'Parade herself like a cheap whore for everyone to see?'

Her father's friends would see it. His father would see it. The shopkeepers, the neighbours, the boys who already looked at her too long, all would, and they would keep the pictures.

Ishaan trembled.

'It is a respectable magazine.' Her voice came quiet but steady. 'The pictures came out well.'

The rage came swiftly. His palm connected with her cheek before he had registered moving. The crack echoed against the walls. She stumbled backward, caught herself against the table, a thin line of blood appeared at the corner of her mouth.

But that look remained. Not defiance, but something deeper, something he would not tolerate.

The second blow came backhand, catching her across the temple. Her head snapped sideways, hair fanning out. Still, her eyes held his.

The trophy cabinet stood against the far wall, glass-fronted, filled with singing certificates and dance medals. His fingers closed around its frame, muscles straining as he yanked it forward.

Glass shattered. Her mother's scream from the kitchen doorway barely registered. Trophies scattered across the floor tiles, a silver dancing girl, a golden microphone, certificates edged with blue ribbons.

Ishaan's fingers twisted into the neck of her kameez, pulling her close. 'I am going to kill you.'

She threw her head slightly back, turning up her chin.

Memory plays strange games, and he could not figure out whether she did this, or whether his brain filled in the detail later.

The corner of her lip, already darkening to purple, curved upward. She was smiling back at him.

'There was an...incident,' Ishaan said carefully to Ria, his voice level. His hand rose unconsciously to demonstrate the slap, stopping halfway before dropping it to his lap. 'I was upset about something she had done without telling me. The pictures were not decent. We had words. Things got heated.'

'Her father hit her later too, you know.' His fingers rubbed against each other, the sensation of impact still in them. 'When he found out about the photoshoot. Happens in good families, fathers disciplining their daughters. It wasn't just me who thought she had crossed a line.'

'Did her family file a police report?'

'Of course not.' Ishaan's laugh came sharp, dismissive. 'Why would they? Did I not tell you they were upset too?'

What he didn't say was the next memory. Pramila's father standing in their doorway the next morning, voice quivering yet clear. 'Don't come to our house again. Ever. Whatever she did, and I accept she should not have done what she did, you too had no right. No right to hit her, no right to throw down her stuff.'

The man's eyes had darted past Ishaan's shoulder, scanning for signs of his father. That unmistakable fear, the same he had witnessed on shopkeepers as his father had entered their stores, on boys who had lingered too long watching his mother walk past.

Later that night, Ishaan found his father in the living room. He sat in a spotless white kurta and pyjama, a golden chain resting on his broad chest, hair smelling of freshly applied dye. A crystal tumbler rested between his fingers, amber liquid catching the lamplight. The familiar cologne mixed with whisky, that signature combination defining countless childhood evenings. Their pet Alsatian, Boscoe, lay at his father's feet, tongue hanging out.

The magazine lay open on the table. His father looked up, eyes blood-red, swimming in the fever of drunken anger, a look that once meant a beating with his belt was imminent.

But tonight, Ishaan knew the rage wasn't directed at him.

'She posed for that without telling me,' Ishaan said, leaning against the doorframe.

'I know. I heard you went to their house.'

His father swirled his drink, ice clinking against glass. 'Well, I hope she learned her lesson.'

'Her father came by. He was upset about what I did.'

His father shook his head, disappointment evident in the slow, deliberate movement.

'Bakul should have thanked you.' His laugh cut through the room, harsh and certain. 'Bakul and his wife, they are the newfangled types. Happens when the wife goes to work; the husband becomes a pussy himself. If they had done their parenting properly, neighbours wouldn't need to take matters into their own hands.'

He took another sip, eyes narrowing. 'This is a community of decent folk with middle-class values. Not a place for girls who pose like they are a heroine in Mumbai. But yes, mistakes happen. I don't really blame Pramila. She's a kid, a nice kid. It's Bakul's wife who is responsible for her behaviour.'

His father leaned forward, lowering his voice as if sharing secrets. 'Neighbours say she shouts at Bakul, returns late from work, sleeveless blouse, chiffon sari, local Sridevi. Her office is in Park Street, those white buildings where women are hired to show their armpits and flutter their eyelids.' He barked a laugh. 'Her boss drops her home, the paan-wala outside their house says, that too in a Contessa. They sit outside in the car, in the shadows, discussing office work, which for some reason, she and her boss cannot take five steps and do inside her home.'

The sarcasm dripped from each word.

'I am sure he drops all his employees home and spends quality time with them in the dark.'

He shook his head in disapproval. 'Children learn from what they see from their parents, not what you tell them.'

He looked up at Ishaan, satisfaction settling across his face. 'Girls should stay girls. And boys will be boys. And when the lady wears the pants, the men end up in saris. Men were meant to control their women, and those who don't aren't men at all.'

'Your father's name appears a lot in these old news clippings,' Ria said, looking at him intently.

For a second, Ishaan wondered at the coincidence, how she had mentioned his father precisely when memories of him had surfaced.

'Rumours. Innuendo. Slander.'

Anand entered with a tray of food, setting down stainless steel bowls on the glass coffee table. Steam rose from the paneer tikka masala, the scent of cardamom and coriander filling the air. He arranged the naan in a basket, placed raita in a small copper bowl.

'Vegetarian, as requested,' Anand said quietly, backing away.

Ishaan waved his hand dismissively without looking at him. 'My father was a businessman. Had interests in movies, and in real estate. He made money, a lot of it. In those days, when everyone struggled, that made people envious. They could not understand, working 9 to 5 as clerks, how a man like my father got so much. Big house, successful business, respect, cars, and yes, a pretty wife. Since they did not figure it out, they all decided he was a criminal. Let them sleep better. Explain away their inadequacies. And yes, he knew people in the ruling party.' He tore a piece of naan, dipped it in the raita. 'Any successful businessman needs those connections.'

'These connections will come up in the documentary,' Ria said, not touching the food.

'Let them.' Ishaan shrugged, chewing. 'My father is still alive. Lives in my house in Dubai with my mother. He would be more than happy to deal with the documentary people should they try to finger him.'

In his mind, he saw his father as he once was, walking out of his room, muscles straining against his shirt, the buttons undone, white undershirt riding over his belt, Charminar cigarette dangling from his lips, filling rooms with the threat of his presence. Depending on who had challenged him, there would be his bare hands, or he would whip out the heavy leather belt from the trousers. Or he would go to the backroom and bring out his hockey stick, the one with dried blood on the heel, and when things were bad, he would take the big green key and open the iron cabinet by the side of his bed and bring out his beloved 9mm semi-automatic Walther P5.

He was fourteen when he failed arithmetic. His father caught the forged report card, studied it with eyes that narrowed to pinpoints, then slapped him with an almost-indulgent half-smile. But then Ishaan made a fatal mistake, tears streaming down his face: 'Baba, Prasanto-uncle forges signatures on cheques for you. I have seen you take them from him. If that is right, why am I wrong?'

The blows came without warning, hands first, then the belt, whistling through the air before it landed. Ishaan curled into a ball at his father's feet.

Two images burned into his memory: his mother at the top of the stairs, dressed for an outing, watching with practised indifference, waiting for the drama to end so she could leave with his father. And through it all, his father's face, warped by rage, spittle flying as he screamed, 'You dare talk back to me? To me, your father?'

Later that night, his father applied ointment to the welts with surprisingly gentle hands. He sat beside Ishaan's bed as the boy struggled to sleep, every small movement sending fresh waves of pain through his body.

'The beauty of pain,' his father whispered in the darkness, 'is that memory makes it immortal.'

Reality intruded. Ishaan remembered his father now, withered in a wheelchair, one side of his face frozen, mouth working silently, trying to form words that never came.

If they come for me, you show them, Baba.

Ishaan stared at the food growing cold in front of him. They were coming for him now, circling like vultures that had waited three decades for this moment. For the first time, there would be no one to say: 'You go to your room; I will handle this.'

There was only Ishaan, alone with what he had done.

Anand crouched to gather the untouched plates. 'Sir, if I may,' he said, stacking the metal bowls carefully. 'Why do you or Uncle need to talk to this documentary?' His voice remained soft, deferential. 'Better to ignore it.' He kept his eyes on the silverware, years of experience teaching him when to look and when not to. 'People will say whatever they want. All these years later, must we dignify every accusation with a response?'

Ria remained silent, jotting something in her phone, her face impassive.

Ishaan studied Anand's face, searching for hidden meaning. Something cold slithered down his spine. Why was his manager, normally afraid of his temper, offering him advice when he told him twice not to?

'What do you know about how social media works?' The copper bowl of raita still sat untouched, a thin skin forming on its surface.

Anand bowed slightly. 'Nothing, sir. I was just thinking...'

'Next time I will make you wear a T-shirt that says "I am not paid to think",' Ishaan snapped. 'Anand-bhai, I am not sitting quietly while they drag my name through mud. The moment I stay silent, those rival fan clubs will hashtag "coward" and "killer" across every platform. Hell, I am sure Armaan Khan will personally plant that idea through his proxies. The fucker pretends to be my friend and is as unconvincing in real life as in his films.' He shifted his weight, the leather creaking beneath him. 'I have never run away from anything in my life.'

Anand gathered the last of the dishes. 'Of course not, sir.'

Or from anyone, a voice whispered in his mind.

'Will there be anything else, sir?' Anand asked, backing toward the door with the tray.

'No.' Ishaan watched him leave, his mind racing.

'So, Ms Ria, what do you think? Should I talk to them, or just give them the run-around with vague dates?'

Ria set her phone down, eyes steady, professional.

'I agree with Anand. You shouldn't do it.'

Ishaan blinked, caught off guard. He had expected her to side with him. Isn't that what consultants did? Tell you what you want to hear? Sell strategies that padded their invoices?

'Normally,' she said, 'I would advise taking something like this head-on: control the narrative, provide interviews, with lawyers present, an iron fist in a velvet glove. Threaten litigation for anything that's hearsay but otherwise cooperate.'

She leaned forward, voice low. 'But that only works if the celebrity is believable.'

The room went quiet. Anand lingered by the door, as if afraid to breathe too loud.

'I have been testing you this entire conversation. And you failed.'

Ishaan's jaw tightened. 'What did you say?'

'In front of cameras, with a hostile interviewer, you are most likely to break down or worse, go postal.' She nodded toward the untouched food. 'Look at you now, barely holding it together in a quiet room with softball questions. Now imagine multiple cameras, and you obsessing over your angles and how you are coming across, and they will probe, bring out some surprises, and I am really scared of what you will do then.'

Anand stared at the floor.

'You are defensive.' Ria continued. 'Everything is someone else's fault. Every time your father's name comes up, your fists clench like someone is about to draw blood. And when we talk about Pramila, your eyes dart to the side, where I know no one is standing.'

'Tell her she's wrong, Anand,' Ishaan snapped.

Anand's silence said everything.

'Your team walks on eggshells around you,' Ria said. 'Your PR firm has a crisis manager dedicated just to you. Your sexism and misogyny are so ingrained that an interview with curveballs would be an indictment, not a defence. And worst of all, even after I asked for full honesty, even after you verified my bona fides, you have consistently lied about Pramila, about her memories and about your father. Don't lie again that you have not lied. It's your call what to do next, but no, an interview will not go well for you.'

'You have been testing me?' Ishaan's voice dropped to a dangerous whisper.

'It's my job to assess risk. And you, Mr Chatterjee, are your own greatest liability.'

From the corner, Anand's gaze finally lifted to meet Ishaan's, not with fear but with the weary confirmation of a man who had spent years managing outbursts, making excuses, cleaning up messes, and finally relieved that someone had had the courage to tell his boss the truth.

'You are an actor,' Ria said, her eyes meeting Ishaan's. 'And you know how important workshops and rehearsals are. This was one, and it didn't go well.'

Ria rose, gathering her purse and phone with practised efficiency. Through the floor-to-ceiling windows, Mumbai's nightscape sprawled like a galaxy, countless lights shimmering against the darkness.

'I understand.' Ishaan nodded, his shoulders sagging, just a fraction. 'And I thank you for your candour. I am difficult…sometimes…maybe all the time.'

Something in his voice made her pause, a note of genuine sadness beneath the actor's polish.

'Can I ask you a question, Ms Ria? A personal question?'

'Sure.'

'I know you do not watch my films; I know you hated me the moment you walked in,' he said, not looking up. 'But, after talking to me, how much more do you hate me now?'

Ria hesitated, her bag half-closed. 'Why do you think I don't watch your movies? I have seen all your work. Many films more than once. I am your fan, maybe a superfan. *Whenever I am lost in the dark, my hero comes to me.*' She quoted softly, the lines of one of his hit songs.

'You should never meet your idols then.' Ishaan shrugged.

'Yes, I know that saying.' She clasped her bag closed. 'But that's for people who don't want to find that their gods have feet of clay. I always knew who you were. It comes out everywhere, in your interviews, in how your co-stars talk about you when they think cameras are off, in the way you accept awards. Maybe the fact that you are honestly terrible and terribly honest is why I am a fan. Perhaps I love your acting. Perhaps I love the man inside. I do not ask, for I will never know.'

The city lights caught in his eyes as he turned toward the windows, reflecting like distant stars.

'I still had to come,' she continued. 'When Black Envelope discussed the documentary and everything, I felt I had to come. To do what little I can. I know it's not much, but all I have to offer is advice. I know you didn't like it, but it came from the best place I have.'

'I know,' Ishaan nodded.

She looked out of the window and then back at him.

'But I know you won't take my advice.'

'I will,' he said, looking up with an unexpected flicker of vulnerability.

She shook her head. 'No, you won't. You are too used to being who you are. I know that, and I am not using reverse psychology. You are too used to fighting, and when you are fighting, that is when you are you.'

'And what if I am tired of fighting?' His voice cracked slightly. 'What then?'

'I should go,' Ria said.

'Everyone does, eventually.'

Ishaan nodded, suddenly looking all his years and more.

The elevator chimed as Anand summoned it.

'Oh, Ms Ria, you asked for water but never drank it,' he said, pointing to the marble coffee table, and he immediately wondered why he even mentioned it.

'Water waits,' she said softly.

Ishaan felt a chill at her words. 'What do you mean?'

She did not reply, just smiled sadly as she stepped into the elevator.

As the doors began to close, she turned away, presenting only her profile and then just her hair, black and flowing like water in the night.

The elevator descended, leaving Ishaan alone with the untouched glass. Water condensing on its rim, dripping down the side in long lines of tears.

6

A Call and a Search

Rain pattered against the wide windows of Ranadeep's office, blurring the view of Lutyens' Delhi into smudges of green and grey. The monsoon had arrived two weeks early this year, washing away the summer dust and bringing with it the familiar petrichor that reminded him of childhood afternoons in Calcutta.

Ranadeep adjusted his cufflinks, mother-of-pearl set in gold, a gift from Monobina on their fifteenth anniversary, and returned to the papers before him. The latest tranche of Rajya Sabha appointment documents required his signature in three places. They had told him these were the last, but he was sure they were not; each process triggered another, like a Russian doll concealing yet another layer of paperwork within.

Of course, he need not do any of it. The privilege of being a politician in India was that process was for other people. But his orderly civil servant mind compelled him to follow the rules. There was comfort in compliance, a word that Monobina teased him for loving too much.

'Compliance? Compliant to what?' He could hear her voice in his head. 'You do realize you are being compliant to some nameless civil servant, probably dead by now? Even if you could bring him back from the dead, he would not be able to tell you why he wrote this policy, because he too was being compliant.'

She was right, of course. But that was precisely the point. Rules transcended the individuals who made them and also common sense. They were a shared agreement, however arbitrary, that kept the wheels of society turning. His father, a West Bengal Civil Service cadre bureaucrat who spent most of his life at Writers' Building, the seat of Calcutta's administrative power, had taught him this as a boy: break one rule, and then why not break the others? Start pulling at a loose thread, and eventually, the entire fabric unravels.

He could hear Monobina's voice again, 'I get that rules are rules, but can't a woman expect her husband to be a bit of a rebel?'

She had said this last year when their driver fell ill and they had gone to see a concert. He had parked the car almost a mile from the venue and made her walk in her heels rather than leave it in the no-parking zone, where a flash of his government ID would have settled the matter. That's how things worked in Delhi, but not how Ranadeep worked.

It wasn't blind obedience that drove him, but the understanding that civilization itself was just a delicate web of mutual agreements. The moment everyone decided to ignore these invisible boundaries, chaos followed. He had seen it firsthand during riots, during floods, during political upheavals, how quickly order dissolved when the tacit agreement to follow rules collapsed.

So, he signed where indicated, dated where required, and initialled where requested, his signature joining thousands of others in the vast paper machinery of state. A link in a chain stretching back to Independence and beyond.

The greatest comfort in his life was precisely that. Its structure. He woke up at 5 a.m. every day, exactly the time he would wake up as a teenager, and did his morning yoga, Pranayama and a full circuit of asanas that exercised different muscle groups. In school, he would sit to study after that, tackling subjects that needed memorization: Sanskrit, geography and history. Now, with no more tests to prepare for, he used that time for a run, then returned to check his personal emails.

Even though as a top bureaucrat he had an army of staff, he fixed breakfast himself, for Monobina, and when Shayan was home, for him too. He arrived at work by 8.30 a.m., not coincidentally the same time his school had begun. Never late for meetings, never unprepared, he took lunch precisely at 12.15 p.m., exactly when tiffin had been at school. Unless a crisis emerged at work, which happened more often than he liked, he left at 5 p.m., ninety minutes later than school had let out.

From 4 to 6 p.m. in his youth, he had played cricket, football, carrom or attended music practice. Now this time belonged to family and friends, stretching to 7 or 8 p.m. When Shayan was younger, this was when he would sit down with him for studies, but it had been years since he had asked for his help. Then, latest by 8.15 p.m., he retired to study, as in school, reading files, drafting reports, making calls. On rare days without urgent matters, he read books or, if no one was within earshot, attempted to sing again, the Rabindra Sangeet from his childhood, though his off-key notes would make him stop. From 10 to 10.30 p.m., he made it a point to ask Monobina about her day and discuss his own, and unless the prime minister or the home minister had called a late-night meeting, he turned in for the night.

'I think the only time you would ever break the rules would be to protect your routine,' Shayan had once told him, to which Ranadeep had replied, 'I follow the rules precisely because they maintain my routine.'

It was not exactly true; this professed consistent compliance to rules. Rules could be broken, but only if needed to maintain order. As a bureaucrat, he had honed that craft of orderliness, and it would serve him well as a politician. He had learned long ago that sometimes maintaining order required looking away at precisely the right moment. That sometimes the careful architecture of a life depended on which doors you chose never to open again.

His office reflected this precision of mind. Handcrafted teak shelves lined one wall, filled with leather-bound legal volumes and policy manuals, each categorized by subject and relevance. Awards and certificates hung in neat rows behind his desk, their frames perfectly aligned, pictures of him with multiple prime ministers and three US presidents. His most prized possessions, though, lay in a glass case: two signed cricket bats, one by all members of the 2011 World Cup winning team, another by the 1983 champions, a rare privilege to have both.

Ranadeep reached for a tissue to wipe a small ink stain from his pale blue cotton shirt. Monobina had selected it that morning, insisting it complemented the charcoal Nehru jacket better than the white one he had initially chosen. 'Ministers must look distinguished, not like bureaucrats,' she had said, straightening his collar before he left for work.

As his silver-framed glasses slid slightly down his nose, his secretary placed a folder on his desk. The interview for *The Hindu*, a human interest, softball one, or at least that is what they had told him. The answers had been prepared by his press attaché, generic and anodyne, as per policy. Ranadeep scanned them while contemplating what his real answers would be.

Why do you want to get into politics?

His eyes glazed over the answer on the piece of paper. The real reason was that he had realized, years before, that in this country, bureaucrats, even the ones at the very top, had little power in front of a politician, even a mid-level one. He had understood that in his first ever posting, where he was made to personally escort the daughter of a state minister to her MA examinations, waiting, in the car, for her to finish writing them, and dropping her home again. He knew what would happen if he refused: he would be transferred to some district with a Naxal militia problem, where he would die from a landmine, malaria or dysentery.

It had worked out for him well though, for that daughter was Monobina. She had invited him in for tea after the last examination. Then, while stirring his cup of tea, she had looked into his eyes and said, 'I am sorry my father made you do this. He didn't need to. He just does this to show new officials in his district their place.' It was not what he was expecting to hear. It was not also what she was expecting to hear when, on the day he was being transferred out to his next posting, almost a year later, a year he had spent playing badminton with her in the afternoons and discussing dead British poets as the sun set, he had asked her if she wanted to leave with him. She had said, 'I thought you would never ask.'

But the powerlessness of the bureaucrat in front of the politician wasn't a lesson he had learned after joining the Indian Administrative Service. He was fourteen when his father came home, a nervous wreck. As a member of the West Bengal Civil Service, his father oversaw infrastructure projects. There was a bridge tender that had come to his desk, one that his supervisor had said needed to be approved. The contractor was a friend to the ruling party, and two ministers had been ringing about the project non-stop. But the engineers had advised against it. The bridge would collapse given the materials and specifications the bidder proposed.

Ranadeep had stood in the doorway, eavesdropping. His father's hands trembled as he weighed impossible choices: sign off on the doomed project and face criminal liability when the bridge collapsed or resign and not only lose his job but also earn the lasting vengeance of the ruling party.

It had been raining that day, and Ranadeep had slipped out without the umbrella, running to Ishaan's house. Rain pelted his skin, soaking through his clothes by the time he knocked at 9.30 p.m., far later than appropriate for visiting a friend. Ishaan opened the door, surprise crossing his face. Ranadeep asked if his father was in, and that is when Siddhartha Chatterjee emerged from the shadows of the hallway.

He was scared of Ishaan's father, as everyone was, particularly after nine at night, when he was known to be fully drunk. But Ranadeep did not care. He told Ishaan's father everything he had overheard: the bridge, the politician, the names, and the dire situation his father was in. Could he help, Ranadeep had asked, knowing that Ishaan's father was someone whose influence ran high up to the highest in the ruling party.

Siddhartha's expression remained unreadable. He first told Ishaan to take Ranadeep inside, have him shower so he would not catch a cold, and then give him some dry clothes to wear. When Ranadeep emerged, Ishaan's father motioned him to the chair directly across from his own.

'Look, son,' he said, leaning forward slightly, 'I don't know what you think I am. I am not some mafia don from those Hindi movies who makes things happen with a phone call. I am just a small-time businessman. Sure, I may strut around a bit, but my influence is local. Shopkeepers, Durga Pujo committees, nothing really important.'

Ranadeep's face fell. Siddhartha Chatterjee stood, placed a hand on his shoulder.

'Go home, take that umbrella. Leave this to grown-ups, hmm?'

Saturday passed in silence. On Monday evening, when his father returned from the office, Ranadeep overheard him telling his mother in hushed tones: 'The strangest thing happened. Those people changed their bid, accepting everything our engineers suggested.' There was something in his voice: surprise mixed with quiet satisfaction.

A week later, they were all playing cricket at Ishaan's place. One-drop-one-hand cricket, with Ishaan's father in his usual position as keeper, seated comfortably in his chair. During a lull in the game, Ranadeep approached him.

'Thank you, Uncle,' he said softly.

Ishaan's father looked up, the corners of his eyes crinkling as he smiled. 'What thank you? Kids don't say thank you to adults...okay?' He scuffed his hair gently, and said, 'Now go and stand at short leg. Krishanu will hit there, any time now...and stay low for the one-hand.'

Yes, that was how powerful politicians were. Even a local goombah like Ishaan's dad had more capital than his father, and in Delhi, things were even worse.

His eyes scanned the next few questions, flipping through the four pages of prepared answers. He hoped there wouldn't be any about the documentary.

There weren't. Not yet.

But there would be.

He signed his name at the bottom, as per procedure. These answers were now officially his.

Well, if *The Hindu* hadn't asked about the documentary yet, it only meant they were waiting. Because the subject of the next season of *Hidden Secrets* wasn't exactly hidden anymore.

Last Friday, Ranadeep had attended a media event at India International Centre, where some aging journalist with deep ties to Delhi's ruling elite was releasing his autobiography.

Ranadeep hated these events. The pretentious conversations, the fake bonhomie. He would rather be home, reading, talking to Monobina or Shayan, or calling his parents in Calcutta. But now that he was on track to become a minister, he had to network, be seen and appear suitably vacuous. As Monobina said, that was the only way to fit into the Lutyens' crowd.

He stood with a polite smile, pretending to listen as two Delhi socialites discussed carbon credits, both equally wrong in their understanding.

'Why don't you correct people when they talk bullshit?' Monobina had once asked.

'When people are half-wrong, it makes sense to,' he had replied. 'When they are fully wrong, it is not worth my time.'

Suddenly, he felt a tug at his elbow.

He turned to find Amritlal Patel, party president of the ruling Indian People's Front and reportedly the third most powerful man in the country after the prime minister and the home minister.

A joke went around that the reason Amritlal knew all of Delhi's secrets was because he was so short, he could stand beside you without your noticing.

His white kurta-pyjama remained crisp despite the sticky evening, and his bald head gleamed under the overhead lights.

'What is this, Bangali-babu?' Amritlal asked, his voice pitched just loud enough to turn nearby heads. 'We are making you a minister, and you never told me you are Ishaan Chatterjee's childhood friend. My wife is his biggest fan, would definitely leave me for him. So can you please introduce her to Ishaan, and do me a favour?'

He laughed, a booming sound that demanded others join in.

Ranadeep shook his head and laughed along. Not just because this man would soon be his boss, but because, surprisingly, the joke showed more wit than he would usually credit Amritlal Patel with.

Buying rival MPs? Yes.

Blackmailing them? Definitely.

Clever turn of phrase? Not really.

'So, you heard about the documentary?' Ranadeep asked, suddenly alert.

Ranadeep wondered. Why had Amritlal come over to speak to *him*, when far more important people were mingling across the lawns of India International Centre, drinks and vegetable kebabs in hand?

'It is my job, alas, to hear everything,' Amritlal said with a mock-sorrowful shrug, eyes gleaming.

He placed a firm hand on Ranadeep's arm and led him aside. Lowering his voice, he asked, 'So, tell me, I won't tell anyone. Did the superstar kill the girl?'

Ranadeep's expression stayed neutral.

He had learned long ago that showing emotion during uncomfortable conversations only gave the other person leverage.

'Of course not,' he said, steady. 'They found the killer. It was in all the papers back then.'

'Ah yes, the old lunatic who hanged himself.' Amritlal gave Ranadeep a mild nudge. 'Very convenient. We know how that works, right? The files that burn in the accidental fire, the criminal who tries to run while being transported between jails and gets shot in the back, the crusading journalist who gets run over by a drunk truck driver.'

'Nothing like that. The man was a strange sort; there were witnesses, and there was evidence.'

'Yes, yes,' Amritlal said, 'I have seen the files. Only one witness. A friend of yours.'

Ranadeep's shoulders tensed slightly. 'Basab, yes. An IIT topper, MIT PhD, absolute genius. Plus, there was evidence.'

'Ah, yes. Evidence,' Amritlal said, with a twinkle in his eye. 'Not that our police would ever plant or tamper with it. God forbid!'

Ranadeep knew where this was going, but he was going to let Amritlal come to it, in his own way. He took a sip from his glass, using the moment to scan the crowd. Several journalists were watching their conversation from a distance.

'Your friend's career is not going well. You know that, right?'

'I really have not been in touch with him for thirty years.'

A waiter passed with a plate of vegetable kebabs. Ranadeep took one, grateful for the momentary distraction.

'The way I look at it, they are going to pin this on him, this documentary. Otherwise, why would anyone care to watch it?'

'That would be unfair if they did. He did not do it.'

'Honestly, between us, I hope he did. That would get my wife to stop crushing over him. But the person I am concerned about is you. Is there anything you need to tell me?'

Ranadeep nodded. 'I am guessing you read my testimony.'

'Oh yes, Pramila Chatterjee's best friend. Her Rabindra Sangeet partner.'

The way he said '*best friend*', Ranadeep understood the innuendo.

'I wouldn't say best friend. We did not grow up in such times. I knew her, yes, we practised singing together, went to some competitions, but that was it.'

'But I am a man from the times of *Maine Pyar Kiya*. Remember that line? A boy and a girl can never be friends. But don't worry, Bangali-babu, I am not suggesting any impropriety. And the only reason for that is you had Ishaan Chatterjee at the other end. No disrespect, you are a good-looking man, but I doubt even you could hold a candle to Bollywood's Titan in his youth.'

Ranadeep stood silent, with a measured smile. Maybe he should have stayed home and played badminton with Monobina.

'Look, the party stands behind you. But just stay on top of this; these things sometimes acquire legs of their own. I am not saying you guys saved your friend, Ishaan Chatterjee, from the noose, and even if you did, good for you, so many great movies he has given us. But you know these documentaries; they go digging, they pay people money, ask leading questions, and you know our opposition right, muckraking anti-nationals. They have their pet media plants; what I am telling you, you know...all I am saying is whether you talk to the documentary or not, it is your call, but just know I am always a phone call away, you need any help, ting-a-ling, you call me...'

Of course, Ranadeep knew what Amritlal Patel was really saying. He was being made a minister, not because he was a leader of the masses who brought in votes. If he were, he wouldn't have needed the Rajya Sabha route. He would have contested elections for the Lok Sabha. The ruling party was having a problem with the foreign media, endless negative articles in the *New York Times*, *Washington Post* and the *Economist*. Amritlal Patel had concluded they needed a friendly face in the government, someone with a clipped English accent who would be acceptable abroad: moderate, personable, erudite, and most importantly, without scandal.

This documentary threatened to derail that last part.

Another file waited on his desk, part of the transfer process to his successor. He would soon resign from his position to begin his career as a politician. They had compiled a list of projects requiring his insights, his institutional memory made portable for the next occupant.

These were important; he needed them done today, yet his focus kept drifting like a boat slipping its mooring.

The past. It never released its grip. Its fingers reaching across decades to tug at his carefully constructed present. The Musketeers. Thirty years since he had severed those bonds, and yet they grew back, like weeds, more powerful. Krishanu, Ishaan and Basab had coloured the best parts of his youth, and yet now he wished he had never known them at all.

Without them, he wouldn't be facing this documentary, wouldn't be forced to translate the half-formed memories of 1994 into words that could be scrutinized, analysed, judged.

Memories that he had run from, and yet strangely, sought out, during moments of thought, how nice things had once been, knowing fully well they had not.

He thought of what Monobina had said a few months ago.

'I know why he wants to be a minister, the real reason, not the one he tells everyone.'

She had said it one weekend at the Delhi Gymkhana, just days after the Indian People's Front had sounded him out. Ranadeep was collecting his breath after a bruising badminton doubles match, methodically wiping sweat from his forearms.

They had been playing against another couple, a surgeon who owned a specialty hospital and his wife, Monobina's partner in their NGO.

'This will be interesting,' the surgeon said, slapping Ranadeep hard on the back, that chummy, overfamiliar touch he despised and yet the loud, old man, did not seem to catch on.

Before he could recover, Monobina announced, 'You guys may know this, or not, but his childhood friend, best friend, is Ishaan Chatterjee.'

'What?' The surgeon squealed so loudly that a waiter nearly spilled drinks off his tray. Several patrons turned to stare.

'THE Ishaan Chatterjee?'

'The same,' Monobina said. 'I think he has always wanted to one-up him. Now, he finally will, as a minister.'

Ranadeep loved Monobina. But sometimes, though he would never say it aloud, she could be a jerk. Almost like Ishaan. There was no need to bring up his friendship with Ishaan; this trying to live off a celebrity's reflected glory was something he despised. He knew she was teasing him, trying to get under his skin. Their teams had been on opposite sides, and hers had just lost badly, but this was a cheap shot.

He smiled, unbothered on the surface, popping a chicken sausage into his mouth as the conversation shifted to Ishaan: his career, his various rumoured girlfriends, his volatile image and his misogyny.

But Monobina had struck a nerve.

Ishaan had carved himself into Ranadeep during those formative years. Not just him, Krishanu with his eager smiles and nervous laughter, Basab with his brilliant mind hidden behind thick glasses; they had all orbited Ishaan like planets around a sun. Each absorbed his light differently; each reflected it back in their own way.

Ranadeep had always thought himself different. Not socially awkward like Basab. Not approval-starved like Krishanu. But still caught in Ishaan's gravity. Still measuring the arc of his life against that reference point.

That was the thing about the Musketeers. They hadn't been just friends; they had been architects of each other. He had made other connections before and since, but none that rewired his circuitry so completely. Even thirty years distant, with oceans and careers between them, they remained bound by invisible threads. Ranadeep could feel them pulling whenever he achieved something significant – a promotion, an award, his son's admission to Harvey Mudd – as if some part of him still needed to run back to Ramkrishna Park, where he knew the rest were waiting, to prove himself worthy of that circle, to go, to use Monobina's words, one-up not just Ishaan, but all of them.

He wondered.

Did Basab flee to MIT to outshine Ishaan's spotlight?

Did Krishanu stay behind and give up?

And was this ministerial position Ranadeep's final move in a chess game only he was still playing?

Now the thing he had been avoiding, pushing off, ever since he heard of the documentary. He had to get back in touch with them: Basab, Ishaan and Krishanu. He had to ensure their stories aligned, that they wouldn't contradict each other through faulty memory or careless phrasing. There was a third thing he feared, of course, deliberate betrayal, and that too would have to be taken care of.

Krishanu. He knew where he stayed. At the same place he had always been.

The letters had started coming about five years after Ranadeep joined the civil service. Handwritten on cheap, ruled paper, the kind sold at small stationery shops outside schools. They arrived at his office, never his home. Krishanu did not know his personal address. Each envelope bore the familiar slanted script, the 'R' in Ranadeep always a bit too large, as if announcing itself, and ended with 'Forever yours, Master of None'.

'My dear Jack of All Trades,' they would begin, followed by elaborate enquiries about his health, his parents, his career. Krishanu would recount mundane details of his life in Calcutta, the changing neighbourhood, the new flyover being built, before eventually circling to the true purpose buried in the final paragraphs.

'Things have been difficult lately...the bank job doesn't pay what it used to...Mother's medical bills...'

Ranadeep never replied. He told himself it was cleaner this way. A response would imply a desire to keep the connection, would suggest a willingness to be drawn back into Krishanu's orbit.

He had made discreet enquiries. Krishanu was a gambler, an inveterate one, seen frequently at Calcutta's racecourses and fired from a bank for having stolen from the till. They could not prove it, and so he was simply let go with no charges and, most likely, the money.

The last letter came sixteen years ago. The final line visible through the thin envelope caught his eye: 'Knock Knock...'

Inside, Krishanu's handwriting appeared more jagged, less careful. 'I have no idea if these mails even reach you. Perhaps they vanish into some bureaucratic void, or perhaps you receive them and choose silence as your answer. Either way, this will be my last imposition on your time.'

He didn't know if Krishanu had written after that. He never received any more letters. And he was thankful for that.

Now the documentary was forcing his hand. He would have to reach out first, and he knew that somehow, somewhere, this time he would have to pay him. In one form or the other. For the silence.

Then, there was Ishaan. One of the advantages of being a high-ranking bureaucrat in Delhi was that obtaining phone numbers from government documents and filings required merely a quiet word to the right person.

The number he had might not reach Ishaan directly, celebrity buffers were thicker than bureaucratic ones, but a message left with some gatekeeper would suffice.

Ishaan would call back. He was certain of it.

After all, he had the most to lose from a lack of coordination in their stories.

Which brought him to Basab. He had pulled Basab's surrendered passport from Ministry of External Affairs records, a file stamped with the finality of relinquished citizenship. The address listed was the old one from Calcutta, decades out of date. A dead end.

That meant there was only one route open to him.

Good old Google.

Basab's Caltech webpage came up immediately. The familiar face in the faculty photo, older, lined, but with the same outsized glasses, appeared beside his credentials. Ranadeep began to note down the contact information when his eyes caught the black banner across the top of the page.

'In Memoriam: Professor Basab Banerjee (1976–2024)'

His finger froze above the trackpad. A static buzz filled his ears as he clicked the link, watching the page load with excruciating slowness.

The official obituary was brief, clinical:

'The California Institute of Technology mourns the loss of Dr Basab Banerjee, Professor of Theoretical Physics and recipient of National Medal of Science, who passed away at his home on 17 May 2024. Dr Banerjee's groundbreaking work on quantum field theory transformed our understanding of subatomic particles. Students wishing to send condolences may contact the Department of Physics. Information regarding Dr Banerjee's courses may be found on the updated department schedule.'

No mention of how he died. Nothing of the man beyond his academic achievements. Just institutional acknowledgement of a vacancy that needed filling.

Ranadeep leaned back in his chair, the leather creaking beneath him. Genius was gone.

He had imagined this reunion differently, awkward initial conversation giving way to cautious reconnection. Perhaps even a chance to untangle the knots that had bound them together all these years. Instead, there was this, a sterile obituary on an internet page.

What struck him wasn't just the fact of Basab's death, but its timing. Just as the documentary began production. Just as the past threatened to resurface.

A coincidence, surely. It had to be.

He closed his eyes, and for a moment, he saw Basab as he had been at eighteen, hunched over textbooks in the weak light of the Calcutta power cuts, explaining complex equations with simple analogies. He remembered the ritual before exams: dozens of students flocking to Basab for last-minute clarity, hanging on his every word as he unpacked the most difficult concepts with effortless precision.

And then there was Krishanu, who would wait until everyone had left before approaching Ranadeep with his notebook full of hastily scribbled notes.

'Explain it to me again, *yaar*,' he would say, scratching his head. 'Basab is way too super high funda for me.'

Ranadeep would break it down further, translating Basab's genius into something more digestible. Krishanu had a theory about this: 'You digest Basab's funda like a cow digests cud,' he would say with that lopsided grin, 'and I can only digest pre-digested food.'

It had become their private joke, a recognition of the chain that linked them, Basab to Ranadeep to Krishanu.

Ranadeep took off his glasses and kept them on the table, letting the tears come at the corner of his eyes.

Grief has a way of surprising you, especially when you have spent half your life pretending the person didn't exist.

Basab had saved him. He could never say how. And now, never would.

The grief seemed to evaporate now, like camphor. Two names left on his list now, not three. The documentary team would have known about Basab's death. They might even have interviewed him before he died.

He had to know more.

As he searched, he found Basab's professor review page. Years of reviews, hundreds of them. Ranadeep scrolled through each category: the five-stars, the three-stars, and definitely, the one-stars. The word 'genius' appeared repeatedly, the glowing reviews praising him for explaining the most difficult concepts with effortless clarity: 'teaches physics like your mother reading a bedtime story before tucking you into bed'. He could almost hear Krishanu's voice: 'For clarity, remember these are by the standards of Caltech students, not human beings.'

The complaints, fewer but more vivid, criticized his uncompromising grading. One review called him 'as merciful as a Nazi camp commander'. Another mentioned his 'Indian accent', which some ex-student likened to 'hearing Apu from *The Simpsons* explain quantum physics'.

Yes, this was all Basab, unchanged across decades and continents. Demanding excellence without apology. Unconcerned with being liked.

Ranadeep found himself nodding, almost smiling as the tears still flowed, reading through each assessment of his old friend, until the reviews ended and he pressed the back button to return to the Google results.

He scrolled down, without thinking, till his eyes alighted on a link on Reddit:

r/Caltech: Professor Banerjee found dead, what happened?

Ranadeep's hand trembled slightly as he clicked it.

The discussion thread loaded, a cascade of anonymous speculation, but the ones that leaped out at him were:

PhysicsUndergrad22: *Anyone hear what happened to Professor Banerjee? Campus is buzzing with rumours.*

QuantumGrrl: *My sister's dating someone on the Pasadena police force. Says it was disturbing, not just a regular drowning. Something about his face.*

CalBruin4: *He was just served divorce papers. I went to his office and the envelope was lying on his table.*

WaveFunctionCollapse: *I had a meeting scheduled with him yesterday that he cancelled. His email said: 'A documentary crew is coming to interview me; I better get dolled up for the camera.' That was the last anyone heard from him.*

Ranadeep closed the browser and collected his thoughts. Of course, he was not stupid enough to believe anonymous commentators on a Reddit board; this was Gen Z's WhatsApp, but there was no way for the Caltech community to know about the documentary crew unless Basab had told them.

Which meant 'WaveFunctionCollapse' was correct.

Which meant he died on the day he gave his interview.

Wait, what does that even mean? They are two random facts, no correlation.

He had never considered himself a superstitious man, if you discount small things like taking his yellow pencil box to all his major examinations, or first doing *pranaam* to his mother and then his father, and never saying 'I am leaving,' instead saying 'I am arriving,' because that is what his grandmother had told him was the right thing to say. And even these were not superstitions, he told himself, but the comfort provided by familiarity, his desire for order. He never seriously believed in spurious, irrational cause-and-effect.

But when he had heard about *Hidden Secrets* doing their next season on Pramila Chatterjee, he could not help but think, why? Why, of all the 'solved' cases in the world, had they decided to pick this? Well, there was possibly a reason for that: the involvement of a Bollywood superhero. But why now, why thirty years later, why did this have to happen at a time when each of them needed it the least: Basab during his divorce, himself on the verge of becoming minister, and Ishaan when his movies were flopping one after another?

Of the three fates, Basab's divorce, presuming CalBruin4's Reddit comment was true, struck him as the most unthinkable. The most honourable man he had ever known, the one whose moral compass had never wavered, the most docile human he had known – what could Basab have possibly done to fracture a marriage? To use one of Shayan's phrases, that would not have been on anyone's bingo card. The thought unsettled him more than he cared to admit. And then this death – what was that word they had used on the message board, 'disturbing', not a 'regular drowning'.

No, this did not add up.

He remembered the day he had first met Pramila. He had just turned twelve, and his stammering had grown worse. His doctor had suggested enrolling him in a singing class. 'The boy's voice is sweet,' he had said. 'Learning to sing might help unlock paths in his brain that would make the words flow when they get stuck on his tongue.'

He did not want to go. Rabindra Sangeet was for girls. But there he was at Saraswati Academy, his head bowed, his mother's fingers clasped firmly around his wrist as she pushed his reluctant self into the classroom.

'I don't want to go, Ma. Everyone here is a girl.'

'You will love it,' she had whispered. 'Your voice is so sweet.'

Yes, that was exactly the problem. He wished it was not.

The class was indeed full of girls his age, some younger and a few older. They sat in neat rows on the floor, voices rising and falling as they went through vocal exercises. There was one boy, who sat hunched in a corner, a stranger whose gaze Ranadeep avoided. No allies here. The teacher was impossibly old and reed-thin, in an ancient shawl, even though it was summer, and he wondered if the shawl fell off, would he see a skeleton and a voice-box within? When he sat down, the teacher looked at Ranadeep with eyes full of disapproval, as if saying silently, 'Yet another reluctant student.'

Then he saw Pramila, as he would find out later, a year younger than him, spine straight, chin lifted, commanding the room without trying. She had not met Ishaan yet. She was just Pramila then, the girl with a voice that was the blessing of the gods. When she sang, the music teacher's eyes closed in appreciation, his withered hands tapping the edge of the ancient harmonium.

During the first week, Ranadeep's voice caught in his throat whenever the teacher called on him. The third time it happened, Pramila shifted closer during break, her small shoulder nearly touching his.

'The trick is to forget everyone's listening,' she whispered. 'Sing to the sparrows outside the window.'

She was always there, never pushy, but again, there, if he ever needed help. While his tongue still tripped over during times of emotion and syllables snagged in his mouth, his singing voice grew clearer. Pramila nodded encouragingly from across the room, and whenever their eyes met, there was always a smile, 'You are doing great.'

With each class, his stammering loosened its grip. And he found out something about himself: he loved to sing.

Years later, standing backstage at the district Rabindra Sangeet competition, Ranadeep's fingers trembled against his starched kurta. Seventeen now, voice deepened, but the old fear of words failing always lurking. Pramila appeared beside him, her competition sari crisp, the smell of her strawberry shampoo.

'I was so lucky that you were there that day,' he said, the words flowing without hesitation.

She studied him with those steady eyes that seemed to hold more years than they should.

'Where others see luck, the sage sees consequence.'

He remembered those words, and now, they finally seemed to make sense.

Ranadeep crossed to the far corner of his office, where a small painting of the Howrah Bridge hung on the wall. Behind it sat a wall safe, a precaution installed when he became home secretary. His fingers worked the combination from muscle memory: 19-94-07. The lock clicked and the door swung open.

From inside, he removed a small leather case. In it, nested in velvet, lay a flip phone, an ancient Nokia model, the kind that predated smartphones. He had not powered it up in years, but had kept it charged at regular intervals, like maintaining an escape route he hoped never to use.

He connected it to a charger beneath his desk. As the phone slowly came to life, its screen casting a pale blue glow, Ranadeep turned to the window. The monsoon rain continued its assault, sheets of water transforming the city beyond recognition. Rivulets traced chaotic patterns down the glass, merging and splitting like timelines of choices made and unmade.

Behind him, the old phone chirped its startup melody. He picked it up, flipped it open, and thought for a second. Once he dialled that number, there was no going back.

He had one favour he would call in. The Brahmastra, as his father would have called it, the mythical one-use weapon of last resort. For ten years, he had preserved this connection, knowing someday he might need it.

That day had arrived.

His fingers found the only number stored in the phone's memory. It would be early morning in the USA, but she would answer; she always did. Their arrangement was clear. No contact unless necessary, and in return, immediate response when needed. Ranadeep would wait here regardless. The monsoon had made the city impassable anyway.

The connection crackled, then rang. Once. Twice. Six times. Then silence.

A minute crawled by, marked only by the rhythmic tapping of rain against glass.

The phone vibrated in his palm, screen illuminating with an incoming call.

He picked it up, and there was silence at the other end. That was the protocol; no words would be exchanged, unless he gave the code sentence.

'Kabira speaking,' Ranadeep said. It had been his own private joke, to use an iconic line from the Hindi movie *Hera Pheri* as the code sentence for the elite private investigator from San Antonio, Texas, who had no idea what it meant.

'You gonna call in your favour, or this a paid gig?' The voice came from the other end, in a soft Southern drawl.

'My favour.'

'Good.' She said, 'It's time we got even.'

'The name is Basab Banerjee. Caltech professor. I want to know how he died, and why he got divorced. I want the police records and divorce records; if there is something written down or stored on a disc about him, I need it. You have got a week.'

'That's tight.'

'I know.'

'Good thing this is your favour. I am booked solid for seven months.'

'How am I going to get the files?'

'A week later, at exactly this time, a link will come to this phone. Click on that link within 3 hours, or the link will expire. The next one will be billable.'

Ranadeep shut the phone and placed it back in the leather case. His movements were mechanical, practised. The leather case went back into the safe, and the combination lock turned, to be opened exactly a week later.

There were a few other things in the safe, objects he kept here at work, things too valuable to risk being at home, important either due to the nature of his work, or due to his nature. Remnants from his past, he did not trust anywhere else.

Among these objects was a magazine, a specific issue, *Woman's World*, Pujo edition, 1994. Between its pages lay a slip of paper, a handwritten poem in black ink, perfect

English cursive flowing across the page. He did not need to read it.

Thirty years had burned every word into his memory.

The leaves creep along the stone,
A blooming rose stands all alone,
In a place that only shadows know,
Down where the ivy grows.

Where a sliver of day scrapes the cold,
And barren branches cling to light,
Withering flowers cry their woes,
Into the chill of the final night.

Where summer decays with a final sigh,
Perishing as its eyes close,
Where fading stars are left to die,
Down where the ivy grows.

Leaves creep along the wall,
Upon it the white moonlight glows,
As shadows twist and bend, they call,
'Who shall pick the crimson rose?'

With prickly thorns as sharp as knives,
And a colour of the deepest red,
Upon weeping petals it thrives,
Born to live among the dead.

An unfinished poem. He often wondered if she ever completed it. Pramila had given him a book to hold during one of their competitions while she went on stage. She wrote poems when the mood struck her, tucking them between pages of books she read. In the book she had handed him had been this poem, and he never got the chance to return it. The book itself was lost, a Bengali anthology, *Greatest Ghost Stories of the Past Century*, with a lurid cover of a skull dripping blood. But he had kept what she had written, preserved it like a pressed flower.

The only thing he had left of his friend.

Pramila Chatterjee.

He walked to the window and stared out at the rain. A movement drew his eyes upward. Water was seeping through the ceiling in the corner of his office, forming a dark stain. As he watched, droplets collected and fell, leaving trails that branched like veins.

Or like hair, spreading outward in the water.

A chill ran through him. He stepped back from the window, eyes fixed on the growing stain above.

For the first time in years, Ranadeep Saha felt afraid.

7

The White Line

The glass elevator of the Bengal Orient, Calcutta's only seven-star hotel, ascended silently, its mirrored walls multiplying Ranadeep Saha infinitely. He examined his reflection, the pressed linen shirt, the blue blazer, the tasteful watch, the carefully maintained salt-and-pepper at his temples. Home secretary to the Government of India, soon-to-be Rajya Sabha member. Not a man to be trifled with.

He had not meant to dress so formally; he had not intended to wear his power like armour. Yet here he was, outfitted as if for a cabinet meeting rather than reuniting with an old friend. The blazer had been a last-minute addition, plucked from his suitcase after he had already buttoned his shirt.

Why? A question he would rather not answer, even to himself.

Though he had achieved what most would consider extraordinary success, graduated from St. Stephens, cleared the IAS exam on his first attempt, risen steadily through postings that others would kill for, some childish part of him still felt the need to prove himself to Ishaan Chatterjee.

Ishaan, whose face adorned billboards across the country. Ishaan, who had never worked a day in his life by any reasonable definition of work. Ishaan, who had been born into wealth and stumbled into fame.

The thought irritated him, and that irritation irritated him further still. He felt like some of Shayan's friends, humble, but bragging on Instagram, showing off their privilege in the most obvious ways to establish online clout, bratty sons of Delhi's IAS superclass. He would laugh at their immaturity, except they were twenty, and he was nearing fifty, and should be beyond such petty concerns.

Yet as he continued his silent climb, Ranadeep adjusted his cuffs one final time.

The elevator chimed softly, depositing Ranadeep on the twenty-third floor. Room 2307. He had received the text after landing: 'No lobby. Straight to my room. Three knocks. Paps everywhere.' Ranadeep wondered if the paranoia about the media was genuine, or whether this was merely Ishaan clutching onto a comforting fantasy, once rooted in reality, but not anymore.

They had decided not to speak over the phone, agreeing instead to meet in Calcutta, first together, then to visit Krishanu's house. Safer that way. No digital trail, no chance of being recorded. Amritlal Patel, he knew, was always listening, and he would not put it past him to tap his phones, the ones whose SIMs were in his name.

Amritlal liked to keep people in control, and secrets were the currency he traded in.

Ranadeep's knuckles rapped against the lacquered door, three measured taps. Footsteps approached from the other side, a peephole darkened, and then locks disengaged in quick succession.

The door swung open.

Ishaan Chatterjee stood barefoot in the doorway, dressed in just a white undershirt, a *baniyan* that revealed arms still muscled in a way that belied his age, and faded jeans. His hair was damp, pushed back carelessly from his forehead. He had not shaved in a while, and yet this was not the stylish stubble that once made *Time* magazine call him India's 'Brad Pitt', but that of a man who had let himself go, of a garden once manicured now gone to seed.

This was Ishaan unfiltered, unpolished.

For a moment, they just looked at each other.

Time collapsed between them. The carefully crafted sentences Ranadeep had rehearsed on the flight evaporated. There stood the captain of the cricket team, the boy with the big laugh and the bigger heart, and the person whom he had loved spending time with the most, not just as a child, but through all the years from then to now.

Before Ranadeep could speak, Ishaan stepped forward and embraced him. The familiar scent of cologne – some things never changed – mixed with something sharper, medicinal. His arms wrapped around Ranadeep's blazered shoulders, tight, desperate almost.

'Jack of All Trades,' Ishaan whispered, using the old nickname.

Ranadeep's arms, stiff at first, finally returned the embrace.

'Hero,' he replied, the word catching in his throat.

'What the fuck happened to Genius?' Ishaan's voice cracked, fingers raking through his hair, leaving him looking dishevelled and more spent. His eyes were rimmed red, not the practised tears of his melodramas but something raw. Unvarnished.

'The police report says he drowned in his pool. That is all we know for certain.'

'Drowned? Basab? That makes no fucking sense.' Ishaan slammed his fist against the wall, then winced, examining his knuckles. 'He was the best swimmer among us. Remember Digha? He swam out farther than anyone.'

'That was thirty years ago,' Ranadeep said, his voice level. 'People change. Age catches up. Will weakens. Divorce happens. His wife had just served him papers.'

Ishaan scowled. 'How do you know that?'

'I make it my business to know things.' Ranadeep pulled out his phone, checked a message, then slipped it back into his pocket with practised ease. 'Give me three days. I will find out exactly what happened to Basab.'

'How?' Ishaan demanded, his voice carrying the petulance of a man unaccustomed to delay.

'Trust me,' Ranadeep said. 'I have my ways.'

Ishaan's voice softened, vulnerability seeping through the cracks of his celebrity armour. 'Was it the divorce? Was it…'

'Let's not speculate.' Ranadeep placed a firm hand on Ishaan's shoulder, steadying him. 'We will know by Monday.'

The suite was tasteful in its understatement, a rarity among luxury accommodations in India. Heavy damask curtains were drawn across the windows, allowing only a sliver of Calcutta's skyline to peek through, Ishaan's concession to privacy over a view. A simple Murano glass pendant light cast a warm glow over a teakwood dining table, its surface gleaming with years of careful polishing. The marble floors were covered with hand-knotted Kashmiri carpets in subtle indigo and ivory patterns. Carefully curated pieces of Bengali art hung on the walls, their value apparent to the discerning eye. The living area featured leather club chairs in butterscotch brown, positioned around a glass coffee table supported by a bronze base that resembled flowing water. Everything spoke of quiet wealth rather than ostentatious display, the kind of room designed for discretion, for conversations that needed to remain behind closed doors.

'Sit, please.' Ishaan gestured toward the living area of the suite. 'Can I get you something? Chivas Regal? A martini? The minibar is well stocked.'

'Water is fine.'

'What? You don't drink? Am I hearing this right?'

Ranadeep understood the question. Ishaan would steal bottles of rum or vodka from his dad, who had so many lying about the house that he lost count. There was a guard's quarter in Ishaan's house, and when the guard went home to Bihar, that room would be empty. The Musketeers would sneak in with a stolen bottle, and they would have a competition. Ishaan actually drank the least; Krishanu would down the glass in one gulp and then go out behind the room to puke his guts out, but it was Ranadeep who quietly consumed the most, without his words slurring, without any way of anyone knowing how drunk he was. Basab sat apart, with that half-smile of his, Ishaan teasing him with 'Would you like a glass of milk?' but he would not rise to the bait, never touching a drop.

Later, at St. Stephen's, far from home and the watchful eyes of his parents, Ranadeep had found himself drinking alone in his hostel room. No friends, no one to talk to, just the burn of cheap whisky and the textbooks he could not focus on. Those years had blurred into postings across dust-blown district towns where the only entertainment was the bottle kept in the bottom drawer of every officer's desk.

Until the doctor in Patna had shown him the scan of his liver, pointed to the shadowy areas, and spoken in that clinical tone that somehow conveyed more urgency than any shouting could have: 'You have been rotting away from the inside, Mr Saha.'

That night, Monobina had poured every bottle down the sink while he watched, her silence more damning than any lecture. He had kept his promise to her for two decades now, with only the occasional glass at diplomatic functions where refusing would cause offence.

'I am not that person anymore,' Ranadeep said simply, settling into the overstuffed leather sofa. *I was never that person*, he wanted to say but did not.

Ishaan opened the minibar and brought out a chilled bottle of mineral water. Turning the cap, he poured it into two glasses, one with ice, and one without.

'You still like ice in your water?' Ishaan asked, moving to the minibar.

'I haven't changed that much,' Ranadeep said with a polite smile, regretting now the curtness of his last response. Drink was a sensitive topic to him even now. Because he missed it, and no time more so than now: Basab dead, everything coming up that he thought he had buried, and the conversation with Krishanu still ahead.

The ice clinked against crystal as Ishaan poured. His hands were steady, the nails manicured but the knuckles scarred from his action films, or perhaps from fights the tabloids never reported.

'So how is Puchki?' Ishaan settled into his couch, feet turned up and resting on the arm of the sofa. 'I am sorry; I don't remember her real name. She must be in college right now and probably hates being called Puchki.'

'Hah,' Ranadeep said, accepting the water glass. 'Puchki is not in college anymore. At least, I hope not. She is thirty-five, has one daughter, and another on the way.'

A flicker of confusion crossed Ishaan's face.

'I forget,' he murmured, fingering the silver chain around his neck, the same one he had worn since they were teenagers.

'I forget that it has been thirty years. In my head, she is five years old, and I thought...' He didn't finish.

'My sister is doing well.' Ranadeep said, reassuringly. 'She and her husband stay in Sydney. They moved there three years ago from Bengaluru. He works for an Australian bank; she joined Google.'

'And Uncle and Aunty?'

'They are doing fine for their age. We moved out from our old neighbourhood a few months after everything happened, after you left. Baba bought a house in Salt Lake. Nothing fancy, but away from the memories.'

He traced a finger along the condensation on his glass.

'We sold that place too a year ago. Ma and Baba moved into a smaller apartment in New Town. The old place was just too big to maintain. Too many stairs for them now.'

'And what about you?' Ishaan asked, 'Kids?'

'Yes, one. His name is Shayan. He is the one who goes to college now.'

Ishaan's face softened. 'Wow. Your son is the same age now as we were, when we were friends.'

He swirled the ice in his glass, eyes distant.

'You must forgive me, the life I lead, I lose track of time. I play young men for a living, and yes, I know it's a joke at my age, but that's the kind of work I get. My head cannot process time in the way it should. If it did, maybe I, too, would laugh at myself. So, yes, I have convinced myself that time had stood still, and that's why all of this, our becoming uncles, is a bit of a shock. But tell me about Shayan; that is a nice name. Where does he go to college?'

'Harvey Mudd. That's in California.' Ranadeep's voice grew quiet. 'His mother and I just dropped him off last month. Empty nest syndrome for us now.' He straightened in his seat. 'But tell me, how are your parents?'

Ishaan's face clouded.

'Baba had a stroke. He's in a wheelchair now, can't talk, needs a nurse for every little thing.'

He looked down at his hands.

'Ma's physically fine, but her memory's going. They are both in Dubai. Good elder care there, top-of-the-line facilities.'

He tapped his knuckles against the coffee table.

'Expensive, but good. I tell myself that's why I moved them; a good son wants the best for his parents, but sometimes...'

He paused.

'Sometimes I wonder if the truth is that I just can't bear to see them like that.'

Ranadeep nodded, his expression carefully neutral.

'Especially Baba,' Ishaan said. 'You remember how he was, full of life, maybe too full of it. Now he just stares at the ceiling, eyes not blinking, makes these sounds.' He swallowed hard. 'Ma doesn't recognize me anymore. Sometimes thinks she is a princess kidnapped by some king. Says she has a daughter who was eaten by a monster. Doctor says not to argue; just go along like you would do with a little girl.' His voice trailed off. 'I know how it sounds...but I just can't...'

Ranadeep nodded his head. 'That's understandable.'

Ishaan stood abruptly and walked out of the living room into the bedroom. The door was open, and Ranadeep saw him opening his suitcase that was kept on the bed.

'Well, aren't you going to ask me about my wife? Or wives? Or children?' Ishaan called from the bedroom. 'Or grandchildren?'

'I follow entertainment news,' Ranadeep replied. 'I am up on all your updates.'

'Don't trust anything they say.' Ishaan's voice carried a bitter edge. 'Some of my hookups are made up by movie

PR to promote projects. The ones that are true, PR tells me to deny them.'

He emerged with a small leather case, smiling tiredly.

'I have not only lost track of time, but I also sometimes wonder what's even real anymore. How much of me is me? How much of me is bullshit?'

He moved back towards the table. 'How much are special effects? How much is the stuntman? How much are camera angles? How much the hero, how much the villain, how much the boy you knew and how much is just a stranger in the mirror?'

'Hah,' Ranadeep gave a half-laugh. 'That happens to all of us. It's called mid-life crisis.'

Ishaan placed the leather case on the table, unzipping it with practised precision. Inside lay a small mirror, its surface scratched from years of use, a clear plastic bag with fine white powder, a black credit card, and a rolled hundred-dollar bill, creased and worn.

'What the hell is that?' Ranadeep sank into his seat, tensing.

'Are you trying to tell me you have never seen this at those high society Lutyens' Delhi parties I know you get invited to?' Ishaan's lips curled into a wicked smile. 'Relax, as far as you know, it's chalk powder, like the stuff we would have on our hair after fighting near the blackboard.'

'Have you become an addict?' Ranadeep asked, his voice low, a shadow darkening his face.

Ishaan's fingers moved with ritual efficiency, tapping out two lines of cocaine onto the mirror, perfect parallel tracks, startlingly white against the reflective surface.

He leaned forward, placed the rolled bill to his nostril, and inhaled sharply. Twice.

His head snapped back, eyes closing momentarily.

'Been dependent for years now.'

He rubbed his gums with his index finger.

'But what isn't scripted in my life anymore? Even my chemistry is manufactured.'

Ranadeep observed his old friend, noting the slight tremor in his hands, the way his eyes suddenly sharpened with unnatural focus.

'Don't look at me like that,' Ishaan said, opening his eyes. He pinched the bridge of his nose, sniffing. 'Everyone snorts: the stars, the startup bros, the crypto kings and, I will bet, some of the men you click and salute at work every day.'

Ranadeep remained silent, his disapproval hanging in the air between them.

'You have no idea what my life is like.'

Ishaan paced the room, energy coursing through his veins.

'I wake up whenever they want me to, spend three hours in makeup, do forty takes of the same scene, get screamed at by directors half my age, then spend the night wondering if tomorrow they will replace me with some twenty-year-old who will work for half my rate.'

He stopped by the curtains, peering through the narrow gap. 'I used to love the work. But now they laugh, used to be behind my back, now they do it when I am there but turned away. Any day now, they will do it to my face.'

He laughed bitterly. 'And you know why? Because I can't fucking remember my lines anymore. Three pages of dialogue I used to memorize while taking a shit. Now I need cue cards.'

'That is what getting older is,' Ranadeep said flatly.

'It would all be fine if the damned movies worked. But they bomb, each and every one of them.'

Ishaan gestured toward the mirror.

'This? This just gets me through the day. Helps me focus. Keeps me sharp. It's medicinal, practically.'

'You know it is not,' Ranadeep said quietly. 'It's making it worse.'

Ishaan's eyes flashed.

'Don't you fucking pretend to care. If you had, you would have called; you would have stayed in touch. When I left Calcutta, I ran away because everyone whispered "murderer", when my father sold our house and ran, my father, who had never left any field of battle, where were you?'

Ishaan spluttered. 'You think I killed Pramila. All of you do.'

Silence. Neither man moved.

Ranadeep shook his head. 'It doesn't matter who thought what.' His voice emerged measured, each word deliberate. 'The past is irrelevant. The truth too, no one gives a fuck. What counts is our next move. This is why we are here. That's why we need to talk to Krishanu. We present a united front. We stay consistent; we survive this.'

Ishaan stared at him. 'They will try to pin this on me. Just as they did last time.'

'Not if we have our stories straight.'

Ishaan's gaze never left Ranadeep's face, searching for something: confirmation, absolution, perhaps just recognition. Finding none, he looked away, toward the mirror where a few grains of white powder still clung to the glass.

'The truth is that Brajendra Das killed Pramila.' Ishaan said, 'That is the only story.'

'Yes, you are right. But I am not sure Krishanu will go with that.'

Ishaan's head jerked up. 'What do you mean?'

'Has Krishanu ever written to you? Mails? Postcards?' Ranadeep asked.

'Mail?' Ishaan snorted. 'My staff screens everything, and for good reason. I have got women sending letters written in blood; do not ask from where. Got a severed thumb once from a millworker who lost it in an accident and wanted to "gift" it as tribute. Teeth. Yes, people send me their teeth. And of course, threats. Murder and worse. My staff destroys all my mail. Only legal notices and bills get through.'

He shrugged.

'Of course, mail is dead now. All that love and hate comes through Instagram, which again my staff runs. If you ask me, I prefer body fluids and dismembered body parts over social media. At least they are human or once were.'

Ranadeep leaned forward, elbows on knees. 'Krishanu's been writing to me. For years. Desperate letters, always asking for money.'

Ishaan's eyebrows lifted. 'You think he hit me up too?'

'Probably. Makes sense, doesn't it? Your family was always the most generous.'

A dark chuckle escaped Ishaan's lips. 'Must have tried Basab as well, I suppose.'

Ranadeep hesitated, gaze distant. 'Maybe. But somehow, I doubt it.'

'Why?'

'Just a feeling.' Ranadeep's voice softened. 'The thing about Krishanu…he always saw Basab as even worse off than himself. In a way, it was true back then. Both poor, but Basab's dad was crazy on top of it.'

Ishaan's jaw tightened. 'Yeah. Remember how he wouldn't show up at the hospital when Basab was dying, terrified he would have to pay? What a piece of work.'

'I used to read Krishanu's letters,' Ranadeep said quietly, 'before he stopped writing. He wrote like we were still eighteen. Time seemed to have frozen in his mind. Maybe it was just a ploy for sympathy, or maybe...he never really moved on. But to him, I bet Basab's still that skinny kid hustling tuitions to support his family. Not some high-flying American professor in Pasadena. Asking him for money...it probably never even occurred to him.'

'Why did he stop writing to you?' Ishaan asked.

'Because I never replied. Not once. Eventually, he got the message.'

'What message?'

'That I wouldn't melt for his sob story. That there would be no money.'

Emotion roughened Ranadeep's words.

Ishaan's brows knit together. 'Sob story? He's our friend, *yaar*. If we don't help him, who will?'

'Was our friend. Thirty years ago.' Ranadeep set his glass down.

'We were the Musketeers, Ranadeep. Friends for life, one for all and all for one, remember?' Ishaan's voice carried the conviction of his movie roles.

A bitter smile twisted Ranadeep's lips. 'It is not the way the world works.'

'Oh?' Ishaan asked, scratching at his nose with one finger. 'How does it work then?'

'We're dying always, continuously passing away. Have you seen our old photos, the ones at eighteen? Those kids aren't alive anywhere, and I don't mean metaphorically.' Ranadeep's voice softened. 'Our cells die and rebuild; our blood renews every few weeks, at a cellular level. What we call nostalgia, that ache we feel when we hear old songs or watch clips of old cricket games, it's grief. Grief for our dead selves. The Musketeers are dead, Ishaan. All of them. What's left now are just fragments linked by a fraying thread of memory.'

Ishaan stared at Ranadeep, his pupils wide, mouth slightly open.

'Why were those boys, those boys who are dead, friends? Because they wanted to be. Common interests, cricket matches, awful teachers, impossible exams. It was self-interest. Then things changed. Pramila happened. It broke us. We became new people. We scattered, each looking out for himself.'

'That's very poetic, something that the dead Rano would say, after having too much Old Monk.' Ishaan sniffed, rubbed at his nose again.

Ranadeep didn't flinch.

'I know what you are thinking: what a cold-hearted bastard I have become. Maybe. But it's the truth. Harsh? Yes. But real. Even Krishanu, with his letters…all that "how've you been, good old days" routine…it's song and dance. It's a set-up. A prelude to the real ask. Money. It's not friendship anymore, Ishaan, and that is fine. That's just the way the world works now. We have different interests, different needs. Right now, his and ours…they don't align. Not anymore.'

'So let me get this straight,' Ishaan said, opening his eyes wide with mock innocence. 'You are suggesting that since we didn't send Krishanu money or even bother to dignify him with a response to his many letters, he is pissed. So, he is going to take revenge on us by…how? Making up stories for the documentary?'

'He does not have to make anything up. He just has to talk. He has leverage now,' Ranadeep said. 'You are a famous man. I am about to become a minister. Neither of us can afford to have our names dragged into a reopened murder case. Now, he gets to set the terms. He will want money, with interest. And we cannot even pretend we did not hear him.'

'Tell me something, Rano,' Ishaan said. 'Is this what they teach you in the world of safari-suited babus? Leverage and mind games, and how to barter this for that, who gets the high ground and who gets thrown in the ditch? Because I cannot remember the Rano I know, that person, ever thinking like this about a friend.'

'Oh, please,' Ranadeep said. 'As if in your movie world, everyone sings Kumbaya and dances around trees holding hands.'

'They do not. They are vipers. They are export-quality bastards. They smile to your face while sliding the knife in your back.'

Ishaan stood and began pacing, his bare foot on the carpet.

'But they are not us. They are not the Musketeers.'

He jabbed a finger toward Ranadeep.

'I refuse to believe everything is transactional. That the Ranadeep, sitting here in this room, does not carry the love that the dead Ranadeep had for the dead Ishaan or the dead Krishanu. I am sorry; I refuse to believe that friendship is just self-interest in disguise.'

'And who's preaching this gospel of eternal love?' Ranadeep cocked an eyebrow. 'A man who changes girlfriends like most change socks?'

The words hung in the air like smoke. A moment later, Ranadeep raised his palms in surrender.

'I shouldn't have said that.'

Ishaan's face remained unnervingly calm.

'See, that is friendship.'

A faint smile tugged at his lips.

'Not your honesty, but the fact that your teeth are still in your mouth.'

He dropped back onto the sofa.

'Anyone else who said that to my face would be picking their molars from the carpet right now.'

'I didn't mean…'

'You meant it.' Ishaan cut him off. 'You are sorry for saying it out loud, not thinking it. So let me explain.'

He leaned forward, elbows on knees.

'I cannot keep relationships because I am a shit person. I am insecure. I am violent. I drink way more than I should. As you can see, I also do drugs. As I am sure you have read, my views belong in another century, which it turns out, women don't seem to like.'

Something vulnerable flickered across his face.

'But every time, Rano, every fucking time, I have believed it was forever. Not once have I thought about "the next best thing." That's not me.'

Ranadeep looked away. His discomfort said more than words ever could.

'All those terrible tabloid stories – yes, most of them are true, to an extent; that's me desperately trying to hold on to women who are leaving. Makes them leave faster, of course.'

A bitter laugh escaped him.

'Never claimed to be smart.'

'That's not what I…'

'You started this. Let me finish.'

Ishaan's fingers went to the ghostly streaks of white powder on the table.

'Pramila, and I know you think I killed her…if I did, I did it so she wouldn't leave. Maybe that proves your point about selfishness.'

He rubbed his jaw.

'But I never calculate leverage with friends. And Krishanu doesn't either.'

Ishaan's eyes hardened.

'I am surprised that you, the one Krishanu cared for most, think this way about him. Remember when those boys spread rumours that you were gay? The *meetha paan*, that was the nickname they gave you, a guy singing Rabindra Sangeet as a hobby, reciting poetry in competitions, creaseless shirt and perfectly combed hair, and that pretty boy look you had.'

'I remember, only too well.' Ranadeep's fingers tightened around his glass.

'Then you should remember who stood up for you.' Ishaan leaned forward. 'It was Krishanu. The soft one. The one everyone picked on. He confronted them. He loved you. He loved me too.'

'You think he loved you?'

'The dead Krishanu did.' Ishaan's eyes gleamed. 'I guess we will find out what the alive one thinks.'

'Do you remember what you used to call him?' Ranadeep asked.

'What? Krishanu, of course.'

'No. "Doggie Dum Dum."'

Ishaan blinked. Then laughed.

'That dubbed Russian cartoon, about that fat Saint Bernard and his adventures. We were what, thirteen? Fourteen? It was a joke.'

'But you did call him that.' Ranadeep's voice had an edge.

'Okay,' Ishaan said with a light sneer. 'Krishanu *was* fat. I know that is illegal to say now, body shaming and all, but those were not the times we grew up in.'

'You know why he was fat?' Ranadeep leaned in. 'Because he was poor. After Saraswati Pujo, when families gave away their extra sweets, the *kodma*s and the *batasha*s and the *nokuldana*s, he would take them, keep them in jars. To eat. Because his...'

'Oh, fucking please.' Ishaan threw up his hands. 'Basab skipped meals, and he was as thin as a stick. You have seen real poor people, ribs poking out, sunken cheeks, malnourished.'

Ishaan sniffed.

'I heard this at a cocktail party once, two wives of industrialists, decked in diamonds, discussing childhood obesity and poverty. What they did not seem to understand, and I felt no need to correct them, was that what they were saying was true about the US, where poor children eat cheap processed food. It doesn't apply to India. Krishanu was fat because he was lazy and liked to eat sweets. Yes, maybe he didn't know better; no one taught us about carbs and protein, but he did eat like a pig whenever he had a chance. One of my father's friends brought a huge Toblerone bar from the US, and Krishanu wiped it out in ten minutes... and his being fat is somehow society's fault?'

Ishaan's voice softened slightly. 'And yeah, I called him fat, yes, but he did not mind.'

He coughed lightly.

'Please stop trying to use the woke ideas of the now-alive Ranadeep to judge the already-dead Ishaan.'

'How do you know he did not mind?' Ranadeep asked aggressively, though he kept his voice low. 'How do you know he liked you bullying him for his weight? Or his bad fielding because he was fat? You used to shout at him continuously during cricket matches; have you forgotten?'

'If he did feel bad, he would have told me.'

'Told you?' Ranadeep laughed, short and sharp. 'No one told you anything. Everyone was afraid of you.'

'Afraid of me? Am I their dad now?' Ishaan's nostrils flared.

'You pushed us around. You were a bully. We still stuck around because we were obligated to you. You helped

Basab with money. You protected Krishanu, from the real bullies. You bullied him, sure, but not like the other boys did. And being seen with you, the Hero, it gave us what people now call "social capital".'

He exhaled.

'You were the best sportsperson. We wanted you on our team. Your house was the grandest any of us had seen. You got us into trouble, the fun kind. We loved you. You were kind. You cared. Your father...he was like a dad to all of us.'

Ranadeep stared at the bottom of his glass.

'But do understand, we *chose* to tolerate your nastiness. Because it came with the package.'

'It's okay, Rano.' Ishaan tapped the table twice. 'You don't have to backpedal. I get what you are saying. I know I am a bad person and always have been. Where I disagree is your idea that we are always dying and replacing our former selves. Our problem is the opposite: we stay the same, no matter how many breakthroughs my therapist claims we have. I am still Ishaan Chatterjee, after all that "talking through issues" and "meditation" crap. I am sorry; I am, and always have been, a bully. But here is my story: I bully because I care.'

His eyes softened.

'I cared for Pramila. I cared for you, each of you. And I still do. Maybe I just sucked at showing it.'

He rubbed the bridge of his nose.

'Yes, I know, we have scattered, moved on, gone about with our lives. But the nature of love, true love, and yes, you will call it filmy, is that it does not need for people to remember birthdays or call or send flowers. Those are for business associates. True love just *is*. If I have any regret, right now, it is that I was not with Basab at his end. I will not know what happened to him. I was not there to share his pain. I was not there to hold his hand.'

'I will find out, trust me, I will find out.' Ranadeep's voice softened. 'Don't think I do not feel the same.'

'What about Krishanu?' Ishaan slumped back against the sofa, suddenly sounding tired and defeated. 'What do you want to do today?'

'I have told him I will be there at his house, to discuss the documentary. I did not say you would be there.'

'Why?'

'Because I want to catch him off guard.' Ranadeep adjusted his cuffs. 'Yes, I am sorry; I too cannot change who I am. I believe Krishanu is going to try to squeeze us. While he might have thought what he is going to say to me, he has not planned for you.'

Ishaan nodded, sadness settling across his face like an evening shadow.

'Why don't I give him what he wants? If it is money he is after, I honestly do not mind.'

'No, wait.' Ranadeep held up a palm. 'Not just because every rupee you give him proves he can get more, but because if we pay him off, he will sling it back at the documentary: "See? I am being bribed to stay quiet." We cannot afford that narrative.'

'God, you do not like Krishanu.' Ishaan's eyes widened, hurt and realization mixing in his expression. 'What did he write to you in those letters?'

Ranadeep checked his watch, avoiding the question.

'We should leave soon. It will take time to reach his house in this traffic.'

Ishaan's shoulders slumped. 'Fine. Keep your secrets, Jack of All Trades. We all have them, I suppose.'

He pushed himself off the sofa and disappeared into the bathroom.

Water splashed behind the closed door. Ranadeep stood at the window, pulling back the curtain just enough to glimpse the hotel's manicured gardens, geometric perfection of trimmed hedges and sculpted flower beds. A final look at the ordered world he had constructed for himself before stepping back into the chaos of a past he thought he had escaped.

'Did you know the tap is leaking?' Ishaan called out. 'What kind of seven-star hotel has a leaking tap? Probably hiring the same contractors that build our roads.'

More splashing. A muttered curse. Then silence.

The bathroom door opened. The man who emerged was not the dishevelled, barefoot Ishaan who had greeted Ranadeep before.

This was Ishaan Chatterjee, Bollywood icon, hair styled with practised carelessness, cheeks expertly shaved, face subtly powdered to hide the ravages of time and excess. Designer sunglasses concealed his dilated pupils. The white linen shirt looked casual yet cost more than most people's monthly salary.

'Ready,' he announced, slipping his phone into his pocket.

Ranadeep straightened his blazer and ran a hand through his hair. The bureaucrat was back, his vulnerability filed away like yesterday's paperwork.

Together they stood at the door, two middle-aged men in costume, performing roles they had perfected over decades.

'After you,' Ranadeep said, in the way he used to when they would walk out to open the batting.

Ishaan stepped into the hallway, his practised smile already in place. Behind them, the tap continued its slow, steady drip, counting seconds down like a metronome.

8

Samosas and Sweets

The old ceiling fan, its blades bent with age, wheezed overhead, each rotation producing a metallic click and an unnatural sigh. Ishaan looked around, taking in Krishanu's living room. It remained unchanged, the same faded maroon sofa with permanently indented cushions, now more colourless than he remembered. The pale blue paint on the walls peeled away in long scrabs, exposing brick and rusted iron beneath. The large, framed picture of Rabindranath Tagore garlanded with greyed flowers, the glass-fronted cabinet displaying ancient crockery, and the wooden lamp-stand Krishanu's father proudly claimed came from Kashmir, its intricate patterns now buried under dust and grime.

The place was in an advanced state of decay. Just like Krishanu.

He sat across from them, skeletal fingers wrapped around his teacup. Cancer had carved him hollow. His once-pudgy face had collapsed inward, cheekbones jutting beneath paper-thin skin. Only his eyes retained their old animation, darting between Ishaan and Ranadeep with fevered intensity.

'You shouldn't have gone through the trouble,' Ranadeep said as Sunanda arranged samosas and sweets on chipped china plates. 'We are just here for a visit.'

'Oh man, there goes my carb quota for the week,' Ishaan added, eyeing the rows of sweets. 'Sunanda, please take away three of them. They look too tempting, but at my age, I can't work these off like I could at twenty.'

'These are dinosaurs on your plate.' Krishanu gestured weakly. 'Genuine Bengali sweets are going extinct.'

Sunanda moved with quiet efficiency, her movements economical, practised. She wore a simple cotton salwar kameez, her hair pulled back in a no-nonsense ponytail. Ishaan noticed the dark circles, too deep for a girl her age.

'Baba exaggerates,' Sunanda said, 'Let me remove one, but please have the other two. They are really good.'

Ishaan nodded with a smile.

'No, I do not exaggerate,' Krishanu snapped, his voice unexpectedly sharp. 'All the sweet shops from our childhood are gone. Mahaprabhu and Nobokishno Guin from the market are all shuttered. No demand for them anymore, they say. Instead, we have Marwari shops, run by Sethjis and Lalajis, peddling kaju katli and fancy barfi, more silver foil than sweets. Milk replaced by *daal*, food colouring, it is more Holi in my mouth than sugar. And now they have added Cadbury chocolate in sandesh, what an abomination. Changing tastes, they claim. But it is something else. It is the erasure of Bengalis in Bengal, cultural imperialism on all fronts. Hindi words in Bengali movie songs, signboards in Hindi, even in Urdu, and the war reaches its final frontier, our taste buds...'

'Baba...please.' Sunanda pressed her father's shoulder gently. 'No politics. Leave that to your WhatsApp groups.'

'The samosas are good,' Ranadeep said, his voice measured. He sat with perfect posture, knees together, blazer unbuttoned but still formal. 'Thank you, Sunanda.'

'Remember Das Cabin?' Krishanu reached for a sandesh with trembling fingers. 'Those special kobiraji cutlets? There was always a line around the block, and their butter toast for five rupees in the morning.'

'Gone?' Ishaan leaned forward.

'Bulldozed.' Krishanu made a gesture with his hand of being run over. 'A hundred-year-old building replaced by glass and chrome. Starbucks on the ground floor. Second floor houses a school for air hostesses. The third and fourth floors, illegal, built without permits, keep changing tenants. Shifty people from out of state.' Bitterness seeped through Krishanu's voice. 'This whole place has gone to the dogs, floating population now, no community, no neighbourhood.'

Ranadeep sipped his tea. 'Places change, Krishanu, just like people.'

'For the good, yes.' Krishanu's Adam's apple bobbed violently. 'But this is decline. We middle-class Bengalis are being squeezed out by rich yuppies. A Starbucks coffee costs twenty times what it should, but young kids sit there all evening, glued to their phones and laptops, not even tasting the coffee, paying whatever they are charged. Domestic help, I cannot afford it anymore. All these yuppies pay whatever they are asked, give in to all demands, ten thousand rupees monthly and Sundays off. People like us on fixed incomes cannot pay the market rate. Poor Rini does everything now, mopping, sweeping…'

'Baba,' Sunanda cut in, 'why do you keep bringing up politics?'

'Why shouldn't I?' Krishanu flared. 'How often do you have a government minister in your house? By the way,

Rano, much of this decay comes from the politics of the party you are about to join.'

Ranadeep paused his cup of tea mid-air. 'That help is no longer cheap; that they want living wages, or basic privileges like days off, that is not decline. That's progress.'

Ranadeep's voice took on an edge as he met Krishanu's gaze.

'In the US or Europe, most people can't afford butlers or drivers, not because they're worse off than us. If they were, they would be applying to settle here, not the other way around. And this "outsiders displacing Bengalis" narrative, it's not so different from what Americans say about Indians. Think about that.'

'Thank you, Uncle,' Sunanda said, relief washing over her face. 'You say it much better than I can.'

'I am sure you say it better.' Ranadeep smiled wryly. 'But something tells me your father doesn't let you finish.'

'There, now you have a favourite uncle.' Krishanu gave a theatrical sigh, reaching for another samosa.

'What about Ramkrishna Park? Is it still there?' Ishaan asked.

Ranadeep shot him a quick glance, surprised. Ishaan avoided his eyes.

'You really haven't been back, have you?' Krishanu shook his head. 'Gone. All gone. There is a mall there now, one of those gleaming ones with parking lots and security guards. We used to play cricket where they now valet Audis.' He jabbed a bony finger at Ranadeep. 'Your bureaucrat friends approved that construction. *Progress*, they called it.'

Ranadeep placed his teacup carefully on its saucer. 'I know that park meant a lot to us, but it was not much of a park, more a large vacant lot left when they stopped building on all sides. I dislike malls too, but change is good and development inevitable.'

'Development!' Krishanu's laugh dissolved into a rasping cough. 'They demolished all the single screens where we watched movies. Remember? Ten rupees for a ticket. Now it's five hundred. Three screens, or is it five, and overpriced caramel popcorn, not even real popcorn like we had, and recliner seats. Who goes to theatres to sleep?'

'Don't get me started on ticket prices; it's killing the movie industry.' Ishaan muttered. 'If I start on this topic, Sunanda will ask both of us to stop talking politics.'

Ishaan paused, and then asked softly, 'And our school?'

'Progress there too.' Bitterness dripped from the word. 'Closed down. An international school stands there now, glass walls and security cameras. Fees fifty times higher, though Rini says they are not comparable to what we had growing up: Spanish lessons, programming bootcamp from age five, teachers who reply to students on WhatsApp, teachers sending students…what is that thing, Rini?'

'Memes,' she answered flatly.

'Yes. Memes. Imagine Shibashish sir sending us memes. And all children get counselling. I tell Rini we got counselling too from our teachers: two tight slaps and hair yanking till our scalps buzzed.'

Ishaan laughed. 'True. I prefer what we had.' He mimicked a playful slap. 'They are raising a generation of namby-pamby wimps now. They need trigger warnings every few words.'

Krishanu nodded, 'I swear.'

Sunanda returned with more tea, pouring without saying a word.

'The tea is very nice,' Ranadeep said. 'Thank you, Sunanda.'

'She works too hard,' Krishanu said, pride leaking through his complaint. 'Mobile shop all day, then comes home to this wreck of a house and her wreck of a father.'

'Baba, please,' Sunanda began, 'everyone works hard.'

'Sure, they work hard. One makes one face when punching people, another when running around trees,' Krishanu continued, ignoring her startled look. 'The other pushes papers and whispers to ministers. And me? I just waste away, counting my days. Master of None, remember?'

Ishaan gestured to Sunanda that they were not offended. 'You look good, Krishanu,' he lied. 'That new regimen Sunanda mentioned must be working. The doctors must be optimistic.'

'He has been eating better these past weeks,' Sunanda said, flicking at the crumbs on her father's plate.

Krishanu ignored her comment. 'Optimistic?' He widened his eyes in mock cheer. 'Absolutely. They are optimistic I will die by December, not November. As for the new regimen, I am a guinea pig, a hamster on a wheel generating a big bonus for some pharma CEO. Rini believes it will cure me, but cancer always comes back. This chemotherapy cocktail merely delays my death, delays Rini selling this place and having her own life.'

'Baba!' Sunanda's voice sharpened.

'Fine.' Krishanu waved a skeletal hand. 'My daughter believes if we do not mention death, it won't find me. As if death hides in the corridor, thinking, "Oh, they're ignoring me; better leave them alone."'

Ranadeep's eyes met Sunanda's briefly. Krishanu caught it.

'Don't give her those bureaucrat's eyes,' Krishanu said. 'That "poor thing dealing with this difficult man" look. She is used to me. Keeps me alive through sheer stubbornness.' He reached for her hand. 'Too stubborn, my Rini.'

He took another samosa. 'One benefit of Ranadeep's vaunted progress, real estate prices have gone through the roof. Pramila's, Basab's and Brajendra Das's houses?

All gone. Replaced with new construction. Promoters, Marwari naturally, swoop down, buy cheap and sell high. I have held out, partly for better prices, but also because I don't want to die elsewhere. I want to close my eyes in my real home. Then Rini can cash out and fly away.'

He took a bite, then set it down. Looking up at Sunanda, who nodded and said, 'I will leave Baba with you for a bit.'

Ishaan and Ranadeep exchanged glances, preparing for the real conversation.

'I know how you both see it.' Krishanu's voice sharpened once Sunanda left. 'I am sure Basab felt the same. This neighbourhood is the shithole you escaped. The erasure of what was is good news for you with your fancy lives elsewhere. That's why Bollywood's Titan and Mr Minister never once returned in all these years.'

The room fell silent except for the ceiling fan's persistent click.

'There was nothing to return to,' Ranadeep finally said, his composure beginning to fray.

'Wasn't there?' Krishanu gestured with his skeletal hand to include them all. 'Here we are, still bound by what happened. Why you ran, why you are back now. One name. *Pramila*. Still carrying her like stones in our pockets.'

Ishaan set down his cup, its rattle against the saucer sharp in the quiet room. 'Let's discuss it then, this documentary.'

'Oh,' Krishanu threw his head back mockingly. 'Now you want to talk. How convenient.' His voice dropped to a hiss. 'What about when *I* wanted to talk? When I sent handwritten letters every few months? Then yearly? No response, not once, until I understood the truth. You had left for good.'

His trembling fingers clutched his cup.

'I didn't expect visits, but not one reply? Not even a one-line acknowledgement? Really?'

Ishaan visibly tensed up. 'I never saw any letters. My staff handles all mail, fan mail, hate mail, business proposals, scams, letters written in blood, body parts. I haven't opened my own mail in twenty years.'

As Ishaan spoke, Krishanu's gaze fixed on Ranadeep. Ranadeep sat quietly, studying his palms.

'At least, Rano here respects me enough to not lie to my face.'

'If Ishaan says he didn't get your letters, he didn't,' Ranadeep said evenly.

Krishanu's tongue darted across cracked lips. 'You are right. He is telling the truth. No disrespect, Ishaan, but you are no Om Puri. I can always tell from your eyes when you are fibbing.' His smile cut like a razor. 'But what's your story, Rano?'

Ranadeep shifted uncomfortably. Before he could answer, Krishanu raised a hand, blue veins visible beneath translucent skin.

'Let me simplify. I asked for money.' His voice rasped. 'And either because I asked too much or because you are fundamentally opposed to giving friends money, you chose silence.'

Ishaan glanced between them, his face unreadable.

'Three lines in a ten-page letter,' Krishanu continued, eyes narrowing, 'but those three lines killed any chance of connection, is that what you are telling me?'

'You know what that kind of request looks like,' Ranadeep said, not being able to meet Krishanu's intense glare.

'So instead of honesty, "Krishanu, I will not give you money", or even a polite lie like, "I cannot afford it right now", you chose silence.'

Krishanu leaned forward, his hollow chest rising and falling with each laboured breath. 'A poor choice, given what our friendship should mean to you. Do you think, as a man praised for judgement, a man soon to be minister, that your decision was wise?'

Ranadeep exhaled slowly, smoothing his pressed linen pants. 'I did what seemed necessary. It felt impolite to say no outright. I thought silence is its own message.'

'Perfectly typical, just like the IAS types handling department files,' Krishanu whispered, smiling faintly. 'Ignore what's uncomfortable until the ink fades and the file is forgotten. *Silence is its own message*, as Rini would say, meme material.'

They sat motionless in the heavy air.

'Tell us about the documentary,' Ranadeep said quietly.

'Ah, yes.' Krishanu's eyes lit with feverish intensity. 'Those people. Here last week. Asked about Pramila. About the night she died.' He leaned forward, his kurta slipping off one shoulder. 'About you, Ishaan. And your father's political connections and stories.'

'What did you tell them?' Tension tightened Ishaan's jaw.

'The medicine, the chemotherapy,' Krishanu swayed slightly. 'It has fried my short-term memory. But the past? Clear as glass. Every catch I dropped, every time you mocked me for being clumsy, all burned into my memory. But what I said hours ago? I honestly don't remember.'

'You don't remember?' Ishaan pressed.

Krishanu grinned widely. 'I swear on my big tumtum, woofie woo, toodlie doo, Doggie Dum Dum.'

Ishaan gripped his seat handle, asking slowly, 'What did you tell them about my father?'

'Nothing they wouldn't learn from old-timers,' Krishanu said flatly. 'Nothing worth the famous Ishaan Chatterjee temper. At least, not yet.'

'What do you mean, "yet"?' Ranadeep's formal demeanour cracked.

'They're coming in a few days for a longer interview.' Krishanu's expression twisted between amusement and contempt. 'And I have been considering what to say.'

Ishaan stood up abruptly. 'Are you threatening us?'

'Threaten?' Krishanu laughed, the sound rattling in his chest. 'I am just sharing plans with old friends. That's what friends do, isn't it? Share important news?'

'Sit down,' Ranadeep commanded Ishaan. 'Let me handle this.'

Sunanda returned with fresh tea, carefully avoiding the room's tension. 'More tea, Uncle?'

'No,' Ishaan snapped, barely containing his anger.

'Yes, please,' Ranadeep countered calmly. 'Thank you, we are being such an imposition.'

'Not at all, Uncle.' Sunanda glanced fearfully at her father. 'Baba always enjoys company.' She had clearly been eavesdropping, unavoidable in the cramped apartment, and was now alarmed at the sudden shift in tone in the conversation.

'This is how we Musketeers talk,' Ranadeep reassured her. 'We are being mature adults so as not to frighten the little kids.' He nodded slightly, implying she was the child, and then smiling again, trying to defuse the tension.

Ishaan sat sullenly, glaring daggers at Krishanu. Sunanda offered a shy, unconvincing bow.

Ranadeep waited until she had left before continuing. 'What exactly are you planning to tell them?'

'I really do not know,' Krishanu fixed his gaze on Ishaan. 'I might repeat what I said before. Old gossip. Nothing explosive. Or something else entirely. I wasn't joking about memory gaps from this new chemo cocktail, really scrambles up my mind.'

'What do you want?' Ishaan demanded. 'Not that I fear the truth, nor does Ranadeep, but your stories harm us. Reputations cost money.'

Ranadeep slapped his hand against his thigh. 'I told you to let me handle this.'

'What do I want?' Krishanu repeated the question, his voice hollow in the air. 'You make it sound as if I am blackmailing you.'

'I was hoping you wouldn't use that word,' Ranadeep said. His jaw had tightened.

'Yes, it's a bad word. I apologize.' Krishanu's lips pulled back in a ghastly smile. 'Let's just say I am renegotiating our friendship. It has been one-sided for a while. I am just putting it back on an even keel.'

'Fine. I am waiting.' Ranadeep stared at Krishanu, face emptied of emotion, a technique learned in those interrogation sessions, dark rooms with a single hanging light. The weight of silence.

'The documentary team is paying me. A trifle really, but money is money.' Krishanu's fingers trembled against the armrest. 'From you? Asking for cash would be petty. We know what that looks like. Instead, I want to make a request. Just a simple request.'

'What is it?' Ranadeep maintained his mask.

'If we had met two years ago, when I was technically still alive, I would have asked you to simply be a witness to my life…*just see me*.'

'What the fuck does that even mean, *just see me*?' Ishaan cut in. Ranadeep's glare shut him up.

'Why do you think kids today post everything online?' Krishanu continued, 'The selfies, the filters, the "here is what I am having for lunch today". Why do you think they do that? Because life is not just about living. It is about being seen. Being seen by strangers, yes, but more than that, being seen by people you care for. Family. Friends.'

His voice cracked.

'I want to be seen, dammit. You, Ishaan, I see you everywhere; turn on the TV or open a newspaper, and there you are.'

He paused, catching his breath as saliva gathered at the corner of his mouth. 'Ranadeep and Basab, you are all over Google. You matter to the world. Me? I am a cockroach in the dark, behind an old trunk. The only time I have ever mattered is when I am being hit by the bottom of a shoe. Once the blows become too much, there I am, running back, lurking again in the darkness, scraping for crumbs.'

His eyes, yellowed with disease, fixed on them.

'Do you see me? Have you ever seen me, both of you?'

Ishaan leaned back, a vein twitching at his temple. 'I don't know how we could have seen you the way you mean.' His face softened, sadness etching the lines around his eyes, 'I would have helped if I had gotten your messages. But I couldn't change how life treated you. I am sorry. I am only a hero on screen. And lately, not even a good one.'

Krishanu leaned forward, a fine mist of spittle escaping with his words. 'I know you had to leave after what happened to Pramila, after the media circus outside your house. I heard the whispers here, at school. Your father did what he had to, moving the family away. But why didn't you come back? Years later. Just to check on a friend? Was a plane ticket from Mumbai really so expensive you couldn't afford it?'

He turned to Ranadeep, eyes burning with decades of abandonment. 'And you? Your family fled too. What was your excuse? The papers weren't hounding you. Yes, I know your father got transferred. We heard that story. At least, Basab stayed for a while. I would like to believe he cared, but I know the truth: his family could not move even if they wanted to, they were as poor as we were.'

Krishanu's eyes had that faraway look, as he remembered.

'It was never the same once the group shattered, and Basab and I barely spoke, just a nod or smile passing each other at school or on the street. But that was more than I ever got from either of you.'

His voice dropped to a whisper.

'Why did it have to be this way? Why could we not move past Pramila? I know she meant a lot to you, Ishaan, and to you too Ranadeep; she was your friend. But what about us, weren't we special? We loved each other. We were tight as a fist...'

'It was life, Krishanu. Life happened.' Ishaan shook his head. 'It would have happened someday, moving away from each other. I understand you being angry we lost touch, but that is not really your complaint, is it? You are angry we are not still playing cricket together in Ramkrishna Park as fifty-year-olds. That is pure sentimental nonsense.'

He gestured vaguely toward the window. 'You just said they built over Ramkrishna Park. What does that tell you? The world moved on. We moved on. Expecting us to stay frozen in time. That is just...' He exhaled heavily. 'What can I tell you?'

Krishanu raised his feet onto the couch, reclining back. Even on the small old sofa, he seemed to disappear into the cushions, his body swallowed by cancer and time.

'I know what you are thinking. How can we *see you*, *you failure*, when you did nothing with your life?' Krishanu's voice gained strength despite his weakness. 'So let me tell you what happened to me. Humour a dying man with some of your precious time. A year after you two left, Baba died. My uncles decided to take my widowed mother to court to force us out of our house. The house my father bought with his own money.'

He fixed his gaze on Ishaan. 'While you were somersaulting off buildings with a heroine on your arm,' then turned to Ranadeep, 'and you were exploring Delhi colleges, and Basab was building his career at IIT, I was sitting every day at Alipore Court, bunking college, shuttling between crooked lawyers. For years, alone.'

His fingers trembled against the armrest. 'We had sold my mother's gold, endured humiliations I will not describe since I know Rini can hear what I am saying. I had no place to go to. I started writing to you, Ishaan, hoping your celebrity status might help us get a court date, cut some slack with a judge. And to you, Rano, for money, when they nearly threw us onto the street...' His eyes glowed from within his sunken face. 'But I beat them. I won in court. I pulled their trousers down. I evicted those bastards. I did it all alone.'

He took a laboured breath. 'Then things got better. Bank job. Marriage. Then Sunanda was born. Thought I was doing okay. I know you would think, "Haha, yeah sure", but as good as I could hope for. Then God struck again. I got into trouble at the bank. It was a small clerical error, that was all it was, while the bank was transferring the ledgers from paper to digital. The bastards threatened jail. I lost my job, and, in this place, everyone knows everyone. I couldn't get within a hundred yards of a teller's booth ever again. The horses started losing, yes, I gamble, then Sunanda's mother was killed by a speeding truck outside her office. And finally, God looked up at me and gave me cancer.'

'Baba, that's enough.' Sunanda rushed into the room, glancing anxiously at Ishaan and Ranadeep. 'I think it's time...'

'No, leave us,' Krishanu commanded, colour briefly returning to his face. 'Come back only when I call you.'

Sunanda seemed to crumple under his harshness, scurrying away with downcast eyes.

'Was that necessary?' Ranadeep asked, his bureaucrat's composure slipping, 'To raise your voice at your daughter?'

'Don't pretend to care for her. At least give me that respect.' Krishanu paused, gathering his remaining strength. 'You want to know what I would like from you? A job for Rini, government job. Permanent. Not contract. I know you can do it, Mr Minister.' His voice softened to a whisper, hollow eyes filling with something gentler than bitterness. 'She is educated. She is smart. She is honest. She would have gone so far ahead in life had it not been for me.'

His gaze drifted toward the door where Sunanda waited unseen. 'While she should have been building her future, she has been watching mine end. All these years, she has carried me when it should have been the other way around.'

He pressed a withered hand against his chest. 'In a better world, I wouldn't have to resort to this. I would simply ask my friends, as I once had the right to, to look after her when I am gone. To do what I would have done for your children had our positions been reversed.'

Tears welled in his sunken eyes, but he held their gaze. 'But we don't live in that world. So, call this what you will, extortion or blackmail or a dying friend's plea. I don't care anymore. Just give my daughter a chance at the life my choices stole from her. Please.'

Ishaan said nothing, his face a mask of emotions. Sadness, anger, and pity warred across his features as he stared at Krishanu's withered form. He reached out his hand and held Krishanu's trembling hand in his, just for a moment, with surprising tenderness.

Ranadeep showed no outward emotion. He cleared his throat and simply looked at his watch. 'Government positions are complicated, Krishanu. There are examinations to be taken, processes to be followed, waiting lists stretch for years, filled with candidates who have gone through the proper channels. You know all this; you have worked in a bank.'

Krishanu's eyes hardened, the momentary vulnerability vanishing. 'So that is your answer? Bureaucratic excuses? You forget that having worked in a bank, I know very well that for the right people the answer always is "Yes, sir" and "How high should I jump, sir?"'

'I didn't say no,' Ranadeep countered, his tone measured. 'I am in Calcutta all week. If Sunanda could visit my office, there might be opportunities on my staff when I take the ministerial position. Some roles are discretionary, and this is a good time, when I have a budget of my own and the power to get something done.'

Krishanu studied him, searching for deception. They met each other's eyes, and whatever Ranadeep was thinking, nothing seeped out into the room.

'Fine,' he said finally. 'She will come.'

'When would be convenient?' Ranadeep asked, reaching for his phone.

'As if the convenience of beggars matter to the kings.' Krishanu's bitter smile returned. 'Tomorrow afternoon. She works mornings at the mobile shop.'

Ishaan stood abruptly. 'We should go.'

Ranadeep followed, placing his teacup carefully on the table. 'Thank you for the tea, Krishanu. It was…good to see you.'

'Was it?' Krishanu didn't rise to see them out.

Sunanda materialized from the shadows of the hallway, eyes red-rimmed but composed. 'I will show you out, Uncle.'

At the door, she lowered her voice. 'He is not always like this. You saw how it started off. He was so happy when you came, and then the medicine kicked in and he went all unstable. He has been doing much better with the new therapy, but he forgets things and doubles back. In a few hours, he will say what a pleasant interaction this was.'

'No need to explain,' Ranadeep said gently. 'We understand.'

'He loves you.' Her gaze was direct, unblinking. 'He talks about you three constantly. The Musketeers. His whole life, even now.'

Ishaan looked away, unable to meet her eyes.

'Tomorrow afternoon, then?' Ranadeep confirmed.

She nodded. 'I will be there.'

The rain had started when they emerged onto the street, fat drops striking the pavement with unusual force. Ishaan stopped at the edge of the sidewalk, his attention caught by the building next to Krishanu's. Where Pramila's house once stood, grey and decaying, now rose a four-storey modern structure with glass-framed balconies gleaming darkly in the sudden rain.

Their driver waited with the engine running, wipers cutting arcs through the downpour. Ranadeep reached for the door handle, then realized Ishaan wasn't beside him. He turned to find his friend motionless on the sidewalk. Rain plastered shirt to skin. His gaze stayed anchored upward.

Ranadeep followed that gaze to the second-floor covered balcony, exactly where Pramila's room had been thirty years before. A girl stood there, perhaps sixteen or seventeen, long black hair falling in familiar waves around her face. She wore a school uniform, fingers at her tie, adjusting it with a gesture that made something stir in Ranadeep's memory.

Her eyes found Ishaan's across the distance. She smiled.

The smile widened, revealing teeth too white in the gathering darkness. Her black kohl-rimmed eyes locked onto Ishaan's, too steady for comfort.

Water streamed down Ishaan's face as he stood frozen. His chest rose and fell in shallow, rapid movements.

A metallic taste filled Ranadeep's mouth. A schoolgirl recognizing a movie star, he told himself. Yet something in her stillness, in the way she stood at that exact spot, made his certainty waver.

The girl raised one hand in a small wave. It was the same wave that someone else, dead for years, used to give Ishaan when he went out to bat, standing at a distance.

Then, her gaze shifted to him. Their eyes met across the rain-filled space, and Ranadeep immediately looked down and away. This was the right thing to do, to not make eye contact with a teenage girl as a fifty-year-old man. But he knew he was lying to himself, and he knew he had grown to be very good at that.

As he looked away, his eyes caught movement in Krishanu's window. There he stood, watching them, his smile mirroring the girl's, teeth bared in what might have been a goodbye or something else entirely. His hand rose, fingers curling in a wave that echoed the girl's perfectly, as if they were performing a choreographed duet, one young, the other withered, yet somehow linked, like marionettes, by the strings of an unknown puppeteer.

Ranadeep seized Ishaan's arm, recoiling at the unnatural chill of his skin through the wet fabric. He pulled him toward the car, keeping his back to both watchers, and shoved him inside with unexpected force.

None of them spoke.

Ranadeep watched Calcutta slide past the window, blurred by the squiggly lines of rain cutting across the glass, each droplet vibrating with the pulse of his heart.

He should have never come back to that street. Never.

'So how did you think that went?' Ishaan's voice cut through the sound of traffic and the patter of rain on the roof of the vehicle.

'No better than I thought it would.' Ranadeep responded. 'But at least, we know what he wants.'

'I could give him money,' Ishaan said, running his fingers through his wet hair, 'That is what he needs right now: serious money. After all, how much would his daughter possibly earn in a government job?'

'I told you. That would be unwise,' Ranadeep said, not looking at him. 'You giving him money would be wrong at this time for all sorts of reasons. We discussed this in the hotel.'

'Then through you. You pay him. I pay you. That would not trip any alarms.' Ishaan turned to face him. 'Whatever time he has left, Krishanu deserves some happiness. A year by the sea, maybe, or up in the mountains. Not sprawled out in that little shithole that looks even worse than him. They need cash, right now.'

Ranadeep studied Ishaan for a long moment.

'He got to you, didn't he? That last little speech about his daughter, it really cut through the grime, didn't it?'

'What the hell are you implying?' Ishaan asked, half-turning to Ranadeep, the muscles in his arm clenching up. 'I cannot believe you are saying this after what we just saw.'

'That outburst, supposedly a side-effect of his meds, was calculated,' Ranadeep said, a sad smile playing at his lips. 'First: "Feel sorry for me." Then: "Don't feel sorry for me." Then: "I am angry because I care." And finally: "I care so much I will hurt you if I have to." It was a performance.

A perfect tutti frutti. One scoop of guilt, one of nostalgia, layered with threats, topped with an "or else". They teach us this in the service: how to make people see things your way. But Krishanu, he figured it out all on his own.'

'Holy shit,' Ishaan exclaimed, loud enough that the driver glanced at him through the rear-view mirror. 'You really are trying to tell me, without laughing out, that that unhinged rant we just sat through was planned out, rehearsed?'

'Not rehearsed. Improvised. Like jazz. Or a small classical recital, where the ustad reads the room, bends the mood, manipulates the air with each note. No two are the same. That is what makes it art. What we saw was not scripted. It was engineered.'

'Well, I don't know what to tell you,' Ishaan said, his voice betraying his disbelief.

'You don't need to say anything. Just think.'

Ranadeep leaned forward, balancing his elbows on his knees.

'He gave us time to settle in. Let our guard down. Then came the food, from the one surviving place from our youth. Comfort food. You know what that does, it messes with time. Puts you back in a space where you feel safe, happy. Disarmed.'

'Brings alive the dead selves?' Ishaan said, dryly.

'Exhumes their ghosts,' Ranadeep replied. 'He brought up multiplexes and single screens, which just so happened to be the topic you spoke on at that conclave last month.'

'You think he watches that kind of thing, in the state he is in?'

'That is all he does,' Ranadeep said. 'He told us, didn't he? He has been watching us online for years. All of us. Stalking us. That was his real complaint, that we did not *see him*, while he did.'

'But you have been stalking him too.' Ishaan smiled bitterly. 'You knew about the gambling, the bank stuff. Why not just tell him "I have been watching you too, boss"?'

'That would have pissed him off the most,' Ranadeep said. 'To know that I have seen through the act. That I have kept tabs on him all this time. Because then he would know that I know that he, himself, has been an architect of his own destruction. That was not a typo in the bank ledger, as he seemed to casually suggest. He was trying to shift money off the books when they were going over from analogue to digital, and he got caught. If he knew I knew, it would have knocked him off script. And then he might have actually become dangerous. But now? He is right where we want him.'

'Wait, how does that make sense? If what you are saying is right, that Krishanu was making us feel comfortable and nostalgic, with the food and the "How nice things once were", why was he continuously snapping at you? He was blaming your party for the city's state, if you recall. Are you telling me that too was part of his master plan?'

'It was.' Ranadeep smiled faintly.

'You remember how we used to argue as kids, about cricket, football, music? Sachin versus Lara, Maradona versus George Best, Kishore versus Rafi. That was our rhythm. He baited me back into it. Got me comfortable, nostalgic. And he knows, everyone knows, I am happiest when I am challenged, when I get into my debate mode. You, on the other hand, like being agreed with. That is who we have always been. And Krishanu? He remembers exactly what makes us feel like ourselves.'

'So, what if he does?' Ishaan's voice rose again. 'Does that make his pain any less real? Is the cancer fake? Did you see him, Rano? He is disappearing.'

'I am not saying don't help,' Ranadeep said, softening his tone as the car slowed in traffic. 'I am saying don't forget why we are helping him. I will meet with his daughter. Go through the motions. Keep him pacified until this documentary madness blows over. We still need him for now.'

'And then?' Ishaan asked, already knowing the answer.

'And then I will quietly let her go.' Ranadeep's tone was matter-of-fact. 'New minister, staff reorganization. Happens all the time.'

Ishaan stared at him. 'That's cold, my friend. Calculating.'

'It's survival,' Ranadeep replied. 'Something I learned in Delhi.'

The traffic hemmed them in: trucks, tempos, private cars pressed together in honking futility. Outside, vendors waded through knee-deep water, selling plastic-wrapped snacks and cigarettes to stranded drivers. The rain had thickened into a monsoon curtain, turning the battered streets of Calcutta into shallow, sloshing rivers.

The driver, a middle-aged man with a grey-streaked beard, muttered something under his breath and tightened his grip on the wheel. He glanced back at them.

'Sahab, good thing we took the Bolero. Road ahead is flooded. Only SUVs and buses can make it. But it will take time.'

'Don't big people like you get lights?' Ishaan muttered, cracking his knuckles, agitation thick in his voice. 'I am drenched to the bone. I have got a flight to Dubai in a few hours.'

'No more *lal batti*, Supreme Court banned it ten years ago,' Ranadeep said, watching a woman balance precariously on bricks, trying to cross the street without soaking her sari's hem. 'Very few get that privilege now. I am not one of them.'

He paused, noting the edge in Ishaan's voice.

'Sorry if my company's been so bad you are counting the seconds to get out of this car.'

'No, Rano,' Ishaan said, offering a grin that didn't reach his eyes. 'I love being with you. It's just…the things you said about Krishanu, they are burning me up inside. You called him "dangerous." The guy's dying.'

He looked out the window at a group of schoolchildren huddled under a shop awning, uniforms soaked, shivering as they waited for the rain to let up.

'I talk like that about movie people all the time. Because they play me. I play them. That's fine. But they are not the Musketeers. With them, I didn't bunk tuitions to watch movies. Or play football in the rain. Or sit on a broken bench and just…talk.'

Ranadeep sat quietly, letting Ishaan go on. Outside, a cycle rickshaw pushed through the flood, its driver's thin legs straining against the water's resistance, determination etched on his weathered face.

'What I am trying to say is that I get what you are saying, but I am not buying it,' Ishaan continued, his voice softening. 'Yes, he is threatening to make life difficult for us, that part I get, but unlike you, I see it as something natural. It comes from desperation rather than avarice. Which is why the word "dangerous", I cannot get past it. It is not right to even think that of Krishanu. Among us, he has always been the most harmless.'

The driver cleared his throat, adjusting the small Ganesh idol on the dashboard before pointing to a less congested road ahead.

'Sahab, I think we can take this side street. It might be faster.'

'Do that then.' Ranadeep said and then turned to Ishaan.

'Let me ask you something,' Ranadeep said, his voice barely rising above the rain's steady drumming. 'Why do you act in movies?'

'Money,' Ishaan answered simply.

'Maybe at first,' Ranadeep said, watching a child splash through puddles while his mother called after him. 'But you and I, we are past that point. Think about it, you have enough in the bank right now to go somewhere quiet and live well. Not like you do now. But better than we ever imagined growing up.'

The windshield fogged with their breath as the cold seeped in.

'Same for me, though I make far less than you. We could both walk away, to some small town, somewhere peaceful. It would be simpler. Would not that be worth it? To escape all the bullshit our work throws at us? To be, I don't know... happy?'

'What are you saying?' Ishaan asked.

'I am saying we do not work for money. We work for hope,' Ranadeep replied, finding a rhythm to his words. 'That is what drives us all. We are chasing futures that do not exist yet. For you, maybe it is making it in Hollywood. For me, it is having my picture hanging in Parliament after I am gone.'

He glanced out again through the window.

'Hope, it is the most powerful word in the world. It is why poor people vote for the interests of the rich. They think of themselves as "potentially rich". Not poor, just *not yet rich*. That is the trick of hope.'

The car inched forward while outside, Calcutta blurred into watercolours.

'Money and fame matter,' Ranadeep continued, 'but only as the currency of hope. I hope for more money. I hope for recognition. I hope for the corner office. I hope for the fancy car. And maybe most importantly, I hope for more time.'

His voice softened. 'We all know we will die, but why is a death sentence the most terrible punishment known to man? Because it tells you *exactly when*. It strips away the hope of uncertainty. That is what makes it unbearable.'

He looked at Ishaan.

'Krishanu is almost there, at death's door. His only hope left is to see Sunanda taken care of. He will do anything for that last hope. That is why I called him "dangerous". He knows I could fire his daughter after this documentary mess is over, or after he is gone.'

He paused.

'But hope does not need guarantees, just a chance, just a path forward, just a comforting hand as you ease into your sleep, for the night or forever.'

Ishaan rubbed his neck.

'So, you are saying if he loses his hope, he will make sure we lose ours, my deal with Netmovies and your ministership?'

'Wherever we go, we go together,' Ranadeep replied. 'All for one, one for all. That hope is what defined the Musketeers. We did not lift him up, at least that is what he feels, and so now he will take us both to where he is going. Down where time ends, and with it, hope.'

They stayed quiet, both the men, as the weight of the words sank in.

Then, Ranadeep added, almost to himself.

'You know what worries me most? I keep thinking about what Basab would say if he were here.'

He turned to Ishaan.

'But then I remember, he is already there, at that place.'

9

Kairos

Ranadeep propped pillows against the headboard, adjusting for the familiar ache in his lower back. This was not his childhood room, they had moved years ago, but the bed from his youth remained, now placed in the guest room of his parents' New Town apartment. The old frame let out its familiar creak. For a moment, he braced himself for his mother's voice calling from the next room: 'Rano, have you not slept yet?'

Only silence. Ma was deep under medication for early-stage heart failure. Baba too had turned in, one of those rare nights when his back pain and ulcer had called a truce.

Coming home used to feel simpler. Unlike most of his college friends, he had always looked forward to returning. He would drop a bag of unwashed clothes in the living room and curl up on this very bed, shedding adulthood like a coat. Home was a sanctuary. Here, Ma cooked, Baba ironed his shirts, and they all talked past midnight without ever mentioning a 'generation gap'. Even after marriage, even after he became a bureaucrat of consequence, it had remained that way. Until now.

His parents had grown old. Each visit brought a quiet jolt at how bent and brittle they had become. Yet somehow, they looked exactly as they had the last time. It was his memory that lied, still holding on to a younger image of them, a happier illusion.

His Nokia buzzed right on time.

Ranadeep unlocked the ancient device. A link and a line of text: 'same old key', ticking down from three hours. He copied the link to his iPhone, then opened a Telegram bot tied to a secure, password-protected file server. A code word, leftover from field operations, granted access. A single folder appeared:

Target.

Those years came rushing back. Five years buried under the title of 'special liaison to foreign office on deputation'. Five years tracking separatists and extremists across North America, men who thought distance offered immunity.

He had never pulled the trigger. That wasn't his role. He read patterns, made connections others missed, and decided who warranted action. RAW's chief had pulled him in directly. Unlike other officers fluent in spreadsheets and dinner diplomacy, Ranadeep had delivered. That record had caught Amritlal Patel's eye.

And among the many external assets he had worked with, she had been the best. An American with no ties to India. No ideology. Just precision and detachment.

Then came Operation Pavan. Bad intel. Worse planning. Her cover blown by a leak in the chain. She was left cornered, wounded, one step from capture and exposure of India's extrajudicial operations on foreign soil.

Ranadeep had made a choice. He broke protocol, risked his post, jeopardized international relations. But he pulled her out, called in debts from people who owed him nothing, arranged a backchannel evacuation meant only for diplomats.

She lived. Recovered. Went back to work.

'If you ever need anything,' she had told him, voice cool and dry. 'One time. One favour. Anything.'

He had waited ten years.

Now, for Basab, he had called it in.

The folder opened. Twenty-three JPEGs. Three videos. One PDF, the Pasadena Police Department case report.

Now, with the city asleep, he could examine the folder's contents. AirPods in ears, the screen's cold blue light painted his face in ghastly relief.

He tapped the first image file.

Ranadeep's second posting had been as an Additional District Magistrate in rural Bihar, in the middle of a gang war between rival mafia barons. No month passed without slaughter, twisted bodies, weeping survivors, buzzing flies, emaciated children staring past their fathers' corpses, young widows beating their heads against walls. As a junior, he worked on-site while seniors stayed behind desks, drinking and plotting transfers. He would shower repeatedly at home, trying to wash away death's stench that soap and water couldn't remove.

But no amount of violence had prepared him for this.

His stomach twisted.

Basab floated in his jacuzzi like a discarded doll, arms splayed in final, futile defence. Morning sunlight struck his face at a cruel angle, highlighting his hollow cheeks. Underwater lights still glowed, casting an eerie blue halo around the corpse.

What struck Ranadeep most wasn't the clinical evidence markers dotting the poolside. It was how wrong Basab looked in death, how utterly abandoned, how alone.

Tears streamed down Ranadeep's face unbidden.

First Pramila, now you. Both of you in water.

The connection, which he had made before, returned without warning, halting his tears and replacing them with something else, something he could not yet name.

The second image forced a sharp intake of breath.

Basab's face, captured in death's unflinching portrait. His eyes bulged from their sockets, bloodshot and staring at something beyond the camera's frame. His lips had pulled back in a rictus of terror, teeth bared as if his final moments had held something so horrifying that even death could not relax his features.

Basab, brilliant, composed, the boy with the smart smirk, whose eyes spoke volumes, now reduced to this mask of primal fear.

What did you see, old friend? What could frighten a mind like yours?

The clinical objectivity of the police photographer somehow made it worse. This was evidence, not grief. Pixels arranged in the shape of what had once been his friend.

The third image showed Basab's hands, claw-like in their post-mortem state. Nails broken, one torn completely away, blood dried around the cuticle. The forensic scale beside them only emphasized their desperate violence.

He had died a terrible death. He had drowned. *Like Pramila.*

Ranadeep blinked twice, trying to dislodge the thought.

One lesson the chief had drilled into him: never construct narratives from fragments. Never leap to conclusions and cherry-pick evidence. Stay open. Stay sceptical.

He told himself to obey.

Yet still, the fear, irrational, intrusive, swelled in his chest.

But how could he ignore it?

The next image showed a single crimson rose floating near the body. The rose had been photographed both in situ and after retrieval. Someone had placed a ruler beside it once removed from the water, showing its precise dimensions. A deep red, fully bloomed specimen, its petals unfurled as if freshly cut. The thorns remained intact on the stem. A supplemental note stated there was no explanation for how the rose had come to be there: the nearest rose bush was on the other side of the property, and there had been no wind that night.

There was something unnervingly deliberate about its placement.

As if it had been staged for an audience.

Without warning, the words of Pramila's poem surfaced in his mind:

Leaves creep along the wall,
Upon it the white moonlight glows,
As shadows twist and bend, they call,
'Who shall pick the crimson rose?'

With prickly thorns as sharp as knives,
And a colour of the deepest red,
Upon weeping petals it thrives,
Born to live among the dead.

He flipped through the remaining pictures, not of Basab, but of his house. Lavish and opulent compared to where he had grown up, yet cold and harsh, too empty, drained of life, no less unnerving than the dead body in the pool.

Somewhere in the silence of the night, two stray dogs began fighting.

The coroner's report came next. Ranadeep scrolled through it, his eyes trained to extract critical information from bureaucratic language. The document was comprehensive, ninety pages of clinical analysis, with detailed anatomical diagrams, toxicology tables and procedural notes. Certain phrases stood out with alarming clarity:

- Male, 48, of South Asian descent, 173 cm, 76 kg
- Blood alcohol content 0.11% (legally impaired)
- Pulmonary fluid analysis confirms death by drowning in chlorinated water matching pool sample
- Microscopic evidence of acute stress cardiomyopathy (Takotsubo syndrome), a condition linked to sudden emotional shock
- Ketamine detected in femoral blood at a modest concentration of 0.12 mg/L
- Expression fixed in a state of extreme terror, with facial muscles contracted beyond normal rigor
- Time of death estimated between 12.15 a.m. and 1.30 a.m. based on body temperature and livor mortis
- Hyoid bone intact, ruling out manual strangulation as primary cause of death
- Subdural haemorrhaging suggests significant physical trauma shortly before death
- No water in sinuses, suggesting victim was facing upward during drowning event

The report concluded with an unusually candid assessment:

'While drowning is the immediate cause of death, several highly unusual and potentially linked anomalies warrant immediate investigation. The extreme fear response evident in facial muscles, and the presence of acute stress cardiomyopathy, suggest a death involving an unknown terror stimulus. The physiological evidence indicates the subject experienced a fear response severe enough to potentially compromise cardiac function prior to the drowning event. The position of the body, alcohol and ketamine presence (none of them high), and missing situational evidence create a medical-forensic puzzle that defies conventional accidental drowning, suicide, or standard homicide classifications. Recommended: Priority investigation with psychological consultation and specialized forensic review.'

The most disturbing note came on page four, highlighted in the PDF with a yellow marker, presumably by his contact:

'Subject's facial muscles contracted in a manner consistent with sudden extreme fright. This physiological response is rarely seen to this degree outside of cases involving electrical shock or neurotoxins, neither of which are indicated by toxicology. Rigor mortis appears to have set in while subject was in a state of extreme physiological distress, resulting in unusual fixation. Cause unknown, though fear response suggests subject perceived a threat immediately before death. Of special note: this expression mirrors descriptions in medical literature of thanatophobia-induced cardiac arrest, but with survival long enough for drowning to occur. In layman's terms, subject appears to have experienced terror sufficient to potentially stop the heart yet remained conscious long enough to drown.

'Cardiac examination presents a complex timeline question: the subject's heart shows clear evidence of stress-induced cardiomyopathy, a condition where extreme emotional distress triggers heart dysfunction. However, the presence of water in the lungs indicates the subject was alive when submerged. This creates two possible scenarios: 1) Subject experienced extreme fear triggering partial cardiac compromise, then drowned while in weakened state, or 2) Subject drowned first, with final cardiac arrest occurring during terminal phase of drowning. The extensive fear response evident in facial musculature suggests scenario 1 is more probable, pointing to a terrifying stimulus preceding the drowning event. The nature of this stimulus remains unidentified.'

'In thirty-two years of forensic psychology, I have never seen physiological evidence of fear this extreme in an otherwise healthy adult.'

Ranadeep looked up medical terms he did not understand. 'Thanatophobia-induced' meant 'caused by fear of death' and 'Takotsubo syndrome' was 'a sudden weakness in the heart muscle triggered by extreme stress'.

He reviewed the remaining images, notes taken by officers at the scene. Nothing sensational, except that the security cameras facing the driveway had captured only Basab on the night of his death. The house's perimeter security had been armed, and no alarms triggered. There were no security cameras covering his pool. The officers had reviewed security footage from neighbouring properties and found no unaccounted vehicles parked near the house.

Something had terrified his friend to death. Something that left no trace, triggered no alarms, and made him drown in his own jacuzzi. Something that delicately placed a rose beside his corpse.

Outside, the stray dogs had fallen silent, as if they too were listening for sounds that shouldn't be there.

There was a text file, he noticed now, a README.txt file, and he opened it.

'Police notes, crime-scene photos, forensic report, divorce papers, full transcripts of pre-divorce arbitration proceedings between Basab and Sandra Banerjee, video of Basab Banerjee's Q&A during arbitration (could not access Sandra Banerjee's despite my efforts, sorry).'

Ranadeep's finger hovered over the folder labelled 'DIVORCE'. A boundary existed here that felt wrong to cross. Basab's death was one thing, a criminal investigation, a matter of public record despite its horrors. But this was different. These were private moments, the dissolution of something intimate. The exposure of wounds that Basab had never shared with him.

He remembered how Basab would close his notebook whenever anyone walked past, how he would turn away when eating to hide his mouth, the way he would share the least of his life. Privacy had been Basab's sanctuary.

And yet.

The rose. The bruising. The fear frozen on his friend's dead face.

Something had changed in Basab's life before his death. Something had broken. The divorce might explain the ketamine in his system, the alcohol level, for a boy who never touched a drop, who they always teased with, 'Shall we get you a glass of milk?'

Forgive me, old friend.

He clicked on the first video file.

The timestamp indicated this was recorded three months ago. The camera angle showed a conference room with the bland, inoffensive décor of a law firm. Basab sat alone at one end of a polished table, wearing a button-down shirt that looked too big for him. His hair was unwashed, his posture defensive. Despite the video's resolution, Ranadeep could see the shadows beneath his eyes, the slight tremor in his hands as he reached for a water glass.

A female voice spoke from off-camera.

'Dr Banerjee, can you please state your name and occupation for the record?'

'Basab Banerjee, Dr Basab Banerjee, Professor of theoretical physics at the California Institute of Technology.' His voice was flat, clinical, but his fingers tapped against the table in that familiar rhythm Ranadeep remembered from exam days.

'And you understand why we are here today?'

'We are finalizing the terms of my divorce from Sandra.'

Another voice, male this time, with the practised calm of someone accustomed to managing emotional situations. 'Dr Banerjee, the terms we have outlined are, frankly, extremely generous given the circumstances. Your wife is not pursuing criminal charges. You retain the Pasadena residence. There are no ongoing alimony obligations. However, before we finalize, Ms Banerjee requires your acknowledgement of the actions that led us here.'

Basab's eyes narrowed, that familiar look whenever anyone challenged a calculation he had made.

'I have already acknowledged them.'

The male voice continued, 'For the record, Dr Banerjee. We need explicit acknowledgement that you accessed Ms Banerjee's trust fund without authorization and diverted approximately eight million dollars to fund your private venture, Kairos.'

'It was not "unauthorized". We are married. It is our money.'

'The Carrington Trust was established prior to your marriage, Dr Banerjee. It remains Ms Banerjee's separate property under California law. You bypassed multiple security measures to access and transfer these funds.'

Basab's expression hardened. 'The security was elementary. Anyone with basic understanding of...'

'That is not the point, Dr Banerjee,' the female voice interrupted. 'The ease with which you committed the offence does not mitigate its criminality.'

Basab leaned forward. For a moment, Ranadeep saw the boy he remembered, the one who never accepted being wrong.

'Look, the algorithm was perfect. I had validated it, following the best mathematical practice. I had tested it with smaller amounts, and the gains had been astronomical. Kairos could analyse market patterns no human could detect, leverage quantum solutions to trading problems that conventional predictive AI could not touch. I was creating a system that would have made us billions.'

'And instead, you lost sixty per cent of your wife's inheritance in a single day.' The male voice was deliberately calm, which seemed to infuriate Basab further.

'Because of government interference! An external variable no model could predict.' Basab's hand slammed against the table. 'The day I executed the main strategy, that idiot Treasury secretary announced cryptocurrency regulations. The market tanked before the algorithm could adjust.'

'Dr Banerjee,' the female voice said, 'you do understand that what you have described is criminal fraud? That under normal circumstances you would be facing federal charges?'

Basab waved dismissively. 'It wasn't fraud. It was an investment.'

'An investment requires consent, Dr Banerjee.'

'Sandra wouldn't have understood. Her degree is in art history. She doesn't grasp computational finance.'

'So, you decided for her?'

'Yes!' Basab's eyes lit with a fervour Ranadeep recognized. The same look he would use to explain organic chemistry theory to them on the school roof. 'The same way you do not explain calculus to children. You make decisions in their best interest because they lack the framework to comprehend. If I had succeeded, which I would have, had I been given time to recover the capital lost, Sandra would have thanked me.'

Basab leaned forward suddenly, his demeanour changing. 'But I need to discuss the custody arrangement. These terms. They are unacceptable. I am their father.'

The male voice replied, measured but firm. 'Ms Banerjee has offered visitation at her discretion. Given the circumstances…'

'At her discretion?' Basab's voice cracked. For the first time, raw emotion broke through his academic detachment. 'They are my children too. I have a right…'

'You had rights, Dr Banerjee,' the female attorney cut in, 'which you essentially lost when you stole their college funds along with their mother's inheritance.'

The camera captured Basab's stunned silence.

'The twins' trust accounts were accessed as well?' The male voice asked, seemingly for clarification.

'Yes. While Ms Banerjee has restored those funds from her remaining assets, that fact remains relevant to custody considerations.'

Basab's face drained of colour. 'I would have replaced it. Multiplied it.'

'Ms Banerjee is being extremely generous,' the male attorney continued. 'She is allowing you to see the twins, but it will be entirely at her prerogative. You get nothing guaranteed legally. Most judges would grant her request for sole legal and physical custody, given the circumstances you yourself have accepted.'

'But the twins…' Basab's voice was barely above a whisper now.

'They need stability, Dr Banerjee. Predictability. Something your recent actions have demonstrated you cannot provide. You have stolen from your children; there is no other way to put it.'

Ranadeep watched as his friend, the most logical, rational person he had ever known, struggled to process this information.

The great Genius, confronted with a problem he could not solve with equations or algorithms: the human cost of betrayal.

'Let me be absolutely clear.' The male voice had lost its practised calm. 'You stole eight million dollars, lost nearly five million of it, and your defence is that your wife, a woman with multiple degrees, who sits on museum boards, who managed her own finances successfully for years before meeting you, was too stupid to understand your brilliance?'

'Not stupid; I never used that word.' Basab countered, as if the distinction mattered.

'Unprepared. Lacking specialized knowledge. Like most people.'

Ranadeep winced. Even through the screen, he could feel the collective discomfort in that conference room. The childish arrogance, that had been an endearing quality of his once upon a time, seemed to hang hollow, leaving Basab looking like an arrogant man out of touch with reality.

The questioning continued, with Basab growing more defensive, more condescending. He kept returning to the same themes: the algorithm's perfection, the government's interference, the inevitability of his success had he been given more time. Never once did he acknowledge the violation of trust, the betrayal of his marriage vows.

Ranadeep paused the video, suddenly exhausted. There was more, three hours more, according to the file's duration. But he had seen enough to understand.

This was not the Basab he thought he knew. Or perhaps it was, with the qualities that had made him brilliant as a boy – certainty, focus, uncompromising belief in his own intellect – curdled into something toxic with age.

He scrolled through the transcript, looking for anything that might connect to the strange circumstances of Basab's death. Most of it were variations on the same theme: Basab's refusal to acknowledge wrongdoing beyond a technical error in his algorithm's predictive capacity.

Then, near the end, a passage caught his eye:

ATTORNEY WILSON: Dr Banerjee, throughout these proceedings, you have characterized yourself as someone who can solve any problem. Yet you failed to predict a major market event that financial analysts had been discussing for months. Do you see the contradiction?

BANERJEE: There is no contradiction. I solve problems every day that would break most minds. I have published papers that changed how we understand the universe. One setback does not erase that.

ATTORNEY WILSON: Ms Banerjee describes a pattern of you taking similar actions throughout your marriage, making unilateral decisions because you believed yourself smarter than everyone else, incapable of error. Would you agree with that characterization?

BANERJEE: [No verbal response]

ATTORNEY WILSON: Dr Banerjee?

BANERJEE: I am thinking.

ATTORNEY WILSON: About whether you agree?

BANERJEE: No. I am thinking about your phrasing. 'Incapable of error.' I have never claimed that. I have only claimed that I can solve any problem if given enough time. The difference is subtle but important.

ATTORNEY WILSON: And you do not consider your current situation – losing your wife, your family, potentially your reputation – a problem you failed to solve?

BANERJEE: [Extended pause] I did not anticipate this outcome.
ATTORNEY WILSON: That seems to be a recurring theme, Dr Banerjee.

The next video file showed Basab alone in the conference room. The camera was still recording, but the attorneys had left. He sat motionless for almost two minutes, staring at nothing. Then, abruptly, he buried his face in his hands.

Ranadeep had never seen Basab cry, not when he nearly died on the cricket field, not when the geography teacher had humiliated him in class for wearing a shirt with stains. Yet here he was, shoulders heaving, making ugly, desperate sounds that seemed torn from somewhere deep. No one was there to witness it. No one except the camera he had likely forgotten was running, and now, Ranadeep.

He ran his fingers across the screen, as if he could reach through it, across space and time, to wipe away the tears, to embrace his old friend, to tell him that things would be all right again.

And then Basab looked up.

His face held something Ranadeep had never seen there before: defeat.

Pure, absolute defeat. His lips moved, forming words too quiet for the microphone to catch.

Ranadeep leaned closer, tried to read his mouth. He rewound the footage, slowed it down. Tried again. But the words remained shadows on a shattered face.

Whatever Basab had whispered to himself in that empty room, it was a burden he had carried alone into the night he died, a night when something had terrified him beyond reason, something that left a rose floating beside his corpse.

He closed the video, feeling like an intruder in his friend's private hell.

Whatever had happened to Basab in that pool, the seeds of it might have been planted here, in the ruins of his marriage, in the collapse of the certainty that had defined him since boyhood.

Genius brought low.

The rose. The water. The impossible hand span on his throat.

He thought again of Pramila's poem. *'Who shall pick the crimson rose?'*

Was there a connection, the rose, the documentary, Basab's unnatural death, or was his shaken mind manufacturing patterns where none existed?

The chief would caution him against such leaps. So did the rationalist within him.

And yet, the memory of Basab's corpse and of him alive, crying, refused to leave him, as he closed his eyes. He could not decide which of them was more terrifying.

And then, there was that other thing.

The truth Ranadeep had kept locked away in his mind, as securely as he kept the Nokia phone and Pramila's poem in that office safe, to be brought out and considered in times of emergencies.

Like now.

The brilliant, incorruptible Basab had lied before, long before he had touched his wife's trust fund.

He had lied about Brajendra. Lied to the police. Committed perjury. Sent an innocent man to his death.

Back then, he had been clever enough not to be caught. His reputation for honesty had made the lie all the more convincing. But time had eroded his brilliance, just as it had eroded all of them. Or perhaps his luck had simply run out.

The stray dogs began barking again outside, their voices rising into a frenzy that matched the racing of his heart.

10
The First Episode

Forty thousand feet above the Arabian Sea, the first-class cabin of Emirates flight EK501 hummed with silence. Ishaan sat alone in the opulent pod, the curved walls giving him the illusion of solitude. The champagne in his crystal flute had gone flat, tiny bubbles clinging to the sides like dying stars.

His phone vibrated against the lacquered table.

Anand's name flashed on the screen, the third call in thirty minutes. Ishaan let it ring, watching until it stopped. Five seconds later, a message appeared.

They are dropping it tonight. My source at the production company confirmed. First episode goes live at midnight IST.

Ishaan took a long swallow of champagne. Through the oval window, darkness stretched unbroken. The sensation of suspension, of being nowhere at all, usually comforted him on these flights. Tonight, it felt like purgatory.

He typed back: *What is in it?*

The three dots appeared immediately. Anand must have been clutching his phone, waiting.

Only what my source is telling, sir. Very bad angle on you, sir, and your father also. Too much focus on your 'controlling behaviour'. Making you look like guilty man who escaped because of Papa-ji's money and setting.

Ishaan closed his eyes as the flight attendant approached. She wore the distinct Emirates uniform with its crisp beige cloak and red pillbox hat, make-up perfect, despite the late hour.

'Would you like me to take that, sir?'

Ishaan nodded, handing her the empty glass. 'Another, please.'

She hesitated. 'Perhaps some water as well?'

He looked up, making eye contact. The moment stretched, her professional smile faltering as she took in his bloodshot eyes, the tremor in his hand.

'Just the champagne.'

When she left, Ishaan turned back to his phone. Another message was waiting for him.

They interviewed that Pramila girl's parents. And R.K. Roy, the inspector who first investigated. He is saying your father purchased the senior officers. Always he was thinking you were guilty.

What about Krishanu? Ishaan typed, his thumb hovering over the send button.

'Some bits here and there. My source is telling producers will get more out of him in later episodes only. Maximum public shock they are wanting.

Ishaan set the phone down as the flight attendant returned with a fresh glass. The cabin lights dimmed, casting most passengers into shadow. In the soft glow of his reading lamp, Ishaan caught his reflection in the window.

The face staring back looked like a stranger's, cheekbones too sharp, skin too tight across the forehead, eyes hollow from the comedown. He barely recognized himself.

His phone buzzed again.

Also, sir, they do not record all episodes together and release. They put out episode, then public is giving tips and stories, then they make next episode from what people are sending. Like those crime shows where audience is solving the case only.

Ishaan's stomach clenched. *So after the first episode drops, they will wait for the public reaction before filming the next?*

Yes, sir, exactly that only. They want public to give new dirt on you. Then they will use footage they already have, the ones they don't show in first episode, to create more drama. It is reality show, in dress of documentary.

Then more messages. *Sir, just now my friend at Democracy TV was calling. They are doing big show after episode comes: 'Breaking down the Ishaan Chatterjee allegations.' Full panel they are bringing, those criminal mind doctors, retired judge types, filmi journalists. Prime time slot, sir. Very bad situation. Someone has already leaked the contents of the show to the press in advance.*

Ishaan stared through the window at the vast Arabian darkness. Truth had always been pliable in his world. Press releases crafted to hide affairs. Leaked videos as part of film promotions. Rumours planted about rival actors. There was a time early in his career when the editor of a major newspaper came to his house, threatening to go public with an incident involving him unless he agreed to be the compère at their awards show.

But this was different. This was about a dead girl, a bucket of water and thirty years of running.

There would be no coming back.

The flight attendant's voice startled him.

'Would you like dinner now, Mr Chatterjee? The chef has prepared your special meal.'

Ishaan shook his head. 'Not hungry.'

She nodded, withdrawing into the dim cabin.

His mind drifted to the conversation with Ranadeep and their visit to Krishanu's home. Ranadeep's cold calculations. Krishanu's bitter accusations.

Who would stand with him? Who would turn?

His fingers trembled as he navigated to YouTube. The *Hidden Secrets* channel appeared immediately in his search results.

He connected his AirPods, adjusted the screen, and waited, ordering another champagne when the attendant passed.

The documentary began to play. Ishaan found himself jabbing at the timeline, impatient through the opening sequence, letting sections play before skipping ahead whenever anything struck too close to home.

A montage of India's contradictions filled the screen, gleaming tech hubs beside sprawling slums, ancient temples alongside modern skyscrapers. The female narrator's voice carried a slight British accent.

'India, the world's largest democracy, a land where tradition and modernity collide daily. In the early 1990s, as economic liberalization transformed the nation, old power structures remained firmly entrenched. Nowhere was this more evident than in Kolkata, formerly Calcutta, once the jewel of British India.'

Ishaan grimaced as the documentary cut to political rallies from the era, Communist flags waving beside images of violent street protests.

'Against this backdrop of political volatility and rigid social hierarchies, our story unfolds. A tale that encapsulates India's most pressing contradictions: wealth disparity, gender politics, corruption, and celebrity culture.'

'Ah, god damn,' Ishaan muttered, 'this is more cliché than the worst of what I have done.'

'In 1994, Pramila Chatterjee was found drowned in her home in Calcutta, India. Her head submerged in a bucket of water, bruises around her neck. The case seemed solved when her neighbour, Brajendra Das, was arrested and later died in custody. But thirty years later, questions remain.'

The title card appeared: HIDDEN SECRETS: THE MURDER OF THE ROSE.

Ishaan's jaw tightened as the opening featured old newspaper clippings, including one with his teenage face. It was the only one from that era that had captured him on camera. *Within the hour, this will be everywhere, dug up, like everything else.*

The camera cut to a dimly lit interview room, where a grey-haired man with thick glasses spoke directly to the camera.

'The social dynamics of 1990s Calcutta were unique,' the academic explained, extremely conscious of the camera. 'The city operated under unofficial power structures. Certain people, through connections to politics, business and sometimes criminal elements, existed above the law. In fact, they were the law, the apparatchiks of the ruling party.'

Ishaan unclenched his fist, realizing he had been digging his nails into his palm. On screen, the documentary cut to black-and-white photographs of his father, younger, standing beside politicians whose names might not hold any significance to the generation of today, but once held weight in Bengal's power circles.

'Siddhartha Chatterjee was one such figure,' the academic continued. 'Not a politician himself, officially a film producer, but a man whose influence extended into every corner of the city's power machinery.'

Ishaan drained his champagne. The documentary shifted to a residential street, his old neighbourhood, though barely recognizable now. The camera panned slowly to a modern apartment building.

'Here once stood the home of Pramila Chatterjee,' the narrator explained. 'In a modest section of Calcutta where middle-class families lived in cramped quarters. While just a few streets away stood the lavish bungalow of the primary suspect in her murder, Ishaan Chatterjee, son of Siddhartha, and the boyfriend of Pramila Chatterjee.'

The screen split to show a recent promotional photo of Ishaan at a film premiere alongside his teenage yearbook picture.

'Now one of India's most recognized film stars, Ishaan Chatterjee, was then a privileged teenager with a reputation for volatility.'

The scene shifted to an elderly couple sitting on a worn floral sofa. The woman's eyes were cloudy with age, but the hardness in them was unmistakable. Pramila's mother, Ishaan recognized her immediately. She had never liked him.

'We knew it was Ishaan. We knew it the moment we discovered her body, face down in that big nailed-down bucket,' she said, her Bengali accent thick beneath the English subtitles. 'Who else could it be? Our daughter feared him. He controlled everything: where she went, who she spoke to, what she wore.'

Her husband nodded, his thin hand covering hers. 'When she tried to break free, to become her own person, he could not accept it.'

The documentary cut to photographs of Pramila, school portraits, family pictures and then the magazine cover that had started everything. The glossy image filled the screen: Pramila with bare shoulders, eyes challenging the camera, a serene confidence in her smile.

'This photoshoot for the *Woman's World* magazine apparently triggered a violent confrontation,' the narrator explained. 'According to multiple witnesses, Ishaan Chatterjee physically assaulted Pramila in her own home after seeing these images.'

'I blame myself. I was afraid of his father.' Pramila's father said, 'Everyone was. When Ishaan came to our house that day and struck my daughter, I did nothing. I said nothing. Well, I did, actually.' The man's eyes filled with tears. 'I hit her too, for shaming us and besmirching the family name. How can I walk in the streets? What will people say? That is what went through my mind when I slapped her, my little flower of a daughter. But when Ishaan killed her, that monster, those same people I was worried would say things about my daughter, said nothing. They looked away.'

As the man broke down into tears, his wife shook her head.

'They were all in on it. The police were in Siddhartha Chatterjee's pockets. There was never going to be any justice. If there is anything I blame myself for, it was leaving Pramila alone in our house. We could have taken her along with us, but she did not want to come. She said she wanted to meet Ishaan and end it for good, and it never once occurred to me, not even once, that he would not let it end, unless he ended it himself.'

A woman appeared on screen. 'Shibarati Mukherjee: friend of Pramila Chatterjee' appeared in the text below her.

Ishaan squinted. He had never heard of her. Maybe he had known her by her nickname, but the face didn't register.

'I went to school with Pramila. She was my best friend; we shared every secret that girls do.'

'Ishaan was, of course, every girl's dream even then.' Shibarati continued. 'Good-looking. Charming. Confident. Good in sports. Would win all dancing competitions in school fests. He loved Pramila – chocolates, roses and Archies cards for every occasion. Yes, that is what we thought. He loved her. What I didn't know was…' She stopped, eyes flicking off-camera for a fraction of a second, 'that, even then, he was a good actor.'

Whoever she was, that last line was too scripted, too coached, to be something she came up with.

'Ishaan was possessive, madly possessive, in a way we didn't question back then,' she said. 'If she talked to other boys, he would twist her arm later. If she wore something he disapproved of, he would shout until she changed. We somehow believed that's how men showed love, through jealousy, through control, and that women were just people men owned.' She nodded sadly at the camera, 'When he realized she was going to leave him, he decided to ensure that no one else would have her.'

The documentary cut to a montage of clips from Hindi movies of the 90s with lyrics overlaid: 'If I do not have you, no one else will' and 'You may say "yes", you may say "no", but you are mine.'

'Bollywood, India's dominant film industry, has long been criticized for normalizing controlling behaviour as romance,' the narrator explained. 'Ishaan Chatterjee's own career offers a particularly troubling case study.'

The clips transitioned from the 90s classics to his own hit movies: scenes of him grabbing actresses by their wrists, yanking them close; finding an actress had gone out wearing a skirt, setting fire to all her Western clothes until she later dances with him in a sari. Ishaan skipped through scenes he had seen countless times before, till he landed on an interview he had given to the BBC years ago, in 2008, one he thought had been lost to time.

'Indian women say no when they mean yes.' A much younger Ishaan says with a knowing smile, 'This is how it works in our culture, madam. Western feminism doesn't understand Indian relationships. Indian women expect to be pursued. They don't want to appear to be "easy". They want to see how much the man will do for them, how far he will go. The value of anything is how much you desire it. It is because the West has forgotten all of this that you see divorce rates as they are; you have killed romance and replaced it with domestic partnerships.'

A young female film critic appeared, one Ishaan knew always gave his movies 'one star' without fail. Her expression was severe.

'For decades, we have questioned whether Bollywood merely reflects Indian patriarchy or actively shapes it. The truth is both. Stars like Ishaan Chatterjee don't just perform toxic masculinity on screen. They embody it in their personal lives, creating a dangerous feedback loop.'

'As Bollywood seeks global partnerships and international legitimacy,' the narrator continued, 'the industry faces increasing scrutiny over the values it exports. Western studios now conducting background checks on potential collaborators might find Ishaan Chatterjee's history particularly concerning.'

The screen displayed recent headlines about Ishaan's rumoured deal with an American streaming service.

'The patterns of behaviour displayed in Chatterjee's roles don't just echo disturbing accounts of his teenage relationship with Pramila,' the narrator intoned. 'They represent the very attitudes that global entertainment companies now claim to reject.'

Ishaan's stomach dropped. They knew about the Netmovies deal.

This wasn't about a cold case. There was no pretence of balanced inquiry. No neutral reconstruction. This was war, packaged in the guise of documentary. And the fact that they had front-loaded all of it, his worst moments, the most incriminating visuals, in the first half of episode one, the part that would have the most viewership, told him what he already suspected.

His enemies were behind this.

And he was certain he knew exactly who.

Bunty Grewal. The pig had undercut him in two roles that he wanted, cutting his remuneration in half to squeeze out Ishaan. His fan club was the one that specialized in dank memes on him, and that stand-up comic he had punched, whose name he could not remember, had Bunty Grewal as a regular on his shitty podcast.

Okay, he told himself, *two can play this game. Let me get back to Mumbai. I will take a flamethrower to your two-hit career. I will make you regret the day you decided to bankroll this hit job on me and my dad.*

He pressed his fist against his mouth, tasting blood where he had bitten the inside of his cheek. He swiped at the screen, skipping through the talking heads until he stopped suddenly.

'Ishaan ran with three of us,' Krishanu said, his skeletal fingers tracing patterns on the armrest. 'The Musketeers, they called us.'

The camera pushed in on his hollowed face, capturing the fever-bright intensity in his sunken eyes.

'I remember when it happened. Same school, same class. This teacher caught Ishaan cheating and dragged him to the front. Slapped him hard across the face.' Krishanu's lips twisted into a smile. 'Now, we all got beaten back then. Rulers across knuckles, ears twisted till they burned. Usually deserved it too.'

He leaned forward, voice dropping. 'But Ishaan? He slapped the teacher back. One clean shot. The man's glasses flew across the room and cracked against the blackboard.'

The interviewer murmured something off-camera.

'Expulsion? Oh yes. The entire staff marched into the principal's office, threatened to walk out unless Ishaan was gone by morning.' Krishanu's laugh dissolved into a wet cough. 'A week later, Siddhartha Chatterjee donated enough money to renovate an entire wing. Never another word about it.'

He looked directly into the camera, eyes glittering with what might have been admiration. 'When Ishaan came home that day, we were all there. His father just laughed. "Next time you beat someone up," he said, "make sure I don't have to pay this much." That was Uncle, always had our backs. The kind of man who could fix anything. We all wished our fathers were like him.'

Krishanu's trembling hand rose. 'We were untouchable, understand? Nobody dared cross us. When we played cricket in tournaments, local community tournaments, the umpires knew better than to cheat against us. People crossed the street when they saw us coming. Everyone knew who we were, Ishaan Chatterjee's friends.'

He fell silent, gaze drifting toward the window. 'But if you think Ishaan was Ishaan just because of his father, you would be wrong. What really gave him power was being Pramila's boyfriend.'

The screen filled with faded photographs: a teenage girl with knowing eyes and a half-smile that suggested secrets kept.

'Pramila outshone him. She turned heads without trying. Everyone knew she was destined for movies someday.' Krishanu's voice softened. 'Boys didn't have girlfriends back then. But Ishaan did. Like owning a genuine Sunridges bat or having a computer at home, a status symbol. And not just any girl. Pramila. She elevated him in our eyes. "There goes Ishaan, Pramila's boyfriend." Mind you, Ishaan was something himself, a good-looking guy with a body, but there were others like him. But, Pramila, there was no one like her.'

The interviewer's voice cut in softly. 'Was there violence in their relationship?'

Krishanu's expression shifted, becoming carefully neutral. He paused, as if choosing his words with great care. 'Ishaan was…protective of her. Very protective. But that is how it was back then. Different times.'

'Some have described his behaviour as controlling.'

'People love to judge the past by today's standards.' Krishanu shook his head slowly.

'Do you think Ishaan was capable of what he was accused of?'

Krishanu's face went completely still, the silence stretching for several uncomfortable seconds.

'I think,' he finally said, his eyes never leaving the camera, 'that question can never be truly answered. We can never say with certainty what anyone, even ourselves, is capable of. When pushed to desperation, when people have nothing to lose, or worse, everything to lose, they are capable of the unthinkable.'

Ishaan paused the video. Krishanu was speaking to him and Ranadeep through the camera, warning them that if his demands were not met, then yes, he would do the 'unthinkable' in a subsequent episode.

Ranadeep was right. These were not random ramblings of a terminal patient, but the calculated moves of old Doggie Dum Dum, angry at being abandoned and left to die. He was baiting the hook, waiting for Ishaan to bite.

There was more of Krishanu, a lot of him, but Ishaan skipped forward, stopping when Inspector Roy's face filled the screen, older now but with the same intense gaze Ishaan remembered from those interrogation rooms.

'From day one, the investigation was compromised,' Roy said firmly. 'My senior officer, Inspector Bhattacharya, I sometimes wondered whether he was investigating Ishaan Chatterjee or acting as his lawyer.'

The interviewer asked, 'Can you give specific examples of interference in the investigation?'

Roy's face hardened. 'In a case like this, standard procedure was to bring the suspect to the station. Depending on who they were and the severity of the crime, we would make them sweat in a room without a fan, keep them waiting for hours, perhaps a few slaps across the face. And if that failed...' his voice dropped '...well, yes, we were allowed to use the "third degree". But for Ishaan Chatterjee? We had to go to his house like supplicants to record his testimony, and only when his father permitted it.'

He leaned forward, hands clasped together. 'Throughout the questioning, Ishaan's father hovered, coaching his answers. Two of Calcutta's highest-paid lawyers flanked him. You must understand, this was 1994 India, not America. For a murder this stomach-churning, a girl drowned in her own bathroom, lawyers wouldn't even enter the picture. The boy would have been tied to a pole and beaten until he confessed. That's what Ishaan Chatterjee deserved.' He paused. 'I can say that now that I am no longer on the force.'

'And your superior allowed this special treatment?'

'He actively enforced it.' Roy's face flushed with decades-old anger. 'Once, I merely raised my voice at the boy. It was my second murder case, and I knew very well which way the toast was buttered, and I had been very careful. But, once, yes, I lost my composure, just for a moment. For that, Inspector Bhattacharya dragged me outside. Berated me for twenty minutes. Called me unprofessional, threatened traffic duty.'

Roy's eyes narrowed. 'The worst came when I suggested we validate Ishaan's flimsy alibi, so thin a gentle breeze would shred it. Right there, in front of everyone, Siddhartha Chatterjee looked at me and asked, "What were you doing on the night of the murder, Inspector Roy?" Then, with a smile, he added, "I would love to ask around about you. Maybe visit your house; your son's Montessori is on Gurusaday Avenue, isn't it?"'

'You felt he was threatening your family?'

'It was not subtle.' Roy shook his head. 'The intimidation was creative. The next day, a brand-new Ambassador car was parked outside my house. Just sitting there. When my wife ventured out to the market, it followed. When my son went to school, it trailed his bus.'

He shifted uncomfortably. 'Twice, I returned home to find my front door unlocked. Nothing stolen or disturbed. Just… open. My desk at the station would be rearranged, pencils moved, papers straightened. Small things, impossible to report, but the message was clear: we can reach you anytime.'

'Why do you think Inspector Bhattacharya was protecting the Chatterjees?'

'Siddhartha Chatterjee's influence reached the very top. And I mean, the very top.' Roy's mouth tightened. 'A month later, Inspector Bhattacharya moved into a new house in Salt Lake. You do the math.'

'And what happened to you?'

Roy smiled bitterly. 'Pramila's pictures and other belongings were "conveniently" discovered at Brajendra Das's house, and guess who led the raid? Yes, Inspector Bhattacharya himself. The case against Ishaan crumbled. Three months later, I was handed transfer orders. They claimed I had launched a personal crusade against Siddhartha Chatterjee's son. The party office had deemed me "ideologically suspect".'

Roy looked down, holding his wrist.

'So, I spent the next few years near the Bangladesh border, investigating bicycle thefts and disputes over which farmer's goat had eaten which farmer's bush.'

He waved further thoughts away.

'But forget about me. Basab Banerjee was the truly fascinating figure. The boy whose testimony freed Ishaan was the real piece of work.'

'Why would you say that?'

'First, he was Ishaan's best friend. In any other country, his testimony would have been thrown out. But here, the whole case against Brajendra hinged on Basab saying he saw the man leave Pramila Chatterjee's side gate, acting strangely. Second, the boy's family was dirt-poor. His father had been unemployed for years, with a houseful of sisters and daughters to feed. I would wager every paisa I have earned that Siddhartha paid handsomely for that testimony.'

'The boy went to America to study. Imagine that, America. A kid whose father once begged neighbours for grocery money.'

Roy's voice dropped.

'But that is not why I called him a piece of work. He lied. From the first word to the last. And yet, he was brilliant. Cold. I have interrogated hardened criminals and not seen anyone stay this calm. Every time I thought I had him, he slipped away. Needless to say, Bhattacharya was always there to bail him out. When Ishaan lied, you could see it all over his face. But this boy…' Roy leaned back, voice low, '… his eyes never wavered.'

He gave a short, bitter laugh.

'They called him Genius, and I agree. 1986. It was like being the Belgian defence to a Maradona in his prime; the boy is feinting, going left while looking to the right, and every time I try to trip him, he seems to gather even more momentum, dribbling the ball away. Feinting left while looking right, slipping past every question like a ghost. The more I tried to trip him, the faster he moved.'

He paused, gaze unfocused now.

'You know how you spot a liar? The eyes. They move. They are windows to the soul. But that boy, Basab Banerjee, I am not sure he even had one.'

'So you are claiming the evidence was planted by the police?'

'Not the first time, not the last. But I am claiming something worse.'

A long silence followed.

'I have thought about this for years. And I think Basab did see something, just not on the day of the murder. He had seen that old man enter Pramila's house. Knew the rumours: lonely, perverse, a hoarder. And he knew exactly what the man was stealing. So, he built the perfect trap. Not with lies, but with half-truths.'

Roy looked up, eyes burning.

'And nothing is more dangerous than a truth that points in the wrong direction.'

He skipped past a segment analysing the autopsy report, stopping when he saw photographs of Brajendra Das filling the screen.

The scene shifted to a professional office. The light fell softly on familiar features, Basab, sitting upright in an office chair, his expression guarded.

'Dr Basab Banerjee, now a respected physicist at Caltech, was another of "The Musketeers",' the narrator explained. 'His testimony about seeing Brajendra Das behaving suspiciously on the night of the murder became the cornerstone of the prosecution's case.'

Tears welled in Ishaan's eyes as he watched his dead friend defending him, throughout, despite the persistent sceptical questioning. Basab looked tired, stressed, nothing like the brilliant boy Ishaan remembered. But still loyal, still standing by him, even as his own life was falling apart, still sure of his original testimony.

There he was, from the great beyond, 'This is the reality TV conundrum, and like the Grand Unified Theory conundrum, there seems to be no solution to it. All I will say is that I have said what I had to say, now, as I did thirty years ago. And to use Walter Cronkite's closing lines: "And that's the way it is."'

The documentary cut to text on a black screen: 'Dr Basab Banerjee was found dead in his home swimming pool hours after this interview. His death was ruled accidental drowning.'

The narrator's voice returned. 'As we continue our investigation into Pramila Chatterjee's murder, we invite viewers with information about the case to contact us. What really happened that night in 1994? Who killed the Rose of Calcutta? And is her killer still walking free?'

The *Hidden Secrets* logo appeared, accompanied by a helpline number and website.

Ishaan stared at the blank screen, tears streaming down his face. A sob threatened to escape his throat, but he swallowed it back. The memory of Basab, defending him until the very end, was unbearable. And now he was gone, drowned like Pramila.

The cabin lights dimmed further as the other passengers settled for the night. In the cocoon of his private pod, Ishaan pulled out the small leather case from his jacket pocket. He needed a line, he desperately needed one, but he knew better than to bring powder to Dubai. Instead, he reached inside to bring out the tablets, all legally procured under prescription, and he needed a few now to steady himself.

This will break social media. And most likely, his career.

As he bent forward, he caught movement in his peripheral vision. Looking up, he saw a flight attendant he had not noticed before standing in the aisle. Not the one who had served him earlier, this one was younger, her uniform somehow different.

'Sir,' she said, 'would you like some water?'

Her voice seemed to echo strangely in the quiet cabin. As she stepped closer, light caught her face.

Ishaan's heart hammered against his ribs.

The flight attendant smiled, the familiar tilt of lips, one he had not seen in thirty years.

'You look like you have seen a ghost, Ishu,' she said.

She held out a glass of water, her fingers impossibly pale against the crystal. A waft of familiar scent reached him, not the Emirates perfume but something else. Strawberry shampoo. The cheap kind sold in sachets.

Ishaan jerked backward, the leather case spilling across his lap. When he looked up again, the aisle was empty.

The glass of water stood on his table, beads of condensation running down its side.

The plane continued east through darkness, carrying Ishaan toward a past he could no longer outrun. Beyond the window, clouds parted briefly, revealing the black mirror of the Arabian Sea miles below. Somewhere in that darkness, he imagined Basab's face staring up at him through water, saying words he could no longer hear.

Ishaan reached for the glass of water. It was ice cold against his palm. He drained it in one swallow, the liquid burning like acid down his throat.

When he set it down, he noticed something that had not been there before. A single red petal clung to the bottom of the glass, vibrant as fresh blood against the crystal.

11

The Office Visit

Ranadeep looked across the table at Sunanda Batabyal, hearing her voice but barely absorbing her words. All he could think of was Shayan. The similarities struck him like a physical thing. She was a few years older than his son, but when they leaned over their phones, explaining what was happening in the world while he was too 'out of it' to know, they mirrored each other. The same inflection, the excited flutter of eyelids, the quiet joy in the shifting power dynamic. Even though they were freshly minted adults, they felt that the adults around them still treated them as children. When they knew more about something – tech, trends, the chaos of online life – they pushed the advantage. It was a feeling Ranadeep wasn't so old that he couldn't remember experiencing himself.

So, he sat, watching her with benign, feigning attention.

'They are calling him Killer Chatterjee now,' she said, scrolling through her phone. 'Bunty Grewal's fan club started it. The hashtag is trending. You know who Bunty Grewal is, Uncle?'

He had a vague sense – some new Bollywood star, hot property these days – but he said, 'I don't follow these things, so no,' just so she would explain.

It was a trick he had perfected with Shayan, this feigned ignorance, this manufactured interest. A small deception that opened doors between generations. He would pretend not to know some band or game or viral trend, and Shayan would light up, words tumbling out with the lightness of someone confident in his expertise. Those moments, his son's face animated with importance, Ranadeep would try to imprint on his mind, knowing how quickly such things disappeared.

He now understood what had taken him years to learn: memory was like water, and who we are, our present selves, is the bucket. Memory reshapes itself to fit us, filling the contours of whoever we have become. He missed Shayan as a baby, as a child, as a teenager, not because he hadn't been there, but because those versions of his son no longer existed. Each Shayan had been replaced by another, leaving only ripples behind. And so, he was grateful for these small subterfuges, for having the foresight to keep the tap on, gathering what he could while it lasted.

No, this wasn't Shayan sitting across from him. But spending time with Sunanda, just the one hour they had been talking, felt like echoes of those moments with his son, like listening to the cover version of a favourite song. It made no logical sense, yet he found himself playing the same games, floating with the currents of memory without questioning it too deeply, another skill acquired too late, like so many others.

'It's everywhere.' Sunanda's eyes reflected blue phone-light. 'Ishaan's fans are fighting back with #LiesNotEvidence and #BuntyGrewalIsAFool. It's like watching two monkeys throw faeces at each other.'

Her laugh was startling, bright and unrestrained in a government office, a temple of measured responses. It reminded him of himself, as he used to be, a long time ago, when he would laugh because something was funny, and not because it was the polite thing to do or because he needed to make a statement.

'The first episode did more damage than I expected,' Ranadeep said.

'It's not just the episode. The news channels have picked this up. It's almost as if all the country's problems have been solved, and Ishaan Chatterjee is the only topic worth discussing. Everyone's running an exclusive, and everything is "big breaking, big breaking".'

He had not imagined, an hour earlier, that the conversation would unfold this way. Before Sunanda arrived, he had mapped the encounter precisely: fifteen minutes on his calendar, a position in Calcutta that bore the government stamp but none of its stability. She would be hired through a contracting agency that supplied temporary workers to plug bureaucratic gaps. Just enough to satisfy Krishanu's demands while leaving Ranadeep with clean hands when it ended. After the documentary faded from public interest, after Krishanu was gone, her employment would dissolve with the changing winds of administration. No responsibility. Merely the natural order of things.

Fifteen minutes. Initial pleasantries. An email address for the contractor. A handshake. Done.

Yet here he sat, an hour later, listening to tales of rivalry between Bollywood titans as if they were matters of state.

The trajectory had shifted the moment she appeared in his doorway, awkward, clutching her purse like it held something that might escape. At Krishanu's house, she had been background noise, a daughter-shape moving at the edge of vision. But here, in his office, she emerged as Sunanda.

She belonged to Shayan's generation, yes, but wore time differently on her skin. Where his son carried the lightness of assumed possibility, her eyes held the wary calculations of someone who had learned early that life's math rarely balanced in her favour. The things Shayan never questioned as his birthright – education, opportunity, the breathing room to make mistakes – were luxuries she had clawed toward with bloodied fingers. She had grown up in a world that showed her its teeth, while his son was still being shown its promise. Ranadeep had seen enough people to read all of this in one glance, in the posture with which she stood at his door.

Once he had invited her in and pointed to the chair, she had started speaking. 'I am so sorry about Baba,' she said, setting down her purse. 'What he is doing, using the documentary to pressure you, it's wrong.'

Ranadeep blinked. 'Excuse me?'

'I know why I am here.' Her shoulders squared. 'Baba really threw Ishaan-uncle under the bus in his interview. There was no need to bring up stories from his school. I wish I could apologize to Ishaan-uncle directly. I know he is bartering his nuisance value for my job. I don't endorse that in any way. You must understand, Baba is not this kind of person. It's the sickness. The desperation.'

He had prepared for many conversations – defensive pleas, calculated gratitude, veiled threats. Not this. Not a blunt, clear-eyed confession that cut through his carefully laid plans like a scalpel through tissue.

'I understand if you need to promise him something until the documentary ends. I just want him to have peace in his final months.' Her fingers twisted in her lap. 'I will resign once all this is over, or feel free to fire me any time you want.'

'That was not what I...'

'It's okay.' She smiled, and for a moment, there was Krishanu in the curve of her lips. 'After Baba's gone, I intend to sell the house, move to Bengaluru, stay with a friend and restart my life there.'

'Would you like something to eat?' Ranadeep asked, the question surprising himself as much as her.

'No, I am good, Uncle,' she said with a smile. 'I am full. I would just like to know the next steps, and I will go tell Baba.'

Something in the quick dart of her eyes told Ranadeep she was not 'good'. That something was the quiet radar that fatherhood had installed in him, sensitive to signals no bureaucratic training could detect.

He rang for the attendant and ordered two biryanis and water.

'Uncle, I am being honest. I am fine.'

'But I am not,' Ranadeep said. 'It's time for my dinner, and I don't like eating alone.'

That part wasn't true. Ranadeep usually skipped dinner when at work, his body trained to ignore hunger until it became a dull background noise. But he wasn't going to let her leave without a proper meal.

'Do you like biryani? This place we'll be getting it from is quite good.'

'Mmm...okay,' she said, quickly looking down, but not before Ranadeep caught the flicker in her eyes that confirmed what he had suspected; she was hungry.

The simple human need beneath her dignity touched something in him. That practised pretence of the proud when they need something they are afraid to ask for.

It reminded Ranadeep of Basab, how at Ishaan's house or his own, when food was plentiful, Basab would eat the least, though he was running on fumes. He took small portions, chewed slowly, left food on his plate, all so no one would notice the quiet desperation of a boy whose family measured rice by the handful.

'How is your father?' Ranadeep asked.

'Some days are better than others.' She looked down. 'The new treatment helps with pain, but the side effects...'

'And you? How are you managing?'

The question seemed to surprise her. 'One day at a time. The medical bills, the collection agencies...it is like trying to empty the ocean with a teacup.'

The practised detachment Ranadeep had cultivated through decades in service cracked slightly. This girl, merely a woman, carried burdens that would crush most of her peers.

As they waited for the food, he asked more questions about Krishanu's condition, and she told him about his diagnosis, the new medication he was on, her mother's death and how Krishanu had taken that very hard.

'I don't know if you will believe anything I say, Uncle, based on what happened that day, but Baba really, and I mean really, loves and admires you guys. He mentions you all constantly.'

Her voice shifted, taking on Krishanu's cadence and inflections.

'"You know superstar Ishaan Chatterjee; he sat here in this very sofa you are sitting on", or "You think I look small, well, you have no idea, how many friends I have in high places, Ranadeep Saha, yes top IAS guy, you are lucky I am not going to him and complaining about you", or "You know who I learned physics from in school, my friend, he is in the US, at Caltech, he won the highest medal for science there, so do not come poking around here with your ignorance."'

She transformed before him, back straight, chin jutting, finger wagging in perfect mimicry of her father. But beneath the performance, Ranadeep saw Krishanu from decades ago: the same gift for observation and imitation, the same delight in becoming someone else. Through Sunanda, memories surfaced like ripples across still water, each widening circle touching shores of his mind long left unvisited.

'I know Krishanu cares a lot about us. I know we were like the family he felt closest to,' Ranadeep said.

'Thank you for saying that, Uncle. It would mean a lot to Baba to know you understand how much you all matter to him. He spent most of his youth fighting with his own family in court, his own uncles and cousins. He hates them, absolutely hates them. That is why you three, I mean, two now, were so important. Even though none of you are around, you still exist larger than life in his imagination. That is why I was so surprised, so distraught, hearing him speak that way to you and Ishaan-uncle, especially when both of you were so nice and understanding.'

Dinner arrived, and Ranadeep divided the biryani onto their plates, steam rising with its warmth and spice. When he asked if she wanted more, she nodded, and Ranadeep quietly served himself only a quarter portion, transferring the rest to Sunanda's plate in small, unremarkable increments. He brushed aside her soft protests with a dismissive wave. The reversal wasn't lost on him. Basab had once gone hungry so no one would notice; now Ranadeep ensured someone else wouldn't have to.

They spoke about the fallout from the documentary's first episode, and she gave him the backstory of Ishaan Chatterjee's long-standing feuds – with other actors, their fan clubs, the hashtag wars. It felt strange hearing about his friend through the voice of Krishanu Batabyal's daughter, like viewing a familiar landscape through unfamiliar glass.

Ranadeep found himself opening up too. He told her that he had agreed to speak in the second episode of the documentary, with rumours swirling that it would be released at noon on Saturday.

'So, Uncle,' she said, glancing at the window, where darkness had settled like ink, 'it is getting late, and trust me, I would love to chat more, but the buses start running empty, and Baba tells me not to travel in empty buses. So... what are my next steps?'

'Well,' Ranadeep said, 'I had something in mind for you. But now, I am thinking of something better. It would be on my personal staff, as a junior policy analyst. You could start here, I understand you need to look after Krishanu right now, but it would eventually require you to move to Delhi.'

'Your personal staff? A junior policy analyst?' She laughed, a startling, open sound. 'Uncle, I sell mobile phones and fix cracked screens. I have a Bachelor's in English lit from a second-rate college. How does that make me qualified for policy work?'

'You will learn. I am confident.'

'Uncle, thank you, really. But forgive me, I think that first job you had in mind before I walked in here...that's probably better for everyone concerned.'

'Why do you say that when you don't even know what the first job was?'

'Because I trust your judgment, Uncle.' Her gaze met his, unflinching, calm. And for a moment, he saw Pramila in her. 'Before I came in, you had already decided what I was worth. You weighed my situation, my father's pressure, and you made a call. Now, after we have talked for, let's see, about two hours, you feel bad for me. Watching me wolf down almost two packets of biryani must have made you feel worse.'

She paused, her voice softened, 'You barely touched your share, kept moving it onto my plate. Yes, I was so hungry, I ate it, nonetheless. But now, on a fuller stomach, I must, with respect and gratitude, say "No." For now. If in the first job I do well enough that you think I deserve this other position based on my ability, and ability only, I would be only too happy to work for you.'

Her words carried the weight of someone who had learned early that kindness often came with strings, that people gave only to take something else away. There was Krishanu in that caution, but also Basab's quiet pride, Ishaan's directness, and Ranadeep's own analytical clarity.

She carried pieces of all of them, yet remained entirely herself.

'Well, then, can I at least drop you home?' Ranadeep asked. 'Krishanu is right, the city is not safe for women, not that it ever was. And now, there is a quick shower forecast, so the buses will empty out even earlier.'

She nodded awkwardly.

Thirty minutes later, they sat in silence as the car crawled through Calcutta's rain-swollen arteries. Water transformed the city into a fever dream, buildings bleeding into one another, streets dissolving beneath them. His driver navigated potholes with practised precision while Ranadeep watched the world outside lose its edges.

Sunanda sat with her purse clutched to her chest, eyes forward, as if the rain might find its way inside the car to claim her too.

They passed the mall that had replaced Ramkrishna Park, its glass façade fracturing the rain into kaleidoscopic patterns. Billboards loomed through the downpour.

Ishaan's face twenty feet tall, advertising cologne, water streaming down his perfect features like tears.

'He was different back then,' Ranadeep said.

Sunanda followed his gaze to the billboard. 'Baba says the same. Says he was the sun your lives revolved around.'

'We were just boys,' Ranadeep murmured. 'We thought we were immortal. And the time we were in, that was forever.'

'Baba still thinks that, somewhere in his mind. That he is still in that "forever time". I hope that in the end, when it comes, he dies in that dream.'

She paused.

'Can I ask you a question, Uncle?'

'Sure, go ahead.'

'How was Pramila-aunty? I know she died at a younger age than I am now, but I think somewhere she is still alive, and I need to call her Aunty.'

Ranadeep did not reply.

The question lingered in the mist.

Outside, rain tapped against glass like impatient fingers.

'Baba does not talk much about her, and I figured out that they were not particularly close, but he told me that you were, that you were her best friend.'

It was then that she turned to the side and looked at Ranadeep.

He was weeping.

'I am so sorry, Uncle, I am…' She reached out her hand to touch Ranadeep's shoulder. 'I should not have. I am really sorry.'

Ranadeep sniffled, paused, then pulled himself together.

'No, it is a good question to ask. In all this, if there is someone we have forgotten, it is her. She is the one who has remained frozen in time, and all of us have moved on. No, not moved on; we have run away. Ishaan ran; his family could not take the media scrutiny. I ran too. I could not go to my singing lessons after that. I could not walk past this street. I stopped playing cricket. And, perhaps most telling, I stopped singing after that.'

He looked out of the window.

'I was pretty good, at a competitive level. I just could never start a stanza knowing that she would not be there to pick it up. Her favourite Rabindra Sangeet was "*Daanriye acho tumi amar gaaner opaare*" ("You stand on the other side of my song").'

Ranadeep stopped talking. Sunanda did not look his way again, knowing what she would see. Instead, she spoke out the second line of the song, 'My tune reaches your feet, but I can no longer find you.'

'Yes,' Ranadeep said. 'It was always in the song. When you sing it as a teenager, you do not understand what it means. The words just flow out, but the true significance, the "why". That hits you years later.'

He exhaled slowly.

'She was a good person. She helped me get through my stammer. Helped me find myself. And what I hate, truly hate, about the documentary, all of it, is that she has been turned into a trope. Like some kind of Black Dahlia figure. A mystery, a symbol. A question mark.'

He paused, the words catching.

'But no one cares who she *was*. They care about how she died, but not the lives she touched. Not the people she saved.'

There was a silence.

'You will say that to the crew, won't you, Uncle?' Sunanda asked.

'I will,' he said. 'But something tells me they will edit it out.'

They turned onto Sunanda's street. The buildings seemed to lean inward, pressing closer, as if listening.

'This one,' Sunanda pointed.

The car stopped outside Krishanu's house. Ranadeep kept his eyes on the dashboard, afraid of what memory might ambush him if he looked up.

'Thank you for the ride,' she said. 'And for...everything.'

'Take care of yourself,' he said. 'Not just your father.'

She stepped into the rain, hunching against its force, and hurried toward the door. Despite his resolve, Ranadeep watched her through the fogged window, struck by a sudden, irrational urge to call her back, to tell her things he had never spoken aloud.

The truth was that the Delhi posting had not been a gesture of charity. It was selfish. He wanted it for himself. For Monobina. Shayan's room was empty, and it would be good to have someone in it again, someone young, someone as endearing, someone his age, to fill that space they both knew would otherwise stay hollow. Because otherwise, he could already see it: he and Monobina, withering in silence, husband and wife orbiting a quiet phone, waiting for calls that would grow fewer, shorter, colder, as Shayan drifted further away into his world and they stayed frozen in time, just like Krishanu.

Sunanda paused at the door, turning to wave. Rain plastered her hair to her face, and for a heartbeat, time folded over itself like wet paper.

It wasn't Sunanda standing there.

It was Pramila.

Same height, same slightness, same way of tucking hair behind her ear. Rain clung to her eyelashes, and even across the distance, he could see the question in her eyes, the one she had asked that final day, voice warm: *Will you come by tomorrow? I have something to tell you.*

Cold sweat broke across Ranadeep's forehead. His chest constricted as if gripped by an invisible hand. He pressed his palm against the window, mouth dry, heart hammering.

The guilt surged up, dark and tidal, ready to drown him where he sat.

When he blinked, it was Sunanda again. She waved a final goodbye and hurried in.

The driver turned to him. 'Where to now, sir?'

'My parents' home, New Town,' Ranadeep managed, though his voice sounded like it came from underwater.

The car pulled away from the curb, tyres slicing through puddles. In the rearview mirror, Krishanu's house receded into rain-blur.

But Pramila, her ghost, her memory, her unfinished song, remained a passenger in the back seat that only he could hear.

12

The Second Episode

The elevator doors parted with a soft pneumatic sigh, opening directly into the vast living area of the penthouse. Anand stepped out in his grey safari suit and black shoes, polished to a dark sheen, phone chiming with morning alerts, and froze.

Darkness.

Ishaan Chatterjee's suite, usually flooded with morning light through floor-to-ceiling windows, remained shrouded in shadow. The automated curtains remained closed against the Mumbai morning. No relaxation music from hidden speakers. No workout equipment on the yoga mat. No women's lingerie tossed across chairs from last night's escapades.

Only the gigantic television dominated the space, its blue glow the sole illumination in the manufactured night.

'Sir?' Anand called, peering into the gloom. He checked his watch. Seven o'clock. No matter how late Ishaan had partied the night before, how much powder he had snuffed, or whisky he had chugged, or women he had entertained, he would be sitting right now, after his workout, draining his protein shake in large gulps, bare torsoed and sweating, usually in his shorts, angry or happy or caustic, but never, ever silent.

Ishaan was there. Anand could feel his presence.

But even as he stepped in, the silhouette before the screen did not move.

'Sir? Are you all right?'

No response.

Ishaan sat unnaturally still in his throne-like chair, perched on the raised marble pedestal that allowed him to look down on visitors. Yesterday's white linen shirt clung to him, creased and stained. The coffee table before him told the story of his vigil: an empty whisky bottle, overflowing ashtrays, a bottle of sleeping pills, and an expensive crystal bowl, a gift from some international fan club, now full of ash.

He had been using one of his trophies as an ashtray.

That was as strange as him just sitting there, unkempt and silent and off his schedule.

Anand approached cautiously. The stench of stale cigarettes hung in the air, a vice Ishaan had renounced five years ago after his pulmonologist's warning.

'You have the *Film Companion* photoshoot at eleven,' Anand said, pulling out his phone, trying to act normal. 'Should I call Sanjay to come early for hair and makeup?'

Ishaan's eyes never left the screen. He kept on sitting exactly as he was, like a statue.

On the television, the second episode of *Hidden Secrets: The Murder of the Rose* played, the host's voice filling the silence.

Anand observed some movement. Ishaan's fingers trembled slightly as they gripped the remote.

'You didn't sleep,' Anand observed, now noticing that the bottle of sleeping pills had its sealed cap on.

'*Glamis hath murdered sleep, and therefore Cawdor shall sleep no more,*' Ishaan said softly, in an impeccable British accent, and Anand had no idea what he just said, or why. Anand had not read Macbeth and was not likely to.

'How can I sleep? They have been at it all night,' Ishaan whispered, his voice ragged. 'Playing it over and over.'

Anand glanced around, seeing no one else in the room. 'Who has, sir?'

Ishaan gestured vaguely at the walls, the shadows, the corners where night still lingered. 'Everyone. They are all watching. Listening.'

Anand thought it would be best to try to pretend that this was normal, that maybe bringing up business would bring Ishaan back from wherever his mind had travelled.

'Sir, the PR agency is messaging me, saying you have not replied to their...'

Anand took a step forward, and that is when he felt something crunching beneath his foot. In the near darkness, he made out the shattered remains of an iPhone.

'Well, I see you have found my phone, Anand-bhai.' Ishaan's perfect teeth glowed in the darkness. 'It was laughing at me, ping-a-ping-a-ping. The messages kept coming through the night, expressing concern, asking questions, mostly gloating. So, I shot the messenger. As they say in Hindi, if there is no bamboo, the flute plays no more.'

'Let me draw the curtains, let's get the sunlight in, let me call the cleaning service...' Anand said, with a falsely cheerful voice, 'And everything will be as right as rain.'

'No sun,' Ishaan's voice was hoarse as if he had been shouting all night. 'The light hurts my eyes. I want the darkness. I don't want to see those traitors.'

'Traitors?'

'You heard me. Traitors. My staff. The serpents I feed with milk I pay for.'

Anand had heard of Ishaan being paranoid of everyone: his movie industry friends, his ex-girlfriends, the media, his directors. But never, *never*, of his own staff.

'They all adore you,' Anand said. 'They...'

'They sell information about me to the paps. As if the money I give them, to work, to keep shut, is not enough.'

He stopped, and then said, almost tenderly, 'I don't mean you. You are the only loyal person I have, Anand-bhai.'

'No, sir, they are all loyal, they have been here for...'

Usually, any contradiction would spark a tantrum. Today, Ishaan remained eerily calm, as if all the fight had drained out of him, leaving only a cold, humming wire.

'They look at me, Anand-bhai, I can see their eyes in the dark. Watching. Judging. Wondering if I did it.'

'Did what, sir?' Anand asked, before realizing what he meant, but he must have said it too quietly, because Ishaan did not seem to hear.

He was drifting again.

'They hang there, the eyes. Like lights on a string. Mocking, pitying, hating. Dancing from side to side. I can't stop the eyes. I just want to stop the bodies attached to them.'

He turned to Anand now, gaze sharp in the darkness.

'No lights.'

'Can I fix you something then? You haven't had...'

'Fix me? No, I don't think you can.' He tilted his head, swaying slightly, as though he were hearing a melody from another world. 'I broke that night when Pramila died. I broke into a million pieces, and they built a fucking mall over my remains.'

He smiled without warmth.

'You will not find me there; I am gone.'

Anand pulled out his phone. Fingers flying, he began cancelling the day's appointments. Photoshoots, meetings, interviews – none of it mattered now.

Ishaan stared at the screen again, its glow painting ghostly contours across his face.

Ishaan looked towards the screen.

'Most notable in our continuing investigation,' the narrator intoned, 'is this passionate defence from Ranadeep Saha, childhood friend of Ishaan Chatterjee and current home secretary to the Government of India.'

The scene cut to Ranadeep, his bureaucratic composure barely containing simmering anger. Wearing a Jawahar coat and seated in a high-ceilinged office, he looked every bit the embodiment of power.

'I find it telling,' he said, his voice clipped, in an impeccable accent, 'that your entire first episode focused on building a case against Ishaan, while barely acknowledging Brajendra Das's well-documented proclivities. Ask anyone from our neighbourhood; his behaviour toward young women was common knowledge.'

He removed his glasses, rubbing the bridge of his nose.

'I question the integrity of any documentary that claims to be seeking the truth while ignoring inconvenient facts and presenting only one side. Brajendra Das was not arrested based on Dr Basab Banerjee's witness statement. He was arrested because the police found incriminating evidence in his house.'

He paused, letting the line settle in.

'Ishaan's father may have had ties with the ruling party. But you neglected to mention that Inspector Roy, after the government changed, was promoted beyond his turn. You also missed mentioning that he stood as an MLA candidate for that party. Now, I am not casting aspersions on Inspector Roy's competence. Maybe he was exceptional, but those facts matter. It needs to be stated because he has been given ample time in front of the camera to insinuate – no, make that directly accuse – that the investigation had been directed by Ishaan's father, without being made to disclose his own political background.'

He leaned forward, voice firm.

'And, finally, and this bears saying, Brajendra had his day in court. The judge gave his verdict. What you are doing isn't journalism. It's character assassination, besides being an attack on our judicial system.'

Ranadeep paused, visibly restraining himself. It was rare, even for those who knew him well, to see such emotion slip through.

He then looked straight at the camera.

'Pramila was my friend. She helped me overcome my stammer. She gave an awkward boy the confidence he needed to stand up and speak. I owe her memory something. And that is why I am telling you, your documentary has reduced her to a body in a bucket. An agenda against one person, in the guise of caring…'

Ranadeep's eyes flashed.

'Why not talk to all of Pramila's classmates? Why not interview her singing teacher, Mainak Mukherjee, or anyone who knew her as more than a victim? I know you spoke to one person, and here is the thing: I have never ever *heard* of her. Pramila was a very good friend of mine, and I knew all of her friends. Do your research better, or rather, do not cherry-pick only people who support your slant. And I hope you carry all this, as you have committed to.'

The scene shifted to a dimly lit interview room. A middle-aged man with an eye that looked like it had been gouged out stared into the camera, unblinking.

'I shared a cell with Brajendra. Poor man had it rough inside,' the man said, scratching at a scar along his jaw.

He gave a half-smile, brown and yellow teeth in an advanced state of decay.

'We all got kids, back home, you know? You touch a teenage girl, you pay. Guards looked the other way when he used to get beaten every day. Slapped around, punched in the stomach, kicked on the ass when he was looking elsewhere. And this was during the day. Once the lights were out, I hope I do not need to tell you what they would do to him.'

'Suicide because of guilt?' He snorted. 'Well, he used to say he was innocent, that he was set up.'

He again ran his finger up his scar, 'Well, there was this one time he did fess up to the fact. Said he killed the girl.'

The man raised a finger to his face.

'That was after Blind Sharma got to him. The bastard was not really blind. They called him that because he would burst people's eyeballs with his index finger. He said he liked to hear them pop.' The man pointed to his eye, 'Got me too.'

He chuckled. 'But, yeah, Brajendra did confess to the murder. That part was true. Though I wouldn't put much stock in what a man says after his head has been dunked in the jail bucket, the one for the sick ones. You know. The ones who can't make it to the latrine.'

He laughed again, wheezing.

'Drink in a mix of dried shit and wet piss, and you will confess to whatever they tell you to.'

The documentary cut to interviews with former co-stars and assistants, each recounting incidents: Ishaan slapping a makeup artist for making him wait; hurling a phone at a female director who suggested a script change; abusing a female journalist who asked him an uncomfortable question; Ishaan confining his girlfriend in his bedroom while his pit bulls ran around in the living room, simply for signing a film with his rival. All the stories, one after another, with the most damning quotes.

Ishaan Chatterjee reached forward for the remote on the coffee table. But instead of turning the TV off, as Anand expected him to, he changed the channel, from YouTube to Democracy TV.

The huge spinning logo of the globe spun into view, followed by Arun Mathur's face, his expression grave yet somehow ravenous, the performative outrage of a jackal who had cornered wounded prey.

Arun Mathur, India's self-proclaimed number one news anchor, had a long memory. Anand remembered the night it all went wrong. An up-and-coming Arun had approached Ishaan at a film premiere, starstruck and hopeful. Ishaan, in a mood for cruelty, had looked him over and asked, 'Where are the starters?' Ishaan's date had burst out laughing. The suit Arun wore did resemble the waitstaff's uniform. Ishaan had clapped him on the back. 'Just kidding', but the damage was done. Mathur never forgot.

Arun Mathur had never forgotten the slight.

'Why, sir?' Anand squealed out in dismay, 'Why do you want to subject yourself to this now?'

'Hah.' Ishaan's voice held no emotion. 'They have been playing this on loop since last night. See this. See this, to understand why I am sitting here in the fucking dark, railing against my staff. See this clown show.'

The studio lights burned against Arun Mathur's forehead, highlighting the unnaturally smooth skin stretched too tight across his face. His finger jabbed the air with mechanical precision, voice rising to a pitch that threatened to shatter glass.

'I have said, many a night, ladies and gentlemen, that Bollywood is a cancer, a metastasizing tumour consuming our culture, backed by Jihadi mafia dons and the CIA.'

Arun Mathur thundered, his perfectly knotted tie quivering with indignation. 'For saying that, I have been attacked by Lutyens' media, lampooned, mocked on social media, but nothing in the universe, nobody except God, will make me stop speaking truth to power.'

He leaned toward the camera, nostrils flaring like a bull scenting blood. 'I normally do not like to talk about these so-called stars; they are, after all, insignificant insects without an iota of originality. But today, viewers, Bollywood has crossed another line. When a senior bureaucrat, a man being groomed for ministerial position, defends an alleged killer in an international documentary, an alleged killer who is a Bollywood superstar with a very problematic history with women and who flies to Dubai every few days, we must ask: is this official government policy to defend Ishaan Chatterjee? Let us dissect, the lines are open, the hashtag is #BollywoodGovernmentNexus, and you are on India's most popular news channel.'

Six faces stared back from split screens, their expressions ranging from eager agreement to weary resignation. None dared interrupt Mathur during his opening salvo, not if they valued their microphone privileges.

'Breaking news! Exclusive debate!' His voice dropped to a theatrical whisper. 'Who is protecting Bollywood's fallen titan? Why?'

Behind him, the screen splashed lurid graphics: MURDER, POWER, SECRETS.

Beneath these words, two photographs: Ranadeep Saha in formal attire at a government function, and Ishaan Chatterjee at a film premiere.

'Panel!' Arun Mathur barked, glasses sliding down his nose. 'I ask you directly, when Home Secretary Ranadeep Saha defended Ishaan Chatterjee, claiming that the case against Brajendra Das was legitimate, was he speaking as a private citizen or a government representative?'

Amita Desai, former film critic turned cultural commentator, attempted to respond. 'If we examine the actual interview...'

'No diversions!' Mathur slammed his palm against the desk. 'Answer my question! Government spokesman or old friend covering up murder?'

From another screen, retired judge, Prakash Gupta, sighed visibly, and said, 'Mr Mathur, without all the facts...'

'So, you refuse to condemn this clear conflict of interest. I am not surprised. Not everything has nuance; there is the murderer, and there is the victim. Simple as that.'

He spun to his next target.

'Rajiv! Simple question: does this government officially endorse violence against women by supporting Ishaan Chatterjee?'

'That is not what I...'

'The evidence speaks for itself!' Arun Mathur spun toward the camera, eyes blazing, 'When Home Secretary Saha attacks this documentary's integrity, he attacks truth itself.'

He paused, breathing heavily, then lowered his voice to a conspiratorial rumble.

'But there's more. We have obtained, exclusively, a bombshell revelation. I should correct myself, not one, but two.'

The camera cut to a young woman standing on the footpath outside Ishaan Chatterjee's building, wearing a blue jacket and carrying a microphone emblazoned with the channel's logo. She was nervously adjusting her hair, but the moment she realized the camera was on her, she suddenly became hyper-animated.

'We now move to Reshma, our investigative reporter, who has been camping outside the building whose top penthouse suite is occupied by Ishaan Chatterjee. She has, and you will get this only on this channel, obtained information that will change the way you have seen the story so far, dear viewers. Reshma, Reshma, tell us what is happening now.'

Reshma, on cue, waved her hands animatedly with a sheaf of papers. 'I have, in my hand, evidence from a whistle-blower within Ishaan Chatterjee's staff. The staff member says that Ishaan Chatterjee has recently visited Calcutta, where he met with Ranadeep Saha, and we have the flight number and receipts.' Saying this, Reshma started to run, and the camera followed, bouncing wildly as a large black Mercedes rolled through the front gate. She brandished the microphone forward and, between gasps of breath, said, 'We have reason to believe that Ishaan Chatterjee is in that vehicle, ladies and gentlemen. He is running away. He is avoiding the media. Even if he has refused to speak to the documentary, we shall have answers.'

With that, Reshma started thumping on the tinted glass of the Mercedes, theatrically trembling her voice. 'Ishaan sir, I know you are there inside. Answer the question. Did you murder Pramila Chatterjee?'

'That's not even your car,' Anand said, exasperated. 'Why watch this? He clearly hates you. None of it proves anything. A flight ticket does not prove a secret meeting.'

'I know, but he is right. I did meet the home secretary, and we did talk about the documentary, and we went to Krishanu's house.'

'He cannot prove it. No one can.'

'They cannot prove I killed Pramila. But everyone, and their grandfather, believes I did. But, forget that for a second. What pisses me off is someone on my staff has decided to sell my whereabouts to the channels. You, Anand-bhai, think I am paranoid when I say I am being watched, right here, in my own house. And yet, this.'

He turned his head back from the screen to Anand. 'Why are they doing this to me? Have I ever been bad to them?'

Anand knew better than to give the real answer, and he was contemplating how to move ahead without saying anything when Ishaan said, with a sigh, 'Yes, I know I have been bad to them. So, yes, I had this coming. I had been nasty with Arun Mathur, for no good reason; the poor chap was fishing for an interview. So that part too, yes, I understand.'

Ishaan hunched forward, his right elbow digging into his knee, chin resting heavily on his knuckles, his body folding inward like a tight fist, still like he had turned into stone. When he spoke, his voice came out choked with tears.

'But, Basab, he did nothing wrong. My friend. My best friend. He is dead. Why are they still going after him?'

'Sorry, sir? What?' Anand asked.

Ishaan increased the volume until Arun Mathur's voice filled the darkened penthouse, drowning out the hum of the air conditioning, the faint traffic sounds from thirty floors below, even the sound of their breathing.

The screen showed Arun Mathur brandishing court documents with strategic sections highlighted in neon yellow.

'Basab Banerjee, the same man who provided key testimony against Brajendra Das, testimony that sent him to prison and eventually death, has been called, under oath, by his own wife…' Mathur paused for dramatic effect, 'a pathological liar.'

The camera zoomed into Arun Mathur's face and held its focus there, for effect.

'Let me repeat that. The primary witness, whose testimony sealed Brajendra Das's fate thirty years ago, described by his own wife as someone who lies, and I will use her own words: "lies without any hesitation", "gaslights", "no moral compass", "suffers from God complex"?'

Arun Mathur removed his glasses, polishing them slowly.

'These divorce proceedings, obtained exclusively by us, show Sandra Banerjee, ex-wife of Basab Banerjee, stating unequivocally that her husband fabricates stories. A little bit of context here, viewers. Basab Banerjee, apparently the "best friend" of Ishaan Chatterjee when growing up, tried to scam his wife and his children out of their inheritance and got caught. He signed a confessional statement himself as part of his divorce proceedings. Why did he sign this? Because he got a formal assurance from his wife that no criminal or civil charges would be filed against him if he confessed. Think of that, ladies and gentlemen.'

Arun Mathur replaced his glasses, peering over them at the camera.

'If he lied to his wife, if he robbed his own children, what else did he lie about, what other terrible things did he do?'

The split screens erupted in chaos, voices climbing over each other while Arun Mathur watched, face set in grim satisfaction.

'One at a time!' he roared, though his expression suggested he preferred the cacophony. 'Judge Gupta! Does this new evidence warrant reopening the case?'

The ex-judge cleared his throat. 'First of all, this is not a formal court judgement, and also, without reviewing complete depositions in a family court…'

'So, you will not commit! Fascinating!' Arun Mathur swivelled to his next target. 'Professor Kapoor, you are an expert on human psychology and pathological behaviour.

Could an eighteen-year-old boy, for that was what Basab Banerjee was thirty years ago, fabricate evidence sophisticated enough to fool Calcutta police?'

The academic opened his mouth, only to be cut off by Arun Mathur's raised hand.

'Before you answer and try to accuse me of calling into question law enforcement, remember Ranadeep Saha explicitly questioned this documentary's methods. Attacked its integrity! Said we should listen to the neighbourhood instead and then tried to undermine the testimony of a female witness. Maybe there is a pattern here, to all of Ishaan Chatterjee's associates: misogyny and lying. Maybe we should investigate Ranadeep Saha too; let us see how many skeletons he has in his cupboards, after all, don't they say, a man is known by the company he keeps?'

Professor Kapoor blinked. 'I am not sure how these points connect…'

'They connect precisely here!' Arun Mathur jabbed his finger at the camera. 'Government officials, at the highest level, protecting Bollywood elites who champion anti-Indian, anti-traditional values. The same government that claims to represent our culture.'

Froth gathered at the corners of his mouth as he continued, 'The hashtag #BollywoodGovernmentNexus is taking down the internet; look at the tweet counter on the left. The lines are off the hook, it is off the Richter, and India is speaking up against Bollywood, against Ishaan Chatterjee, against the mollycoddling of these murderous men-children by our government.'

He pivoted toward a young woman who was yet to speak. 'Priya! You are a women's rights activist. Does this alliance between the government and a man accused of violence against women send a message to Indian daughters?'

Priya leaned forward. 'Yes, of course, it does…'

'We are running out of time!' Arun Mathur slashed his hand through the air. 'Ten seconds!'

'This case raises serious questions about how...' she said, earnestly trying to make her point.

'There you have it!' Mathur turned triumphantly to the camera. 'Women's advocates condemn this unholy alliance between bureaucracy and Bollywood.'

The ticker at the bottom of the screen accelerated: BREAKING NEWS: Wife called star witness 'pathological liar' • Government defends accused murderer • Exclusive interview with the prison guard who 'found' Brajendra Das dead.

'Stay with us!' Mathur's voice descended to a theatrical whisper. 'After the break, the return of #UrineGate, as yet another incident of peeing in the high skies comes to light. We have to ask the authorities, is it safe to fly, and can we stay dry? Democracy TV, asking the questions others fear.'

Ishaan pressed a button on the remote. The screen died. Darkness reclaimed the penthouse, save for thin blades of sunlight that pierced through gaps in the heavy curtains, illuminating the silence that hung between the two men in the vast room, like cold air between corpses.

'They are coming for us, Anand-bhai, one by one. The people whom I have loved.' Ishaan's words came flat, stripped of emotion.

'My father, dying alone, barely alive; his name dragged through mud. I do not know how old Basab's children are, but one day, they will find this on YouTube. Even if their mother does not tell them, this is how they will remember their father...'

His voice caught, and Anand knew he was weeping.

'I can't even say the words aloud. It's a lie. Basab was the most honourable person I have ever known. But now he will be known as exactly the opposite. Why? *Because he was my friend.*'

A blade of light slashed across Ishaan's face, revealing nothing behind his eyes, windows to an abandoned house.

'At least Basab is dead; he will never know what they have made of him. But Rano, he will. He will see his world collapse. He will see his dreams splinter and break. And why? Because of me, because they want to go after me.'

'This will all blow over, sir,' Anand said. 'It always does; you have been through worse. And Ranadeep sir is powerful; he will also survive. Who knows, maybe, the notoriety might help him in politics.'

Ishaan's fingers worked at the loose thread on his shirt cuff, pulling until it unravelled like his thoughts. 'Strange, isn't it? I was always the one who protected them. The Musketeers.'

He looked down, as if the memory itself burned.

'When Basab cracked his skull on the cricket field, I carried him to the hospital. That was quite a distance; there was too much traffic for him to make it in time. When Rano got heckled for singing like a girl, I broke the jaw of the boy who laughed at him. When Krishanu nearly drowned in that filthy pond, that time we took the train to play the invitational shield up in Burdwan, I dived in and pulled him out.'

He tugged harder at the thread, the expensive linen surrendering to his fingers.

'I never realized when it all went to hell. When I became the one who needed protection. Me, cowering twenty floors above the city while the rats gnaw at my name.'

He gestured vaguely at the shattered phone.

'When did I change? I don't know anymore. Time smears together in the dark. Nothing feels real anymore.'

Anand couldn't remember ever seeing his employer like this. He had seen him break things in rage, screaming obscenities. He had seen him laugh so hard he bent double, anger collapsing into spasms of laughter, something Anand had never seen in anyone else. He had seen him cry. He had watched him exorcise his demons at the gym in sessions so intense they bordered on inhuman.

But never this.

Never this silence.

And it terrified him.

'The Hollywood deal is dead,' Ishaan said, in that same unnatural stillness. 'That's why the phone is in pieces. I threw it when the message came.'

'Sir, we don't know that for certain…'

But Anand knew. This was the end.

The accountants had been calling for weeks. They had hoped the bank might write off part of the loan; after all, this was Ishaan Chatterjee. But the tone had changed. Penalties were piling up. Advertisers had stopped returning calls, even after Anand slashed Ishaan's endorsement rates by eighty per cent. Whatever few brands remained would abandon them now, and Anand could only hope for early termination fees, if they did not have to go to court for them.

The Netmovies deal had been the lifeline. The cash would have covered minimum loan payments. The hype might have brought back sponsors. But now, it was gone.

The bills would snowball. Then the lawsuits. And Ishaan had burned so many bridges in Bollywood he would not even get uncle roles, roles he would not take, even if offered.

The only viable option now was exile. Dubai. Maybe forever.

Ishaan did not notice Anand's expression. He was adrift in his own storm.

'One of them, whichever bland voice belonged to their legal department, said they had conducted "internal interviews" with actresses who have worked with me. Then they started talking about "the toxic effects of Hindu patriarchy" and how they "understand the cultural context" of my upbringing.'

His jaw clenched. 'My father – they talked about my father like they knew him. Called him "a product of his environment" and me "a victim of intergenerational trauma". As if their university sociology courses gave them the right to dissect my life, my culture.'

'What did you tell them?'

Maybe they were giving him a way out. Maybe all Ishaan had to do was apologize, craft a statement, anything. Anand would convince him to do that, once he had cooled down. But then he remembered Ishaan was already calm.

'You are right, Anand-bhai,' Ishaan said, reading Anand's thoughts without looking at him, 'They did say they could work with my PR to craft a statement, basically the adult version of what Poltu sir would make us do in school for not doing homework, get on your knees, and hold your ears.'

He laughed, a short one of remembrance.

'He never made me do it. He tried his best, clutching onto my shoulders and exerting pressure with the full weight of his hundred-kilo body. He was fat, that man, fat like a pig. "Kneel down, kneel down, Ishaan," he kept shouting. I still remember it as clear as if it were yesterday: broken plastic glasses slipping off his shoulders from the sweat of his exertions, his entire leg coming out of his dhoti, panting and breathing like his heart would run out, and yet I stayed straight, looking into his eyes as the entire class laughed. You should have seen me then.'

Anand knew what Ishaan had done. He had told them to fuck themselves.

Yet, he had to confirm, if only to know what he needed to do next. He needed to know for sure if they were past the point of no return.

'Let me call the PR team, and let me tell them to…'

'Too late. If old Poltu sir could not get a thirteen-year-old me to go down on my knees, a bunch of pigs sitting in Los Angeles do not have a chance with me now. I think I might have used some expletives, or what Rano would call "unparliamentary language" while giving them examples of the kind of behaviour they had tolerated for so long in Hollywood, with no-disclosure contracts and suchlike, before telling them they could shove the deal up their ass. And that is when I think I threw my phone down, and it exploded into parts.'

He moved to the window, pulling back the curtain just enough to see the city sprawled beneath him. It was beautiful, Mumbai from high above, the city of dreams.

And now, the nightmare he had fled from had found him, as it had his friends.

'I am going to talk to them.' Ishaan let the curtain fall. 'The documentary people.'

'Sir, no,' an alarm flashed across Anand's face. 'That would be a terrible mistake. You are exhausted. You haven't slept…'

'I am tired of hiding.' Ishaan's voice hardened. 'Tired of others speaking for me, about me. I have lived with this shadow for so many years. People pointing when they think I can't see. The rumours following me from set to set. Me hearing the whispers and pretending not to.'

'You need to think this through.' Anand moved toward him, hands raised as if approaching a cornered animal. 'Let me call Ms Raghunathan from Black Envelope. She was a nice lady. She cared for you. She specifically advised against…'

'She left. Don't you remember? But even if she had not, you see the problem, do you not, Anand-bhai? I cannot open my mouth without asking for permission. What kind of hero requires others to write his courage?'

Anand wanted to say that was precisely what actors were: people who needed writers for their words, directors for their movements, producers for opportunity.

That is what stardom is.

But he said nothing.

'My father never brought me up like this. To cower behind handlers and lawyers.' Ishaan continued, 'And what does Black Envelope Public Relations know? This is not about managing a scandal. This is about ghosts.'

His voice came out haunted.

'What do they know about ghosts? About waking up every morning wondering if today is the day they finally come for you?'

'Please, sir…no one is coming for you.'

'Ghosts.' Ishaan whispered. 'In Hindi, we call them *bhoot*.'

Ishaan's eyes took on a feverish look.

'The same word *bhoot* also means past. Today's ghosts and yesterday's sins are one and the same.'

He stepped back from the window and walked to his chair, his posture hunched. The dais gave him the illusion of stature, but his body had already begun to fold inward.

'Call them. Tell them I will do the interview. No conditions, no pre-approved questions, no lawyers present.'

'Please, sir,' Anand's voice cracked with desperation. 'At least wait until you have rested. Until your head is clear.'

'My head hasn't been clear since 1994. And it never will be.'

'Please, at least have your lawyers sit in.' Anand pleaded. 'Please read the questions beforehand.'

'You do not understand. I have nothing left to lose.' Ishaan sighed. 'The studios are gone. The fans have scattered like cockroaches when the light comes on. My father, whatever is left of him, sits in a Dubai nursing home drooling, with tubes in his arms. Basab is dead. Krishanu is dying. Only Rano remains, and after today's news cycle, I worry for him, too.'

He looked at Anand.

'Why keep running?'

'Because some things, once said, can never be unsaid.' Anand remained standing, holding his hands together, pleading. 'Some doors, once opened...'

'I think I know what's behind the door.' Ishaan's eyes reflected nothing, vacant as a doll's. 'I am ready for whatever comes through.'

'It does not need to be this way.'

He straightened to his full height, an old habit from his leading man days.

'A hero doesn't lie low. And neither will I. Not anymore.'

A long moment passed. Then Anand nodded, accepting what couldn't be changed, and retreated to make the call that would set everything in motion.

Ishaan stood at the window, his reflection superimposed over Mumbai's glittering skyline, awash in the morning sun.

This time, when he looked at himself, he didn't see the aging star with the fading box office.

He saw the boy from Calcutta, the one who had sworn brotherhood with three friends, vowing to stand together through whatever the world might throw at them.

He smiled. Then, he raised his hands to his face to wipe away the tears.

13

Moonwalking

Ishaan stood before the three-panelled mirror in his walk-in closet, an emperor surveying a diminishing kingdom. The custom Italian suit hung on his frame with calculated precision, midnight blue with a subtle sheen, tailored to disguise the softening at his middle, the slight slope of his shoulders. His fingers, steady despite the cocaine and pills, fastened mother-of-pearl cufflinks that caught the recessed lighting.

The ritual of dressing had always centred him. Since childhood, his appearance had been the one constant he could control. While other boys arrived at St. Matthew's with wrinkled shirts and scuffed shoes, Ishaan's uniform had been impeccable, tie perfectly aligned, pleats knife-sharp, shoes polished to reflect the morning sun. Krishanu's perpetual disarray, traces of snot near the nostril, samosa stains on his collar, untucked shirt, one leg of the trouser stuck in his sock, the faint smell of sweat that clung to him even in winter, had always filled Ishaan with anger. And he would not be shy in telling him, 'Doggie Dum Dum, if they gave you clothes to wear, show them that respect.' This was something his mother had drilled into him. 'You may not control the world, but you can control how you present yourself to it.' It was perhaps the only maternal advice he had truly ever heeded.

Today, of all days, he would maintain that control. They might call him a murderer before the night ended, but they would never call him unkempt.

He studied himself critically, noting how the suit's cut created the illusion of his younger self. The tailoring, by his own bespoke tailors from Singapore, was masterful, adjusting for the changes time had carved into his body while preserving the silhouette that had graced a hundred film posters. Every crease precisely where it should be, every line contributing to the fiction that Ishaan Chatterjee remained undiminished by age.

The walk-in closet stretched behind him like a cathedral to vanity, an expansive room larger than his own bedroom. Custom cedar shelving housed hundreds of suits arranged by colour and occasion, a chromatic journey from midnight blacks through navy blues to summer whites. Shoes lined the opposite wall on illuminated shelves, each pair nestled in its own spotlight. Glass cases displayed watches, cufflinks and sunglasses atop black velvet, protected as if they were crown jewels. The air smelled of leather conditioner, the controlled temperature preserving fabrics worth a small fortune.

This room told the story of his ascent, each garment a chapter, each accessory a 'punctuation mark' in the narrative of Ishaan Chatterjee. A museum to the man he had been, not the one reflected before him now.

From below, the muffled sounds of the crew setting up drifted upward through the floorboards. Equipment cases snapped open with metallic clicks. Lights being positioned with hushed instructions, the electric tension of a production coming together. He was the highlight of the documentary; at least they had given him the respect of not sending over a rookie with a cheap camera.

Anand had brought the PR team and lawyers anyway, ignoring his explicit instructions. Ishaan smiled thinly at this small rebellion, this acknowledgement that Anand-bhai no longer trusted his judgement. Once, they would have scrambled to comply with his every whim. Once, a word from him could empty a room or fill it. Now, they moved around him like nurses around a difficult patient. Cautious. Professional. Detached.

Soon, they would abandon him to his own devices.

But not tonight. Tonight, he was in control.

He selected a burgundy tie from the motorized rack, the mechanism humming softly as it rotated dozens of options before him. This particular shade, not quite red, not quite purple, had been Pramila's favourite colour, though he had not admitted this to himself in decades. The silk felt cool between his fingers, expensive in that subtle way that whispers rather than shouts of wealth. As he looped it with practised motions, his reflection in the mirror was replaced by a memory that cut through him.

St. Matthew's Annual Day, 1993. The school auditorium transformed from a utilitarian space into something approaching magic by strings of coloured lights and hastily painted backdrops. Five hundred students, teachers and parents packed together on folding chairs, the air thick with anticipation. Backstage smelled of nervous sweat and rat droppings, the wooden floor sticky and dusty, both together, as if decades of spilled Pepsi and forgotten props had soaked into its grain.

Sixteen-year-old Ishaan adjusted the single sequined glove while Basab crouched beside a contraption of his own making, a modified overhead projector connected to coloured filters and small motors that would produce strobe effects during the performance. The suit Ishaan wore concealed Basab's true masterpiece; sewn into the lining were tiny packets of flash powder and metallic confetti, a miniature pyrotechnic system triggered by a nearly invisible string at his wrist. Basab had spent weeks perfecting the entire system, skipping meals to work on the calculations, stealing parts from the physics lab when the teachers weren't looking.

'You sure this will work, Genius?' Ishaan asked, nervous despite himself, despite being the boy whom nothing could touch.

Basab looked up, glasses sliding down his nose, a smudge of grease on his cheek. His narrow shoulders hunched over his creation, protective as a mother bird.

'Just don't pull the string before the beat drops. The timing has to be perfect. Lights first, then the flash, then immediately into the moonwalk.' He had replied, the pride in his voice unmistakable.

From beyond the hastily erected curtain came the sound of Ranadeep making announcements, his perfectly clipped British accent in that slightly effeminate voice that had earned him so much mockery. The scuffling of shoes, the hushed whispers, the raw energy of hundreds of teenage bodies held in temporary check filled the air with crackling expectation.

Then there was Basab whispering something Ishaan didn't catch, because the music had started, the unmistakable opening beats of 'Billie Jean' flooding the auditorium, sending a current through the crowd. Ishaan stepped onto the stage, heart hammering in his chest despite his outward calm, and something electric passed between him and the audience.

A connection, a current of mutual recognition. They wanted to believe in magic, and he would provide it.

Each movement was perfect, each slide and spin executed with supernatural precision. The fedora tilted at just the right angle, catching shadows dramatically across his face. His body moved as if gravity had loosened its hold, feet gliding across the scuffed wooden stage as if it were ice. The kickball changes, the shuffle, the spin, executed with a precision that belied his age.

As the song built toward its climax, Basab's strobe lights flickered to life, bathing Ishaan in pulsating blue and white. The crowd gasped, unprepared for this technical marvel in their modest school auditorium. Ishaan felt the music crescendo, counted the beats in his head, one, two, three, and pulled the hidden string at his wrist. What happened next burned itself into the memory of everyone present. The flash powder ignited in a controlled burst as metallic confetti exploded from his suit, catching the strobe light and transforming him into a creature made of pure light. In that exact moment, he launched into the moonwalk, his body seeming to defy physics itself, moving backwards while leaning forward, a human optical illusion.

The crowd erupted into near hysteria. Students leapt to their feet, screaming his name. Even stern-faced teachers abandoned their reserve, watching open-mouthed at the spectacle before them. This was not just admiration; this was worship. This was power; this was what it meant to be alive. To hold hundreds in the palm of your hand with nothing but your body and will. The roar washed over him in waves, each cheer and scream carving itself into his memory, into his very cells.

He finished with a flourish, the strobes catching his final pose, the last glittering confetti drifting down around him like metallic snow.

In that moment, he wasn't a schoolboy in a homemade costume; he was transcendent. He was inevitable.

As he descended from the stage, sweat plastering his white shirt to his back, the crowd parted before him like the Red Sea. Boys clapped him on the shoulder; teachers nodded with rare approval. Girls from St. Agnes reached out to touch his arm as if checking whether he was real. And there, standing in the centre of this human corridor, was Pramila in her school uniform, radiant against the sea of blue blazers and grey trousers.

Unlike the others, she didn't reach for him. She stood perfectly still, a focal point of calm in the surging crowd. Her white blouse and navy skirt were precisely regulation, her hair pulled back with a simple band, yet she outshone the girls who had risked detention by shortening their hemlines or applying forbidden makeup. Something about her stillness drew him forward, a gravitational pull he couldn't have resisted had he tried.

She took his hand when he reached her, her fingers cool against his stage-heated skin.

'You were incredible,' she whispered, her words almost lost in the continuing roar of the crowd, but her eyes spoke volumes. They were filled with stars, not just admiration but wonder, as if he had revealed to her possibilities she had never imagined. As if he had shown her a door to another world. Her gaze held something he had never seen directed at him before: pure, unguarded awe.

In that moment, he had known what he wanted: not just to be loved but worshipped. To see that same look in a thousand eyes, a million eyes. To never step down from the stage. To live forever in that breathless space between performance and adulation, where reality itself bent to his will. It wasn't enough to be wanted or desired; he needed to be necessary, like air.

In twenty-five years of stardom, in the eyes of countless women who had been with him, one-night encounters with fans or relationships that had seemed serious at the time, he had searched for those same stars. But they were never quite right, too calculated, too transient, too easily purchased with his fame and wealth. Sometimes, in unguarded moments between sleep and waking, he wondered if he had imagined those stars in Pramila's eyes. If memory had gilded what was merely teenage infatuation. But then he would recall the precise angle of her head tilted up to his, the small intake of breath before she spoke, the way her pupils had dilated in the dim light of the auditorium, and he knew, it had been real. And he had spent his life trying to recapture it.

He remembered Pramila again, captured in that moment in his memory, and he had looked down at her and said, 'You will always be incredible.' Pramila looked back at him, and smiled, but there was something different now, the pinpricks of light had blown themselves out, replaced by the vacant stare of a drowned girl.

'You broke me.'

Pramila's voice.

Ishaan's fingers faltered. The silk slipped from his grasp. He steadied himself against the mirror, breathing hard, waiting for the vision to pass. His heart raced, a drumbeat of fear in his ears, as he dropped his head to his chest, scrunching his eyes to blot out the memory.

When he looked up again, only his reflection remained, older, lined despite the surgeries, fear lurking behind the practised confidence. The face that had launched a hundred films, that had stared down from billboards across India, now seemed to belong to a stranger. He turned away, unable to face himself.

On the marble-topped vanity, three neat lines of cocaine awaited. The white powder contrasted starkly with the black marble, arranged with the precision of ritual offerings. Beside them sat orange prescription bottles, labels facing discreetly away. Sleep aids for nights when the past pressed too close. Anti-anxiety medication for the panic attacks that had begun after Basab's death. Painkillers for the knee that had never healed properly after that action sequence in Kashmir, when he had insisted on doing his own stunts to prove he was still young.

A collection of pharmaceutical shields against reality, against memory, against the ticking clock of mortality that grew louder with each passing year.

He bent, inhaled quickly through a rolled hundred-dollar bill and straightened up. The familiar numbness spread across his sinuses, followed by the artificial certainty coursing through his veins. Chemical courage. The temporary conviction that he could face anything, say anything, be anything. He would face them now. He would tell his story. Not the sanitized version his publicists had crafted over decades, polished and re-polished until it shone like fool's gold, but the truth that haunted his dreams.

His father's voice emerged from memory with sudden, crushing clarity: 'Did you kill her?'

The question had come the morning after Pramila's body was discovered. They stood in his father's study, all polished teak and leather-bound books that no one ever read, crystal decanters filled with amber liquid, a fortress of masculine power designed to intimidate. The curtains were drawn against the morning light, against the reporters already gathering at their gates like vultures scenting death.

Ishaan, still in yesterday's clothes, hair unwashed, eyes bloodshot from shock and sleeplessness, had stood motionless under his father's scrutiny. The events of the previous day played on an endless loop in his mind: Pramila in the park, her voice steady as she ended things between them. The rage that had flooded him, turning his vision red. The hours afterwards remained a blur, punctuated by fragments of clarity, his knuckles raw, though he couldn't remember why. Then the phone call at dawn, the news spreading through the neighbourhood like fire.

'No, Baba. I did not.' His voice had been steady then, certain.

His father had studied him, eyes narrow, searching for the lie. Siddhartha Chatterjee had not built his empire by trusting; he had built it by seeing through men's façades to the rot beneath. By knowing their weaknesses better than they knew themselves. By understanding that everyone had a price.

In the doorway, his mother had appeared, dressed up as if she was going out for a party, even though she was not. She carried a purse, the red one with glitter, and she had laughed, and given an airy, devil-may-care shrug.

'What does it matter?' she had said, her voice floating down, distant and cold as a mountaintop. 'Men in this house can only kill. Whether he killed her now in an instant or would have killed her over the years, who cares? She was dead the moment she met him, either way.'

His father had turned on her then, rage transforming his face from the handsome mask he showed the world to something primal and terrifying. 'Get back to your room, you stupid woman!'

She had flinched, a small movement that spoke volumes of their private life, then disappeared into the shadows of the upper floor, taking her accusations with her.

When she had gone, his father had gripped Ishaan's shoulders with hands that could break bone. Fingers digging into flesh hard enough to leave marks that would linger for days, physical echoes of this moment.

'Listen to me,' he had said, his breath hot against Ishaan's face, smelling of expensive whisky and desperation. 'It doesn't matter what you did. The girl is dead, and people will believe you did it.' His voice had dropped to a whisper, meant for Ishaan alone, though the house stood empty but for them and his retreating mother. 'Even your mother thinks you killed her. As for me, I do not care. I only asked you because the cops are going to. Say it to them exactly the way you said it.'

'But I am not lying; I did not kill her.' Ishaan had entreated.

'Yes, sure,' his father had said, and then got busy calling every lawyer he could afford, and every politician and hood who owed him a favour.

Once they had charged Brajendra, and the police had said they no longer needed Ishaan for questioning; they had packed their belongings and fled Calcutta. The great Siddhartha Chatterjee, who had faced down business rivals and politicians, who had built an empire from nothing, fled Calcutta, not from the police but from whispers, from the stain that threatened to spread from his son to himself. Sold their beautiful house for a fraction of its worth, abandoned their possessions and disappeared into the vastness of Mumbai, where money could buy a fresh start.

Now, in his penthouse bathroom, Ishaan swallowed against the memory's bitterness. He opened the orange container and poured the white pills down his throat, no water. The pills stuck in his throat for a moment before sliding down. He examined his reflection one last time: the perfect suit, the expertly styled hair, the eyes that betrayed nothing. An actor preparing for his final role.

The intercom buzzed. Anand's voice, tinged with concern he couldn't conceal: 'Sir, they are ready for you downstairs. The camera is set up, and the interviewer is here.'

Ishaan touched his reflection, fingers leaving smudges on the glass. 'I am coming,' he replied, his voice steady, as it had been that morning in his father's study. He looked down at his phone, an older iPhone he no longer used, but now had to, after he had broken his latest one. Of all the old ones that he had, this one was the only one that could still hold its charge. Well, he told himself, I can throw this at their heads if they get too intrusive in their questioning.

Smiling at his joke, he stood up. But the smile vanished immediately, as something caught his eye. Within the folds of his suits, in a far corner, was his school uniform.

Strange, I thought this was left back in Calcutta.

He walked to it, and, no mistake, it was his uniform, that familiar insignia of St. Matthews, that familiar shade of trouser blue, the slightly off-white shirt. There was not a crease on it, as if it had just been ironed, exactly the way he liked it before he wore it.

How did it get here? Why have I never seen it before?

Ishaan ran his fingers over the shirt and the trousers, and as he did, he realized they were damp, not soaking wet, but wet, as if they had been splashed with water.

Ishaan stepped back, filled with a sense of dread. The school uniform was no longer there.

It must be all the shit I had. But no, they don't act this fast.

No, the uniform had been there; it was not a hallucination. He touched his fingers with his thumb; they still felt wet.

Turning around, he almost ran to the door, not wanting to look around at what had been his familiar world.

As his hand touched the doorknob, Ishaan heard a whisper, a whisper that was in Basab's voice, the voice he remembered from thirty years ago, exceptionally deep from someone so slight, but not quite his, like a tape being played back at a much slower speed.

But unlike that day he had moonwalked on stage, there was no music this time, and the words hung heavy, every one of them, in Basab's voice.

'It's time.'

14

Driving the Maserati

Ishaan Chatterjee stopped at the head of the stairs, looking down. The marble floor absorbed shadows cast by tripods. Equipment cases lay open, cables snaking across his living room floor. There was Anand, of course, in his trusty grey safari suit, nervously chewing paan, looking carefully this way and that, his reptilian eyes half open, as if waiting for a fly to buzz past, the red spit at the corner of his lips.

The two lawyers seemed too young to inspire confidence, children playing dress-up in tailored suits. Galgotia had sent his B-team, clearly. To think he had danced at the man's daughter's wedding without charging a fee. For twenty years, the firm of Galgotia had been his lawyers, first the dad and then the son, and yet, at the first sign of real trouble, Galgotia had fled, leaving these boys, whose balls had likely not yet dropped, to witness his misery.

At least the cameraman looked like he had been to many rodeos, Ishaan thought with a satisfied smile. The lighting was good. The sound technician seemed to know his shit, testing levels, listening to his private little symphony, jaw settling into a satisfied smirk.

Now, who was that lady standing there, near the window? Ishaan figured she must be from the PR firm; all of them looked like they had been generated from the same mould. Her name must be Priya.

Yes. She looked very much like a Priya.

And there was Maya Sen. The presenter from the documentary. The architect of his demise, he thought wryly. As her blue blouse caught the harsh light, casting a halo that seemed to separate her from everyone else in the room, Ishaan thought of Bunty Grewal. Had Maya Sen approached him with this hack job, or had he reached out? No, of course, Maya Sen had done her research, seen the potential of the damage she might do to him and had reached out to Bunty to slip a few soiled tenners in her purse.

Aah, well, Bunty, Ishaan said to himself, you got me here. You old bastard, you got me good.

He stood there, hoping they would all look up dramatically at the same time, up at a star. But none of them did. They seemed to go about their work, each in their own little world. For a second, he wondered if he had become invisible. He knew what it felt like, to feel small. He had been a debutante once, and he had walked in on his first day, the hero to be launched, and no one had made eye contact. He might have been the spot boy in khaki shorts bringing tea in a glass. But he had not cared then. He was already in love.

For a set was a magical realm, a blank canvas, lights waiting to transform, cameras hungry for movement, the air electric with unwritten action. As he started giving one hit after another, he was no longer invisible. His arrival, deliberately late, would trigger a ripple of excitement, grips adjusting lights, assistants scrambling, media people crowding around his vanity van as security shooed them away.

He would march past, pretending to everyone that he did not care.

That was the best acting he did.

He would show up half-drunk, often a full shift late, with no idea of what scene they were going to shoot. Once he had shaved off his beard on a whim, a beard that was vital to continuity, sending the director into paroxysms of silent rage as he had to reshoot nearly a quarter of the film. He loved doing that, wasting other people's time and money, just because he could, and there was nothing anyone could do. Projects went overbudget, he would intentionally triple-book his dates, and then wait, as the biggest moneybags would line up at his house, begging for him to show up, at which point in time, he would make whatever demands he felt like, just to see when they would say 'No'. They never did. And then, while on outdoor shoots, he would give them the slip, and fly away to some island in the Pacific, and wait for them to rush there and grovel some more.

It had been fun.

But then somewhere down the road, something had changed. Sets became workplaces. Then obligations. The magic had calcified into routine. The hit machine stalled. He flubbed dialogues. The directors would no longer work around him, giving his lines to other junior artists, while he would throw tantrums at poor Anand-bhai for the director changing the script and then editing out his best sequences in the final cut.

Ishaan Chatterjee took a step down, and then another. The tie felt like a noose around his throat. Descending into his own living room, now transformed into an interview set, he felt only the cold dread that his career had become for him over these last few years.

He knew this chill. He had felt this way during the interrogation sessions at his house after Pramila was murdered. They would sit like this in the living room, Inspectors Bhattacharya and Roy, as he would walk down the stairs just like now. Before that, breakfast would be brought to his bedroom, and they would barricade and lock it as the lawyers coached him, and after they were done, his father. He remembered their eyes, Inspector Roy's especially, waiting for him to make a mistake. And he did, from time to time he would fumble and be caught in an inconsistency, and then the lawyers would step in. But mostly his father would.

But he was no longer there. There was no Siddhartha Chatterjee at his side, whose forearm he could clutch onto.

Just Ishaan. Alone.

And Bunty Grewal's net closing in on him, with Maya Sen pulling the drawstring.

Ishaan had now reached the bottom of the stairs.

Thrusting his chest out and extending his arms, theatrically, Ishaan announced, 'Welcome to my house of sin.'

And even then, no heads turned at his declaration. Anand, busy whispering to one of the baby-faced lawyers, his face thick-set with worry, did not even register his arrival. The sound technician continued adjusting levels, the light man fiddled with a barn door, the PR woman adjusted her hair and took a selfie.

Only Maya Sen had the decency to look up, her expression professionally neutral. 'Mr Chatterjee. Thank you for joining us.'

He walked to his chair, the throne-like seat positioned on the raised marble platform. He smoothed his jacket and settled into the leather with practised ease.

'Shall we start?' Maya Sen asked, with the detachment of a doctor going over his bloodwork.

'Don't you want to do a sound check first?' Ishaan asked, adjusting his collar. 'Maybe check the lighting?'

The cameraman glanced up briefly. 'Already done, sir.'

Already done. They had prepared everything without his input, without asking his preference for key light positioning, without enquiring about his good side. In his own home.

They intended to make him look bad. In every which way.

'We will begin then,' Maya said, nodding to the cameraman. 'Unless you need a moment?'

'I am ready when you are.' Ishaan crossed his legs, adopting the relaxed posture he had perfected over thousands of interviews. The slight smile, the easy confidence. Muscle memory.

Whatever Bunty had paid Maya Sen, he was going to make her work for it.

The red recording light blinked on. Maya Sen composed her features into serious journalism mode.

'Mr Chatterjee,' she began, voice measured and professional. 'Thank you for agreeing to this interview.'

'Let's skip the pleasantries,' Ishaan said. 'I want to know who gave you that information about Dr Basab Banerjee. That was a dick move, what you pulled on Arun Mathur's show, dragging a dead man's reputation through mud.'

Maya Sen's expression remained neutral. 'I understand your concern for your friend, but our team had nothing to do with that segment. We don't operate that way.'

'No, of course not.' Ishaan lifted his right eyebrow, 'You want this documentary to be Pulitzer-worthy.' He gave a hard laugh, making no attempt to be pleasant. 'I know your type, Ms Maya Sen. You are the kind that likes to sit on the high ground and then look down at the world through the bridge of your nose. You want to make money, but you don't want to look bad doing so.'

A flash of surprise crossed Maya's face. Her shoulders slumped for a moment, before regaining her composure. Across the room, one of the baby-faced lawyers shifted nervously. Anand's eyes widened in silent warning, waving his hand once, as if telling his employer to stop.

'If I were a betting man,' Ishaan continued, not caring for the disapproval that swept across the room. 'I would say that you planted this filth with Arun Mathur. It is exactly the kind of thing he would do, so you don't have to. And now that the memory of my friend has been dragged through mud, based on dodgy accusations from an ex-wife, you and your financiers have reviewed the watch time of your squalid little reality show, sorry, true crime documentary, and patted yourselves on your backs.'

Maya Sen's expression retained its detachment, but her eyes seemed to go harder. Glassier.

'Perhaps we should focus on Pramila Chatterjee instead?' she said. 'This documentary is about her, not Mr Banerjee.'

'Not, *mister*. That's Doctor Banerjee for you.' Ishaan snapped, his voice rising, 'And I can guarantee you that his genius is no lie.'

'I apologize,' Maya Sen said at once. She flicked a glance at the cameraman, and then back again at Ishaan, 'No disrespect intended.'

'Yes, well. Too late for that,' Ishaan said, his lips pursing into an aggressive line.

Maya coughed sharply, resetting the room.

'Let's talk about Pramila,' she said. 'Your friend Ranadeep Saha felt we haven't focused enough on who she was as a person. So, let's start there. From the person who knew her the best. What made her special? What are your memories of her?'

Ishaan opened his mouth to speak.

But then he heard it.

Laughter.

Bright. Feminine. Mocking.

It sliced clean through his thoughts.

One moment, it was there, ringing in his ear, and then, gone.

The lights seemed to flicker. A half-second stutter in the world.

Ishaan froze.

Maya Sen's lips were still, her face politely expectant. The sound had come from somewhere behind her, but there was no one there.

Ishaan scanned the room. Only the Priya-woman could have made that sound, but she was scrolling through her phone, oblivious.

No one else seemed to notice. Not the flicker. Not the sound.

'Mr Chatterjee?' Maya Sen prompted, 'What were your memories of her?'

She emphasized it this time: *your* memories.

The laughter came again, louder. Like bells ringing underwater.

It darted from one side of the room to the other, left to right, right to left, in a wild, zigzag motion.

Ishaan's eyes followed it, his head jerking back and forth like an animal scenting danger.

Then a voice.

You don't remember me as a person at all, do you? The voice was unmistakably Pramila's, though it had been thirty years since he had heard it. Ishaan stopped, not daring to breathe.

The voice had come from behind Maya Sen's lips.

But her mouth had not moved.

She was still looking at him, waiting for an answer.

All your memories of me are just memories of you, Ishu.

The voice again, Pramila's voice, but this time the voice came out like an angry hiss.

I was just a mirror for the great Ishaan Chatterjee. The perfect audience for your dance moves, your cricket stories, your father's money. But me? I was never there.

'Mr Chatterjee?' Maya leaned forward now, her lips pursed, eyes narrowed with clinical precision. 'Is something wrong?'

'Nothing,' Ishaan replied quickly.

But when he looked down, he saw his chest was rising and falling in rhythm, as if he had just got off after a brutal session of high-intensity interval training. Maybe, he thought, maybe now the powder was working, maybe the pills were kicking in, but this was not how it was supposed to be.

He needed courage. He needed focus. He needed to tell Maya Sen and Bunty Grewal, or whoever the fuck was behind this, that he was not going to go down without bloodying their nose too.

'Could you tell us about her?' Maya asked, gently now, almost indulgent. 'Who was Pramila Chatterjee to you?'

Like a teacher coaxing a difficult child.

Ishaan opened his mouth. *Childhood sweetheart. First love.* The phrases should have come easily. But now, the words felt inaccessible, like artefacts locked behind frosted glass.

'She was...' he began and then faltered.

'Beautiful?' Maya offered, her tone even. 'Devoted? Your possession? Your pet?'

It was Pramila's voice. Not Maya's. The same intonation, the same razor blade softness. Ishaan knew it like he knew his own reflection.

And it came again, not from Maya's lips, which remained pressed in a line, but from somewhere within her, through her, using her.

His face changed. The veneer cracked. The muscle memory of a thousand interviews abandoned him. His jaw slackened, his pupils shrank to points and sweat burst across his forehead like rain on hot stone.

They didn't hear it. None of them did.

Only he could hear the laughter.

Not joyful, not playful, vindictive. It vibrated in the air now, thick and invisible, like a second heartbeat in the room. It didn't dance around like before. It stayed, hovering directly in front of him, mocking him, daring him to pretend it wasn't real.

Ishaan's fingers shot to his tie. It was wet now, though it hadn't been. His other hand clutched the armrest, holding on like the room itself was about to tilt.

The cameraman exchanged a look with the sound technician. One of the lawyers started to rise, sensing something was deeply wrong with their client, and sat down, as Ishaan started speaking.

'She was beautiful,' Ishaan managed, but even he knew the words rang hollow.

'No, not just that. She was talented. Smart. She sang like...'

His voice trailed off, unravelling into the silence.

Anand took a step forward again, palms out in surrender. 'Sir, I think we need a moment. Perhaps some water?'

Ishaan waved him away, more out of habit than clarity. He was struggling, clawing his way back to the version of himself that had always been able to lie without blinking.

'You were asking about Pramila,' he said, his tone stiffening into something more formal, more defensible. 'Rabindra Sangeet. Her voice…'

The sentence didn't finish. The words fell apart, floating like ash on still water.

And that's when he saw it.

The blouse Maya Sen was wearing.

He had thought it was blue. But now, under the lights, it shimmered grey, the exact grey Pramila had worn on that evening.

The evening she died.

His body shuddered, a full-body ripple of something unseen, and now everyone in the room noticed. His eyes, glassy and wide, didn't blink, but then his lids began fluttering rapidly, bizarrely, as if caught between sleep and seizure, though his body remained frozen, unnaturally still.

'Let's talk about the magazine,' Maya said, ignoring Ishaan's agitation, as she reached into a folder. She pulled out the *Woman's World* issue, its glossy cover preserved despite the decades. Pramila's face stared up from the page, confident and radiant.

'How did you feel when you saw this?'

'I think we should stop,' one of the baby-faced lawyers said, his voice too deep for someone that slight.

Turning to the cameraman, he said, brusquely, 'I think you should pack up.'

At that moment, Anand took two long strides and put his body right in front of the camera.

'You heard the man, stop recording.'

He pressed his palm to the lens, firm enough that the cameraman had to steady the tripod to keep it from toppling. Chaos stirred. The PR woman stepped forward, siding with Anand, her voice high-pitched. 'This was not discussed. The magazine was clearly meant to provoke our client.'

Maya stood. As she did, the light shifted. Her blouse, earlier the colour of wet slate, shimmered blue again. Ishaan's shoulders loosened, just slightly. Something had relaxed in him.

The cameraman tried to peer around Anand's broad back, his weathered face pinched with professional frustration. 'Sir, please, this is expensive equipment.' He spoke directly to Ishaan, hoping the actor would rein in his staff.

Ishaan sat deathly still, his frame rigid beneath the tailored suit. The magazine in Maya's hands caught the studio lights, casting a momentary halo around Pramila's face. His pupils shrank to pinpricks despite the dim ambience. A muscle twitched in his jaw, once, twice. The pulse in his temple throbbed visibly. He stared not at Maya but through her, his focus pinned on some invisible point between memory and hallucination.

The cameraman's voice snapped him back like a rubber band snapping against skin. His nostrils flared. He inhaled sharply. His eyes locked back on the present, on the studio, on the room.

And something dangerous flickered.

'Who told you to interfere?' Ishaan's voice sliced through the commotion, targeting Anand and the lawyers with unexpected venom. His eyes flashed with rage as he lurched to his feet. 'No one is going anywhere. I agreed to this interview without conditions, and I intend to finish it.'

The lawyers flinched, shrinking into the cushions. The younger one flushed red, swallowing beneath Ishaan's glare. The senior partner clutched his briefcase to his chest like a child with a pillow in a thunderstorm.

'Sir, please. This is not in your best interest,' Anand pleaded, his hand still shielding the camera lens. Sweat darkened his safari suit under the arms.

'Move your hand, Anand-bhai,' Ishaan said, his voice deadly quiet.

'I cannot do that, sir.'

'Yes, you can,' Ishaan said, sitting back, and moving his fingers to smooth his hair back. 'I can manage this…I can manage…the truth.'

A long silence stretched, taut as piano wire. Anand's hand hovered for another heartbeat, then dropped. Defeated. The camera blinked awake again. Anand retreated to the margins of the frame, lingering behind Ishaan's chair, close but non-intrusive. His thumb hovered near his phone. Ready.

The PR woman's phone chimed. She furiously messaged her team. The blue glow illuminated her face as she backed into the corner, lips moving silently, rehearsing pre-approved narratives that now felt like jokes.

The lawyers remained seated, though stiff. Their posture had shifted, from protectors to accessories. They would bear witness, not shield.

Maya eased back into her seat. Her face betrayed nothing. No triumph. No concern.

'Shall we continue, Mr Chatterjee?' she asked, her voice neutral as she gestured toward the magazine still lying open between them. 'You were about to tell me your reaction when you first saw this.'

The cameraman exchanged a quick glance with Maya Sen, who gave an almost imperceptible nod to continue. The red recording light remained steady, capturing every moment of Ishaan Chatterjee's unravelling.

Ishaan looked at the magazine. Pramila's face smiled up at him, shoulders bare, eyes challenging the camera.

Something twisted inside him, not memory but re-experience. The rage flooded through him exactly as it had thirty years ago.

The magazine stand. The vendor's leer. Boys from National making obscene gestures. His girlfriend, his Pramila, exposed for all to see. His fists had clenched then, just as they clenched now. His vision had narrowed then, just as it narrowed now, the world reduced to that glossy cover, that defiant smile.

'When you ask, what my reaction was, let us cut to the chase.' Ishaan smiled, sinisterly, the camera lights reflecting off his teeth. 'What you really mean to ask is, did I want to kill her?'

Behind Ishaan, Anand's breathing stopped. The PR woman's phone slipped from her fingers, landing softly on her lap. Her lips parted, blood draining from her face as the ultimate PR nightmare unfolded before her eyes. The younger lawyer pressed his palm flat against the sofa cushion, preparing to rise, then sank back as the senior partner subtly shook his head.

Only Maya Sen leaned forward, her body language shifting from interviewer to confidante. The sound technician's eyes widened above the boom mic, but his hands remained steady, capturing every syllable of what might be the confession of the decade.

'And did you?' Maya asked, her voice soft, almost intimate. The question floated between them, simple, direct, devastating.

'Yes, I said I was going to kill her,' he heard himself say.

The words landed like gunshots.

The sound technician paled but didn't flinch. The mic kept rolling.

Ishaan didn't care anymore. Let them record. Let them broadcast. Let the world know.

The only thing that mattered now was the voice.

The voice that hadn't spoken in a while. That voice.

Maya's lips hadn't moved. But the room seemed to hum with her presence. Not her, the one inside her.

'Mr Chatterjee,' Maya Sen continued, voice steady despite the revelation, 'witnesses say you went to her house after seeing the magazine. What happened there?'

He was reliving it, that sensation, the blood throbbing to his temples, drunk on his adrenaline, and Pramila just there, unrepentant, unapologetic, as if she had done nothing, nothing at all. He closed his eyes to flush out the memories.

'Well, it was just a small slap,' he began, but different words emerged: 'Yeah, so I hit her so hard her trophies fell…who cared about those silly little trinkets anyways…it's not as if they were the Oscars.'

His hand leapt to his mouth. The tie tightened against his throat. Had someone adjusted it? He tugged at the knot, found it exactly as it had been.

And then: laughter. Not Maya. Behind him. He turned. The PR woman was in the shadows, but her eyes had lifted.

The angle of her neck, wrong.

Tilted far too much, as though her spine had snapped sideways.

Oh ho, Ishu, so that's when you felt like a man? Here is a little secret, babu. The only time you feel like a man is when you hit a woman.

The voice went straight through his skull.

'I think we need to stop recording,' Anand shouted, panic fracturing his professional veneer. 'This has gone too far.'

'No one is going to come in between,' Ishaan snarled, his voice a wounded animal's. 'Let them ask. Let them ask everything.'

Maya Sen's professional mask slipped momentarily; fear flickered in her eyes, like fish beneath ice, before she recovered. A glint caught the light on her cheek: a perfect droplet, too full to be sweat, too solitary to be a tear, gleaming impossibly in the bone-dry air.

'The last time you saw Pramila alive, you brought her roses,' Maya said, her voice steady despite the tension stretching between them. 'You went to Ramkrishna Park. She wanted to end the relationship. Did you take the roses to convince her to stay?'

'Yes, she wanted to break it off,' Ishaan replied. 'I was surprised she would want to, because the way I saw it, it was she who had not been honest, who had hidden something from me.'

Maya Sen looked up at him, her expression unchanged.

'So just to be clear, you felt that you were the aggrieved party, despite physically assaulting her and breaking her property?'

'Yes,' Ishaan responded. 'If *my body, my choice* allows women to break the social contract, you know, the one where she does not pose half-naked on the cover of a magazine, why is it that when a man acts on his instincts, to lash out, that he becomes a…'

The rest evaporated.

Maya had not asked that question.

The words had surfaced from somewhere else, somewhere he couldn't face. Her startled expression confirmed it. The room tilted. Boundaries between memory and the present, real and the imagined, melted like metal in acid.

'Err…' Maya hesitated, thrown off her script. She glanced at the cameraman, then returned to her mark.

'So, you were surprised by her reaction,' she continued, recovering her rhythm. 'So both of you chose to break off this relationship. You feeling betrayed, and her drawing a line at the abuse.'

Ishaan opened his mouth to correct her, but nothing came. Maya's face shimmered under the lights, her features distorting like a reflection in disturbed water. The droplet on her cheek multiplied and slid down in a single glistening line. Her lips moved, but the voice that came was not hers.

Oh, Ishu, will you not tell them what you said? I will die if you leave me. Boo hooo, do you remember how much you wept? You wept like a little girl. I had to hug you to hush you up, like a baby.

The memory slammed through his drug-fogged mind: him on the park bench, tears running down his face, begging her not to leave. Her expression, not triumphant, but sad. Gentle, even as her words undid him. Her arms wrapped around him, soothing *his* heartbreak, not hers. He had been a fever she had sweated out. All the pain that remained was his alone.

You remember, don't you, Ishu, how you begged? You always knew you would never be able to hold onto anything. Not your liquor, not your fame, not your money, not your fans, not your friends. As for love? You can lock them up, set your dogs on them, or slap them across their face, but they leave. They always do.

The voice no longer mocked. It was mournful now. And Ishaan tasted it, his own tears, bitter on his tongue.

'Mr Chatterjee?' Maya Sen prompted. Her voice seemed to come from underwater now, muffled and distant. 'What about the beggar?'

Ishaan's heart seized. He sniffed back the tears.

'What beggar?'

'The man who slept on the footpath near Pramila's house.' Maya Sen shuffled her notes with deliberate slowness. 'He told the police he saw you walk toward her house that night, after the park. His testimony was never entered into the file. It directly contradicts Dr Banerjee's statement, who said he saw you go the other direction.'

'That's…impossible.' His breath thinned. Every word cost him more air. 'No beggar ever testified. I would have remembered that.'

'Police records suggest otherwise.' Her eyes locked onto his, unblinking. 'Inspector Roy removed certain statements out of the official file. Accounts that contradicted what the police wanted, which he believed would be destroyed. He kept it in the hope that one day he might be able to prove the truth.'

'Inspector Roy hated my father. You know why? Same reason why people hate me. They see my success and think, "Hey, that should be me." Then spend their pathetic little lives trying to tear me down, crapping on films they haven't seen, trolling me online. Insect-men. Inspector Roy was that sort. I have no idea which beggar saw me go in which direction. As far as I am concerned…'

The words choked his throat, and the air seemed to wheeze out of his lungs, like they were escaping a deflating balloon.

Then, a sound. A whisper, almost sing-song.

Ooohhhh…Ishaan Chatterjee is a puppy who follows home…oho…

A wet touch grazed the nape of his neck, like hair brushing skin. Ishaan turned sharply. No one there.

Just Anand, frozen by the bar, face blank, staring through him.

'Are you all right?' Maya Sen asked, but Ishaan ignored her.

Water. He saw it first at the edges of the room. Not flooding in, but seeping, dark patches on the pristine walls, spreading like bruises on skin. Droplets forming on the ceiling, defying gravity, growing fat before tracking down in rivulets.

He blinked hard. The walls were dry.

'Mr Chatterjee?'

Ishaan turned back to Maya Sen.

'This beggar's testimony...it never came up during the investigation.' His voice echoed, thin and brittle. 'Not once in thirty years.'

'Perhaps someone wanted it buried.'

Maya Sen's blouse was Pramila-grey again. When she tucked a strand behind her ear, the movement reminded him of Pramila's habit, that familiar gesture from decades ago.

'The beggar described you perfectly,' she continued. 'Your walk. The way you carried yourself. How you stared straight ahead, never looking back at the park where you had left her. He said you looked like a man possessed.'

His heartbeat kicked up.

'But the most interesting detail.' She leaned forward, her eyes now somehow glassy, reflective like the surface of still water. 'He said you walked with purpose, like a man who knew exactly what he was going to do when he reached that house.'

That voice again, closer to his ear, not the interview's, but someone more familiar.

Puppy came home. Came home to drown the rose.

Ishaan gripped the armrests, leather creaking under his fingers. The cameras kept rolling, unblinking.

Then it came.

The question he knew they would ask.

Maya asked it. At least, he thought she did.

'Did you kill Pramila?'

Four words, sharp as a slap, under the studio lights. His answer, the one he had prepared, dissolved on his tongue.

Behind Maya, the water returned. Pooling on the floor. No pipes, no leaks, but there it was. Spreading like ink on silk.

No one else saw it.

'I did not kill Pramila,' he croaked. 'Yes, I followed her home. I…I thought she would turn around. You know, see me and feel bad. But she never turned around. Not even once.'

'So, you did follow her home? Are you accepting you killed her then?'

'No, no,' Ishaan screamed, his eyes open wide in terror. 'I never entered her house. I swear. I left. I left because of what I said. She did not turn around. She no longer cared for me. I tell you I did not kill Pramila Chatterjee.'

A low laugh echoed from everywhere and nowhere. Every person in the room was now laughing. Not their mouths, but their eyes.

Of course he did. He killed me every day. Every day he drowned me in his bucket, and now he will cry his career away in a bucket of tears.

His eyes snapped back to Maya Sen. Her face…something was happening to her face. The change was subtle at first, skin losing elasticity, taking on a waxy pallor. Her cheeks seemed to bloat slightly, the flesh puffing outward. Her lips, once narrow and professional, appeared fuller, bluer.

'Are you sure about that, Mr Chatterjee?' Her voice carried an echo now, and she was smiling now, teeth bared.

The water rose, invisible to everyone but him. He felt it around his ankles, cold and insistent, like the truth he had been running from for three decades.

'Who the fuck are you?' Ishaan tried to stand but found himself anchored to where he was.

Maya Sen's transformation accelerated. Her hair darkened, lengthened before his eyes, now hanging in wet ropes around features no longer hers. The bone structure shifted, cheekbones higher, nose more delicate despite the bloating. Her eyes, once brown, now appeared black, the pupils expanding to consume the iris entirely.

'*Who am I?*' she asked, but the voice belonged to another. '*I am what you always wanted me to be. I am your mirror. Why? Don't you like what you see? Does it scare you, Ishu?*'

He recognized the remnants of the navy-grey schoolgirl uniform materializing, how he had always remembered her. White collar darkened by water. The silver necklace he once gave Pramila as a gift, now a tarnished chain around this impossible neck.

'You are not real,' Ishaan whispered.

The water reached his waist, though nobody else in the room reacted. The camera operator adjusted a setting. The boom operator suppressed a yawn. They stood in water up to their knees, yet felt nothing.

Pramila, fully formed now where Maya Sen once sat, leaned forward. Her face showed the unmistakable changes of drowning. The slightly distended features. The blue-tinged skin. The strange rigidity of death. The face frozen in terror.

'*I am as real as your fear*,' she said, water spilling from her mouth with each word, cascading down her chin, '*the fear you put in me, the fear I lived with, the fear of your family, the fear of offending you in any way and bringing your wrath down upon me.*'

The taste of metal filled Ishaan's mouth. His lungs constricted as if being crushed by invisible hands. The room tilted, the water rising faster, now at his chest, his neck.

Nobody moved to help him. They only watched, cameras rolling, documenting a breakdown they couldn't possibly understand.

'I can't breathe,' Ishaan gasped.

Pramila smiled, and it was the most terrible thing he had ever seen, this expression of joy on a drowned face, and now her face melded with that of the girl in Pramila's old apartment, watching him from the balcony in the rain.

'*Now you know how it feels to drown*,' she whispered.

The brackish water burned his nostrils. His vision dimmed at the edges, darkness rolling in from the sides, till the only thing that remained was her impossible, terrible face. The drowned girl who would not stay dead. The past that would not stay buried.

Something primitive awoke in him, a sinking man's final, desperate lunge for air. For survival. For silencing the truth once more.

Ishaan lunged forward, hands outstretched toward the apparition's throat. His fingers connected not with ghost-flesh but with the very real softness of Maya Sen's neck. Her eyes widened in genuine shock, interview persona shattered by primal fear, as Ishaan's fingers curled around her throat. Her head rammed backwards, as her eyes rolled back into her head.

Maya Sen's face contorted as his grip tightened. Her mouth opened in silent desperation, lips working frantically but producing only wet, choking sounds. Her hands clawed at his wrists, nails scraping against his skin as her body bucked beneath him. A thin, reedy wheeze escaped her compressed windpipe, but Ishaan did not hear it.

All he heard was a monstrous laugh coming from Maya Sen.

'*Look at my boy trying to be a man. Look at him at his very best.*'

That was all that Ishaan heard, blotting out all other sounds. But this time, it was not in Pramila's voice; it was in a parody of his father's.

Ishaan wanted it to stop, the voices, and he kept shaking Maya by her neck, applying the full force of his forearms. Colour bloomed across her face in alarming waves, flushed red giving way to a deeper crimson in her cheeks. The microphone at her lapel captured every strangled gasp, recording the intimate sounds of her struggle. Spittle gathered at the corners of her mouth, bubbling with each failed attempt to draw breath.

The living room erupted. The lawyer nearest to Ishaan sprang up with surprising speed for his bulk, knocking over a glass full of water that shattered against the concrete floor. Anand reached Ishaan next, arms wrapping around his torso, voice urgent in his ear: 'Sir, stop! What are you doing?' Using his full body weight, he yanked Ishaan backward, both men careening across the polished floor in a violent tangle of limbs. As Ishaan's fingers released their grip, Maya Sen scrambled backward, gasping for air, her hand at her throat, leaving bruises like smudged makeup.

Ishaan's mind cleared for just a moment. The water was gone. The vision dispelled. The terror in Maya Sen's eyes was real; no drowning spectre now, just a frightened woman.

But the damage was done.

'Get off me!' Ishaan twisted violently, breaking free from Anand's restraining grip, and jumped up like a toy on a spring. One of the lawyers now jumped on him to restrain Ishaan, but before he could, his elbow connected with the lawyer's jaw, producing a sickening crack. Bodies converged on him, the cameraman, and the sound guy, and even the PR lady, a forest of arms reaching to contain the madman.

Ishaan shoved blindly, his strength multiplied by terror.

'She was here. She has been here.' Ishaan shouted at faces that registered only confusion and horror. 'Don't you see her? Don't you hear her?'

The path to the elevator door cleared, not through his efforts but from people backing away. His living room had transformed into a tableau of frozen figures, afraid to approach the unravelling star. Only Anand still reached for him, pleading: 'Sir, please.'

But Ishaan was past hearing.

Blabbering incoherently, he turned and sprinted for the elevator door. Reaching it in leaps and bounds, his body contorted unnaturally with each stride, torso wrenched to the left as if half-drowned, limbs moving at wrong angles like a marionette with tangled strings. He jabbed at the private elevator button frantically, glancing over his shoulder, though no one pursued.

The polished doors slid open with luxurious smoothness, welcoming him into their mirrored sanctuary. He punched the lobby button, then hammered the 'close door' repeatedly until the exit sealed, leaving behind a room of stunned witnesses to his insanity.

As the elevator began its descent, a soft plink drew his attention upward. A droplet of water formed on the ceiling, defying the laws of physics, growing fat before falling. It landed on his cheek, cold as a death touch. Another formed. Then another. Soon a steady drip filled the silence of his descent.

Thirty floors passed in suspended time, water pooling around his handmade Italian shoes. The elevator chimed pleasantly at the lobby level, doors opening to reveal the marble-floored atrium. The droplets vanished, leaving him dry but shaking.

Security guards looked up from their station. The head concierge stepped forward, concern etched on his practised features. 'Sir? Is everything all right?'

Ishaan barrelled past them without acknowledgement, his thousand-watt smile nowhere to be found. The automatic glass doors parted before him as he burst into Mumbai's humid evening air, right into his private garage.

'Sir! Sir!' The youngest security guard called after him, phone pressed to his ear. No doubt Anand had already called down with warnings, instructions.

Ishaan's Maserati purred at the curb, the valet miraculously manifesting it without being asked. The young man held the door open, expression carefully blank, the face of someone trained never to notice celebrity meltdowns.

Ishaan snatched the keys, threw himself behind the wheel, and twisted the ignition before the valet could fully back away. The engine roared to life, its familiar vibration the only solid thing in his dissolving reality.

He slammed the gearshift into reverse, tyres squealing against the polished concrete floor of his private underground garage. The Maserati's headlights swept across the cavernous space, catching expensive motorcycles and vintage cars that stood like silent witnesses to his breakdown. He floored the accelerator, the car's rear sensors blaring warnings he ignored as he careened toward the exit ramp.

The private security guard at the garage booth barely had time to register the approaching headlights before slapping the emergency override. The reinforced barrier gate rose with mechanical reluctance, too slowly for Ishaan's frantic pace. He swerved around it with inches to spare, metal screeching against concrete as the Maserati's side mirror shattered against the partially raised arm.

Tyres squealed as he burst onto the deserted service road behind his building complex. The digital dashboard clock glowed 2.17 a.m. in accusatory blue light. Mumbai at this hour belonged to a different world, streets emptied of daytime chaos, replaced by long shadows and pools of yellow street light. The occasional taxi drifted by like a ghost ship, its driver eyeing the speeding Maserati with professional indifference.

Through the rearview mirror, he caught a glimpse of figures spilling from the building's service entrance, Anand among them, phone pressed to his ear, his other hand raised in futile summons, his figure shrinking to insignificance in the midnight darkness.

Ishaan knew there was no coming back. Now he was running. Again. Just like his father had taught him.

Sweat slicked his palm against the steering wheel despite the air conditioning whispering arctic currents across his skin. His chest heaved with sobs that tore through him like violent storms, raw and uncontained. Tears streamed down his face in thick rivulets, blurring his vision until the road before him wavered like a mirage. He had not cried like this since that day in the park when Pramila had walked away, her back straight, her decision final. Back then, he had crumpled onto the bench, pride abandoned, begging her to stay while she stood unmoved by his tears.

Now, as then, his weeping came from someplace primal, a wounded animal's howl. His shoulders heaved, mucous and tears mixing freely. The sobs wrenched from deep in his gut, each one leaving him hollower than the last. The speedometer needle trembled higher as his foot pushed the pedal to the floor. The engine's growl deepened, the only voice that didn't demand explanations he couldn't give.

The old phone rested heavy in his pocket, the one he had thrown in a drawer years ago. The one he had pulled out after smashing his iPhone against the bathroom wall. Something had made him charge it before the interview. Something had made him bring it. Just as something now made him pull it out, balancing the steering wheel with his knee while his thumb slid across its ancient screen.

One message waited. Not from Anand or the PR team or the lawyers yelling at his back as he fled the penthouse.

From Basab.

'This is Genius. Call me.'

The message transported Ishaan back thirty years, to cramped Calcutta apartments and precious phone calls. Back then, Basab would call, let it ring once, then hang up, their signal. Ishaan would then call back from his father's deluxe push-button phone. 'I am here,' he would always say, those three words carrying the weight of their friendship.

But how could this be him now? Basab was dead. Basab, his best friend. Basab, who always had his answers.

Ishaan's vision blurred. Not from speed but from tears that gathered and fell, tracing hot paths down cheeks once adored by millions. With one hand still on the wheel and his foot pressed firm on the accelerator, he typed back, from habit and from hope.

'Hello, I am here.'

The Bandra–Worli Sea Link loomed ahead, a concrete serpent stretched across the black waters. Its lights reflected in the Arabian Sea below, creating the illusion of stars drowning beneath dark waves.

Something caught Ishaan's attention, a movement in his peripheral vision. He turned to the passenger seat, previously empty. A red rose rested there, petals unfurled in perfect bloom despite the lack of water, its crimson intensity visible even in the car's dim lighting.

His heart thundered against his ribs. There was no reason for a rose to be here. Yet here it was, impossibly present, impossibly fresh, impossibly perfect.

Ishaan reached for it with trembling fingers, his eyes leaving the road for just a moment. Just one moment.

The Maserati swerved violently. His hand jerked back to the wheel, overcorrecting. The car careened sideways, tyres screaming against asphalt as they lost their grip. The steering wheel spun beneath his fingers, useless against momentum and physics and fate.

The concrete barrier of the Sea Link rushed toward him, filling his vision with grey certainty. Time stretched, elastic in its final moments. Ishaan saw the speedometer frozen at 210, saw the rose tumbling through the air as the car tilted, saw the black water waiting beyond the barrier like an opened mouth.

The impact came as a symphony of destruction, metal crumpling, glass shattering, the car's frame groaning as it broke through the barrier. For one suspended moment, the Maserati seemed to hang in the air, defying gravity like a dancer at the height of a leap.

Then the fall.

As the car plummeted toward the waiting water, a sequence of memories flashed by like paper flickering in the wind. Pramila turning around to look at him in front of the Pujo pandal, the flowers in her hair, the scent of tuberose wafting through time to fill his nostrils with impossible sweetness. Krishanu dancing in the rain, splashing in puddles that scattered mud in all directions, his face alive with a joy so pure, it burned to witness. Ranadeep's eyes closed as he moved his face close to the microphone, the poetry of Rabindra Sangeet pouring from his lips, sad and beautiful, each note a tear given voice. Basab, carefully putting on his cricket gloves, adjusting the helmet straps over his oversized glasses, expression solemn as a priest preparing for sacred rites. The images dissolved into crowds, thousands packed into stadiums, all yelling 'Ishaan, Ishaan' as he came out to the beat, their voices a single wave crashing against the shore of his existence. Fragments of announcements from what had been his life, 'The best actor award goes to Ishaan Chatterjee', drowned out by thunderous applause.

Now only the rush of wind, the groan of metal, the whisper of approaching water.

'You are here now, Ishu.' A soft, female voice whispered in his ear, intimate as a lover, cold as the grave.

Ishaan's tears stopped abruptly. A preternatural calm settled over him as he turned toward the voice.

In the passenger seat where the rose had been, Pramila sat watching him. Not the vengeful apparition that had haunted his nightmares, but the girl he had known, young and beautiful in her school uniform, dark eyes reflecting the moonlight filtering through the windshield. Water dripped from her hair, from her fingers, from the hem of her skirt, pooling on the leather seat beneath her. Yet her presence brought not terror but a terrible, aching relief.

'Yes,' he whispered, his voice steady for the first time in hours. 'I am here.'

The car struck the water with the force of a meteor, metal howling as it surrendered to impact. The windshield imploded, sending a shower of glass across Ishaan's face like diamond tears. Water rushed in with hungry violence, swallowing sound, swallowing light, swallowing time itself.

Ishaan's neck snapped at impact, and yet consciousness lingered, stretched across the threshold between life and death like morning fog. In this liminal space, the burgundy tie, Pramila's favourite colour, floated upward in the rushing water before tightening around his neck, a silken noose drawn by invisible hands.

As darkness crept inward from the edges of his vision, Pramila's hand found his, her fingers twining with his as naturally as they had thirty years ago, cold yet impossibly familiar.

'Sleep now,' she said, though no bubbles escaped her lips, though no sound could travel through water rushing into the car's carcass. Yet he had heard her, not with his ears but with whatever part of him was already crossing over.

With her words, the last tether to consciousness unravelled. The man who had once commanded millions from silver screens surrendered to the deep, to her, to whatever waited beyond the veil between worlds.

Ishaan's past and present merged completely underwater, the boy who had moonwalked across a school stage to thunderous applause became the man who had taken Mumbai by storm, now lying in its watery depths. The circle closing, becoming nothing. Just another whisper in the city's eternal noise, a ghost story that would be told, and retold, and then buried under other such stories until only the rose remained, crimson and perfect, washing up on shores where nothing blooms.

15

Ranadeep Reflects

Ranadeep checked his watch. The IndiGo flight to Calcutta was now delayed by eighty minutes, meaning arrival close to midnight. He sat alone in a leather armchair in the VIP lounge, surrounded by potted plants, a natural barrier against unwanted conversation. He disliked small talk with strangers, though at least with them, he did not have to tell them who he was. Worse were the distant faces from receptions or meetings approaching with calculated smiles, who already knew who he was.

These interactions were not just pointless; they were invasive. Each encounter an extraction, people wanting something: a favour, a connection, an introduction, a 'quick meeting'. He thought of them as time thieves, pickpockets who stole not money, but something far more precious, the dwindling hours of his life.

Today, more than ever, time felt critical. Four days had passed since Ishaan died. And he had found neither the time to grieve nor to piece things together.

The final episode of the documentary was short, a surgical slice of sensational moments. They showed

Ishaan's erratic interview, the darting eyes, the cornered-animal desperation, the wild outbursts. He kept glancing off-camera, as if tracking something no one else could see. It was just enough to shatter viewership records. They repeated the incident of violence with the interviewer ad nauseam, never showing the footage. The message was clear: Ishaan Chatterjee was a murderer who chose suicide over justice for Pramila Chatterjee.

His staff rushed to sell their stories. The media amplified whispers, drug abuse, paranoia, a thirty-year-old cover-up, Basab Banerjee's false testimony, an innocent man executed.

But beyond the carefully curated clips, the full interview told a different story. The unedited version had been seized by the government from the documentary crew. Ranadeep had seen every second.

If this had been a scene from Shayan's found-footage horror movies, he would have laughed it off as too absurd, for trying too hard to be scary.

But this was real.

Say what you will about Ishaan, but coward was not one of them. Even as a teenager, he had courted physical danger just for the rush. The world saw a star who did his own stunts, but Ranadeep knew even more: Ishaan sought out fear, often in a foolhardy, reckless way.

Ishaan Chatterjee did not scare easy. Or ever.

Which is why that look – pure, unfiltered terror – defied logic. This was not drugs. This was not panic over a cancelled deal. Something had entered that room with him. Something no one else could see.

And then there was Basab.

Two deaths. Both by water. Both men terrified in their final moments. Just like Pramila.

It was the most tired trope of cheap Hindi movie horror, the vengeful female spirit, the ghost seeking retribution.

These were the stories they watched on grainy VHS tapes during their teenage years: black eyes in white saris with terrible special effects, laughing until their stomachs hurt.

Yet what else explained this?

Coincidence?

Occam's razor: the simplest explanation is usually correct. But coincidence required more mental gymnastics than believing the impossible.

Sagan's standard: extraordinary claims require extraordinary evidence. Was what he had seen on the video extraordinary enough?

It likely was.

He remembered the conversation with Shayan on the way to the airport. The FaceTime call had appeared suddenly, disrupting the pattern of their recent communications: precisely twelve minutes, same time each weekend.

Ranadeep had begun to recognize this regular call as the transformation of their relationship from dependence to duty. The empty nest syndrome that had hollowed his chest corresponded to Shayan constructing his own world, a natural progression where the emotional space once dominated by parents gradually contracts, compressed by the expanding territories of friends, lovers and, eventually, one's own children.

Monobina had voiced this fear recently, 'Don't you find Shayan distant?' and Ranadeep had responded with nothing but a distracted 'Hmm', pretending absorption in work while the question echoed his own unspoken dread.

Yet he recognized this diminishment as part of life's relentless cycle. It had happened to him with his own parents, this gradual emotional relocation.

Love remained but transformed, no longer the centre of one's existence but a tributary feeding into a larger river of connections.

We are continuously dying, our past selves linked to our current selves by a tenuous chain of memories. What he had told Ishaan wasn't merely rhetorical. It was the truth as Ranadeep understood it, the fundamental impermanence at the core of all relationships, all identities.

Each version of us disappears, replaced by another that claims continuity but is, in essence, a stranger carrying borrowed memories.

And yet, this sudden call disrupted the narrative he had constructed. This was the old Shayan who would check in on him all the time, even though he might be in the next room.

'Baba? You okay?'

Ranadeep had straightened, arranging his features into a passable imitation of composure. The performance of fatherhood, something his position as a bureaucrat had prepared him for better than any parenting book.

'I am fine, Shayan. Just tired.'

Shayan's eyes narrowed. Even through the pixelated video, Ranadeep could see the scepticism. He had acquired that look from his mother, the ability to dissect a lie without saying a word.

'I mean, after what happened to Ishaan-uncle.'

'Well,' Ranadeep had said, with a wan smile. 'At this age, you must prepare yourself for the demise of friends. I am at the age of *vanaprastha*, what our ancients recognized as the age for conscious decoupling from attachments, preparing yourself and the world for your death. So, I have been…'

'Baba, enough with the overdramatic, fridge-magnet philosophy. And leave your non-answers for the TV channels, Mr MP.' Shayan had interrupted, surprisingly assertive. 'You know what I mean. The death of two friends, so close together and…'

'Yes, I know,' Ranadeep had said, 'I am still trying to understand what happened.'

'Did Ishaan-uncle kill Pramila? Is that true? Did Basab-uncle cover up for him?'

'Let me guess. High school friends asking you this question on your WhatsApp group.'

'Nah,' Shayan had said, 'I do not have friends like you had. Our high school alumni WhatsApp groups are either stupid birthday wishes or political flame wars or dumb videos.' Shayan had stopped and looked directly into the camera. 'Things are different now, Baba. People talk to AI apps, because they are trained to make you feel better. Most get their dopamine high scrolling on Insta or X, or making clans with strangers and playing Fortnite.'

'Well, still having trouble fitting in?' asked Ranadeep. 'They haven't been bullying you, right? No hazing?'

'No,' Shayan said firmly. 'Everyone here is polite; no one bullies you. Strict rules against hazing, zero tolerance. It is just what I have told you; I am not part of any cliques. I just get ignored. Politely ignored. Like a third wheel.'

He sighed, looking away from the screen. 'I so wish I had what you had growing up. The Musketeers.'

The names echoed in Ranadeep's mind.

Genius. Hero. Jack of All Trades. Master of None.

Friendship is not what it is made out to be. It is, once you remove all the fluff, merely a temporal convergence of souls at specific crossroads of existence: children kicking footballs in dusty fields, students hunched over shared textbooks, adults in adjacent cubicles sharing coffee and complaints, old men at tea stalls cataloguing complaints about their physical ailments. We shed friendships like seasons shed leaves, growing new connections from the compost of the old, and lamenting their dissolution is like mourning a faded cinema ticket discovered in a forgotten jacket, evidence of a fleeting shared reality of fun, preserved in paper but emptied of significance, a memorial to moments that belong to versions of ourselves who no longer exist.

That was what Ranadeep was going to tell his son. But what came out surprised him, even as the words poured out of his mouth.

'Yes,' he said, fingers tightening around his phone, 'I was lucky. Deep friendship among boys, like we had, is a strange thing.' His voice softened, as if speaking from a place he rarely visited. 'Literature rarely captures it properly, in my opinion. It is all teenage romance, never bromance. And yet the dynamics of teen friendship between boys remain unexplored. There are some in which the devotee-boy attaches to the hero-boy because he wants to be him. Sometimes the connection is like the one you have to a puppy who followed you home. If you do not love him, who will? Some friendships are based on dependence, attaching to others because they provide protection, social currency, like wearing a brand.'

Shayan nodded, leaning closer to the screen. 'The popular table phenomenon.'

'And some are based on shelter,' Ranadeep said, the ache in his heart deepening. 'When friends become the only family you know.'

'Which one were the Musketeers?' Shayan's eyes searched his father's face.

The question felt like a trap. Because the answer was all of them, and none. Because the truth was more complex than the neat categories Ranadeep had created to distance himself from what happened.

That night that Pramila died.

'Such deep friendship ultimately turns toxic,' Ranadeep continued, his throat tightening. 'It starts healthy, but the expectations, the unspoken rules...They create a dependency that can consume you, and you ultimately spend your life, consciously or unconsciously, trying to run from it.' He paused, swallowing hard. 'I know this is all very confusing, but trust me on this, you are better off with your WhatsApp friends. I might have had more fun than you had, to be honest, but you will have fewer regrets than I will.'

'Did you spend your time running from them?' Shayan's voice dropped to a whisper. 'Was Ishaan-uncle running away from the same thing when he died?'

Ranadeep stared at his son's concerned face, thinking of the price they had all paid for that friendship. How their lives had been defined not by what they had built, but by what they had hidden. How one terrible night had bound them together even as it pushed them apart.

'Look at the time,' Ranadeep said, glancing at his watch. His hand trembled slightly. 'Don't you have that physics lab in the morning?'

'Baba, you are deflecting.' Shayan's jaw tightened in that familiar way.

'And you are turning into your mother.' Ranadeep's smile did not reach his eyes.

They looked at each other for a second, father and son, and the 5G connection became better, and his son's face seemed to solidify on screen.

'I love you, Baba.'

It was strange for Ranadeep to hear that. It had been years since Shayan had said anything like that, and he wondered why he did, till he realized that he too had likely appeared in high resolution to Shayan, and his son could make out how he had broken these last few days.

'Now see who is being overdramatic,' Ranadeep said, covering his hurt with a smile, fingers reaching out to touch the screen.

'Take care, Mr MP.' They both disconnected at the same time. Ranadeep could never say the last goodbye.

There was one thing he did not tell Shayan. Nor had he told Monobina yet.

He was no longer going to be a Member of Parliament. The meeting with Amritlal Patel that morning had made that perfectly clear. He had been trying to get in touch with Amritlal ever since the Arun Mathur attack episode on Ishaan Chatterjee. He had not picked up the phone, nor messaged him back. Last evening, Amritlal's secretary had called Ranadeep to fix up an 8 a.m. appointment in his boss's office.

When Ranadeep had walked in, Amritlal was sitting enthroned behind his giant mahogany table, swaddled in a crisp white kurta-pyjama that gleamed under the fluorescents. Gold-rimmed spectacles perched on his nose, as he took a sip from a large glass of milk, and scrolled down on his phone, with a yawn. As Ranadeep entered, Amritlal stood with theatrical solemnity, hands pressed together.

'What a tragedy about your friend. My condolences.' His lips barely moved. 'Ishaan Chatterjee was a true icon, a great son of India.'

'You leaked Basab's arbitration files to Arun Mathur.' Ranadeep remained standing, his voice ice.

Amritlal's face twisted into practised shock. 'And why exactly would I do that?'

'To create a diversion,' Ranadeep said. 'The US defence deal was going to the Joint Parliamentary Committee. You needed something to dominate the news cycle. So, you leaked my friend's most damaging secrets to the press, files taken from a closed deposition.'

'You are upset,' Amritlal shrugged casually, taking one more long sip from his glass. 'The documentary found those files on its own.'

'Stop insulting my intelligence.' Ranadeep's voice sharpened. 'You dragged one friend through mud and pushed another to his death.'

Amritlal leaned back, mask dropping into a wolf-like grin.

'Your friends were no saints. A liar who framed an innocent man. A degenerate who killed his girlfriend. The world is better off without them.'

'I thought we were both on the same side.'

'I am only on one side: the smart side. And I used to think you were on it too. But then you defended a murderer on TV. You used our government's most expensive contractors for personal gain, and if that was not bad enough, you seemed to think we would not know. I realized I may have to think about how smart you are again.'

Ranadeep stood perfectly still, absorbing the blow.

'Given your...prominence in Arun Mathur's broadcasts, the party has decided you should maintain a low profile.' Amritlal took another deep gulp of milk. 'Now that the opposition has realized we neutralized their attack on the US defence deal, they will target you instead.' Taking a contented burp, he continued, 'As a private citizen or even a big Babu, they will ignore you. But get into Parliament, they will rip you to shreds.'

'Thank you for your concern.'

'I like your sarcasm, but I am serious. How do I know you will be able to take the heat? Maybe you will drive your car off a bridge or drown in your bathtub. I am saying this as your friend. The planets are not aligned for you.'

Ranadeep stared at the man. The message was clear.

'Who have you promised my Rajya Sabha MP-ship to?'

'First of all, it is not yours. It is the party's. And it is Viswanathan, since you asked.'

'Which one? The father or the son?'

'Neither. It is the daughter-in-law.'

Ranadeep gave a tired laugh and acknowledged his defeat with a nod.

'Who knows?' Amritlal said, savouring each word, 'We win the next general election, and in two more years, we try again. All this would have long blown over by then. You are an asset, one of the best administrative minds in the country. But then…'

Ranadeep interrupted Amritlal, 'I think we are done here.'

Ranadeep turned. Amritlal called after him, genuine bewilderment in his voice.

'Why did you do it? People do the worst things for their sons; I understand that. They do terrible things for love. I understand that too. They kill for their family; yes, I have seen that. But school friends? People you barely kept in touch with for decades? Why the hell would you bring it all down, for a bunch of people you played cricket with once upon a time?'

Ranadeep sat quietly in the lounge, his eyes glazed over, leaning back, looking up at the ceiling, remembering the reply he had given before walking out.

'You will never understand.'

Even he did not truly understand this bond beyond biology.

Friendship.

Beautiful. Suffocating. Terrifying.

Once back in Delhi, he would have to tell Monobina. He had been married long enough as to know exactly what she would say. 'Good riddance, I don't know what had gotten into you. Want to be a minister, hah, as if you did not have enough politics at work. Now stay home, and for heaven's sake, look through your collection of shirts and trousers, and see what you can get rid of. In this house, the man has more clothes than the woman.'

But between his last word and Monobina's first, there would come a silence, brief, almost imperceptible, but inside it he would see everything fall apart. Through her eyes, he would glimpse the quiet collapse of dreams she had already begun to build, dinner invitations rewritten, saris mentally picked for oath ceremonies and the belief that the sacrifices they had made had finally led somewhere. And then the words she always found would come: soft, supportive, rehearsed, the kind that masked disappointment with grace. That shard of silence between their voices, when reality slipped in before performance could catch up, that is what he dreaded most.

With friends, it would have been so much easier. He would say it. They simply would not care.

'Want to play carrom?' 'Want to catch a movie?' 'Have you seen that new girl who moved into the floor above Mangal-da's store?'

The announcement came through, in that airport voice, on the overhead speakers.

'May I have your attention, please? Flight IndiGo 6E 474 to Calcutta will now be boarding at gate number 15. We will be commencing boarding immediately.'

Ranadeep Saha stood up, picked up his briefcase, looked around once to check if he had left anything behind, and then proceeded to the boarding gate with measured, heavy steps.

He was going home.

16

The Cleanup Crew

Rain slid off the corrugated metal awning above Krishanu's door in irregular sheets. Ranadeep stood beneath an umbrella, watching the house hunker before him, a black void against the ambient glow of the city. Once white, the façade had aged to the colour of weak tea, water stains mapping decades of monsoon seasons and neglect.

Eleven at night. Despite his raincoat, Ranadeep felt a wet chill spreading through his bones. He had barely stepped out of the Uber; there hadn't been enough time for the rain to penetrate his waterproof layers. And yet, the dampness came from within.

He knew why. The memories of this house. The memories of that night. While everything else had changed, this house had not, a reminder that while the world may move on, some things do not.

The call had come at around nine. He had been at his parent's place in New Town, working on his official laptop, when the phone, on silent, buzzed across his table. Seeing

Krishanu being the caller, he had wondered, for a moment, whether to pick it up. Then he picked up.

Krishanu's voice was hollow, raspy, barely recognizable.

'Please, come now. Come to my house.'

There was something in that urgency that immediately caught Ranadeep's attention. As he closed the lid of the laptop, he asked, 'What is it?'

'Please come to my house. Please.' The line was bad, but Ranadeep thought he heard a wheeze, the kind that comes from someone who has been weeping.

'Look, Krishanu, it is late. I have let my driver go home for the night. Can't this wait till morning?'

'No,' he said, trying to steady his voice, 'I need you here now. Look, Rano, I promise I will never ever call you again after today. You will never hear of me again. Please. For an old friend. Please.'

Ranadeep had wondered if Krishanu was having a drug-induced breakdown, some variation of the episode they had witnessed the last time they had gone to visit him.

'Give the phone to Sunanda,' he said firmly. 'I want to talk to her first.'

'No, no, no,' Krishanu whispered, convulsing on each word. 'Not her. Not her. You come to me. Me.'

Now in the rain, Krishanu's house crouched like a malevolent sentinel. Ranadeep squinted through the gloom, searching for any sign of life. Not a single window showed light. Strange for Krishanu to call so urgently, then sit in darkness.

The silhouette of the building wavered at the edges, as if viewed through rippling water. Ranadeep blinked away raindrops from his lashes, but the effect remained, the building's contours refusing to settle into fixed lines. Despite staring directly at it, his mind struggled to hold onto the complete shape; it remained frustratingly indistinct, like a half-forgotten face from a dream.

Ranadeep took a step closer, his shoe splashing in a puddle he had not noticed. Something about the structure's absolute stillness against its shimmering outline made the hair on his neck rise.

He paused, listening. The rain pattered around him but seemed to fall silent as it touched the walls. Like entering a soundproof room, sudden, disorienting. His own heartbeat was now the loudest thing.

The windows were dark, not with the passive emptiness of an unoccupied room, but with a kind of active refusal, as if the darkness was pushing back. He reached for his phone's flashlight, then stopped, suddenly reluctant to announce himself.

The scent of wet concrete filled his nostrils, mingled with something older, like the cold water from the tank in the backyard. Why remember that now? He had not thought of it in years. They used to wash up there after muddy games of football. Strange how some things surface when least expected.

He tightened his grip on the umbrella. He was a grown man, not someone taken to irrational fear. And yet, standing before this house, he felt sixteen again.

Uncertain. Afraid.

And worst of all, complicit.

He had run away from this place for thirty years, but now he was back here again. The house knew. It was waiting.

Krishanu's mother used to feed the stray dogs, despite the neighbours' complaints. Sunanda had told him her mother did too, and so did she. The dogs learned that under the metal awning, they wouldn't be chased away. They would be fed.

Four dogs were there now, huddled under the same awning. Something about their posture unsettled him. They stood immobile, tails straight, all facing the door with their backs to him.

He froze. They didn't growl. They didn't move. Even as he approached, they didn't turn to acknowledge him. Just stood there, as if hypnotized by whatever lay beyond the door.

Maybe I am imagining things, Ranadeep thought. My nerves are shot. They are just sheltering from the rain.

But he had owned dogs all his life. He recognized the tension in their bodies, muscles taut beneath wet fur. This wasn't hunger. It was something else. As if they sensed something he could not.

He walked past them, unnerved by their silence. At the door, he pressed the bell. The chime echoed inside, familiar, unchanged. For a moment, he half-expected Krishanu's mother to appear, smiling in recognition, offering tea and Marie biscuits.

But they were all gone now.

He checked his phone. Seven missed calls to Sunanda. Five to Krishanu. No voicemail.

He raised his hand to knock, then noticed the door was slightly ajar.

That detail triggered another memory. Krishanu's father with his obsession for security. Five separate locks and bolts installed on the front door, a fortress against imagined intruders. 'The less we have,' Krishanu used to say with that familiar sad smile, 'the more Baba obsesses that they will come to take away even that.'

An unlocked door, on a night like this, in this neighbourhood?

His instincts screamed at him to turn back.

Call the police. Come in the morning.

But if Krishanu needed help, if he was struggling due to the medication, or facing something worse, something Ranadeep still refused to name, then who else would come?

Who else could understand?

He placed his palm against the wood. The ancient door surrendered with a low, protesting creak.

Darkness. A sound came from within, a low, wheezing noise, somewhere between a sob and an animal growl. It came from a fixed point, unmoving.

Ranadeep froze. Water pooled at his feet.

His hand moved by instinct, finding the switchboard on the wall. Third switch from the left, his body remembered. How many times had he walked into this house as a teenager?

The light snapped on, harsh and cold.

Krishanu sat on the threadbare couch, hands clasped between his knees. He wore a light blue Punjabi kurta and white pyjamas, fabric too clean, too crisp for the decay around him. He did not resemble the man Ranadeep had seen weeks ago, nor the pudgy boy from their youth. He had filled out, shoulders broader, face no longer gaunt.

But this new solidity only deepened the unease. He looked like a man inflated from within, as if something alien had taken root in him, shaping him to its own design.

His face glistened. Not sweat, but tears. They poured from sunken eyes that seemed to have collapsed inwards, dark pits in a crumbling face. Ranadeep had seen grief before: mothers beside their dead children, men standing amid charred homes.

But never like this.

Krishanu wept like a man possessed, his body leaking from every pore, purging something unspeakable. Mucus clung to his upper lip. His chin trembled. The collar of his kurta was soaked through, clinging to his throat.

The sound continued, rising and falling, not words, not even human. It was the keening of a creature in a trap, unable to understand what had wounded it.

But worst of all were the eyes. Through the deluge of tears, they remained fixed on Ranadeep, recognizing, knowing, accusing.

Ranadeep closed the door and twisted each lock into place, muscle memory guiding his fingers through the familiar sequence. The harsh clang of metal sliding against metal echoed in the quiet house. He remained frozen by the switchboard, unable to approach the weeping figure, an energy that he could not understand pushing him back.

'What has happened, Krishanu? Are you all right?' He tried to keep his voice, low, normal almost, but the surging panic inside him still seeped through at the end.

Krishanu's shoulders heaved beneath the light blue fabric. 'I cannot remember...' The words crumbled into that animal wheezing, a sound that seemed to come from somewhere deep inside his chest, as if something inside was trying to escape.

'What can't you remember?' Ranadeep flicked across the room. There was nothing out of place: a half-empty glass of water perched on the side table, a faded framed photo, an ancient radio from the 90s, long-dead covered by a floral cloth, a glass shelf affixed to the wall with audio cassettes, a single slipper abandoned in the corner.

'Where's Sunanda?'

'I might have done something terrible.' Krishanu's hands trembled as they wiped uselessly at the tears streaming down his face, leaving shining trails that caught the harsh overhead light.

'I was again myself, as I once was. I was in a dream. I did something terrible. I do not know what is real any more. Help me...'

The incoherent babbling continued, fragments of sentences spilling out between sobs. Each broken phrase sent a cold current down Ranadeep's spine. He edged closer, careful as if approaching a wounded animal, despite the primal urge that told him to bolt out the door. The smell of Krishanu's sweat mingled with the acrid tang of medicine, his cancer treatment, perhaps.

'Where is Sunanda?' he demanded again. His fingers curled into fists at his sides, nails digging into palms. 'Where is she, Krishanu?'

The air in the room felt too thick to breathe properly. Outside, the rain intensified, drumming against the windows with relentless urgency.

'Where is she? Where is she?' Panic clawed up Ranadeep's throat, bile rising with each desperate repetition. His heartbeat thundered deafeningly in his ears, drowning all but Krishanu's wet, ragged breaths.

Krishanu's eyes, red-rimmed and haunted, shifted toward the narrow passageway leading to the back of the house. One trembling hand rose, finger pointing. The blue sleeve of his kurta slid back, revealing a wrist so thin the bones seemed to wobble.

The smell, it hit him again, the smell of stagnant, cold water.

Ranadeep moved before thinking, feet carrying him down the familiar corridor. The walls seemed to close in, the passageway narrower than he remembered from childhood. Framed photographs watched his progress, generations of Krishanu's family, their eyes following him accusingly.

The back door stood open, swinging slightly in the restless night breeze, hinges crying out with each movement. Rain pattered on the cracked concrete beyond, forming small rivulets that ran toward the ancient water tank in the centre of the yard.

He fumbled for the exterior light switch, ancient plastic cracking under his desperate fingers. A harsh flood of light spilled into the courtyard, revealing every detail with unforgiving clarity.

There, at the ancient water tank, the *choubaccha*, a figure knelt. Sunanda, body bent forward at the waist, her head submerged in the dark water. Her long hair floated on the surface like black seaweed. Her arms hung limp at her sides, fingers curled slightly as if they had tried to grasp at something before strength failed.

For a disorienting moment, Ranadeep's vision flickered like an old television losing signal. Reality seemed to shift and buckle. The kneeling figure blurred, shifted, became Pramila in her school uniform, then Sunanda again in her simple house clothes, frozen in the same position, with the same terrible stillness.

A scene separated by decades yet identical in their finality.

A wave of nausea crashed through him, his stomach contracting violently. He stumbled backward, colliding with the wall, the impact sending a framed photograph crashing to the ground, glass shattering, splintering the silence. His legs threatened to give way, knees buckling under the weight of recognition.

Then he was moving, running back to the living room where Krishanu remained, grabbing his shoulders, fingers digging into the crisp blue Punjabi. The fabric bunched between his fingers as he pulled Krishanu forward.

'Wh-wh-wha h-h-have you-you-you done?' Ranadeep's stammer from his childhood returned, jagged and raw, the one he had battled all his life to suppress.

It had come back once before, the night Pramila had died.

He shook the man whose tears had not ceased, Krishanu's head snapping back and forth.

'Wh-wh-what h-h-have you-you-you done, you ba-ba-ba-stard, wha-wha-what h-h-have yo-u d-d-done?'

Krishanu looked up at him, recognition dawning in those hollow eyes. A dreadful clarity seemed to settle over his features, the confusion giving way to something worse, understanding.

'The same thing,' he whispered, voice steady for the first time. 'The same thing again.'

Ranadeep's fingers dug deep into Krishanu's shoulders, enough to bruise. His tears fell freely now. The careful distance he had maintained his entire adult life, from his emotions, from his past, collapsed in an instant.

'Wha-wha-what d-d-did you-you do?' The question emerged as a ragged whisper. Then louder, thundering through the small room: 'H-h-how d-d-did you-you d-do-do this?'

His gaze caught on an overturned side table near the passage to the courtyard. A framed photo of Krishanu and Sunanda lay shattered, their smiling faces splintered forever, glass fragments scattered across the floor.

The girl with her bright eyes and quiet determination had reminded him of Shayan. The way she had looked at him with such hope when they talked about her future. Gone now. Her head in that filthy tank like a grotesque baptism.

Krishanu's body went slack beneath his grip, head lolling forward. 'I cannot remember,' he said, voice hollow. 'I thought I was dreaming…remembering.' His chest heaved with each laboured breath. The stench of chemicals and sickness rolled off him in waves. 'I do now…vivid dreams since they increased my dosage.'

Something clinked against Ranadeep's shoe. He glanced down to see a woman's bangle, purple with red enamel work, rolling to a stop against the wall.

Krishanu looked up, eyes suddenly focusing. 'The medicine…it's beautiful, Rano.' His voice took on a dreamlike quality. 'It helps me relive memories in full sensory detail. I can taste foods I have not eaten in decades. The mustard fish my mother made. I can feel the texture on my tongue.'

Ranadeep noticed dark smudges on the wall, fingerprints, smeared, leading toward the back door.

A sickening realization clenched his gut.

Krishanu's fingers twitched, curling as if holding an invisible cricket bat.

'I play full matches in my head. Every ball, every run. I can feel the leather against my palm, hear the crack of willow.' A ghost of wonder crossed his ravaged face. 'That's the magic of this drug. It made what little time I had left beautiful…reliving the best moments of my life. You know, I never got the life you or Ishaan or Basab had. This drug, it has helped me get the most mileage I could out of the very little good times I have ever had.'

A chair lay on its side, one leg splintered. Had it always been broken? Ranadeep couldn't remember from his last visit. His bureaucrat's mind catalogued each detail automatically, building a timeline of violence, or illness.

Krishanu's expression crumpled. 'And then when I came to…' His fingers twisted in the fabric of his pyjamas, knuckles white. 'My hands were wet. I had no idea how I had got her head into the tank, trust me, it is a complete blank. Rini, she was dead.'

The name died in his throat, replaced by a sound Ranadeep had never heard from a human before, something ancient and broken, the noise of something fundamental tearing apart.

They wept together under the merciless light.

'My daughter,' Krishanu moaned, rocking forward and back. Each forward motion brought his forehead almost to his knees. 'My flower-like daughter. Oh God, please.' He beat his head on his palms. 'Take me to the police. Call them. I will confess. I will confess everything.'

Ranadeep's gaze fixed on a lamp cord pulled from the wall, the socket dangling. Signs of struggle, or evidence of Krishanu's declining coordination? The uncertainty made his throat tighten.

Krishanu looked up suddenly, gaze penetrating through tears. 'Pramila. Rini.' Each name fell like a stone between them. 'I need to die. I need to pay for my sins.'

A faint scent caught Ranadeep's attention, something floral and slightly sweet beneath the medicinal smell. A perfume. One he had not smelled in thirty years.

Something shifted in Ranadeep's expression, a tightening around the eyes, a calculation visible even through grief. The bureaucrat reasserting control, assessing damage, measuring consequences.

Krishanu caught it immediately, his lips twisting into something between a grimace and a smile. 'I will not take your name. I promise.' A harsh laugh escaped him, edged with thirty years of resentment. 'All that blackmail. I was never going to take your name. I just needed some money, just a bit of cash to tide over my bad times. Trust me, I would never ever open my mouth about you.'

The lights flickered, drawing Ranadeep's attention to a water stain spreading across the ceiling, fresh and growing. Directly above them. It must be the rain, he told himself, but he was not sure.

'Don't you see?' Krishanu whispered, leaning forward as if sharing a secret. 'It's Pramila. She's making me pay by taking away my daughter.' His voice dropped lower still, forcing Ranadeep to lean in despite himself. 'So that I understand the pain.'

The distant strains of a song came from afar, '*Madhumaloti Daake Aaye*', Pramila's favourite.

Fresh tears carved new paths through the half-dried tracks on Krishanu's face. 'I understand the pain now. I never did before.'

His gaze locked onto Ranadeep's, clarity emerging from the madness. 'I never understood the pain because she was never really my friend. She respected Basab, loved Ishaan, and, more than anyone else, it was you, Rano, you who she trusted most in the world. As for me, I was just the fat, pimply kid, the clown, Doggie Dum Dum, the Master of None.'

Ranadeep wiped his tears with the back of his hand, leaving a streak of dirt across his cheek. His breathing steadied as cold pragmatism settled in his eyes, the familiar calculation of a man who had spent decades navigating political crises.

'I am going to handle this situation,' he said, his voice steadying to the professional tone he used in ministerial meetings, the stammer receding, but still lurking.

Krishanu looked up, face hollow beneath the harsh overhead light. 'Just call the police,' he whispered. 'I do not have the strength to do it myself. Just call them and let this all be over.'

'That would benefit no one.'

'I promised I will not take your name.' Krishanu's fingers clutched at air, as if trying to grasp something invisible. 'I just want to atone for what I have done.'

Ranadeep moved to the window, drawing back the curtain an inch. The street remained empty, rain lashing against the pavement in silver sheets. The dogs still had not moved from their vigilant position.

'It is too late for that.' He let the curtain fall back into place. 'The cancer gives you what, three months? Four? Would you rather spend those final days in a police lockup? In Presidency Jail?'

The water stain on the ceiling had grown larger, dark liquid seeping through the plaster in an expanding pattern. Drip. Drip. Neither man acknowledged it.

'I made a mistake,' Ranadeep continued, his voice softening with an emotion he could not quite identify. 'I should have taken better care of you.' He glanced at his reflection in a small mirror on the wall, unrecognizable to himself. 'Ishaan always did handle these situations. But he is gone now. I will do what needs to be done.'

'What exactly are you planning?' Krishanu asked, each word a struggle to form.

'First, we will handle this. Then, I will send over a nurse to manage your meds and make sure you are looked after. Don't worry about the costs; you are my responsibility now.'

'No,' Krishanu said, shaking his head slowly, 'I don't want you to handle this. I want you to take me to the...' He could not finish the sentence; his breath seemed to give way from all the exertion, and Krishanu half-closed his eyes, only to be jerked back to wakefulness. Then, he started crying again.

'Krishanu, I am not asking,' Ranadeep said with authority. 'I am telling you. This time around, you listen. Do you understand?'

'What are you talking about?'

Ranadeep pulled out his phone and checked something. 'I know specialists. Men who clean up situations like this.' His thumb scrolled through contacts before stopping on one without a name, just a string of numbers. 'They will be here in four hours. You will remain exactly where you are while they take care of Sunanda.'

Krishanu's face twisted in horror. 'You can't mean…her body? Who are these people?'

'The government requires certain situations to be… managed.' Ranadeep's voice had become mechanical, detached. 'Terrorist eliminations. People who provide them support. India doesn't officially acknowledge such operations, but they happen. These men are professionals; they clean up crime scenes as if nothing happened.'

He moved to the front door, steps precise and controlled despite the chaos surrounding them. The dripping from the front door had synchronized with the leak from the ceiling, a macabre duet.

'Lock this door behind me. When they arrive, they will knock three times. Let them in. Do not speak. Do not interfere. Do not question.' Ranadeep paused, hand on the doorknob. 'Have you understood what I have told you?'

Krishanu remained motionless, a fixture in the room like the furniture. His breathing had slowed to barely perceptible movements of his chest.

Ranadeep crossed the room in three strides, crouched, and gripped Krishanu's shoulders. The fabric of the Punjabi felt damp beneath his fingers. 'Did you understand me?'

Krishanu lifted his head slowly. His eyes held the resignation of a man already dead. 'I am sorry for everything, Rano. All the blackmail, the threats.' He swallowed hard. 'I just wanted what we had back. The four Musketeers. I never wanted to lose you all. But I did anyway.'

Something cracked in Ranadeep's carefully constructed façade. He pulled Krishanu into an awkward embrace, the first time they had touched with any genuine affection since they were teenagers.

'We will be together again,' he whispered, trying not to break down.

He released Krishanu and stood. Without looking back, without daring to look back, he stepped into the rain, pulling the door closed behind him.

The street glistened black under the sporadic street lights. The dogs watched him, mute sentinels as he made the call. His voice barely rose above the storm; he gave precise instructions, the address and an authorization code that would unlock unseen powers.

For fifteen minutes he walked through the downpour, his expensive leather shoes ruined, his tailored shirt plastered to his body. The rain washed away his tears but not the weight that had settled in his bones.

The next morning, Ranadeep sat in his parents' living room, staring blankly at the television while his mother prepared breakfast. The news ticker scrolled across the bottom of the screen:

FATHER AND DAUGHTER FOUND DEAD IN APPARENT JOINT SUICIDE

The female anchor's practised solemnity matched the gravity of her words: 'Krishanu Batabyal and his daughter Sunanda were discovered in the early hours of the morning, both drowned in the family's backyard water tank. While police are investigating all possibilities, initial reports suggest a suicide pact, potentially linked to Mr Batabyal's terminal cancer diagnosis and financial difficulties.'

The camera panned across the small crowd gathered outside the house: neighbours, journalists, curious onlookers. The reporter continued: 'Authorities have found no signs of forced entry or struggle, though investigators noted a broken vase containing fresh roses near the scene.

Sources close to the family indicated that Mr Batabyal had become increasingly despondent in recent weeks.'

Ranadeep switched off the television. His mother called from the kitchen, asking if he wanted tea or coffee. He did not answer, staring instead at his reflection in the black screen, wondering which of the men in the glass was real: the ambitious bureaucrat, the loyal friend, or the accomplice to murder, twice over.

17

Thirty Years Ago

The evening air clung to Ranadeep like a second skin, humidity pressing against him as he navigated the narrow lane toward Pramila's house.

He had slipped out of chemistry tuition early, a calculated move that required sitting on the last bench, a place he had never voluntarily chosen before. Throughout Dr Adhikary's lecture on organic chemistry, carbon bonds and molecular structures had dissolved into meaningless diagrams as his fingers kept returning to the note hidden in his pocket, creasing and smoothing it with nervous energy.

He held in his hands a torn half-page from an exercise book. Earlier this morning, as she had walked past, outside school, Pramila had shoved it into his hand without saying anything.

Please come. Need to talk. Important. 7 p.m. Parents not home.

At the bottom corner: simply P, followed by a rose sketched in fading red ink.

His first reading had sent his stomach into knots. His palms sweated, running the blue ink on the paper into the lines of his palm, yet he could not help reading it again and again. Why summon him alone? What conversation required the absence of her parents?

Those stolen twenty minutes from Dr Adhikary had been essential. With his own parents still at work, Ranadeep had showered quickly, trading his sweat-stained uniform for his favourite shirt. His grandmother had given him the shirt piece, and it had been sewn by the neighbourhood tailor. He never liked that his father took him to Sri Nataraj Tailors, a place that made Bharatnatyam blouses year-round and only produced boys' shirts before Durga Pujo. The visits always embarrassed him, though his father seemed oblivious to his discomfort and his remonstrances that maybe this year they could go to New Market, as Ishaan did. This particular shirt, however, he genuinely liked. It paired well with his treasured Levi's, a gift from his uncle who stayed in New Jersey. A furtive raid on his mother's drawer had yielded the Chanel perfume that same uncle had given her – foreign, expensive, forbidden – which he had applied with reckless abundance.

Now, with Pramila's house looming ahead, he felt sweat forming along his hairline, threatening both his composure and the borrowed scent. He wiped his forehead with his sleeve, hoping the evening would mask his nervousness.

Seven o'clock almost, and darkness had descended. A mangy dog sniffed at garbage piled against a crumbling wall, looking up with rheumy eyes as he passed. Krishanu's house loomed to his right, a mirror image of the one next door, Pramila's. Krishanu's mother fed the dogs, and so here they would soon assemble when she would come out and pour leftovers from dinner onto the sidewalk.

He reached into his pocket and brought the note out again. Ranadeep had known Pramila for years now, but she had never slipped him a note.

The possibility flashed in his mind, unwelcome and disturbing. The way Hindi movies always insisted that friendship between men and women inevitably transformed into love.

No. The denial came swift and fierce. Even entertaining such a thought felt like a betrayal towards Ishaan. It was friendship with Pramila, always, nothing more, she had helped him with his stammering and his singing, and he felt ashamed even thinking that it could be anything but. They shared music, conversation, laughter, and yes, he enjoyed being with her, more than he would care to acknowledge, but his loyalty was always going to be to the Musketeers.

What most likely had happened was that Ishaan must have broken things off with her, after that magazine and that scene at her house. She was going to meet him at the park this evening, and they were going to fight. They had fought before, of course, but yes, this time it was bad. So, that is why she had called him. She could cry on his shoulder about how cruel Ishaan had been, and he would offer to mediate, and she would say 'Not at all', and then after a week or two, he would see her and Ishaan standing in front of Flurys having ice cream.

But something, this time, felt different. His mind drifted back to the bus ride to Chandannagar, six months ago. Their singing academy had entered Bengal's biggest song competition, Ranadeep for Rabindra Sangeet category and Pramila for Bengali film songs. The academy proprietor and their singing teacher sat together, leaving Pramila and Ranadeep to share their own seat.

The seat was narrow, their shoulders brushing with every bump on the cratered road. Pramila leaned in, her voice barely rising above the engine's rattle.

'I got an offer,' she whispered, eyes bright with contained excitement. 'From the *Woman's World*. They want me on the cover.'

A flutter of pride caught him off guard, what girl in Calcutta wouldn't dream of such glamour, and what boy wouldn't want to be her friend?

But the words that left his mouth were different.

'Ishaan will be mad.'

'So?' The challenge in her voice caught him off guard, like a chess move he had not anticipated.

'So?' Ranadeep raised his eyebrows, attempting an incredulous smile. 'You know what is going to happen.'

Her face hardened, jaw clenched, he had seen that look before, when she decided to be impossible. 'I am tired of asking for permission.'

'Why not just focus on your studies?' he offered, channelling the sensible voice he thought she respected in him, a contrast to Ishaan's immature tantrums.

She turned to the window, fields and dusty villages flashing past.

'I want to be a movie star,' she said suddenly.

Ranadeep laughed, not unkindly, but with disbelief. 'Come on, normal people do not run away to Mumbai.'

Her eyes flashed with something fierce, catching the early morning sun streaming through the dusty window. 'If you are going to talk like old uncles on park benches, at least say it right. Decent girls do not run away to Mumbai. Ishaan can, though.'

The words stung. He was not an old uncle. He was trying to protect her.

'Ishaan can dance,' he pointed out, his voice defensive. 'He can moonwalk.'

'So can I,' she replied, quietly.

She was teasing. Or maybe not. Her eyes had that glint, half mischief, half challenge, that made you question whether the joke was on you.

Then she said something that made his breath catch.

'Would you...' She hesitated, fingers playing with the edge of her dupatta. 'Would you come with me? When I go to the studio?'

He had turned to her then, their faces close enough that he could smell that shampoo sachet in her hair, see the tiny mole near her left eyebrow, count each eyelash if he wanted to.

'I will always support you. No matter what you do. You are my best friend,' Ranadeep said, the words coming easily, truthfully, though even then, something inside him hurt to say it.

He had gone with her to the studio, waited outside while flashbulbs popped behind closed doors. The whole time his stomach had churned with disloyalty. Balancing between them, Ishaan, his friend since childhood, and Pramila, who was also just a friend. Nothing more. Nothing more. The repetition in his mind had become a mantra.

And then she had come out of the studio, clutching her bag, flushed with delight.

He was standing on the opposite side of the street, the cars rushing by like a river between them. She had smiled, radiantly, and then, as he stood open-mouthed, Pramila had executed a moonwalk across the studio entrance, far more perfectly than Ishaan had, stretching out her hand toward him across the divide of traffic, and holding her pose like a statue coming to life.

The image had stayed with him all these months, and he was afraid, would stay with him all his life.

He pushed the gate to Pramila's house open. It creaked on rusted hinges. He went in, climbing the two steps to stand at the front door.

'Pramila?' he called softly, touching the door.

It opened. For some reason that he could not understand, he felt happy.

And he felt full of hope.

Maybe it was going to be different. Maybe, she saw him differently. Maybe he was different.

18

The Bucket

Pramila stood before the bathroom mirror, twirling a rose from Ishaan's bouquet between her fingers, thinking of their argument in the park. The sound came from behind her, a footstep on wet tile. She sensed a presence and turned around, her expression brightening momentarily, her head slanting to the right, throwing her hair back.

The light faded from her face when she saw who stood in the doorway.

'Not who you were expecting, right?'

Krishanu's voice cut through the bathroom air, lower and more controlled than the soft-spoken boy everyone knew from school. In the harsh fluorescent light, his familiar pudgy features had transformed, eyes reflecting a cold, predatory gleam, lips curved in a smile that belonged to someone else entirely.

Pramila's hand froze. The rose slipped from her fingers, landing with a soft pat on the bathroom floor. A few loose petals scattered across the tile.

'What are you doing here, Krishanu?' she asked, backing away, her voice steady despite the wariness in her eyes.

He stepped forward, his movements strangely fluid. Gone was the awkward shuffle, the hunched, self-effacing posture, the clownish geniality.

This Krishanu moved with eerie purpose, each step deliberate.

'Is this about Ishaan?' she asked, chin lifting. 'Did he send you?'

'You know he didn't,' Krishanu said, still advancing.

'But you didn't answer my question, you were expecting someone, were you not? Just not me.'

'Well,' she said, her lips pursing in defiance, 'since you seem to know already, why don't you tell me?'

'Slipped Ranadeep a note, eh?' Krishanu's tone was mocking now. 'Poor boy could not concentrate in organic chemistry. He kept bringing out that note, reading it to himself, and putting it back again into his pocket. Forgive me. I peeked. Hard not to, sitting right next to him. He was so entranced by that rose you drew. Nice touch, by the way. Says everything and yet absolutely nothing.'

He mimicked her voice in a falsetto. 'Parents not home.'

'What's wrong with you?' Pramila snapped. Her back hit the broken tile wall.

Krishanu stepped closer.

'What's wrong with me?' Krishanu asked, still doing his parody of Pramila's voice.

Reverting to his original voice, he asked, dragging out each word: 'No, what's wrong with you?'

'What do you mean?'

The mask, her practised confidence, especially around him, was starting to crack. A slight tightening of her eyes. A faint twitch at the corner of her mouth. Tiny signs, but Krishanu saw them all, drinking in her discomfort.

And she saw something too.

There was something different today about Doggie Dum Dum.

She swallowed hard, her throat working beneath the thin gold chain she always wore. Despite the fear seeping into her expression, she kept her chin tilted upward, her shoulders squared, attempting to project a composure she no longer felt.

Krishanu watched the transformation with quiet fascination. Each flicker that crossed her face, the widening pupils, the sharp breaths she tried to control, the way her gaze darted to the door behind him and back, fed something inside him that had been starving.

'You don't love Ranadeep, do you?' he asked, his voice almost conversational.

'First of all, I know he is your friend, but that is none of your business. And since you ask, he *is* my friend, why should I love him? Again, what's wrong with you?'

'That's what I thought,' Krishanu's chipped tooth gleamed as his smile widened. 'You just want to play us against the other. You want to break us up. You want Ishaan for yourself, and no one else gets him.'

His voice rose, each word more tightly coiled than the last. The fluorescent light caught the sheen of sweat forming on his forehead, making his skin appear waxy, almost artificial.

'Don't act as if you don't know what you do. You love that power, don't you? That rush. It makes you feel strong.' His fingers flexed at his sides, opening and closing in rhythm with his accusations.

'Basab, the sage who cares only for mathematics and physics and chemistry, turns into a quivering bit of jelly when he sees you. Even he walks with a spring in his step after your tutoring sessions. He smiles to himself when he thinks no one's watching. You, who can barely solve a linear equation, you make him behave dumber than you.'

Pramila's eyes widened, her chest rising and falling more rapidly.

'But that's fine,' Krishanu went on, now holding his position, 'We all get our jollies somehow. Basab, at least, opens Irodov, chapter number five, and he forgets all about you. But Ranadeep. That's different.'

The small bathroom seemed to shrink further with each word.

'The poor boy thinks he is smart, Jack of All Trades, right? But he is the biggest fool, of us. Come on, you and I both know that. He is putty in your hands. He is the nice guy, isn't he? That soft earth you can dig into. Take from but never give back to. The sensitive boy who sees you as a person, always there with his shoulder for you to cry on, am I right?'

'I think you should leave,' Pramila said, knowing fully well that Krishanu did not intend to.

'Ishaan slaps you around. What do you do? You run into his arms. You love him. But Rano, with the sweet voice and the kind words, he is a…what did you say now…a friend?'

'Take a step closer, and I am going to scream.'

Krishanu sneered and raised his voice.

'He took you to the magazine shoot. Didn't he? Of course he did; who else would? Why didn't you go alone?'

'None of your business.'

'Since you are his friend, did you stop for a second to think what will happen when Ishaan finds out? He will rearrange his teeth.'

Krishanu took a long step forward, his foot crushing the fallen rose. He slammed his palm against the mirror behind her; glass rattled in its frame. Pramila flinched, pressing back against the wall. There was nowhere left to go.

Now his face was inches from hers. She could feel the heat of his breath.

Out of the corner of her eye, she noticed his hand, black gardening gloves.

'But what do you care?' he whispered. The softness of his voice was more terrifying than his shouting.

'What do you care if Ishaan blames Ranadeep? If we fight? If we break, if we never speak again?'

His voice cracked slightly.

'Do you even understand what this is? What we have?'

His eyes were glassy now. His smile gone.

'You do not. You never did. You do not care about the friendship. You just want to be the jewel at the centre.'

The look in Krishanu's eyes shifted something in Pramila's brain, from fear to survival.

In one fluid motion, she brought her knee up hard between his legs. Krishanu doubled over with a startled wheeze. She shoved his shoulder with both hands, putting her entire weight behind it.

For a heartbeat, freedom seemed possible.

Krishanu staggered back, his hip hitting the sink. Porcelain cracked against bone. Pramila lunged for the door, her feet in the rubber slipper slipping on the damp tile.

His fingers caught a thick handful of her hair, yanking her backward. The force whipped her head around. Pain tore through her scalp as strands ripped free.

She screamed, a short, guttural sound, cut off as her body was flung to the floor. Her spine hit the tile with a dull thud, the breath driven from her lungs. Cold water from the shower soaked through her kameez.

Pramila scrambled, crab-like, palms skidding across slick tile. One fingernail cracked, but she barely noticed. She rolled onto her stomach, pushed up onto her hands and knees.

His shadow fell over her.

Before she could rise, his hand clamped around her throat. Fingers dug into the soft flesh beneath her jaw with shocking force, as though the pudgy, awkward boy had hidden steel cables beneath his skin.

He lifted her by the neck alone. Her toes scraped the floor. Black spots bloomed in her vision. She clawed at his wrist, nails tearing skin, drawing blood, unnoticed by either of them.

With terrifying calm, he guided her toward the metal bucket in the centre of the floor.

'But you see, Pramila,' he said, voice eerily calm as he forced her head downward toward the bucket. 'I am immune to your charms. I know what you are trying to do to us.'

Water splashed over the rim as her face broke the surface. Her body bucked against him, but he leaned his weight onto her shoulders, pinning her against the edge of the bucket. The metal dug into her stomach as she bent double, cutting a red line into her flesh.

He gripped the bucket's rim with one hand to keep it from tipping. The heavy industrial-grade metal should have shifted under her struggles, but he held it in place as if it were bolted to the floor. His other hand remained clamped on the back of her neck, feeling her pulse race beneath his palm.

'I guess I am a dog. Doggie Dum Dum. And you threaten my pack.'

She thrashed wildly, legs kicking out behind her, heel connecting with his shin. He did not flinch. Her hands slapped the bucket sides, trying to push herself up, but Krishanu simply applied more pressure, his arm trembling not with exertion but with controlled power.

'Most of all, you threaten Rano. Ishaan will recover from you. Other girls will throw themselves at him. But Rano cares for you deeply. He will never recover. He feels this world more than any of us.'

Her struggles grew more desperate. Bubbles erupted around her submerged head as the air escaped her lungs. Krishanu shifted his stance, planting his feet wider. With one smooth motion, he lifted her slightly and then slammed her down harder, her forehead striking the bottom of the bucket with a dull metallic thud that resonated through the water.

He rolled his shoulders, adjusting his grip. When her body spasmed particularly violently, he simply countered by applying more weight, his forearm muscles bunched, trembling with madness. The bucket should have overturned a dozen times, but his hand steadied it with impossible strength, gloved fingers denting the metal rim.

'You make him feel like a man. But you and I both know, he is not. Not like Ishaan. But you don't mind leading him on, as long as it makes you feel loved and wanted.'

Water sloshed over the sides, soaking his shoes. Krishanu remained immovable.

She managed to lift her head, gasping.

He shoved her back under: clean, mechanical, unflinching.

'You were tearing us apart,' he murmured, as if confiding a painful truth. 'I won't let you; I would rather do this than let that happen. This is the only family I have left. These are my friends.'

The seconds stretched. Her kicking weakened.

Just as his arms began to tremble with exertion, something strange happened.

The bathroom around him seemed to flicker, its walls dissolving.

Suddenly, he was standing in a dilapidated backyard, his own, yet not the one he knew. It was older, worn by decades of neglect. Before him was not a bucket but the large *choubaccha*, the ancient water tank built into the ground.

And the person struggling beneath his hands was not Pramila.

As he stared into the churning water, Pramila's face seemed to shift, to change. For a split second, he saw another face reflected there, a face he had never seen before yet somehow recognized down to his marrow, a woman's face for whom he felt a kind of tenderness and love he had never experienced before.

Something seized in his chest, an explosively strong grip from inside. Tears welled up, streaming down his cheeks. His hands loosened slightly, his body trembling not with exertion but with an inexplicable grief that seemed to come from nowhere and everywhere at once.

Pramila's head broke the surface.

Water poured from her mouth and nose.

She gasped, coughed, and choked, but then managed a single, strangled word: 'Baba!'

But it wasn't her voice. The sound that reached Krishanu's ears was a grown woman's voice, one he had never heard calling for her father.

He stumbled backward, the dilapidated backyard vanishing as quickly as it had appeared. The bathroom tiles solidified beneath his feet once more. The tears flowed freely now, his chest heaving with sobs he couldn't understand. The monster within him temporarily dislodged by this ghost from a future he couldn't see.

Pramila twisted, gagging, coughing up water. Her fingers clawed the floor. She turned toward the passage and screamed with what was left of her breath.

'HELP...' The word broke off in a wet, gurgling sound.

The strange moment passed. Krishanu's face hardened, the tears still wet on his cheeks, but the weakness gone from his muscles. With a low snarl, he lunged forward, seizing her hair in a brutal grip. Strands came away in his fist as he forced her head back under with renewed violence.

This time he knelt on her back, one knee grinding into her spine. She thrashed beneath him, her body convulsing in desperate need for air. Her nails scratched at the bucket's sides, tearing, breaking against the metal.

'You called Rano here, to use him, to get Ishaan jealous,' he growled over the splashing. 'You had no other intent.'

Her struggles became spasmodic, less coordinated. Bubbles rose to the surface, breaking with tiny popping sounds that seemed obscenely loud in the tiled bathroom. Her legs kicked in diminishing arcs, one sandal flying off to land with a wet slap against the far wall.

'You can't stand what we share, you witch,' Krishanu snarled, pressing harder.

Then, gradually, the resistance ebbed. Her body gave a final, shuddering twitch before going slack beneath his hands. Still, he held her down, counting silently, making certain. One minute. Two. The water grew still around her submerged head.

When he finally released his grip, her body remained over the bucket, motionless. Her hair floated on the surface, black and limp, spreading outward in tendrils. The water had stilled, becoming a dark mirror that reflected nothing.

Krishanu straightened, adjusting his shirt with methodical movements. No gasping, no trembling. He turned toward the half-open door, his face composed, all traces of that momentary weakness gone, though the tear tracks remained on his cheeks.

'You can come out now, Rano,' he said. 'She is dead.'

And there he was. Ranadeep was crumpled against the wall in the passage. His face had drained of all colour, mouth working silently. One hand pressed against the floor as if to ground himself; the other clutched at his throat.

He tried to speak, but no sound emerged, just the passage of air through a constricted throat. His eyes, wide and unblinking, remained fixed on the scene in the bathroom: Pramila's still form bent over the bucket, Krishanu standing behind her, composed and in control.

'I know you have been there for a while,' Krishanu said, adjusting his gloves. 'I smelt you. And she knew you were there too. That was who she was calling out to.'

The only sound between them came from the water as it fell from the edge of the bucket to the tiled floor.

Drip.

Drip.

Drip.

19

The Last Conversation

Night pressed heavy against the narrow alley behind Krishanu's house. The moon, a thin crescent, provided barely enough light to navigate between the two broken brick walls that hemmed them in. Scattered garbage rustled in the faint breeze: discarded newspapers, green plastic wrappers putrid with the smell of rotten fish, and the occasional empty Pepsi bottle reflecting what little moonlight filtered down. A shallow ditch ran along one side, choked with wild grass and the sickly-sweet smell of rotting vegetation.

Ranadeep sat hunched on a crumbling section of wall, his body convulsing with small, uncontrollable tremors. His mouth opened and closed, but only fragmented sounds emerged, as if his vocal cords had forgotten their purpose.

Krishanu paced in tight circles, occasionally glancing up at any of the windows, alert for anyone looking down into the dark chasm between the two houses. The distant sounds of television drifted from houses, providing some amount of cover for the conversation he knew he was going to have with Ranadeep.

Getting here had been a blur. After the bathroom, after Pramila, Krishanu had gripped Ranadeep's arm with surprising strength, steering his shock-frozen body up the stairs to Pramila's terrace. There, Krishanu had guided him across a broken wooden plank spanning the narrow gap between buildings, a makeshift bridge connecting Pramila's house to a small ledge on Krishanu's roof, before removing the plank and throwing it down the side into the space where they both now were.

Ranadeep had moved like a sleepwalker, his feet finding purchase more by instinct than intent. The cool night air had done nothing to clear the fog in his mind.

To avoid detection by Krishanu's parents and grandmother, they had skirted the edge of the terrace, descending an external staircase that led to this desolate alley where neighbourhood dogs sometimes came to scavenge, and children were forbidden to play.

Now, Krishanu crouched before Ranadeep, his face transformed once again, the coldness of the bathroom replaced by something almost like concern. He spoke in hushed tones, though the words seemed to reach Ranadeep from a great distance.

'Can you hear me?' Krishanu whispered, snapping his fingers before Ranadeep's vacant eyes. 'Rano?'

'Y-y-y-o-u…k-k-ki…' Ranadeep's lips trembled violently, the words breaking apart before they could fully form. He closed his eyes, tears spilling down his cheeks, dropping onto his prized shirt, now rumpled and damp with sweat.

'Yes, I killed her. Stop stating the obvious. We have other things we need to get straight.' His voice was steady, controlled, the same tone he had used in the bathroom.

Ranadeep's head lolled forward, then snapped back up. 'W-w-w-h-h-y?' The single syllable seemed to take all his remaining strength.

Krishanu brushed away a mosquito that had landed on his neck, the casual gesture surreal against the context.

'You were there; you heard why. She was going to get you killed. What would Ishaan do if he found out you knew about the magazine cover and that you took her to the studio?'

He bent lower, forcing Ranadeep to meet his eyes.

'I am not talking about him just knocking your teeth out. I am saying what would happen to your friendship, our friendship. She would have told him. If she already hasn't.'

Ranadeep's breathing came in short, rapid bursts. He swallowed hard, trying to force air through his constricted throat.

'A-a-and y-you k-killed her f-f-for that?' He pressed his palms against his temples, as if trying to hold his fracturing thoughts together.

'Yes, I did. Now deal with it.'

Krishanu straightened, moving to lean against the opposite wall. In the dim light, his face appeared strangely peaceful, his movements fluid and relaxed, while Ranadeep's body seemed to fight against itself.

'You do know why Ishaan let you spend time with his girl? Why he let you two go to Chandannagar and Shyambazar for your little singing thingies?'

Ranadeep lifted his gaze, blinking rapidly. A car passed on the distant street, its headlights briefly illuminating the alley before plunging it back into shadow.

'B-b-b-ecause h-he t-trusted me?' His voice rose at the end, plaintive and childlike.

Krishanu guffawed; his grunt barely audible over the distant sounds of a late evening Calcutta.

'Well, okay, if that is what you want to believe. But, no, because he, like everyone, believes you are a bit of a fruit. Not a full homo, but you know, the way you comb your hair, the way you sing, the way you apply perfume, the way you tuck in your shirt, you aren't like…you know…a real man.'

Something shifted in Ranadeep's face, the shock temporarily displaced by a flash of anger. His posture straightened slightly, hands balling into fists against his thighs.

'T-t-that i-i-s n-not true.' The stammer remained, but his voice had gained strength, the tears still flowing as he spat out the words with sudden clarity. 'I am not like that.'

Krishanu's lips curled into a cruel smile. He pushed off from the wall.

'Yeah, well, I think Pramila thought that way of you too.' He pushed his fingers absent-mindedly through his own hair, feeling the sweat on his scalp. 'Again, I am not saying you are a homo, but you are like a bulb without a fuse. Yes, you got the wire, but flick the switch, there isn't going to be any light. That's why she went with you. You made her feel safe. That's why Ishaan felt safe with her being with you too.'

Ranadeep jerked to his feet, turning to face Krishanu. His movements were uncoordinated, like a puppet with tangled strings, but his voice had found solid ground.

'I am not a fruit. I am a man, just like…' The words trailed off as his gaze caught on something in Krishanu's expression, a cold certainty that silenced him.

'Well, I guess so.' Krishanu wiped his hands on his trousers, though they were already clean.

'I mean, you definitely had something on your mind, other than singing a soulful duet, when you came to her house with that perfume, knowing her parents were not there.'

Ranadeep sank back down onto the crumbling wall, the brief fire extinguished. His shoulders collapsed inward as if his spine had suddenly dissolved.

'She was my friend, and you killed her.' The tears had stopped, replaced by a hollow emptiness in his eyes.

Krishanu dropped to a crouch, bringing his face level with Ranadeep's. His movements were graceful, confident, a stark contrast to the broken boy before him. In this hidden alley, far from the awkward, bullied figure he presented at school, Krishanu moved with the assurance of someone who had finally stepped into his true self.

'Bullshit, she was not your friend.' Realizing he had said that out too loud, he lowered his voice.

'I am your friend. She was just using you. I killed for you. That is the difference between who is real and who is fake. Learn to understand the difference.'

Ranadeep's hands trembled as he wiped tears from his face, his breathing steadying slightly.

'I will have to go to the police,' he whispered, voice gaining a fragile resolve. 'I will have to tell them what happened.'

In Krishanu's eyes there was a darkening, like clouds gathering before a storm.

'Oh sure, you can,' he murmured, his voice a silken thread with cold metal beneath. 'But I will say you were there, you saw it happen, and you did not stop me.'

He made a noose with his fingers. 'And we will hang together. I don't mind. I will be with a friend till the end.'

'No.' Ranadeep shook his head, fingers digging into the crumbling brick beneath him.

'I didn't see it. You had killed her by the time I came in.'

Krishanu's laugh was barely a breath against the night air. 'Oh, that's not true. That "Help" she cried out? She did that only after she had seen you. You were there for a while.'

Ranadeep's mind cleared slightly, grasping at logic like a drowning man at driftwood. 'It's my word against yours.'

'Oh no.' Krishanu settled beside him on the wall, their shoulders nearly touching. 'You see, that "my word against yours" would be true if I was saying you killed her, and I didn't. It makes sense only if we were pointing fingers at each other. I am absolutely going to say I did it, and that gives my testimony much weight.'

He stretched his legs out and then brought them back close.

'Plus, your fingerprints are everywhere. Let me guess, on the door handle, on the floor, on the wall.'

He held up his hands, turning them palm up in the dim light. 'You see, I wore gloves.'

Ranadeep's eyes widened, realization washing over him like cold water.

'Now if you decide to stay quiet,' Krishanu continued, calmly laying out his trap. 'They aren't going to wipe the whole house. Even if they do, they don't know what your fingerprints are. But if I accuse you, they will take your prints. I will tell them exactly where to look for them, and *then* there will be a match.' He placed a hand on Ranadeep's shoulder, gentle but inescapable. 'No, we do this together, or we go down together. *All for one and one for all*, remember the motto of the Musketeers?'

'They will arrest Ishaan,' Ranadeep whispered, his voice hollow. 'He will be thrown in jail.'

Krishanu shrugged, the motion almost invisible in the darkness. 'The police will question him. He will be the prime suspect, yes, but he didn't do it. They will never be able to prove beyond a reasonable doubt that he killed Pramila. That's his greatest protection, the truth.'

'You think people who go to the gallows are all guilty?' Ranadeep's voice cracked with disbelief.

'Oho,' Krishanu yawned. 'First of all, Ishaan hasn't passed his eighteenth birthday. That's two weeks away. He is a juvenile; we aren't.'

He ticked off points on his fingers, the gesture precise and controlled.

'Another thing, that "circumstantial evidence" crap happens to people like me who would get court-appointed lawyers. Ishaan will buy the best, and his dad has the city in his pockets.' He leaned back, radiating calm. 'I would be surprised if Ishaan is even charged. As a matter of fact, he will love the notoriety, do you know how the boys will see him if they think he actually killed a girl who dumped him? You think I didn't think this through, all day today?'

A distant dog barked, then fell silent. Somewhere, far away, a conch blew.

'You stay quiet,' Krishanu whispered, 'and this blows over.'

Ranadeep stared at the ground, his gaze fixed on nothing, lost in the darkness between the walls as his mind raced through an impossible labyrinth of choices, each path leading to destruction.

'You don't understand, do you?' Krishanu's voice softened, taking on an almost pleading quality that was more terrifying than his threats.

'What all of this means to me. Only when I am with you guys do I feel like I exist.'

His words quickened, intensity building beneath the hushed tones.

'I am not going to let you and Ishaan fight and make Basab take sides. I am not going to then stand and watch as the only family I have gets destroyed. I see that with my own joint family, quarrelling every day, my father and his brothers. They weren't like this, you know, all their lives. This happened after they got married. Aunts started fighting over the kitchen, then they started poisoning the ears of their husbands about their brothers, which of them doesn't contribute to the family finances as much as they should, who eats the bigger portion of fish, and now they are at each other's throats. And I wish someone had stepped in years ago and stopped it. Well, I can't do anything about that. But here, I can. And I did.'

Krishanu stood up, dusting off his trousers.

'We are forever, don't you see? Don't you see even Pramila knew that, and that is why she was trying to break us apart?'

Ranadeep collapsed inward. The brief clarity he had found dissolved into fresh sobs, his body shaking with the effort to keep them silent. He was once again a blubbering mass of emotions, while Krishanu watched with clinical detachment, as if observing a specimen under glass.

Krishanu's voice was now practical, matter-of-fact. 'Go home. Just do normal stuff. Tomorrow, we go to school like always.'

He turned to leave, then paused.

The question came softly, almost tenderly. 'Why didn't you stop me, Rano?'

Ranadeep looked up, caught off-guard.

'You could have,' Krishanu continued, his silhouette motionless against the night sky. 'I know you like Pramila. She saw you and cried out for you to help her. Why didn't you?'

A long silence stretched between them, with their breaths, falling heavy, the only interruption.

When Ranadeep finally spoke, his voice was barely audible. 'I wanted to,' he whispered. 'But I realized if I did, if I saved her, she would take you to the police.'

His fingers twisted in the fabric of his shirt.

'You would spend your adult life in jail.'

He swallowed hard. 'I hesitated. And by that time…it was over.'

Krishanu turned. A window opened across the street, spilling light onto his face. The brief illumination revealed an expression of terrible understanding, and something worse: gratitude.

'Between two friends, you chose me.'

He crouched down again, his movements gentle, almost reverent.

He reached out, his fingers circling around Ranadeep's shoulder. The touch was feather-light, yet Ranadeep trembled as if struck, feeling Pramila's last breaths still clinging to those fingers.

Krishanu smiled, the expression oddly childlike in its joy.

'See? This is what makes it special. Friendship. It flows both ways. It outlasts time.'

'I can kill for you,' Krishanu whispered. 'And you can kill for me.'

In the narrow alley, with the night pressing close around them, these words remained suspended in the air like a covenant sealed in blood.

Ranadeep felt something irreversible taking place, as if the person he might have been was dying, right here in this filthy space between houses, suffocating in darkness.

'The Musketeers,' Krishanu said, raising his right hand as they did before they stepped onto the cricket field. 'Forever.'

And then Krishanu melted into the shadows, leaving Ranadeep alone with the knowledge of what they had become together.

20

The Stay at the Hotel

Ranadeep Saha stood before the mirror in his suite at the Delhi Sheraton, studying his reflection. His fingers brushed against his temple, detecting an unusual warmth. Fever. Slight, but present.

Season change, he told himself, echoing his mother's reassurance. Nothing to worry about, she would say, as he would lie in bed, with that old mercury thermometer in his mouth, as she brought him chicken broth, and then put wet strips on his brow as the red line rose.

He unscrewed the medicine bottle on the shelf, took out two Tylenol pills and swallowed them dry.

The bathroom's recessed lighting made him look unfamiliar. The man staring back in the mirror seemed older, haunted, skin too pale, lips dry and cracked, eyes swimming with moisture that refused to resolve into proper tears. The stubble on his face had now grown wild into a patchy, unkempt beard, black hairs mixed with premature white, growing in uneven clusters across his jaw.

Yes, tonight might be the night the fever really takes hold, he told himself. He could feel it already, the dull ache in his bones.

Three days since he had checked himself in, requesting the top-floor suite, issuing his peculiar instructions to the front desk staff.

'No one enters,' he had said, voice calm and measured. 'Not housekeeping. Not room service. Not even my wife, should she show up.'

The young woman at the reception had exchanged a look with her colleague, brief but unmistakable. The look reserved for difficult guests, for eccentrics, for the potentially unstable. Still, they knew who he was, and his position carried weight. They had nodded, made notes in their system, promised discretion.

Occam's razor, he reminded himself. The simplest solution is usually the correct one.

Basab drowned in his pool. Ishaan crashed into the sea. Krishanu, well, he had planned that one himself, having the men place both bodies in the water tank to make it look like suicide.

Three of his friends, all dead in water. What were the odds?

Even though he had arranged Krishanu's death that way, part of him wondered if he had merely been following a script written long ago. Had he chosen water for Krishanu? Or had something chosen it through him? Had he been the instrument rather than the architect?

The thought of Krishanu brought an unexpected pang, not guilt exactly, but something that resembled it. The fever opened a memory: Bhulu, his uncle's German Shepherd. It was a dog his uncle had rescued. His original owners would regularly beat him, keep him chained outside and give him very little to eat. His uncle had told Ranadeep, *Bhulu resource guards. Don't get too close.*

Of course, as a child then, he did not listen.

Oh, how he had loved that dog. The way Bhulu would rest his massive head on Ranadeep's lap during summer afternoons, tongue lolling, eyes watchful, and how he would lick his knees, and look up at him with those eyes, melting with love.

Until the day Bhulu bit him. Not savagely, a warning nip when Ranadeep had startled him awake. But enough to break skin and draw blood. Enough that he had shown the wound to his uncle, concerned but not thinking of consequences.

Three days later, he watched from the backseat of his uncle's Ambassador as they drove Bhulu to the vet. The dog's tail wagged happily in the front seat. He had no idea where he was going or why.

The memory still stung like the bite itself. How he wished he had hidden the bite, said nothing.

One mistake and Bhulu had paid with his life.

Krishanu had been like that too, dangerous, unpredictable, with a guarding tendency toward what he valued. He had always told himself that is why he had hesitated, because he did not want to do a repeat of what happened to Bhulu with Krishanu. He had hoped that if the bite remained hidden, if the identity of Pramila's murderer stayed buried, the problem would solve itself, and everything would go back to the way it was.

Except it never did. And that's why he had to euthanize him now. Doggie Dum Dum.

Not that it had hurt any less.

The fever made these memories sharper somehow, more intrusive. Three deaths. All by water. And whatever supernatural explanation his rational mind rejected, there remained the undeniable pattern. It was water he had to avoid.

He wondered whether he was going mad.

He looked around the bathroom, at what he had done for the past few days.

He had located the water line going into the bathtub and the shower. The blasted hotel had hidden it behind a false panel, and he had to first find it, and then break the front. It had not been easy, he did not have a hammer, and he was not going to ask the hotel for tools, of course. So, he had to bang at it with whatever he could lay his hands on from the room: coat hangers, the travel iron, the base of a lamp.

He could not do it too loudly. The last thing he wanted was some bellhop to come and knock on his room for the noise.

In the end, he had to use his nails to wrench away the final trappings of the false cover, and he looked down at his fingers, the nails broken and still bleeding. Then he had turned the inside metal valve off. But even that had not felt secure. So, he had taken extra sheets from the closet, jammed them into the spout, then managed to unscrew the showerhead with his bare hands.

Of course, the commode still had water. So did the sink. But that could not be helped.

It made perfect sense, rational sense, to reduce his exposure to water.

Given what he knew, this was the most logical course. Minimize threat exposure; that's what they taught during assignment training. He was simply applying it now: no showers, no shaving, no brushing teeth, no handwashing. Just bottled water. Sealed. Drunk only when thirsty, not out of habit.

Sure, from the outside it might look crazy. But no one else knew what he did.

There was something about the bathtub, the moment he had stepped into the room three days ago. He had felt a sense of foreboding. Very luxurious, the porcelain gleaming under the fancy lights, almost crying out to him to step in and wash away the tiredness of the last few days. But he had resisted that call, sensing something wrong about it. Not after Basab, no way. Maybe there would be an electrical short circuit with him in the water, or who knows what else.

He couldn't explain it, but there was something about the water itself. Not the plumbing. The water.

It had begun last night. Every time he flushed the toilet, he caught himself stepping back, almost running from the sound of churning water. His eyes would snap up to the ceiling, away from the swirling water circling down the bowl.

Something in it unsettled him. Turned his stomach.

'Good thing I didn't take that shower,' he muttered, touching his forehead.

The fever had risen.

He stepped out of the bathroom and into the bedroom. The light seemed too bright, the sheets too white.

How long could he stay here? That question had pressed against him since he had arrived. Eventually the hotel staff would demand entry. Eventually someone from work would insist on a meeting. His leave would run out. His family would expect him back.

But the alternative, returning to the world, returning to water, felt unthinkable.

Krishanu had died thirty years to the day Pramila had. That detail had not escaped his notice. If this were one of those horror films his son enjoyed watching, the vengeful spirit would have already claimed him on that anniversary. Classic horror tropes dictated that supernatural revenge followed precise timelines, usually culminating on significant dates.

And yet, here he was, still alive. How? Had he avoided the curse?

Perhaps it meant nothing. Perhaps the deaths of his friends were merely tragic coincidences, and his fevered mind was constructing patterns where none existed. Or perhaps, and this thought chilled him more than the others, whatever waited for him operated on rules that even he could not decipher.

It was seven o'clock. Normally at this point, he would unlock the door, glance down the passage, once to his left and then to his right, and pull in the tray that he had ordered from room service. His dinner. For the last few days, he had only ordered factory-sealed food, nothing cooked, inspecting each package before breaking it open.

But today, he didn't open the door.

He was not hungry. On the contrary, he worried that with the fever coming on, food might make him vomit, and that would require another interaction with water.

Instead, he climbed onto his bed. For the past few days, that was all he did, lie there with the television on until sleep came, then wake in the middle of the night, shivering beneath the blanket, the AC cranked to full blast. He was doubling his prescribed sleeping pills. At least they kept the dreams away.

He missed Shayan. Missed talking to him on the phone. Sometimes, sitting up in his bed, he would find himself weeping inconsolably, the stammering that had plagued his youth returning, words getting stuck in his mouth. Then he would calm himself down, trying to analyse the sadness, break it down logically, as he always had.

Was he grieving his friends? Was it something else?

He had lied to Shayan, as he had to Monobina. Told them he was on assignment in a place where phone communication was restricted for national security reasons. After what had happened to Sunanda, any contact, even over the phone, might put them in danger.

But why was he crying like this?

The answer made him cry harder.

He was never going to see Shayan again. There was no logical reason to believe that. But the certainty settled in his gut like a heavy stone. He told himself this was inevitable, the parting; everyone dies someday, all fathers leave one day.

But the voice inside whispered otherwise.

He wasn't weeping for the future. He was mourning the past.

All the times he could have been with Shayan but chose not to: working late at the office when he could have gone home early, watching television programmes he didn't even like while Shayan sat in the next room with nothing to do, scolding him over trivialities, bad scores in his mid-terms, an unmade bed, a harmless lie about homework. Nothing big, nothing necessary for parenting, just the small cruelties that leave behind hairline fractures that never fully heal.

It is those small things we remember, he realized, and the realization made him weep harder. Not the grand gestures or important moments, but the casual dismissals, the impatient sighs, the phone calls cut short, the raised eyebrow, the dismissive sigh. They crowded him now, the consequences of these choices. In that dark room, alone, he saw for the first time shadows of timelines he would never experience.

To ward off the gathering darkness, he sang quietly to himself, sitting on the bed, the songs he used to perform as a teenager, in competitions and for practice. Sometimes, just sometimes, he thought he heard another voice joining him, a female voice, delicate and distant, echoing his melody. He told himself it was his imagination. Because if what he feared was truly out there, it wasn't singing duets.

But tonight, Ranadeep did not even feel like singing. He lay down, pulled up the sheets and looked up at the ceiling.

Twenty-four more hours, and he would check himself out and go back to his life.

No, he told himself, not back to his own life, but a different one.

He would resign. Enough of pushing files. Whatever time he had left, if he had any, he would spend doing things he wanted to do, go back to music, take guitar lessons, start singing regularly again. Yes, finances might be tight, with Shayan's tuition fees at Harvey Mudd. But he would figure out some way. Maybe do a little government consultancy work on the side, just enough to cover the bills, so that Monobina also does not feel he had chosen to transition to becoming a bum.

And maybe he would write a book.

A biography on Ishaan. From his childhood to his fame to his demise. Publishers would line up for it. He, after all, had a perspective no one else did.

And maybe, just maybe, he could say out loud what only he and Krishanu had known for certain: Ishaan did not kill Pramila Chatterjee.

But then a colder voice spoke inside him.

Maybe Ishaan hadn't killed her. But he wasn't innocent either.

He had abused her, belittled her, humiliated her. He had broken something inside her. And whatever had come for retribution had not spared him.

If that hadn't spared him, why should public opinion?

These weren't serious thoughts, he told himself. Just fever dreams. Brain fog.

He turned over, closed his eyes, and tried to sleep.

When Ranadeep Saha woke up, it was still pitch dark. But he realized he was not alone in the room.

There was a single-seater sofa near the floor-length window, next to the table, and there was someone sitting there in the shadows. He could not make out the person, but he was sure of the presence. His hand moved instinctively toward the bedside switch.

Then the rational voice spoke.

Don't bother.

There's no one there.

And if there is, it's only because it's dark. The light will make it vanish.

If the thing truly existed, if it meant to reveal its no-doubt terrifying visage, it would have done so when the lights were on. If it wanted to harm him, it would have already.

What was the point? He did not have the energy for this game.

If it was a trick of his fevered mind, the light wouldn't make a difference anyway.

So, he left the light off.

'Why did you do it?' The voice asked. A voice he had not heard for decades.

He knew what the next words would be, and he was right.

'You were my friend, Rano.'

'I wanted to save you,' his voice came dry and panicked. 'But I panicked.'

Fear would not help him now. Only logic. Maybe, just maybe, he could do what he had always done: talk his way out of it.

The silence stretched, as if waiting for more.

'You would have sent Krishanu to jail. He would have died there. And he was a friend too.'

His voice broke with the next words.

'I chose him. Between you and him, I chose him.'

The presence spoke again. But now it was his own voice, echoing back across the years.

A memory: Shayan, fifteen, falling in with the wrong crowd. Drunk bureaucrats' sons at a Delhi pub. A fight. The police bringing him home. That night, Ranadeep had said these exact words.

And now, he heard them again, coming back to him like a verdict: 'A half-truth is also a lie. It's the worst kind of lie because you don't just lie to the other person. You lie to yourself. You convince yourself it is the truth because you never said anything technically false. But deep down, you know what you left out.

'The truth is there. And you have to say it.

'Where the end of your lie and the beginning of the truth converge.'

The voice trailed off.

'Say it,' the voice in the room whispered.

Now it sounded like all of them – Pramila, Krishanu, Ishaan, Basab – a chorus in unison.

'Say what you never said. The real truth.'

Ranadeep's throat constricted. The words, that had never been spoken aloud in thirty years, rose from somewhere deep within him, ugly and raw.

'The reason I watched you die was because, at that moment, I wanted you to die.'

The confession ripped through him.

'Krishanu was right. Every word he said when he was drowning you. It was the truth I had always known. But never had the courage to say. Even to myself. When I heard him speak it aloud, it hit me, and I hated you for it.'

His voice grew stronger, the words pouring out now.

'I hated that I was only ever a friend to you. That I would *always* be just that. As if there was something missing in me, some deficiency, that I didn't even register as someone who could see you differently. That I was not really a man.'

The room seemed to grow colder.

'I never thought you were playing me against Ishaan, the way Krishanu said. For that you would have to consider me equal to him. And you never did. I knew you had no intention of going back to Ishaan. I had seen it in your eyes when you looked at me and asked for help, and I stayed still. In your eyes, I saw someone who had decided to move into some other world where neither Ishaan nor I existed, a world where you could be free.'

He swallowed hard, tasting something bitter.

'So yes, between someone who never saw me as I saw her, who was going to disappear into a life I could never be part of, I chose the person who would never leave.'

The final words came out as barely a whisper.

'Yes, Pramila, I chose Krishanu. Because he was more of a friend than you were. Because friends stay. Friends don't make you feel like you are not enough. Friends don't want to break away.'

When Ranadeep woke up again, he wasn't sure if he had been dreaming.

Or if he had left the dream at all.

But there was something else bothering him intensely that had pushed the memory of that half-dream out of his mind: the air-conditioner. The room had become like a refrigerator. He knew it must have been the fever, but it was not just the chill that was tingling around his bones. It was the draft, the wind circulating, and he was feeling it on his cheeks and his exposed skin like little blades, like the string they would coat with broken glass shards for kite fighting during Viswakarma Pujo to slice through other kites in the sky.

He stood up, fumbling with the buttons of the air-conditioner, but it refused to turn off. It was one of the newfangled 'smart' systems, and through his fever-clouded mind, he could not figure out the touch-screen interface. No matter what he touched, the AC seemed to roar louder, circling air more aggressively, sending icy currents directly at his face.

Ranadeep wrapped all the hotel blankets around himself, cocooning his body, but the draft found every gap, every exposed inch of skin. He nearly tripped once, his movements clumsy and desperate. Nothing he did would stop the relentless flow of air.

He could call housekeeping, but he could not do that, not with the state of the bathroom, not with his fears about bringing anyone into his room. No, he would have to solve this himself.

The suitcase. He had brought changes of clothes. He would wear all of them, multiple layers to trap air between the fabrics, create insulation. Two pairs of jeans, as many shirts as he could manage, one over the other. The air between the layers would be still, protected. Yes, he just had to wait it out, wait till the fever broke, till this hypersensitivity to every breath of moving air finally subsided.

Turning on all the lights in his room, he began pulling clothes from his suitcase with trembling fingers, his skin flinching with each fresh wave of air from the relentless machine. It was not the cold, he realized he was recoiling from, but the draft, as if he was terrified of it.

He remembered as clearly as if it was yesterday; the night Pramila had died, there had been a breeze. He had felt it sitting in the passage outside the bathroom and later in that narrow alley between the buildings. The same sensation of air moving across his skin that had accompanied his terrible choice. The terror of that night flooded back through this strange draft, linking past to present in a way his rational mind could not dismiss.

He stood and shivered, not from cold but from recognition. His body was recoiling from the very movement of air as if it carried something more than just temperature.

It carried the memory of him watching Pramila being murdered and not wanting to do anything about it.

Still trembling, he reached for the bottled water on the table. It must have been almost a day since he had water. Despite his aversion to it, he wondered if he was also dehydrated. But the moment his hand touched the bottle cap, Ranadeep Saha felt it, as if fingers were clamping down on his throat, not his own fingers, but someone else's. Cold, strong fingers wrapping around his windpipe, pressing until his air was cut off.

He remembered that scene again, from thirty years ago. Pramila's face underwater, her throat working desperately for air that couldn't come, Krishanu's hands on her neck, the way her body had convulsed. And now, impossibly, he was experiencing the same sensation, the crushing grip, the inability to breathe, the panic rising like bile.

His throat muscles seized, cramping violently as if his own body was reenacting Krishanu's grip. The water bottle fell from his nerveless fingers, rolling across the carpet. He grabbed at his neck, trying to loosen an invisible hold, but the spasm only intensified. His windpipe felt like it was closing, the muscles contracting in violent waves that sent him gasping and choking.

'Do you feel it, Rano?' The voice said in his head, 'Do you now know how I felt?'

The sensation washed over him now, of being held underwater without the water, just the crushing airlessness, the terror of suffocation, the knowledge that no amount of struggling could make it stop.

The water that had spilled on the carpet began to spread, forming a dark, creeping stain. Ranadeep watched it expand across the expensive hotel carpet, each dark tendril reaching out like fingers. An intense terror seized him, not at the water itself, but at the sight of it spreading, finding form, moving with purpose. He stumbled backwards, his layered clothes making him clumsy, and rushed to the bathroom, desperate to escape the liquid that seemed to pulse with malevolent life.

In the bathroom mirror, he caught sight of himself and froze in horror. Saliva dripped from his mouth in thick, viscous strands, far more than he had ever produced in his life. It hung from his chin like wet spider silk, silver-white and bubbling under the lights. The sight of his own face triggered a wave of revulsion and terror that left him paralysed. He was becoming something else, something that produced too much saliva, something that could not control its own basic functions.

His hand trembled as he tried to wipe the drool away, but the moment the warm, sticky liquid touched his palm, a fresh surge of irrational fear coursed through him. His own saliva felt alien, dangerous, as if it belonged to someone else. He stared at his wet hand, transfixed by horror at this simple bodily fluid that now seemed to carry disease, death, corruption.

You were my friend. You let me die. You wanted me to die.

Pramila's voice drifted through the bathroom, soft but clear. It was not inside his head anymore. He spun around, expecting to see her, but found only empty space.

Desperate to clean himself, to wash away this terror, he reached for the tap. His rational mind had fled completely, all thoughts of avoiding water forgotten in his mounting panic. As his trembling fingers grasped the chrome handle, he glanced into the mirror to look away from the water flow.

That's when he saw them.

Basab, Ishaan, Krishanu stood in a line behind him, reflected in the mirror. Their faces were wrong, their eyes completely white, no pupils, no irises, just blank stares from eyeballs turned inside out. They stood perfectly still, watching him with their terrible empty gazes.

And then they smiled at him, all together, as if responding to some unheard signal. The smiles extended beyond what human muscles should allow, curving upward nearly to their ears in perfect, synchronized grins. Their cheeks distended, skin stretching paper-thin across their faces as the smiles grew wider still, even though their heads remained perfectly still.

'Don't you want to play?' They asked in unison, but their lips did not move.

A scream tore from his throat. Pure terror exploded through his nervous system. Without conscious thought, he lunged forward at the mirror, needing to destroy these horrific images. His head collided with the glass with tremendous force. The mirror exploded into a thousand fragments, sharp pieces raining down around him. Jagged shards cut deep gashes across his forehead and cheeks. Blood poured down his face, mixing with the saliva, creating pink streams that dripped onto his shirt.

Pain and panic drove him into pure flight mode. He burst from the bathroom, crashing through the hotel room without fully seeing where he was going. His mind split between present terror and past memory, running the same way he had after Pramila died, Krishanu's strong hand yanking him up those stairs. But this time was different. This time he felt wet hair, thick, dank strands heavy with water, wrapping around his neck like a living noose, tightening with each step he took, pulling him forward.

Unlatching the door with feverish fingers, Ranadeep exploded into the hotel corridor, blood streaming down his face, multiple layers of clothes making him look like a madman. Hotel guests screamed and pressed against the walls. He ran blindly forward, the blood obscuring his vision, the drool wetting him through to his bones, and hands that weren't there clamping on his windpipe.

Then the strangers' hands became real. Hotel security, other guests, were all converging on him, trying to restrain his flailing body. Their voices merged into an incomprehensible roar: 'Someone call security!' 'He's bleeding!' 'Get him down!' 'Call an ambulance!'

The hands pulled him to the ground. The last thing he saw before darkness took him was the hotel ceiling, spinning like a carousel. And then he realized he was looking at the bottom of a metal bucket.

His mind fractured completely as consciousness fled, leaving him suspended between terror and oblivion.

'Help,' he cried out, but the word died in his throat, a strangled whisper lost in the chaos around him.

As he lay pinned to the cold hotel floor, he felt it: wet hair sliding against his cheek, water dripping onto his skin. A presence so close that her lips brushed against his ear. Pramila's voice, no longer in his head but intimately, impossibly real.

'No one is coming to help you, Rano,' she whispered, her sodden hair intertwining with his, cold water seeping from her scalp to his. 'Just like you did not come to help me.'

The water was now everywhere. He knew he would never again be free of it.

21
The Protocol

Monobina Saha stood beside the hospital bed, her eyes fixed on her husband's still form. Ranadeep lay motionless beneath a web of tubes and wires, a central line running into his chest, an endotracheal tube between his lips, secured with white medical tape. The tube connected to the ventilator that dominated the room with its rhythmic sounds: the mechanical inhale, the pneumatic hiss as it pushed oxygen into his lungs, followed by the longer whoosh of exhalation. Phssssh…whoooosh. Phssssh…whoooosh. An unnatural, mechanical breath that made her own breathing feel deliberate and strange.

The EEG electrodes attached to his scalp, small metal discs held in place, mapped brain activity she could not comprehend onto a screen of dancing green lines. A feeding tube ran through his nostril, taped securely to his face, delivering nutrition directly to his stomach.

The private room was quiet apart from the ventilator's persistent rhythm and the steady beeping of cardiac monitors. Fluorescent lights cast a harsh glow that made Ranadeep's skin appear waxy, almost translucent. His once-expressive face now slack and empty, the plastic mouthguard preventing him from biting down on the tube itself.

Her mind kept replaying the conversation with Dr Mehta earlier that morning. The neurologist's voice had been gentle but direct as they stood in the corridor outside this very room, clipboard in hand.

'The test results are positive for rabies,' he had said, looking up from the file, his glasses catching the overhead light.

'Rabies?' Her voice had risen in disbelief. 'That's impossible. He has not been bitten by any dog, as far as I recall, for years.' She remembered feeling her knees weaken, grateful for the wall behind her.

Dr Mehta had shaken his head. 'Not necessarily a dog. Has Mr Saha travelled internationally in the past two to three months?'

'Yes, we were in the United States. Los Angeles.' The memory felt distant now, like something from another life, when they had gone to drop off Shayan at Harvey Mudd. 'But he was not attacked by any animals there.'

'In the United States, bats are the most common rabies vector.' The doctor's eyes had narrowed slightly behind rimless glasses. 'Did he have any contact with bats? Even minor?'

And then she remembered, that evening on the restaurant terrace, Yamashiro, under the string lights. The hillside view of Los Angeles spreading out below them, glittering in the dusk. How Ranadeep had hopped over a decorative fence to pick a rose for her from a garden bed. She recalled the small scratch on his hand that he had dismissed, a bat, emerging from beneath the shrub, startled by his intrusion.

'There was…a bat,' she told Dr Mehta, her hand rising unconsciously to her mouth. 'It scratched him, I think. Or nipped him. It was minor; we didn't think anything of it. I didn't even know bats could transmit rabies. Isn't it a dog thing?'

Dr Mehta had sighed, deep lines appearing at the corners of his mouth. 'That is a common misconception. Bats are the leading cause of rabies deaths in the United States. Even a minor scratch or bite that breaks the skin can transmit the virus.'

The guilt had crashed over her then; they should have known, should have sought treatment immediately. Now it was too late.

'What can we do?' she had asked, her voice barely a whisper.

The doctor had explained the Milwaukee Protocol; a medically induced coma combined with antiviral medications. The only approach that had ever resulted in survival once symptoms appeared, though the success rate was dismally low.

'It is experimental,' Dr Mehta had cautioned. 'The chances of recovery are extremely slim. But without it…' He had not needed to finish the sentence. Without it, death was certain.

'The coma is induced with ketamine and midazolam,' he had explained, his voice taking on the careful tone doctors use when explaining complex procedures. 'We suppress brain activity to a near-flatline state while administering antivirals. The theory is that by shutting down brain function, we give the body's immune system time to develop antibodies against the virus.'

Her hand had trembled as she had signed the consent form, the pen nearly slipping from her grasp.

'At minimum,' he had added, his voice softening, 'the induced coma will spare him the psychological and physical suffering that rabies inflicts in its final stages. The hydrophobia, the hallucinations – he will not experience any of it.'

Now, standing beside Ranadeep's bed, Monobina tried to reconcile the man she knew – brilliant, composed, logical – with the wild-eyed, bleeding figure hotel security had restrained. The hospital had initially diagnosed him with acute psychosis until the excessive salivation and throat spasms prompted testing for rabies.

She brushed her fingers lightly across his forehead, careful not to disturb the EEG leads. His skin felt cool now, the fever controlled by medication. The ventilator continued its mechanical breathing, the sound both reassuring and terrifying. The stubble on his face had grown longer, coarser in the three days since his admission. His cheeks were sunken, the bones more prominent than before. The scratches across his face from the broken mirror had been cleaned and dressed, thin lines of red against his pale skin.

Shayan was on a flight from California now. She had called him immediately after speaking with the doctors, the weight of explaining his father's condition nearly crushing her. Their son had switched from disbelief to determination in seconds, booking the first available flight home.

'He will be here by tomorrow morning,' she whispered to Ranadeep, though she knew he couldn't hear her. The ventilator responded with its unrelenting rhythm, breathing for him when he could no longer breathe for himself.

As she adjusted the thin hospital blanket over his chest, something on the bedside table caught her eye: a single red rose in a slim crystal vase. The stem was wet, water droplets clinging to the green surface like tears. The petals were vivid crimson, almost unnaturally so against the sterile white of the hospital room.

Monobina froze, her hand halfway extended toward it. She had not brought a rose. None of the nurses had mentioned bringing one in. Ranadeep had been in isolation since his arrival, with access strictly limited due to his condition.

The water in the vase seemed darker than it should be, almost murky. A single drop had escaped, sliding down the crystal to pool on the laminate surface of the table. As she watched, the drop seemed to expand, spreading outward like an inkblot.

'Who brought this?' she asked when a nurse entered to check Ranadeep's vitals.

The young woman glanced at the rose, her brow furrowing. 'I am sorry, ma'am. I don't know. It wasn't here during morning rounds.'

Monobina's gaze returned to the flower. In her mind's eye, she saw her husband reaching for a different rose, one that had set these events in motion with a bat's startled bite. A chill spread through her that had nothing to do with the hospital's air conditioning.

She reached out tentatively and touched one crimson petal. It felt cold and wet against her fingertip, as if freshly plucked from water. When she drew her hand back, a drop of water clung to her skin, dark, almost opaque. It remained there, refusing to roll off her finger or evaporate, a perfect sphere of liquid that seemed to pulse with a life of its own, like a memory that refused to be buried.

22

Dreams in the Dark

In the darkness of his mind, Ranadeep's nightmare continued.

He saw it again, that day, every moment, in vivid technicolour, from the time he entered the gates, his heart full of hope, to the scene he saw from the passageway. He relived it again and again, like a bad VHS tape stuck in the head of the machine, and every time he felt the horror as if it was new. This time the choice of which friend to save was not one he took, but one his memory had taken for him; it was set in stone, no second chances even in that half-alive, half-dead space he was in, no redemption. Pramila died every time, the water spilled out the same way every time, and he sat with his back to the wall, shaking with terror, not just at what was happening in front of him, but with the full cognizance of what the ramifications of his actions would be, on him and on the rest of his friends, thirty years later.

The darkness wrapped around him like a shroud. The water pressed against his skin, neither cold nor warm, just there, unyielding.

'You thought it would be over,' Pramila whispered, her voice coming from everywhere and nowhere. 'You thought you could wash it all away.'

Her face materialized in the darkness, grey-skinned, waterlogged, mascara tracks frozen down her cheeks.

'Occam's razor,' she said, using his words. 'The simplest explanation is the right one; isn't that what you say? And the simplest explanation is that you are a murderer, and you are a coward. And even worse than that, you are a bad friend.'

The water around him began to churn. From the darkness, three shapes materialized, floating around him in a slow circle: Basab, his face frozen in terror, eyes wide and unblinking; Ishaan, handsome features distorted by the steering wheel fragment embedded in his skull; Krishanu, emaciated and empty-eyed.

'Jack of All Trades,' they chanted, voices bubbling through the water. 'Master of None.'

Ranadeep wanted to close his eyes, till he realized his eyes were already closed.

'We are the Musketeers,' they chanted, voices melding together. 'One for all.'

'All for one,' Ranadeep whispered.

The whirlpool tightened. Ranadeep felt the water pressure increase, squeezing his chest, pushing against his eardrums. He tried to swim upward, but there was no up or down anymore, only the circling dead.

'Please,' he begged, 'I have a son.'

Pramila's face appeared before him, close enough that he could count the water droplets clinging to her lashes.

'I had parents,' she said. 'I had dreams. I wanted to be on magazine covers. I wanted to fall in love. I wanted to grow old.'

Now, his friends were there again, forming a circle, but this time, they were moving away from him slowly.

'Am I dying?' Ranadeep asked.

'You have been dying for thirty years,' Krishanu said.

'Since the moment you stood in that doorway,' Ishaan added.

'And did nothing,' Basab finished.

In the hospital room, the monitors began to wail. Monobina screamed for the doctors. Nurses rushed in, pushing her aside. Paddles pressed against Ranadeep's chest. Once. Twice. Three times.

Ranadeep realized he was in both places at once, outside looking in, inside looking out.

In the darkness, the water began to drain away, leaving Ranadeep suspended in empty black space. He could still see the four of them, but they were fading, becoming transparent.

'Wait,' he called. 'Don't leave me here alone.'

'You chose to be alone,' Pramila said, 'when you chose to watch me die.'

He saw his friends vanish into the space, and he floated there, not feeling anything, not touching anything, in the vast empty void.

The last lines of Pramila's poems came to him from beyond time:

With prickly thorns as sharp as knives,
And a colour of the deepest red,
Upon weeping petals it thrives,
Born to live among the dead.

And then, Ranadeep Saha heard the machine flatline.

Epilogue

Ramkrishna Park basked in the slanted light of a winter afternoon. The sun hung low in a pale, rinsed-out sky, casting long shadows across the dusty earth where four boys gathered their scattered cricket gear.

Krishanu sat cross-legged on the ground, struggling to fit the wooden stumps into the fraying canvas bag. His round face was flushed from exertion, a fine sheen of sweat still visible on his forehead despite the winter chill.

Crumbs from the *phuchka* he had devoured between overs dotted his sweater.

'These things never go back in properly,' he complained, forcing the third stump into the bag. 'Like trying to stuff an elephant into a matchbox.'

'Like stuffing the syllabus into your brain,' Ishaan quipped, spinning the cricket ball on his fingertip, before deftly pocketing it with a magician's flourish. His white T-shirt remained remarkably clean despite the diving catches and boundary chases of their three-hour match.

Even his trousers showed only the faintest traces of red dust at the knees.

'Some of us,' Krishanu retorted, yanking at a stubborn zipper, 'actually have to study to pass exams. Some of us don't have daddies running big businesses.'

'Studying is for chumps and Basab,' Ishaan proclaimed, flashing his movie-star smile.

On a nearby bench, Basab methodically wrapped batting tape around the handle of his prized Kashmir willow bat. A blue sweater-vest layered over a neatly buttoned shirt; glasses fogged slightly in the crisp air.

'We all do what we are good at.'

'You guys want the treat, or are we going to keep talking until next winter?' Ranadeep asked, fingers nimbly flicking through the notes in his wallet.

An expensive digital watch gleamed on his wrist, a birthday present from his parents that morning.

'Good innings today, Basab, by the way. Your fifty saved us after Krishanu's duck.'

'It was not a duck,' Krishanu snapped. 'There was an inside edge onto my pads, and I was hit outside the leg stump. The umpire was blind.'

'The definition of out for zero,' Ishaan teased, 'is an excuse.'

'That is enough, now,' Krishanu muttered. 'And Rano, if your idea of a birthday treat is Pepsi and that sad chicken cutlet from Tiffin Corner again, I swear I am going home. Sher-e-Bengal does mutton biryani at twenty-eight rupees. That's a sign from the gods.'

'After dragging us to that awful movie you insisted on,' Ishaan said, mock-wounded, 'you are lucky we are not making you pay. Plus, you going home and not having free food? I call your bluff, that is never going to happen.'

They began strolling toward the park gates, still bantering about the film, the dry grass crunching underfoot. The sun warmed their backs; their shadows stretched long and blurred together on the asphalt path. In the distance, younger boys had commandeered a patch of field, the thwack of ball on bat and joyous shouts ringing in the still air. An old man sat feeding birds from a torn newspaper cone, grey wings flickering around him like ash.

'Sixteen,' Krishanu said suddenly, watching the young boys. 'Weird to think we are sixteen now. Feels like yesterday we were those kids. Oh yes, I forgot, our hero here, Ishaan is still fifteen.'

'And yet I have been shaving longer than all of you,' Ishaan said smugly, stroking his chin.

Ranadeep gave a small nod, his voice quieter now. 'My father says this is when life starts getting serious. Boards. Colleges. The works.'

'With eighteen comes adult movies,' Ishaan grinned. 'No more sneaking in behind the guy selling peanuts.'

'Some of us have to think about the future that does not include adult movies,' Basab said.

'The future!' Ishaan spread his arms wide, theatrically, narrowly missing hitting an elderly couple walking past. 'My future is already decided. Bollywood is waiting for me.'

'First you have to pass twelfth standard,' Basab said, deadpan.

'Details, details,' Ishaan waved his hand, brushing aside reality like lint.

Basab stopped. Looked up. The sky was turning a deeper blue now, dusted with a few wispy clouds.

'Days like this,' he said softly, 'I wish we could keep them. It was perfect today.'

'That movie was perfect?' Ishaan asked. 'You are losing it from reading physics books two grades ahead.'

'Come on, we all enjoyed the movie,' Krishanu said, defensively. 'Sure, it was bad, but we laughed our heads off in the theatre.'

'Some days,' Basab added, stepping beside Ranadeep, 'it all clicks. I want to frame this day and keep it on my table.'

'What's with the sudden poetry?' Ishaan asked. 'Getting sentimental in your old age of sixteen?'

Basab shrugged, looking sheepish. 'Just thinking.'

'Always thinking,' Ishaan said. But there was affection in his voice now.

'That's what memory is for,' Basab continued, slipping into that tone that always made them groan in mock protest. 'When the bad times come, and they will, it's this that carries us. This day. This feeling.'

Ranadeep kicked at a pebble, sending it skittering into a large puddle that had formed after the unseasonal rains. They watched the ripples expand outward.

And then Ranadeep spoke. 'The horror is this. That we fade. These days will vanish. We will leave, lose touch. It's inevitable.'

'Look who's getting dark now,' Basab said, but his smile was softer than usual.

'Not me, I am going nowhere.' Ishaan said confidently. 'I am staying right here, becoming famous. You will all come to my film premieres and then you can fade away to your heart's content.'

'Will we get to meet the actress?' Krishanu asked, 'Will we get to dance with them in the rain?'

'Only if you behave,' Ishaan winked.

'But we will remember this day wherever we go,' Basab said, returning to his earlier thought. 'We will share them wherever we are…'

'You mean we are going to call each other and say, "Hey, remember that one day", like they do in bad movies for exposition?' Ishaan asked, raising his eyebrow.

'Of course not,' Basab smiled. 'We won't need to. We'll carry it, all of us, even in silence.'

'Like water,' Ranadeep said, 'shaping itself to whoever we become, but still the same underneath.'

They reached the gates, and the world returned: street noise, cycle bells, vendors yelling, buses sighing past in plumes of smoke. The sweet-sour perfume of syrup from the *misti* shop floated by, cut with diesel and dust.

'Look,' Ishaan said suddenly, pointing across the street. 'Is that Pramila?'

Across the street, a girl in a peacock-blue salwar kameez stood at a magazine stall, her hair falling like ink over her shoulder as she leaned in to read. A silver anklet caught the dying light.

'Oh God, not this again,' Krishanu said. 'You have been trying to be friends with her for a while now.'

'Stay away from things you don't understand,' Ishaan said solemnly, adjusting his hair. 'Like women.'

Ishaan used his fingers to adjust his hair and pulled the creases of his shirt self-consciously.

Krishanu turned to Ranadeep. 'You know her for a long time, don't you? You go to that singing school with her, right, harmoniums and girlie stuff?'

Ranadeep said nothing, just nodded. His gaze followed Pramila.

'How is she?' Basab asked, softly.

'She is nice.' Ranadeep said, 'Sings very well.'

Ishaan turned to them all. 'Okay, here is the way it is going to go. I am going to cross the street now and say hello to Pramila,' he said, with a smirk. 'Watch me act as if I just accidentally ran into her.'

Basab sighed, looking at Ranadeep.

'She's not your type,' Ranadeep said, eyes still on her. 'I guess you don't know her that well.'

'Oh, my dear Rano.' Ishaan gave his most arresting smile. 'All girls are my type. You ladies run along now, and I will join you…where are we going again?'

'Sher-e-Bengal,' Ranadeep said, and Krishanu gave a happy double thumbs up.

The remaining three watched him go, watched as he approached Pramila, saw her face light up with recognition and then something more, a softening, a glow that transformed her already pretty features into something luminous. Ishaan said something that made her laugh, the sound carrying faintly across the street.

'The beginning of the end,' Krishanu said under his breath.

'What did you say?' Ranadeep turned.

Krishanu blinked, as if coming back from somewhere far away. 'I said I hope they have those hot gulab jamuns today at Mahaprabhu Mistanna Bhandar. The ones swimming in syrup.'

'Swimming,' Basab repeated thoughtfully. 'You are going to get diabetes very soon. If you don't have it already. My youngest uncle lost his eyes to it, you know? And it's not just that, high blood sugar increases the chance for every terrible disease, cancer, heart-attack…'

'Aw, screw you,' Krishanu said. 'Your heart is going to stop before mine does. Write that down.'

Across the street, Pramila laughed again at something Ishaan said, her hand briefly touching his arm. She tucked a strand of hair behind her ear.

Basab watched the interaction across the street with an unreadable expression. 'Some things you can't hold onto,' he said finally. 'Water through fingers.'

'That's why we remember,' Ranadeep replied. 'So that nothing that matters truly disappears. As for forgetting, that's for geography, and history, and all the other stuff that is not important.'

The winter sun slipped lower, gilding the edges of buildings and faces. For a moment, the four boys – three waiting, one across the street – were suspended in amber light, preserved in that moment before shadows lengthened and consumed them.

'Happy birthday,' Krishanu said suddenly, clapping Ranadeep on the shoulder.

'Remember this day,' Basab added.

Ranadeep smiled at his friends, something wistful and knowing in his eyes. 'I will,' he agreed.

In the growing dusk, the water in the puddle behind them darkened to black, reflecting nothing but the first emerging stars. Across the street, Ishaan gestured animatedly, fully alive in the moment, while Pramila watched him with eyes that held both present joy and, if you looked real close, a bit of sorrow.

And somewhere, in the future, a bucket stood, filled with water. Waiting patiently, as water always does.

Afterword

This novel began with a gift.

On my birthday last year, my eleven-year-old daughter Anahita handed me a folded piece of paper. She knows I write horror stories, though it's not her favourite genre. Still, she had written me a poem about a deadly rose that grows 'down where the ivy grows' where it 'thrives upon weeping petals, born to live among the dead'. The entire poem is attached at the end, a fragment of which was used in the book you just read, forming one of its motifs.

The poem haunted me – in a way I could not fully put my finger on. Out of that twilight feeling was born *The Bucket*, a story of men, the same men, at eighteen and then almost at fifty. Yes, there is a murder mystery at its heart, and it might be called 'psychological horror', but more than that, it's about male friendship in all its contradictions – the beauty and the toxicity, the way we hold each other up and tear each other down, often in the same breath.

There's something about being eighteen that mirrors being fifty, though we rarely acknowledge it. At eighteen, the world spreads before us like an unmapped country, full of promise and uncertainty. At fifty, that same world seems to be closing in, possibilities winnowing down to the near certainty of our ultimate fading away and demise. Both moments demand a kind of courage we are not sure we possess. Both make us desperate for our friends, friends who understand what we are going through because they are going through the same themselves.

The men in this story find themselves caught between these two poles of uncertainty, reaching back to the boys they once were and forward to the men they have become. They discover that the friendships forged in youth can become either lifelines or nooses, depending on how tightly we grip them, that the things we are most scared of are the unknowns of the future, and the knowns of the past.

Anahita's poem gave me the map to trace those fears. In her rose that kills those who seek its prize, I found a perfect metaphor for the dangerous allure of the past, for friendships that demand everything and give back just enough to keep us coming back for more.

She may not realize it yet, but my daughter understands something fundamental about human nature: that we are drawn to things that we shall never have, and that sometimes the very act of reaching for what we want most can destroy us.

This book is for her, and for the boys who became the men I know, and for anyone who has ever stood at the edge of eighteen or fifty and wondered what comes next while looking back at what has happened before.

And so, I leave you with the poem that started it all.

Down Where the Ivy Grows
by Anahita Ray

The leaves creep along the stone,
A blooming rose stands all alone,
In a place that only shadows know,
Down where the ivy grows.

Where a sliver of day scrapes the cold,
And barren branches cling to light,
Withering flowers cry their woes,
Into the chill of the final night.

Where summer decays with a final sigh,
Perishing as its eyes close,
Where fading stars are left to die,
Down where the ivy grows.

Leaves creep along the wall,
Upon it the white moonlight glows,
As shadows twist and bend they call,
'Who shall pick the crimson rose?'

With prickly thorns as sharp as knives,
And a colour of the deepest red,
Upon weeping petals it thrives,
Born to live among the dead.

There stands that twisted rose,
Be warned, though, its beauty lies,
Tossing its head with a graceful pose,
Killing those who seek its prize.

Don't let yourself want, don't give in,
Resist the desire from within,
Pluck the flower or dare to try,
And from your skin, the devils cry.

Violent red, its brilliant colour,
Tinted by what falls from your hand,
The petals brighten and the skin grows duller,
As your blood seeps into the thirsty land.

Once it starts, it shall dry you out,
Like dripping rain from a waterspout,
A brutal end for those with greed,
So is your fate if you refuse to heed.

Forgotten there, among the flowers,
Alone to die in those final hours,
Buried in time, as many before,
Killed for always wanting more.

Silver dawn lies in a trance,
The land sings the song of crows,
Petals fly and branches dance,
Down where the ivy grows.

The leaves creep along the stone,
A blooming rose stands all alone,
In a place that only shadows know,
Down where the ivy grows.